Spirit
of the
Knight

by

Debbie Peterson

Spirit of the Knight

Cover Art by *Debbie Taylor*

The Wild Rose Press, Inc.
PO Box 708
Adams Basin, NY 14410-0708
Visit us at www.thewildrosepress.com

Publishing History
First Faery Rose Edition, 2014
Print ISBN 978-1-62830-275-2
Digital ISBN 978-1-62830-276-9

Published in the United States of America

"You're goin' to acknowledge my presence now, aye? 'Twould be discourteous to do otherwise, Murriah Jennins, after our eyes met not once, but twice."

Mariah's hand flew to her mouth. She choked on a breath and stared. After swallowing past the knot in her throat, she shook her head slightly and stepped back. In so doing, she tripped over her own foot and collided with the turret wall. The impact made her lose her balance, and at once she fell backward. In the same instant, her knight wrapped a hand around her wrist and gently tugged her forward. He held onto her hand until she regained her footing.

"Watch your step now. We cannae have ye tumblin' over th' side of th' castle," he said.

She ignored his comment as well as his concern, for, most assuredly, neither of them existed.

"No, you can't be real. Such a thing just isn't possible," she murmured aloud. Despite the rationale of her statement, her gaze remained fixed on the solid image that stood so close she could touch it without effort. Her fabricated vision folded his well-muscled arms against his chest, and tossed her a lopsided grin.

"That depends upon what ye mean by real. If you're speakin' of a man made of flesh, then no," he replied. "Despite th' lack, th' rest of me is real enough, I assure ye."

Mariah squeezed her eyes shut. The moment she opened them again, he'd be gone. Her imagination, as one might expect in an ancient castle, simply worked overtime. Especially after her earlier conversation with Evan. She licked the bottom of her dry lips, and then peeked up through her lashes.

Praise for Debbie Peterson

"I liked the way the author explains history past and present.... My favorite part of the story is Christmas.... It's very sweet and nostalgic."

"Whenever I read a romance with a ghost as one of the main characters (it doesn't happen that often) I'm always a tad worried about how the author will make it work....Overall, the author draws you into this intriguing romance that mixes history and an impossible love. I loved how the story comes together at the end."

"Debbie Peterson has a gift for telling a tale of impossible romance. Part of the delight in her books is sharing the journey and wondering how she's going to bring about an ending that leaves the reader with a contented sigh."

"Along with vivid and memorable characters comes an intriguing mystery...in a story that's best enjoyed through a suspension of belief and lots of faith in HEAs as the author has to dig deep into her bag of magic tricks to pull off the immensely satisfying conclusion."

"One of the sweetest romances I have read. It is a paranormal romance combining history, mystery and suspense all wrapped up into one great read!"

"OH. THIS. BOOK. IS. GOOD! I will DEFINITELY be reading more from Debbie Peterson!"

Dedication

This one is for Brandon and Nichole,
for the joy you have brought and bring into my life!

Chapter 1

The Water Cuddie Pub
Highlands of Scotland
Early May

The scene seemed reminiscent of a Hollywood movie. Female resembling a drowned rat walks inside crowded pub during a raging thunderstorm. The buzz of laughter and chatter instantly ceases. Awkward, uncomfortable silence follows. All eyes turn upon said female and stare. Thus making said female feel as if she'd suddenly sprouted a second head, some mammoth-sized zits, or had something repulsive hanging off the end of her nose. Should she wait for the zombies to converge or just find a seat and sit down?

Mariah opted to sit down. She scanned the room looking for an empty table in the most inconspicuous corner possible. Once located, she drew in a deep breath, scurried over to the polished wooden chair, and settled into the thing. All the while she hoped she hadn't committed an unpardonable sin by attaching herself to someone else's "usual" seat. Somewhere along the way a glass of water and a menu magically appeared—meaning she had no recollection of how or when said items arrived. Nonetheless, she clung to the glass for the support it offered while she perused the menu.

Several uncomfortable minutes passed before the pub's occupants resumed their normal conversations. *If* normal simply denoted speaking aloud. Then again, perhaps normal also included discussing the occasional outsider as if that outsider couldn't hear them. She sighed as she slid the single-page menu to the top of the table and took another drink of water. The action caught the attention of the attractive, sandy-haired man behind the bar.

He wiped his hands on his apron and smiled as he approached. "What will you have then?"

"I think I'll just have the fish and chips." Mariah relaxed her grip on the glass and leaned back against her chair.

"Och, you're an American." His hazel eyes danced with merriment. "We dinnae see many from th' States up here."

A smile touched her lips as she tilted her chin upward and met his gaze. She never tired of hearing the Scottish brogue with their delightful rolling *r*'s. "I imagine not. You're somewhat off the beaten path for the ordinary tourist, are you not?" she countered.

He nodded his head and laughed. "We are at that. Gimme a minute and I'll be right back with your meal."

"Thank you." Once again, the eyes of all the patrons fastened upon her person. She tugged self-consciously at the hem of her damp cotton skirt, took hold of her sketchbook, and formed the lines of a new sketch. At least the activity gave her something to do while the locals ogled and she waited. The wait took longer than anticipated, and her stomach bemoaned the fact. In her quest to arrive at the castle well before dark, she didn't take time to eat after her plane landed. The relentless storm she encountered along the way hindered her travel even further.

"I'm so sorry to have kept you waiting," the bartender said as about twenty minutes later, he set the hot plate in front of her. "But we find ourselves a bit shorthanded today. Linda couldn't make it because of th' rain."

"That's all right. If the food tastes anything like it smells, then it's well worth the wait." Mariah set her sketchbook off to the side and unfolded her napkin. She placed it on her lap and picked up her fork. Most surprisingly then, the man sat down in the chair opposite her. He didn't intend to watch her eat, did he?

"Might I ask if you're just passing through, or have you come to visit someone?" A flirtatious smile accompanied the question. She didn't return it.

"Well, actually, I'm here to do some oil paintings of Laird MacNaughton's castle. These paintings are for the Gallery of Castles project if you've heard of that. So, I'm going to live out there for a time." The comment hushed the crowd. Again.

He stared at her for what seemed like minutes instead of mere seconds. "Surely you dinnae mean to say you're staying inside th' drafty old castle itself?"

She let out a breath of quiet laughter. "As a matter of fact, I am staying inside the drafty old castle. However, Laird MacNaughton has allowed me the use of an empty bedroom inside the cottage should I change my mind."

Another prolonged silence followed the remark. She didn't know what to say to fill in the gap. Finally, he gave her a nod and offered his hand.

"All right then, my name is Evan. Welcome to our

wee village. You'll find us a friendly lot."

"Thank you, Evan. I may need a few *friends* while I'm here." He gave her hand a gentle squeeze before she freed it from his grasp. "My name is Mariah Jennings."

"I'm happy to make your acquaintance, Mariah Jennings." He scooted his chair closer to the table and rested an arm atop it. "I think I remember reading aboot th' castles project in th' newspaper, a while back. They said something aboot th' paintings going on some kind of tour at th' end of th' year?"

Mariah nodded, swallowed the first bite of her food, and followed it with another drink of water. "Yes, that's right. They are. As we speak, there are several artists painting ancient palaces and castles around the globe. Once we have them all complete, the entire collection will go on a ten-year, worldwide tour. The stint will begin in London. Each of the chosen cities will host the gallery for about three or four months, and then they'll travel on to the next city. Afterward, the paintings will return to their countries of origin for permanent placement by the board member representing their country."

"Does old man MacNaughton get to keep any of th' paintings?" he asked.

"Well, I'm not sure about the originals. I suppose Gordon Humphries, your British representative, could give him one or two if he so desires. However, Laird MacNaughton will receive giclée copies of everything I do, regardless," she said. "That's all part of the contract and a bonus of sorts for allowing us to invade and paint his property."

"Th' laird will appreciate that, I'm sure. However,

th' place is so remote, I'm surprised they even considered it for th' gallery. Especially since he doesn't allow tourists on th' property."

"I believe that's one of the reasons the board members wanted his castle included in this project in the first place. They said in comparison to the other castles in the British Isles, very few people are even aware of its existence."

"Only th' locals and th' few visitors that happen by the place." He pointed to her sketchbook then. "I couldn't help but notice you worked on a sketch while you waited for your supper. Do you mind if I have a look?"

Mariah shrugged and as she handed him the book she said, "There really isn't anything that spectacular to see. I just have a tendency to draw when there's nothing else to keep me occupied. So I usually keep a sketchbook close by."

Evan nodded and took a great deal of time flipping through each of the pages. Some of her sketches startled him a bit. Yet, she couldn't see which of her drawings caused his eyes to double in size because he tilted the book upward and tucked his head down.

When at last he spoke, he cleared his throat and said, "I see now why they have hired an artist such as yourself for this project. You have an extraordinary talent for medieval images. I especially like your stalwart knight in his various poses, this one here in particular." He turned the book around so she could see the sketch he referenced. All the while, his eyes probed hers. "I can actually see th' sadness, pain, and anguish reflected in his eyes. Very nice."

"Thank you." Mariah took in a small breath and

slowly released it as she gazed into the eyes of her fourteenth-century knight. She knew them so well she could paint them in her sleep. Although Evan couldn't know it, those penetrating eyes were a most incredible shade of gray. His dark brown hair, trimmed beard, and mustache, set them off to perfection.

She had drawn this same knight in all his various moods and stances for as far back as she had recollection. Her mother often said—to anyone who cared to listen—that she sketched this man incessantly from the moment she could hold a pencil in her hand. She followed that comment by saying it creeped her out.

Nonetheless, whenever anyone asked her about his identity throughout the years, she simply said she didn't know. And in truth, she didn't. She had no idea why his image remained forever entrenched in her mind. Perhaps her psyche created him from a storybook read or a movie seen while in the stages of her early childhood. Either way it didn't really matter. She stopped trying to figure it out years ago.

"So, tell me, is th' man that served as your model from around here?" he asked, pointing to her knight.

She shook her head. "Nope. I can guarantee you he's not from around here."

"Evaann, we need another pint over here," one of the husky patrons hollered out in familiar, friendly fashion.

Evan shrugged and gave her an apologetic smile. "I'm afraid duty calls. Enjoy th' rest of your meal."

A thing easier said than done, Mariah murmured inwardly as all eyes watched every mouthful she took. So she hurried. Yet at the same time, she made every effort not to appear hurried. Once she finished, paid her check, and made her way to the door, Evan bid her goodbye. Just before the door closed, he invited her to return often. He said they'd keep a chair open with her name on it. Pleasant enough comment she supposed. However, just as she exited through the doorway, one of the customers jabbed his companion with his elbow.

"I wonder how long she'll last out there," he snickered, unconcerned as to whether or not she heard him speak.

The other one snorted and said, "I don't think she'll last th' night."

With a slight toss of her head, she got into her car and drove off. She didn't have any difficulty following Laird MacNaughton's simple directions. Within fifteen minutes of leaving the pub, she stepped on the brake just outside a massive set of iron gates. Those gates connected to a stone fence at least six feet in height. Her mouth dropped as she studied the structure that lay just beyond the fence. Without taking her eyes off the imposing castle, she switched off the engine, and stepped out of the car. The recent rain left a trailing mist over the grounds and thick clouds shrouded the castle. She found it both mysterious and enchanting. And—this very setting is how she would paint the main portrait. She'd need look no further for inspiration.

Filled with desire to explore the place in its entirety, she made her way to the towering stone fence. As instructed, she yanked on the third stone down from the top of the wall, left hand side, and removed it. The key and a letter rested atop the crumbling mortar. She collected them both. Her letter contained all the information she needed to find the caretaker's cottage, her rooms, and run the generator. The caretaker, who'd gone on extended holiday with his wife, said the generator could prove a might touchy.

After driving through and securing the gates, Mariah took hold of her bag and exited the car. She retrieved her digital camera and set about taking a wide variety of pictures. Once she photographed the entire exterior from every possible angle, she strolled toward the castle entrance. All the while, she fixed her gaze on the turrets and towers high above her.

Something from those lofty heights demanded her attention. Though perhaps she perceived nothing more than the unique architecture coupled with the mist that cloaked them. Together they formed a fascinating picture. The array of missing stones added a certain charm to the ancient castle and gave it an even more mysterious look. Did those stones break away from the outer walls during a siege? If so, she decreed the courageous knights of this castle as victors over their opponents. Perhaps she could include such a scene in one of her smaller paintings.

She made her way to the large weathered doors, squeezed down on the stubborn latch, and thrust her hip against the splintered wood. The hinges moaned against the intrusion as she entered the great hall. Her gaze swept the entirety of the room. Remnants of ancient furnishings remained within the boundaries of its walls, as did two massive tables set perpendicular to the entrance. Long benches, sturdy in design, sat beneath them. A few bedraggled tapestries hung on the walls. The dais sat empty, void of the ornate chair from which the succession of lords governed the people.

Just as she turned to face the spiral staircase, a

sudden heaviness permeated the air surrounding her. She took in a series of shallow breaths as her heartbeat accelerated in response. The familiar feeling usually meant a ghost or ghosts occupied the space next to or near her. Every muscle in her body tensed as she turned around, expecting only heaven knew what this time. The past two and a half years taught her that not all ghosts appreciated the intrusion of visitors, especially the medieval sort. Such specters could carry a nasty, formidable attitude and amazing abilities she didn't quite understand.

"Hello?" She took a half step forward, swallowed past the dryness in her throat, and assumed a calm persona. "I'm sorry. I don't mean to impose—"

No one responded to the overture. Once again, she turned away from the outer walls and took a step toward the main stairway off to the left of the hall. In that same moment, someone tugged on a lock of her hair. Goose bumps popped out on her skin. She gasped and whipped around to confront her unseen companion. Mariah scanned the room as she wrapped her hands atop her arms and rubbed against the chill.

Did she just hear a deep, masculine chuckle or simply the wind echoing through the crevices? Apprehension made her shiver. As the heaviness dissipated a bit, Mariah released her breath. If a ghost, rather than her imagination, had just greeted her inside this hall, at least he appeared somewhat tolerant of her presence. For now—

She forced all thoughts of ghostly entities into a pen, made her way to the stone staircase, and climbed the steps. According to her letter, they prepared her bedroom on the second floor, west wing, and last room down the main hallway. It didn't take her long to find it.

The wooden door shuddered and groaned as she opened it. Mariah peeked in before she stepped all the way inside. She noticed the antique armoire first and then the highboy dresser. To the left she spied a Victorian era bed, which separated two magnificent night tables. Hurricane style lanterns, with round frosted glass, adorned the tabletops. An ancient stone fireplace, already stacked with wood and kindling atop the iron grate, centered the right hand wall. One electric floor lamp, with the cord still coiled around the base, stood in the corner. A small desk and chair completed the furnishings. In truth, she hadn't expected anything quite so grand.

She made her way to the large arched window located between the armoire and dresser, opened the linen draperies, and gazed at the view. In the distance, tall trees with substantial trunks indicated a very old forest. The woodland lay just beyond the green grassy fields surrounding the castle. Nothing modern marred the area's pristine beauty. Contentment settled in as she rested her head against the casement. If a piece of heaven existed on earth, then surely she found it right here at Laird MacNaughton's castle. Ghosts or no ghosts, she found it a pity her final assignment had a deadline attached.

The light inside the room waned as the sun traveled west toward the hills, and with a bit of reluctance, Mariah turned away from the enchanting view. She made her way to the night table closest to the window, retrieved the matches, and lit both lamps. They cast a warm golden glow throughout the room as well as a couple of eerie shadows that danced along the walls. Right then the disembodied laughter and the tug on her hair popped into her mind. The memory fueled a burning need to activate the generator before darkness filled the castle. Her note said she could find "the beast" in the bailey.

Numerous whispers accompanied her steps as she descended the staircase. Surely the continuous winds traveling through the various chimneys and wall fissures created these haunting sounds. At least, that's what she told herself as she made her way outside to the lower bailey. The generator, a cumbersome rectangular looking thing, sat against the innermost wall. She took the caretaker's letter from out of her pocket as she approached the machine. He told her the main switch lay just beneath the six round gauges on top and just next to the largest two beneath them. She needed to flip the switch and click the start button. If that didn't work, he said, then she needed to turn the hand crank on the opposite end of the generator. He already filled the machine with enough petrol to last several weeks. They stored the surplus fuel inside the carriage house next to the cottage, should she need to refuel.

She flipped the switch and hit the start button as directed. The rusty old generator coughed, sputtered, choked, and then rattled before it evened out to a rhythmic hum. She released a relieved breath and took firm hold of the clunky remote control resting on top of the inner ledge. The caretaker said that the remote would turn the generator off once she climbed into bed for the night. However, it didn't have the capability to turn it back on. She'd have to do that manually each time she wanted to use it. Should she have needs in the darkness of night, the battery-operated torch he placed inside the bottom desk drawer, could guide her steps easily enough.

She spied the long generator cord and followed its course up the wall and through a second story window. If she had the layout of the castle correct, the cord snaked through the room next to hers. She made her way back inside the castle. Soft light now bathed the stairway and the sight surprised her somewhat. The oil lamps from inside her bedroom shouldn't give off such radiance, should they? She halted her steps just as she arrived in front of her door. Her heart skipped a beat as she stared inside the chamber.

The light spilling into the hallway emanated from the bulbs of her electric lamp—not from the kerosene lanterns. The problem with that? She hadn't connected the coiled plug to the generator cord. Once again, unsightly bumps popped out on her skin. She examined every inch of the room in search of the otherworldly visitor responsible for the impossible display. During the process, the focus of her attention settled on her luggage. All her bags sat on the floor next to the bed. Her heart thumped inside her chest as she considered the impossibility of such a sight. She suddenly envisioned her bags floating up the stairway—

The ringing of her cell phone startled her even further. She vaulted from the spot on which she had anchored herself and yanked the phone from the pocket of her jacket. In her haste, she fumbled and almost dropped the thing. Yet somehow, she retained possession and raised the phone to her ear. She gulped a breath and said, "Hello, Mariah Jennings speaking."

"Miss Jennings? This is Kyle MacNaughton."

The moment the man said his name, the lights beneath the crystal shade went out. Her hand flew to her chest. She strained to see in the dimmer light.

"Oh. Hello, Laird MacNaughton. How are you this evening?"

"Just fine, thank you for asking," he said. "I'm calling to see if you found your way to th' castle without mishap."

"Yes, actually I'm here right now and everything is perfect. The bedroom you prepared is just beautiful. Thank you so much. I didn't expect such a fine welcome," she replied as her gaze continued its search of every nook and cranny inside the room.

"My pleasure. But I wish you would reconsider and stay inside th' caretaker's cottage when you're not engaged in painting," he said. "George and Sybil MacGilroy are a lovely couple. Of course, once they return, they'll see to your every need and comfort regardless of where you choose to stay. But, if you stay in their home, you'd have a comfortable bed and a bath with central heating—"

"Laird MacNaughton," she interrupted, "is there a reason you don't want me to stay inside the castle? I don't mean to be a bother to anyone. I just believe my paintings turn out far more retentive in detail when I put myself inside the actual environment. Your castle is the most beautiful and unique structure I've seen to date, and I want to make sure the world has the opportunity to appreciate its grandeur."

"No, I dinnae mind, it's just that th' castle is a...a wee bit...drafty and I dinnae want you to...to fall ill while I'm responsible for your well-being," he stammered. "Not when you're so close to finishing your task. On stormy day's such as this, th' castle can get quite cold, and we have such storms often."

"Yes, I know about the storms. But please don't worry about me. I'll be fine, I promise. I daresay George has left enough wood in my bedroom to keep me warm for weeks. When I want a hot shower or feel like I'm getting the least bit sick, I'll take refuge in the cottage. Will that ease your mind?"

After a lengthy pause the laird heaved a sigh of resignation. "I suppose that'll have to do then," he said. "If I can help in any way please let me know."

"I will," she said. "Thanks so much for calling."

The phone call managed to calm her down. At least it calmed her enough to plug the lamp into one of the power strip outlets and begin the tedious chore of unpacking her belongings. Finally, she hung the last article of clothing inside the armoire, closed the doors, and then stooped down beside her bed. She slid the now empty bags underneath it. But then just as she turned on her heels to stand, she caught sight of a translucent pair of feminine feet beneath a long linen gown. As she drew in a deep breath, her incredulous gaze shot upward, seeking a face to go with the legs. Yet, she no more than looked up, when the backside of a ghostly woman, disappeared straight through the inner castle wall.

Chapter 2

Sir Cailen Braithnoch glanced at the same wall himself. Yet he saw nothing to cause the apprehension that suddenly filled her beautiful, azure-colored eyes. She stared at the stones as if they mystified her in some way. Perhaps she saw naught but shadows and simply allowed her imagination free rein. Not that he could blame her for that. Thus far, he hadn't made any effort to withhold his presence from her knowledge. To his pleasant surprise, she didn't succumb to screaming fits of hysteria once she realized she had unseen company inside his castle.

A slight grin emerged as he recalled her unexpected arrival late this afternoon. From the topmost tower, he and a few of his men stood guard as the white car approached the gates. He didn't expect the vision that presented itself when this bonny, fair-haired lassie stepped out of the vehicle. In fact, he found it nigh on impossible to take his eyes off her. On impulse he followed her while she traversed his property. Mayhap by so doing he would discover the purpose of her visit. She surveyed the castle entrance from all angles with a thing George called a camera, and then fearlessly stepped beyond the thick wooden doors.

"What's she doin' here?" Duncan had asked, as he popped inside the great hall.

Cailen shook his head. "I dinnae rightly know, but

I think she's th' reason George and Sybil readied th' room upstairs."

"Are we goin' to let her stay?" he asked.

"Aye, for now," Cailen had replied.

Duncan raised a mischievous brow and smirked. "Could her comeliness have anythin' to do with your decision?"

"Och, away with ye, and tell th' lads to leave her alone." He shook his head to the sound of Duncan's retreating laughter. His lieutenant's amusement didn't dissuade him in the least from accompanying the girl while she explored his castle.

Cailen leaned against the wall as she placed a hand atop her bed and then rose to her feet. She gazed about the chamber with unexpected thoroughness. He studied her in fascination while she conducted her search. Admittedly, her uncommon beauty had instantly captivated him. A luxurious mane of loose honey colored waves framed the most mesmerizing eyes he'd ever seen. The top of her head just barely matched the height of his shoulders. Yet, what she lacked in height, she more than made up for in spirit.

She reminded him very much of another plucky female who had visited his castle not long ago. Her voice even bore the same strange accent. Perhaps she too, journeyed from far across the sea. At that moment, he had an overwhelming desire to make her acquaintance and ask the questions that plagued him. Yet, caution warned that she might flee the castle altogether if he manifested his form. Such happened often enough through the endless days following his death. But then again, that had been his objective with all uninvited guests. Though he could find no logical reason to support the need, he found he didn't want this particular woman to go, at least not yet.

Still, those nagging questions needed answering, did they not? Just as he moved toward her, the annoying sound of her phone chirped once again. She extracted the thing from her pocket and made her way to the window. This time she focused her attention on the brilliance of the night sky. Starlight glistened through the lingering storm clouds and bathed her face with its radiance. In response, the desire to make her acquaintance strengthened and for a brief moment, he wavered.

The incoming call made the final decision for him. He would wait for a better time to show himself. Yet, despite that decision, Cailen continued the journey to her side. He placed both arms on either side of her body, and rested his hands against the casement, thus temporarily holding her captive.

Before she opened her mouth to speak, he dropped his head close to her ear and whispered, "*Another time, then, Murriah.*"

Her incredulous expression as she whirled around and just collided with his chest almost made him laugh. Probably would have if not for the fact she fixed her gaze exactly with his. She couldn't see him for he hadn't revealed himself. Yet, it truly seemed otherwise, and given the chance, he could quite easily lose himself in those eyes of hers. Just as he prepared to speak aloud, she found her wits and answered her phone. He conjured a disappointed sigh and left her to her conversation.

Most of his companions had congregated in the great hall while he lingered upstairs with his guest.

Their boisterous discussions snapped to a halt the moment he entered the room. Curiosity and anticipation filled their eyes. As expected, Duncan spoke first.

"Well, did ye discover th' purpose of her visit then?" he asked, his impatience obvious in both expression and tone.

Cailen sat down backward on the bench closest to the stairway, leaned back, and propped his arms atop the table. "Aye, she's here to do some paintin's of th' castle for Laird MacNaughton."

The comment caused an immediate buzz of excitement.

"That should break up th' tedium around here a wee bit," Alan said.

"Aye, it might at that." Edmund grinned. His anticipation shone in his eyes as he nodded in agreement.

"I wonder if she'll let us watch?" asked Malcolm.

"She cannae stop ye from peepin', ye dolt!" said Duncan as he smacked the knight's shoulder with the back of his hand, rolled his eyes heavenward, and shook his head.

"Aye, that's true enough," Cailen replied. "But I'll not have any of ye disturb her, is that understood? She's our guest and will be treated with courtesy while she remains."

"Of course, Cailen, that goes without sayin'," Duncan countered. "Ye needn't get your layna in a tangle, man."

"I'm afraid ye dinnae have what it takes to tangle my layna, laddie," Cailen shot back.

****

Mariah stopped dead in her tracks. Did she just

hear the sound of uproarious laughter wafting up the staircase? She turned off the soft music playing on her laptop and turned her head toward the open doorway. Yet, she didn't hear anything out of the ordinary. Not even the sound of the wind disturbed the silence of the chimney. She released a slow breath.

"Stop looking for ghosts where there are none, Mariah," she berated herself. "Or you'll surely drive yourself crazy."

She took her blue silk pajamas out of the bureau drawer. Despite the fine advice she just gave herself, she looked about the room to ensure her privacy. She cast away the desire to leap inside her armoire while she changed her clothes. Yet, all the while, the husky voice troubled her mind. A voice that called her by name in the most charming Scottish brogue she'd heard to date.

Mariah pulled back the bedding and climbed into bed. She selected the off button on the remote control and then snuffed the flame in each of the lanterns. Light from the moon and stars filtered in through the window. She turned to her side in order to face the glorious sight, snuggled deeper into the duvet, and refused even so much as a single thought concerning otherworldly beings. Instead, she concentrated on creating several artistic images of Laird MacNaughton's wondrous castle.

Those very images induced countless nonsensical dreams that plagued her throughout the night. Finally, as the dawn approached she journeyed toward awareness. Yet her current dream continued. She dreamed she wandered through a forest, and it seemed she searched for something important, but couldn't find it. At last, she looked up from her wearisome task and caught sight of MacNaughton's castle in the distance. She needed to get there with all haste because—well, because she needed to get, to get—

Her eyelids fluttered a bit as the rationale of the dream evaporated the moment she opened her eyes. She turned over, yawned, and stretched as she struggled to remember more. Regardless of effort, only brief glimpses of trees and dark castle halls teased her mind before they too flitted away.

The faint light of dawn peeked through her bedroom window. Despite the early hour, she tossed back the blankets and slid out of bed. She had so much she wanted to accomplish today. With her goals in mind, she took a fresh pair of jeans and a T-shirt from out of the bureau and made quick use of the somewhat primitive, late-nineteenth-century bathroom facilities. Once she finished her lukewarm shower and dressed, she descended the stairs. The letter said the caretaker's cottage, and all the makings for meals, lay just north of the castle. A well-worn path would lead her through the trees and to the kitchen door entrance. She couldn't miss it, he said. And of course, she would need to help herself to the pantry, root cellar, and freezer during her stay.

The trail took her through a cathedral of giant trees with thick lush branches. Despite the sun of early morning, the darkened canopy gave the path an eerie feel as she walked underneath and through it. Although quite beautiful, something about the archway made her think of Washington Irving's *Sleepy Hollow*. She half expected his hideous headless horseman to swoop down on her from behind and carry her off.

She banished the absurd thought from her mind as she grasped the door handle, freed the latch, and let herself in. The warmth of the small country kitchen sang out a welcome as she stepped over the threshold. Braided rugs in various shades of brown and dark cherry red lay underneath the round table and in front of the sink. Old-fashioned tin canisters and a vast array of herbal plants adorned the countertops. Gingham curtains in hues of ivory and burgundy framed the window, and a matching tablecloth covered the pine wood table. Potted primrose flowers served as the centerpiece. An old copper teapot sat atop the aging porcelain stove. The shelves in the brick alcove behind it held a most impressive stock of herbs and spices in small glass jars. Homemade labels identified the contents of each container. She approached the pantry next to the shelves, opened the cupboard door, and chose a box of cereal for her morning meal.

After she finished her breakfast, she watered the plants and then paused in front of the narrow stairway just to the right of the pantry. From the open doorway at the top of the steps, she spied the tidy bedroom MacNaughton offered her. She wouldn't need it. The presence of a ghost—or ghosts—would not intimidate her in the least.

She returned to the castle and entered by way of the rear entrance. As her first priority, she needed to find the perfect area to set up her studio. With that objective in mind, she meandered through each of the spacious rooms on the ground floor and spent the better portion of the morning exploring them. Though certainly large enough, none of the rooms gave her adequate light for daytime painting. She didn't want to use her art lamps all throughout the day, either.

She climbed the stairs and continued her quest on the second floor. To the left of the landing she spied a set of double doors just down the east wing. She gripped the black metal latch and let herself in. An exquisite stained glass window behind the altar of the castle chapel captured her immediate attention. If not mistaken, the colorful scene depicted Saint Fergus wearing long robes and holding a cross in his clasped hands. Heaven's light radiated around him. To the right of the room sat the tall cupboard that, once upon a time, housed the sacramental wine.

Mariah strolled down the center aisle and all the while, her gaze wandered about the room. Her imagination took flight. Suddenly, she could see the room's original grandeur, or at least her version of it. She envisioned in vivid detail, various couples standing before the altar while the priest united them in marriage. The christening of their infant children followed. She could even see the movement of tiny feet and hands while the priest performed the rite. After the visions ended, she turned to face the door.

She looked over the pews and envisioned her handsome knight seated on the back row. She imagined him wearing his linen léine underneath his quilted aketon coat, stuffed with wool rather than metal plate. Atop the dark brown aketon, he wore his chain mail hauberk and surcoat. As customary, she didn't visualize anything covering his magnificent, shoulder length hair.

The image she conjured didn't surprise her any. He would fit very well in a castle such as this one. His large, muscular frame all but dwarfed the wooden pews as he leaned back and casually rested his arms along the top of the bench. He grinned at her while his eyes danced with mischief. She returned his flirty smile, made her way out of the doors, and closed them behind her.

Cailen turned his head in bewilderment as Mariah Jennings vacated the chapel without so much as a backward glance. She saw him. He'd swear to it. Their eyes met. She returned his smile. He didn't know what he expected once he showed himself to her. However, he didn't expect this particular reaction. For a moment he sat in dumbfounded indecision. Should he follow and try again? Inane question. He couldn't very well sit here without discovering the reason for her odd behavior, now could he.

He vacated the chapel and made an abrupt halt on the landing just as Evan MacGilroy—of all the unexpected people—burst through the main doors. The lad cradled a large box underneath his arm and a brown paper sack in his hand. What impossible errand would compel him to return to the castle now?

"Mariah?" Evan called out as he stood near the open door with a hand still attached to the latch.

Cailen's eyes narrowed as he gazed down upon the caretaker's wayward son. He called out to Mariah with surprising familiarity. How could he have made her acquaintance? Such seemed impossible. She popped out of the room next to the chapel, and gazed down the stairs.

"Hey Evan," she said as she breezed past him and hurried down the stairs. "I certainly didn't expect to see you out here."

Evan shrugged. "I know, but I thought you might be getting hungry. Have you had anything to eat since you left th' pub?"

"Yes, I had a bowl of oatmeal for breakfast this morning," she replied. "What's more, the caretaker and his wife have left enough food to feed an entire army with plenty to spare."

Evan waved a hand in disdain as he shut the door. "Oatmeal is for babes. What you need is some real fairn. Therefore, I've brought you a chookie and bacon club butty with some crisps and fresh fruit. I hope that meets with your approval?"

"The chicken sandwich sounds delicious. Did you bring enough to share, or do I have to eat by myself?" she asked.

Evan looked pleased as he approached her. "That I did if you're inviting me to stay. If not, you'll have plenty to eat later."

Mariah swept a hand toward the table in response to the comment. Cailen studied the pair as they ambled over to the table together and sat down opposite each other. Curiosity compelled him to stay and listen in on their conversation.

Evan dropped his sack and pushed the box toward her. "Th' delivery man handed me this package at th' gate. There's a few more outside. But I told him I would give this one to you, now."

Mariah glanced at the label. "Thank you for bringing it in. The suppliers called me last night and told me to expect the packages today. Perfect timing since I need this stuff to get started on the paintings. However, I need to find a room with adequate daylight first. I was just upstairs looking for one when you came in."

Duncan chose that moment to pop in beside him.

He nudged his arm. "What's he doin' here?" he asked.

Cailen dropped a curt nod in the direction of the table. "He's brought Murriah somethin' to eat."

Duncan shook his head and snorted in return. Cailen's sentiments exactly. They both knew George and Sybil kept a well-stocked larder and so did Evan. The girl didn't need his offerings.

"I would think th' most daylight would come in from a room that has both south and east windows and th' higher th' better. Perhaps you might find something on th' third floor to suit your needs."

Mariah slid a generous portion of the food toward her guest and then licked the droplets of sauce off her finger. "Yes, I suspect you're right. I just haven't explored the third floor yet."

"She *might* find a room like that?" repeated Duncan.

Cailen shrugged but said nothing.

"Well, it seems you've fared well enough through th' night," Evan said with a bit of nonchalance to his tone. He picked up the sandwich she handed him and took a bite.

She gazed at her visitor for several long moments without speaking. "Did you and your friends think otherwise?" she finally asked as she picked up her own sandwich and raised it to her lips.

"Och, I dinnae know. There are plenty of rumors aboot this castle that might indicate such," he said.

Duncan raised an incredulous brow and shot a disdainful glance at Cailen. "Rumors? What game is he playin' at now?"

Again, Cailen said nothing as he awaited Mariah's reply.

"Ghosts, you mean?" she prodded.

Evan stuffed one of his crisps in his mouth and all but swallowed the thing whole. "Have you seen any then?"

"If you assume I'm expecting otherwise, then you'd assume wrong. I'm thoroughly convinced every castle houses a ghost or two. Believe me when I tell you that during the last few years I've seen my fair share of them."

Evan exhaled a slow breath and gave her a nod. "You have got a fair amount of courage and stamina, Mariah Jennings, I'll give you that. Not many folk would bide here with all th' stories aboot th' strange happenings."

"Think so?" she asked.

"I know so," he replied.

The man didn't listen to what Mariah said at all, Cailen mused. She never once said she *hadn't* seen him. She only said she *expected* to see ghosts. Yet, the omission made him wonder why she would keep that information to herself. Most mortals couldn't wait to divulge something otherworldly to anyone willing to listen to their claims. Duncan slapped a hand atop his shoulder.

"Well, come on, Cailen, she's in good enough hands for th' moment. Th' lads are waitin' outside, and by now, they are growin' a wee bit impatient with us," Duncan said.

Cailen shot a brief glance at the floor and nodded. "I suppose you're right." Despite his reluctance to leave Mariah in the hands of Evan MacGilroy, they disappeared from the grand hall, leaving her in his care.

Chapter 3

Even though she enjoyed Evan's company to some extent, nothing pleased Mariah more than when he vacated the premises and left her in peace. In all likelihood, curiosity as to whether or not she survived the night prompted the visit and far outweighed his concern over her hunger.

And he wanted to know if she had seen any ghosts.

She took hold of the railing and climbed the steps and all the while, her thoughts drifted to the female entity she saw last night. The woman wore an early medieval style léine and the length of her gorgeous flaming red hair all but covered the sash around her waist. She didn't feel any malice coming from this spirit. In fact, besides astonishment, she didn't feel anything at all. Then again, she did only catch a brief glimpse.

As Mariah stepped onto the third floor landing, she determined to put away all thoughts of ghosts and concentrate instead on her work. More than half the day had already passed and she'd yet to locate a suitable work area. She turned toward the east wing and wandered down to the end of the hall. Light spilled into the hallway from the corner room just as Evan suggested it might. She entered through the open doorway and cast her gaze about the roomy chamber. Surely, a more perfect place in which to paint didn't exist. She hastened outside to fetch her packages and all the equipment from the car.

One hour later, she had her studio arranged, with her largest easel and canvas in the center of the room facing the windows. She placed two of her smaller easels on either side of the big one. The smallest table she could find inside the mill tower, now storing various items from the castle's past, sat against the northern wall. She arranged her art lamps and sketchbooks on top of that. Once she had her brushes, paints and supplies organized, she began the first of her paintings by applying a coat of gesso to the freshly dampened canvases. Then, since they would take at least an hour to dry, she set about exploring a little bit more of the castle.

She made her way to the landing and peeked down the hallway leading to the north wing. Her gaze then wandered in the opposite direction and settled on the next set of steps. Curiosity compelled her to climb them to the top. They led her to the southwest turret. She approached the center crenel of that turret for an unobstructed view of the countryside. Beyond the grassy fields that surrounded the castle, she spied sparkling rivers and streams that meandered throughout the dense forest. Lush green hilltops rose just above the tallest trees and a magnificent waterfall danced down the side of the mountain.

Somehow, she needed to include this enchanting scene in one of her smaller paintings. Perhaps she could paint a side view of the castle, with a lady of the court, looking over the top of the turret. In the distance she would see her knight emerge from the forest, leading his weary garrison as they returned from battle.

And then without any effort on her part, she envisioned those same knights engaged in training on the grassy fields below her. The scene burst into life in a way she had never experienced, and the imagined scene both amazed and delighted her. As she absorbed every detail of the spectacle, her eyes fastened on her beloved knight, now directly below her. He wielded his sword against his opponent with an amazing set of skills she had never conceptualized before.

Once he finished the exercise, he shook his hair from off his face, looked up, and locked his gaze with hers. He refused to relinquish her from his gaze while he spoke to his companion. The man nodded in response as he too, gazed in her direction. Seconds later, her knight disappeared from view as did all his comrades on the field. Her mind offered nothing more and the vision faded away. Pity that. She glanced down at her watch and after noting the time, she reluctantly turned around.

"You're goin' to acknowledge my presence now, aye? 'Twould be discourteous to do otherwise, Murriah Jennin's, after our eyes met not once, but twice."

Mariah's hand flew to her mouth. She choked on a breath and stared. After swallowing past the knot in her throat, she shook her head slightly and stepped back. In so doing, she tripped over her own foot and collided with the turret wall. The impact made her lose her balance, and at once she fell backward. In the same instant, *her knight* wrapped a hand around her wrist and gently tugged her forward. He held onto her hand until she regained her footing.

"Watch your step now, we cannae have ye tumblin' over th' side of th' castle," he said.

She ignored his comment as well as his concern, for most assuredly, neither of them existed.

"No, you can't be real. Such a thing just isn't possible," she murmured aloud. Despite the rationale of her statement, her gaze remained fixed on the solid image that stood so close she could touch it without effort. Her fabricated vision folded his well-muscled arms against his chest, and tossed her a lop-sided grin.

"That depends upon what ye mean by real. If you're speakin' of a man made of flesh, then no," he replied. "Despite th' lack, th' rest of me is real enough, I assure ye."

Mariah squeezed her eyes shut. The moment she opened them again, he'd be gone. Her imagination, as one might expect in an ancient castle, simply worked overtime. Especially after her earlier conversation with Evan. She licked the bottom of her dry lips, and then peeked up through her lashes.

"Nay, I'm still here," her amused knight said, and it truly seemed he fought to still his laughter.

Clasped hands trembled slightly as they rose up and touched her chin. She shook her head, but said nothing in return. Time and sanity ceased to exist while she struggled to make sense of this bizarre experience.

"I dinnae ken what's ailin' ye, lassie. Ye just said ye expected to see ghosts in th' castle." Now *he* shook his head at *her* and he sounded a bit exasperated.

Mariah swallowed hard, pointed a finger at him, and said, "Yes, but not you."

"I dinnae ken what ye mean by that?" He drew his brows together and cocked his head to the side as he regarded her.

"Well, I made you up—" She stopped short. For it

suddenly occurred to her that she stood here speaking aloud to a figment of her imagination. Had she gone stark raving mad? Had the accumulative experiences of the past two years taken a toll on her mind? She needed to get a hold of herself. Better yet, she needed to— needed to—she didn't know what she needed. Without giving it further consideration, she whirled around and made a beeline for the door.

Bewildered at best, Cailen stood his ground as Mariah turned her startled gaze away from his and all but ran down the stairs. He discerned the sound of her hurried footsteps leading toward the back entrance of the castle. The door opened and closed. Moments later, he viewed her flight from the turret as she made a dash for the forest. He shrugged off her erratic behavior.

Perchance she needed a moment to come to grips with his presence. Although the lassie said she had seen ghosts, mayhap none of them actually approached and spoke with her. Either that or the girl suffered a bit from the mind muddles. Still, her odd words baffled him. What did she mean when she said she made him up and that she didn't expect to see him? That didn't make any sense at all. Either she expected to see ghosts or she didn't.

"What's all that aboot?" The instant he appeared at his side, Duncan gazed out across the field and tracked Mariah's rapid progress toward the woods. "She couldn't bear th' sight of your revoltin' face or what?" he asked, using a casual tone.

"Nay, my charms simply overcame her. Therefore, she needed a moment to compose herself," Cailen replied.

Duncan stared at him for several seconds before he

threw back his head and roared with laughter. In fact, he laughed so hard and so long, Cailen finally punched him in the chest just to shut him up. The maneuver, which sent him bouncing against the turret, didn't work as well as he intended. Nevertheless, as the fates would have it, Alan chose that moment to appear. He looked from one to the other and then shrugged his indifference.

The man jerked a thumb behind him. "Cailen, I thought ye should know, Evan just now left th' property."

Cailen shifted his focus north of the castle. "What's he been doin' all this time?"

"He went over to th' cottage," Alan replied.

"Why?" he asked. "Murriah told him his parents weren't at home."

"I know, he went over anyway and he took th' back way in. He came out a few moments ago, carryin' somethin' small and black in color. I didna get a good look though, because he tucked th' thing inside his coat," Alan reported.

"That's a wee bit strange," Duncan said.

"Strange, indeed. I thought he collected all his belongin's th' night he left." Cailen put a hand to his beard as he considered what Alan just said. "Ye didna go into th' cottage with him?"

"Nay," said Alan, "I didna see th' need for it at th' time."

Evan hadn't expressed any desire to visit the castle or its grounds for a very long while now. In fact, he hadn't shown himself since the night he lashed out at his parents in heated anger. His presence today would've surprised him more, if not for Mariah.

Although Evan used neighborly concern as an excuse to visit the castle, any man with eyes would find a way to seek her out.

He cast his gaze toward the woodlands. Mayhap he ought to show a bit of neighborly concern himself. He turned to face Alan and said, "All right. Let me know if he comes back."

Alan nodded and disappeared.

"Where are ye off to now?" asked Duncan.

"I better make sure th' lassie doesna get lost out there." Cailen didn't wait around for Duncan's reply. Even so, he couldn't escape the sound of his laughter.

****

Mariah slowed her pace once she neared the river. The melody of the rushing water soothed and calmed her troubled mind. She sat down on the massive trunk of an old toppled tree that looked as though it had fallen along the riverbank ages ago. The clear water rippled over the rocky bottom. For a time, she mindlessly toyed with her fingers as she watched the swirling water run along its course. A gentle breeze trifled with her hair. More than once, she brushed the tousled locks away from her face and tossed them behind her shoulders. She banished all thoughts of insanity and concentrated solely on the beauty of her surroundings. Right now, she needed no more than that.

"Once upon a time, this river used to feed th' moat," the voice behind her said. "Nowadays only th' runoff fills th' trench."

Mariah turned her head toward the sound. Her knight rested a broad shoulder against a tree as he regarded her. She made careful study of every curve and plane of his face and form. Not a single discrepancy revealed itself in the man that dominated a lifetime of sketchbooks. He looked her over just as thoroughly as she did him and all the while, she considered what he just said.

She never really thought about moats before, other than the fact they surrounded many of the castles she'd seen along the way. Whether or not a river fed them never once entered her mind. The term "runoff" never rolled off her tongue during conversation either. Therefore, she couldn't have imagined him saying such things, could she? Did that mean the man she'd sketched and painted her entire life truly existed right here at Laird MacNaughton's castle? If so, how could she have known that?

She said nothing in return as he approached and then sat down opposite her with an ease that suggested he'd done so a thousand times before. And in her dreams, he had.

He gave her one of his flirty grins and said, "We've not been properly introduced, Murriah Jennin's. My name is Cailen Braithnoch, and I'm verra happy to make your acquaintance."

The man looked—well, he looked mortal in almost every way, except she didn't detect any movement of his chest, which would indicate the ability to breathe. He didn't glide or float above the ground—he *walked* upon it as any mortal would. Most amazing? She could hear him speak as if he still possessed a body of flesh and blood. How could he do all that? Better yet, why would he do all that?

She worked up a bit of moisture inside her mouth, swallowed past the dry spot in her throat, and extended a cautious hand toward the incredibly handsome face she knew as well as she did her own. All the while, his eyes bore into hers. He made no move to halt her progress or avoid her touch. Once she arrived at the side of his face, her fingers glided along the length of his jaw and down to his chin. How would she describe the sensation of his ghostly form? Yes, she could easily go through him if she so desired. However, a perceptible barrier existed between his spiritual body and her fingers. She could feel that barrier just as well as she could feel anything else. A touch of humor appeared in his eyes well before it touched the corners of his mouth.

The grin made her feel a bit self-conscious and as she dropped her wayward hand into her lap, he said, "Is this your customary response to a man that introduces hisself to ye?"

The question made her laugh. She dropped her gaze and shook her head. "No, I can't say that it is."

Mariah wanted so much to tell him that somehow they were well past introductions. She wanted to say that only a lifetime of familiarity would drive her to such boldness. And what would he think if he knew that she compared every man she had ever dated to the persona she created and each of those men fell far short of the mark? She couldn't tell him any of those things. For in all likelihood, he would think her insane if he didn't already. She played with her necklace as she sought some kind of reasonable explanation for her behavior.

Finally, she lifted her brows and shrugged. "I'm sorry about that. It's just that I—"

Cailen immediately shook his head. A finger rested against her lips to stay her apology. "Ye needn't apologize, lassie. I'm not sorry for it—quite th' contrary, ye ken?"

The intensity of his gaze caused an unwanted blush. She took in a shallow breath and said, "I guess you could say that I'm feeling a bit overwhelmed right now. I've never, well, what I mean to say is the ghosts—rather the spirits I have, um…" Her hand twirled in small circles as she sought words that wouldn't offend him. Did a spiritual entity abhor the term "ghost"?

"Th' ghosts ye've seen didna choose to interact with ye?" he asked, coming to her rescue.

"Not quite in the same manner you have." She paused for a moment. "You speak as any mortal still living. Very few of the spirits I've encountered actually spoke *with* me. Rather, they spoke *at* me and their voices sounded more—hollow? I think that's the best way to describe the sounds they made. I could tell they stood near me, but when they told me to 'get out' or other such pleasantries, the voices sounded more as if they whispered from afar off and the wind carried their words to my ears, if that makes sense."

Cailen dipped his head. "None of them ever welcomed ye into their home then?"

Mariah lifted a single shoulder. "Actually, several of the spirits I encountered didn't mind my presence. But none of them, friendly or otherwise, sat and talked to me as you're doing right now. And none of them ever manifested themselves as you do. The ghosts I've seen were all transparent, some more so than others. They offered me brief glimpses of themselves from time to time. Except for the hideous monk who delighted in scaring me half to death—usually at night—and one female spirit. She remained completely visible as she glided down an entire flight of stairs. When she stepped onto the ground floor, she turned toward me, gave me a sweet smile, and then faded away. Other than that, most of the manifestations I witnessed appeared in the form of otherworldly abilities."

"Abilities?" he repeated.

"You know, spontaneously producing fire in fireplaces and lamps, moving solid and sometimes very heavy objects, hurling some of those same objects in my direction. More frightening yet? Impossibly balancing those objects on top each other. And the smells! I can't tell you how many times I experienced the odor of rotting flesh, perfume, and even flowers with no possible source. Then, of course, I could feel their emotions—contentment, joy, fear, intense anger, and hatred." She shuddered as the various memories flooded her mind.

Cailen tilted his head to the side as he regarded her. "Well, ye'll find a warm enough welcome here in my castle, I assure ye," he said.

"Your castle?" Mariah sat up a little straighter. "This castle belongs to you?" she asked as she pointed in the direction of the structure.

"Aye," he replied.

"So, you ruled over this castle at one time?" she asked.

"Nay, my father ruled over th' castle. But that was a long time ago," he said.

"Then at some point, you would've governed it, had you not died."

Cailen shook his head. "Nay. My eldest brother

would have inherited that title after th' death of my father if he outlived him, and then a succession of brothers after that. I'm just a knight."

The look that sprang into Cailen's eyes made Mariah shiver. She suddenly felt as if she traveled grounds he'd rather not traverse. Did her question get too close to his reasons for remaining at his castle, rather than moving into the realm of spirits? She sought for a quick change in subject. In so doing, she said the first thing that entered her mind. "So tell me, what is the name of the female ghost who lives here? She seems nice enough."

A look of confusion settled over his features. "Female ghost?"

"Yes," she said. "The spirit with long red hair. I saw her in my bedroom last night just as I finished unpacking."

Cailen shook his head. "We don't have any women livin' here."

"Oh, but you do," Mariah insisted. "I clearly saw her go through the wall."

"Mayhap th' shadows in your room made it appear so," he replied. "All that bide here are my fellow knights."

She didn't wish to argue the point. Who better to know who lived at his castle than Cailen anyway? Besides, his comment perplexed her somewhat, and she needed clarification.

"Are you telling me the entire garrison of knights I saw down on the field with you just now actually exists?" She gulped. "They're not merely figments of my overzealous imagination?"

Sir Cailen Braithnoch turned his gaze heavenward

and laughed over her astonishment.

He rose to his feet, extended his hand in invitation, and said, "Aye, come with me now, my lady, and I will introduce them to ye."

Chapter 4

Excited voices filled the great hall. Each one clamored for her attention now that Cailen had presented her to his entire garrison. Did he really think she would remember each of their names with one quick pass?

She found it obvious that Duncan, the dusky redhead with hazel eyes and boyish grin, found humor in every situation he encountered. His eyes danced with merriment, and she suspected that throughout his entire existence, he actively sought an opportunity to indulge his mischievousness. She remembered his name not only because he made her repeat it several times over, but also because Cailen introduced him as his lieutenant. Despite the introduction, she noticed a far deeper kinship than just that of a lieutenant and his captain. Their familiar banter and friendly insults bore all the marks that arise from spending an entire lifetime in each other's company and not just the afterlife.

The twin brothers, Malcolm and Edmund, had brown eyes and hair as dark as Cailen's. They too, seemed part of her knight's inner circle. As did Alan, the green-eyed redhead who had a smattering of freckles covering his face, and Steven, the blue-eyed blond with a more muscular frame.

The other knights, whose names floated around inside her brain without finding a suitable anchor, didn't possess the same level of familiar camaraderie, but weren't far behind either. She remembered Cailen saying the name John at least three times and William twice. There might also be at least one other Duncan or did he say Donald? Perhaps he also mentioned a Robin or Robert among the fifty or so names that rolled off his tongue. Would she ever learn them all? And why did so many of the knights he personally commanded during his mortality remain earthbound? Surely, they didn't all die at the same time and in the same place. Therefore, how did they all come together? Why didn't any of them walk into the light and move on to wherever it is that spirits go?

"Murriah," Malcolm hollered out from across the room. His lecherous grin made her instantly wary. "Do ye have a husband or is your hand still free for th' takin'?"

Mariah dropped her gaze as the room erupted into boisterous laughter, and all eyes turned toward her. A blush spread across her cheeks in response. From her place atop the table nearest the stairs, she stared down at her feet and for a moment, she watched as they tapped a slow beat against the bench. She lifted her chin and caught Cailen gazing at her most intently as if he, more so than the others, desired to hear her reply.

She cleared her throat. "No, I don't have a husband, yet."

"Well, that's good to know." Edmund nudged Malcolm's ribs and winked.

Duncan shook his head and scoffed, "Not as if she'd be interested in either one of ye weedy, gorbellied half-wits." He turned to face her and rolled his eyes.

His comment made her laugh. Yet before she could

respond, he added, "And neither would her father."

Her father? What did her father have to do with—
Oh. She bit back a smile as comprehension dawned. "I
hate to break it to you, Duncan, but arranged marriages,
at least in the western part of the world, ended centuries
ago. Nowadays women choose whom they want to
marry themselves, and I believe most of the time, they
choose the men they love," she said.

The revelation brought the brawny knights to their
feet. Excited voices once again filled the hall as they
discussed this astonishing information. Their various
comments, both pro and con, filled her with laughter.
Finally, Alan, looking quite perplexed, asked her the
one question she loathed to answer.

"Then why haven't ye chosen anyone, yet? There
must be plenty of men that desire your hand," he said.

The hall grew quiet. She stared at her feet again
while she considered her response. After all, she did
have a wide variety of reasons from which to choose.
She just had to pick one. When she lifted her eyes, she
could see that each of the knights awaited her answer.
Mariah propped her elbows on her knees and rested her
chin atop her clasped fingers. "Oh, I don't know. I
suppose it's because I haven't found the man destined
to claim my heart."

The simple answer Mariah gave pleased Cailen.
Yet, he also sensed her distress over having to give it,
and knowing his knights as well as he did, he sought to
rescue his lady from the crude, boorish questions that
would surely follow. "I have a question of my own, if
ye dinnae mind," he said, breaking through the
laughter.

"I don't mind at all." The pretty blush remained,

yet her eyes looked hopeful as she made her reply.

"Ye've come to paint th' castle, I know, but I couldn't help wonderin' why?" he asked.

She presented him with a charming smile that bespoke her gratitude. He answered with a wink and a single nod of his head.

"The paintings are for a project called the Gallery of Castles," she said.

"What's that?" asked Duncan.

"Well, the answer needs a bit of an explanation. Several years ago, a very wealthy man by the name of Ryan Maitland set out on a personal quest to see the world's greatest palaces and castles. Once he returned from his odyssey, he said it distressed him to see so many of the structures falling into irreparable ruin. That fueled his desire to see them immortalized on canvas before time erased them altogether. Photographs were out of the question. You see, he wanted artists to paint the buildings not only as they are now, but also as they once were. Added to that, he has asked us to create a few imaginative scenes of each structure's past.

"Mr. Maitland found several willing investors for such a project and together they created an international board of directors to oversee it. He charged each director with choosing a specific number of the best castles or palaces in their respective country."

"Why only th' best?" asked Edmund.

"Because it would take more money than what they had available to paint them all," she said. "However, if the project proves successful and has enough monetary return, I'm told they will consider a phase two, a phase three, and so on."

"What are they goin' to do with th' paintin's?"

asked Malcolm.

"Once they're all finished, and each artist now has a six month deadline, the paintings will go on a worldwide tour, which debuts in London," she replied. "Once the ten-year tour ends, the board of directors will take possession of the paintings and find them a permanent home."

Her words filled Cailen with dread. Until she mentioned it just now, he didn't think about the day she'd leave the castle. He certainly didn't consider deadlines. How many more castles did she have to paint in the six months she had left? As he pondered the question, Duncan asked it.

"This is the last castle I'm scheduled to paint," she said in response.

Her answer gave him a small measure of relief. For although six months seemed naught but a diminutive instant in time, six months far outweighed the prospects of only one or two.

"How many have ye painted thus far?" asked Steven.

"I just finished painting my third castle in Wales and I've already painted three in England. This castle is the only one in Scotland Mr. Humphries assigned to me. However, I know there is another artist who has painted several other castles here as well," she replied. "So you needn't worry, this country is well represented."

Malcolm's smile broadened. "Well, as far as I'm concerned, ye couldn't have been handed a better assignment. This is th' finest castle in all of Scotland. I can attest to that."

"I wholeheartedly agree with you," Mariah replied,

pointing a finger in his direction. "However, now that you've brought the matter to my attention, I suppose I'd better excuse myself and work a bit on the principal background before I go to bed. That way the oils on the canvas have a chance to dry during the night."

"Can we watch ye paint?" asked Donald as she climbed down from the table. "We vow to be as quiet as th' dead while ye work."

Mariah dipped her head and laughed. Then as she turned toward the stairway she said, "All of a sudden, that doesn't give me a whole lot of comfort, but of course, you're all welcome to watch anytime you want. I don't mind an audience."

Much later that night and while Mariah slept, Cailen wandered outside the castle and headed for the river seeking a bit of solitude. He approached the secluded area they shared earlier and recollected their brief time together. She had turned and looked upon him with such confusion once she heard the sound of his voice. Yet, with certainty, neither his words nor spiritual form caused her distress. For after she finally accepted the reality of his presence, she fearlessly extended a hand to his face.

If he had breath to hold, he would've held it at that moment. He desired her touch, and more so than he had desired anything else for a very long time. He marveled over the pleasant sensation her fingers provided him as they lightly traced his face and stroked against his beard. He wouldn't have thought such a thing possible.

Though he knew he shouldn't, he looked forward to the coming days he'd spend in her company and with unexpected eagerness. For without doubt, he would take the utmost advantage of each day and each moment they shared, regardless of the consequences—be they good or bad. And why? Because he could feel a most powerful, undeniable, yet inexplicable connection to her soul. He shook his head, stared up at the stars, and said, "Cailen, my laddie, I think you're in a bit of trouble."

****

The alarm sounded and without opening her eyes, Mariah searched for the clock on the night table. She fumbled for and then found the button that would kill the obnoxious buzzer. Surely, it couldn't be time to get up yet. Not when exhaustion destroyed her ability to move, much less rise. She snuggled deeper into the duvet.

Mere seconds later, her cell phone rang. She sat straight up in her bed, rubbed the sleep from her eyes, and retrieved the device that for now, only served to annoy. "Hello?"

Nothing but static responded to her greeting. She closed her weary eyes and tried again. "Hello? Mariah Jennings speaking—"

A series of bizarre tones filtered through the earpiece and nothing else.

Her fingers combed through her tousled hair as she peeked down at the screen on her phone. She blinked a few times to ensure she saw the number correctly. The incoming call originated from the phone she held in her hand. A little creepy, but perhaps the airwaves somehow scrambled themselves. After all, she couldn't blame ghosts on this one. If one of the unruly residents of this castle wanted to speak with her, they'd probably just barge through the door. She wouldn't put it past them to climb atop the huge bed and have a chat with her either—

Fatigue prevented her from giving it any further consideration. Just as she slumped against the softness of her mattress, she glanced at her bedside clock. She gasped, tossed the covers to the side, and leaped out of bed. Far more than mere seconds passed between the sounding of the alarm and her phone call. How could she have overslept? She rushed over to the wardrobe, grabbed a scoop-necked, white T-shirt, a pair of faded jeans, and then raced for the shower.

Twenty minutes later, she stepped inside Sybil's kitchen in search of breakfast. Today, she settled for scrambled eggs, a piece of toast, and a glass of juice. Just about the time she had wolfed down half her food, Cailen appeared sitting in the chair opposite her.

She dabbed the corners of her mouth with the tip of her finger and returned his smile. "Good morning."

"Good morn, my lady. Did ye sleep well?" he asked.

She nodded as she scooped up the rest of her eggs. "I believe I did. In fact, I don't remember turning over or even dreaming. Therefore, you'd think I'd feel a little more rested than I do."

"Ye did have rather an eventful day yesterday. Mayhap it took a toll," he said.

"Perhaps." She swallowed down the last couple bites of her breakfast, finished her juice, and rose from the table. "Still, I don't want to fall behind my schedule. The paintings will look rushed if I do, and your magnificent castle deserves my very best efforts."

Cailen remained silent while she cleaned up the kitchen, and she wondered where his thoughts had taken him. But then just as she turned away from the sink to ask he said, "Yesterday ye mentioned ye were to paint th' castle as it looked in th' beginnin', aye?"

She dried her hands with the kitchen towel and nodded. "Yes, I did."

"I dinnae wish to intrude on your time, but would ye like me to take ye around th' place? I could tell ye exactly what it looked like durin' my mortal life," he said.

Excitement filled Mariah over the prospect. She flashed him a smile, replaced the towel in its rack, and said, "I'd love you to show me your castle—if you don't mind."

Cailen began his account even as they left the cottage. He told her the house had *only* existed for about two hundred years or so. They built the structure for the first caretaker, when the last of his kin finally vacated the premises, and left it in the hands of strangers. Despite the others who professed ownership thereafter, all the caretakers of this land, he said, descended in one way or another from a single freeman of his fiefdom. The fierce loyalty of which, a very pleasant and loyal man by the name of Ewen, passed on to his progeny.

"That's really amazing," she said. "Your Ewen must have been quite a man."

"Aye." Cailen nodded and then pointed to his temple. "We all thought his goodwife a bit dunderheaded though."

Mariah laughed as they entered the gateway to the middle bailey. The baileys, courtyards, and outer fields, he said, had changed very little over the centuries. Of course, all the stones looked much brighter in their original state.

From the bailey, they entered the gallery. They passed through its roomy hall and down the steps leading to the kitchen. Cailen told her then that while his father lived, and for his great love of music, he kept musicians playing from early morning until late at night. He said one always had to step over a musician or two when they entered other areas leading to or away from the vicinity.

"Cailen, do you remember how long it's been since the castle last housed occupants?" she asked. "Well, *living* residents, that is."

"Aye. 'Twas during the time called World War Two," he said. "George's father, a man called George as well, said German planes were droppin' bombs on th' city of London. In an effort to keep th' bairns safe, they sent them out of th' city to safer havens. This castle, deserted for over half a century by then, served as one of those havens."

Mariah drew in a sharp breath. "Really? How many children took refuge here?"

"I believe we provided shelter for twenty-seven bairns and th' six women that cared for them," Cailen replied. "That's when George acquired th' beast outside in th' bailey, so th' wee ones would have light as the rationed fuel allowed them and not be afraid inside th' spooky old castle at night."

"Did any of them ever catch sight of you or your men?" she asked.

"Aye. Some bairns seem to have that gift," he replied. "But we made sure they weren't afraid of us. Some of them even took to followin' us around."

"I wouldn't doubt that for a single minute," she said. "More than likely, you made them feel safe and protected. After all, what are a few bombs in comparison with a host of burly knights?"

After they toured the kitchen, he escorted her into the treasury room. From there they traveled upstairs to the second floor solar rooms, one of which she now slept in. His room, in fact. He described each of them in glorious, vivid detail, so much so that she could visualize them inside her mind.

"I think you might have to tell me this all over again, when I have a sketchbook in my hand," she said. Her gaze wandered around the room in which his father had slept with a succession of wives, after Cailen's mother died shortly after giving birth to her only daughter. "I'll never remember all of the colors and furnishings, otherwise."

He merely nodded and then said, "Come on, I'll show ye th' chapel."

They sat together on the same pew Cailen occupied when she thought him a figment of her imagination. Once he described the original condition of the room, he told her the cleric in residence during his mortal life, used more sacramental wine in one month than the others did in an entire year. When his father confronted the man with it, he directed the fault away from himself by saying, "What with all th' devils that needed adjurin' around th' place, what did ye expect?"

Cailen knew without reservation, he referred to him and his knights. The story of the priest attempting to exorcise the devils possessing the souls of Cailen and his men made her laugh. The tale also gave her a bit more insight as to their mortal shenanigans for his indulgent father to consider such a statement valid.

To finish their tour, they made their way back

down to the great hall. After Cailen described the original furnishings here, he told her King Robert knighted him, along with many of his men there on the dais. Her mouth dropped.

"You were knighted by Robert the Bruce?" She knew she stared. But how often did one talk to someone who personally knew the famous Scottish King?

"Aye," he replied with an indifferent shrug. "He was a verra great man and earned our loyalty and respect many times over."

She shifted her attention to the dais as her imagination envisioned such a scene. Then and there, she decided to paint the image she saw in her mind's eye. She would paint Robert the Bruce knighting Sir Cailen Braithnoch. His closest friends would stand just behind him, while the rest of the men from this fiefdom would observe the proceedings from whatever position they could find inside this hall. The idea of painting a portrait using the men who actually participated in the ceremony filled her with eager anticipation. She would wrench every detail possible from Cailen's memory and make it just as accurate as she possibly could.

"Would ye like to see th' secret passageways?" he asked.

"Hmm?" She tore her eyes away from the dais and gave him her full attention. "I'm sorry, what did you say?"

"I asked if ye would like to see th' secret passageways underneath th' castle," he repeated.

"You have secret passageways?" she asked.

She wondered over her facial expression because the moment their eyes met, Cailen laughed and gently traced the contours of her cheek with a finger. She could feel it.

"Aye," he said. "Over th' centuries, th' knowledge of their existence was lost to th' livin', though."

"I'd love you to show me," she replied.

Cailen led her back through the kitchen and into the buttery. He opened a little door behind the wine shelves almost impossible to see unless one knew exactly where to find it. She saw only darkness beyond it.

"Bide here for a wee moment," he said.

Seconds later, subdued light filtered up the steps.

"Come along now," Cailen called out. "I vow I will not let ye fall."

The sight of the wall torch alight with fire, didn't surprise her.

"How do you do stuff like that?" she asked as she stared pointedly at the flame.

"Like what?" He raised a brow in question as he followed the direction of her gaze.

"Lighting fires to start with," she replied, "and then we can move to opening doors and other solid objects."

"A lot of trial, error, and dedicated practice," he said, "coupled with th' desire to do so. Take hold of th' torch now, and watch your step. Th' stairs are a wee bit narrow around th' curve."

Mariah extracted the torch from its metal brace, and followed her ghostly companion as he led her below the castle foundation. The smell of stagnant air and dampened earth assailed her nostrils. Roots protruded from the rocky walls, and a vast assortment of unsightly bugs slithered and skittered along the ground. She ducked more than once to avoid the spidery cobwebs and their living residents. She suppressed more than one shiver along the way.

"We used th' passageways many times to surprise and surround our enemies once they approached th' castle gates," Cailen told her. "And there were times we used them to keep our women and bairns safe when our enemies attacked the castle."

His off-handed comment drew Mariah's attention away from the bugs. Until this moment, it never occurred to her that her knight would have had a family of his own. Why the thought distressed her, she couldn't say. But common sense told her that even the highest born lady in all of Scotland would happily become his wife. She swallowed past the ridiculous knot forming in her throat and tried her best to sound casual. "So, how many children did you have?"

The question surprised him. He halted his steps, turned around to face her, and then pinned his gaze to hers. "I didna have any," he finally said.

Despite the intensity of his gaze, Mariah wanted clarification. "You never married?"

"No. I suppose I never found a maiden I desired for a wife durin' my mortal years," he replied. "And unlike my older brothers, marriage wasn't a requirement for me. Th' youngest son has his own privileges, ye ken?"

The ensuing relief baffled her, but she wouldn't dwell on the reasons for that now. Perhaps later she could sort through the vast array of emotions her knight inspired.

While they strolled along the passageway, she spied several junctions leading away from the main path. She recalled at least two that veered left and one that veered right. After a time, curiosity got the better of her.

"Where do the other pathways lead?" she asked.

"Mostly dead ends," he said.

A short while later, they exited the passageway through a narrow portcullis near the moat at the side of the castle. An abundance of plant life obscured the metal bars and more than likely, because the moat gave the surrounding foliage ample water, they always had.

She met Cailen's gaze and gave him a smile. "What an amazing experience. I really enjoyed spending the morning with you, Sir Cailen, so thank you very much for the tour."

"'Twas my pleasure, Murriah," he said. "I enjoyed it myself."

Her name sounded like a whispered caress. The way he looked at her filled her with liquid warmth that began somewhere deep inside her heart and spewed outward in every possible direction of her body. On top of that, she tingled from head to foot. The force of the sensation made her a little breathless. She hoped that whatever she said in response made sense, because she had no idea what she said before she excused herself to return to her work.

She carried her bemused state back inside the castle and all the way up the stairs to her borrowed studio.

Yet, the moment she crossed the threshold, shock replaced the bemusement. Her mouth dropped and she sucked in a sharp breath as she cast her gaze across the table. Several of her sketchbooks lay wide open and scattered atop the surface. Several sketches stared back. What's more, she made those impossible sketches herself. They were impossible, because Cailen had just finished showing her the secret passageways.

How then, did she draw them with the precision detailed in her sketchbooks?

Better yet, when did she draw them, and why didn't she have any memory of the incident?

Chapter 5

Mariah glanced up from her work and found Cailen standing in the doorway, watching her progress. Stroke by stroke, during the three and a half weeks that had passed since her arrival, his castle had taken shape on the largest canvas. He seemed very pleased with her efforts thus far. With a critical eye, she stood back and took a moment to study the primary painting. Something about the dark storm clouds provided a bit of mystery to the majestic castle. She saw those clouds as symbolic of all the torrential storms it had weathered over the centuries. Yet through every trial and calamity it faced, the magnificent structure survived. She had spent the entire morning detailing the trailing mist that rose up from the grounds after the rain subsided. Her digitized photograph, displayed on the screen of her laptop, aided her accuracy.

The photo she had taken that afternoon amazed her still. For there on the turret, one could count four, barely discernable spirits as they stood guard over the castle. A thing he and his knights had faithfully done for well over seven hundred years now. She wondered then if they ever tired of that duty or the monotony of their established routine inside a realm to which they didn't really belong.

She turned around and wiped her brush against the palette before she braved the question. "Cailen, do you mind if I ask you a personal question that's really none of my business?"

Cailen tilted his head to the side as he regarded her. "If I can ask a personal question of my own in return," he bargained.

"Fair enough." She took a deep breath. "Well, given the fact you didn't live long enough to see your thirtieth year, coupled with your impressive physical stature, I assume you died in battle and not from disease or some silly accident. Am I correct?"

The corners of his mouth twitched. He dipped his head once, and simply waited for her to continue.

"When your spirit left your body, why didn't you go into the light?" she asked.

"Light?" He lifted a brow and shrugged. "What light?"

"The bright light at the end of the tunnel," she replied. "I've read many near-death experiences. Each person talked about the brilliant light that captivated and then beckoned him or her to enter. They say this light guides spirits to wherever they're supposed to go."

"Near-death experiences," he repeated. He paused for several moments, and then shook his head. "I dinnae ken what ye mean. 'Twould seem to me you're either dead or you're not."

"Well, I've not experienced it myself, so I certainly can't verify the truth of the accounts. But there are those who have officially 'died' for several minutes and then lived to tell the tale. Their stories all bear a striking resemblance to each other. Accident and heart attack victims, those who quit breathing during surgeries, even people who have drowned report seeing a dazzling light that exudes love and serenity from within. They say it compels them to enter and so in they go.

"Most of these people will tell you that once they entered the light, they no longer desired to return to their mortal state. Despite their reluctance, a departed family member, or friend acting as their guide tells them their time to die has not yet come. These guides go on to tell them they must return to their bodies. They give various reasons for the directive. Usually it's because the person still has things they need to accomplish while in their mortal form."

Cailen gazed at her in silent contemplation. "I didna see any tunnel or light once I left my mortal body. I only saw th' death and destruction out there on th' moor of Dupplin. At first, I didna even know that death had claimed me. I didna realize it until an enemy passed through me to engage another. Once I turned around, I could see my mortal body stretched out on th' bloody field. I didna see any light that compelled me to enter, no dead kin waitin' to guide me. Besides those that still lived, only me and th' garrison of knights from my fiefdom stood there on the moor."

Mariah dropped her mouth and stared. "Are you telling me that during that one single battle *every* single knight from your fiefdom died?"

"Those that were with me, aye," he said.

"The same knights that are here with us right now?" she ventured further.

"Aye—"

"And none of you saw a tunnel or a brilliant light out there on the field?"

"Nay," he replied. "Neither of them existed."

She took a moment to digest his account.

"Well then, besides your own men, did you at least

see the spirits of the other dead knights there on the field?" she asked. "If so, where did they all go?"

Cailen looked at her as if the thought had never once crossed his mind. He paused for several long seconds before he shook his head and said, "We didna see any others, although for th' bodies strewn aboot, thousands of good men lost their lives durin' th' battle. I dinnae know where their spirits went."

"Odd. I wonder why you didn't see anyone else." Even though she asked the obvious question, he didn't have an answer for the strange occurrence. "So what then—did you just return here to the castle and resume your life as you had always lived it?"

"To th' best of our ability, aye. Of course, there were obvious adjustments we had to make," he said.

"Did you show yourselves to those who still lived here then or talk to them? You know, let them know you were still around?" she asked.

He met her question with silence and just as she turned to discover the cause, he said, "Upon our return, we found th' castle as well as th' entire fiefdom empty of all folk. Panic ensued as we considered th' possible explanations for such an occurrence. We thought mayhap Balliol had our people removed or they had gone into hidin'. Yet no matter how far we traveled, or how oft we looked, we never saw another livin' soul. At least not 'til many years had passed."

"What do you mean by that?" she asked. "I don't understand."

"As time went on we caught brief glimpses of various people inside th' castle, goin' aboot their lives as if they had never left th' premises. Th' glimpses eventually grew in both time and duration. Then one day, 'twas as if we lived among them again, yet they couldn't see or hear us in return. On that day, we discovered that my brother's infant son, Alasdair, was now an old man. We recognized no one else, though as time passed on, we discovered th' kinship these strangers had with those we once knew. 'Tis th' reason we didna trifle with them." He shrugged as if the incident warranted no further discussion.

She dabbed her brush into the mixture of paint she used for mist, turned back to her painting, and while she worked, mulled over everything he just said. Something about his death experience just didn't feel right—

Cailen fixed his gaze on the painting. The fine stroke of her hand created storm clouds that looked as real as any he had ever seen with his own eyes. In various places on the portrait, she made some of them appear translucent. And if one looked close enough, one could see bits of the castle's foliage and stone behind the mist. Her skill far exceeded his expectations. He couldn't remember a finer portrait ever hanging inside his castle or any other for that matter. No wonder the board of directors chose her for this project. He almost hated to interrupt her progress. Almost.

"I believe 'tis my turn for a question," he reminded her.

She nodded, but didn't divert her attention away from her painting.

"Why did ye ignore my presence inside th' chapel on th' day we met, and what did ye mean when ye said I wasn't real and that ye conjured me? I know that's more than one question, but—" He shrugged. For surely the number of questions didn't matter, only the subject.

She straightened her shoulders and looked upward

for several long moments before she turned around and gazed into his eyes. Her expression seemed troubled. At length, she released the small breath she had held, placed her tools atop her cart, and made her way to the table. She picked up some of her sketchbooks and then turned around to face him.

"I hope you don't think I'm crazy," she murmured as she approached her stool, sat down, and motioned him over to have a look. He couldn't imagine that what she held would explain her odd comments, though. Nonetheless, he positioned himself just to her right and slightly behind her.

She lifted the most worn from among them. "I completed the sketches inside this book over three years ago. This one, over two, and this one contains some of my more recent drawings. Recent, meaning during the past several months while I resided in Wales."

He peered over her shoulder as she opened the first book and looked down at the page. Cailen met the sight with a fair amount of surprise. He could feel her eyes upon him as he absorbed even the smallest detail of her exceptional drawing. She had sketched him without armor. He wore just his léine and brat. She portrayed him leaning over and resting his arms upon the arched wall of a stone bridge with his hands loosely clasped. His face carried a pensive expression. If he didn't know better, he would think that once, a very long time ago, she had caught sight of him and sketched his face while he tarried there. For the bridge truly existed, even if some of the landscape she sketched around it, did not. Mayhap he would show it to her sometime soon.

He looked up from the book, caught, and then held her gaze. Several silent seconds passed between them.

Without looking away, she turned the page. Once again, she tilted her head downward. He glanced at the leaf in her book. 'Twas like looking at his reflection in a pool of still water. More pages and more images followed, each one drawn with obvious detail and care.

"I dinnae ken," he finally said.

She shrugged her shoulders slightly, and raised her brows a tad. "I don't understand it myself," she whispered in return.

"And ye have sketched my image for three years now?" he asked.

She let out a bit of a laugh as if what he said amused her in some way. "Cailen, I have drawn your face for as far back as I have memory. I have hundreds of sketchbooks in a closet at home that contain your image within the pages. All throughout my life people wondered over your identity. I told them all the same thing. I don't know who he is, or where his image originated from. I only know he exists in my mind."

Her eyes begged for his understanding, yet he found no need for such a request. He extended a hand and gently caressed the side of her lovely face. "'Twould seem that somehow our destinies are entwined, my lady. 'Tis obvious th' fates have decreed it. Though I dinnae ken th' reason just now, I cannae say I'm sorry," he said.

"Cailen, I want you to know that I feel like I have always, always—"

At that moment, the chirping of her phone interrupted the response he truly wanted to hear. If he had a sword in his hands, he would have hacked the thing to pieces and killed it. She shook her head in annoyance and then dropped her hand inside her pocket.

"I'll leave ye to your call. When you're finished with your work for th' day, ye'll find us down in th' hall," he said.

She nodded as she lifted her phone to her ear. But then just as he cleared the doorway, she greeted Evan. He halted his exit, and though he knew he shouldn't, he stayed long enough to listen in on their conversation.

"I'm doing just fine, thank you," Mariah said, using naught but an amiable tone. That tone provided him with a great measure of satisfaction.

"Well, you haven't come out to th' pub even once since you arrived at th' castle, and so I worried that something might have happened to you out there," Evan said.

"You needn't worry about me. I'm fine," she replied. "When I get caught up in my work I have a tendency to paint from early morning until late at night, so I—"

"We can't let you work yourself to death," he interrupted. "You need a break every once in a while. They do let you have time off, am I right?"

"My time is mine to use however I see fit as long as I get the paintings done, but it's just that right now, I need—"

"I'm not going to take no for an answer, Mariah," Evan said.

It irritated Cailen the man never let Mariah finish her sentences and he certainly didn't appreciate the stern tone of voice.

"If you don't come out to th' pub for dinner, I'll just have to bring it out there to you then," he threatened.

A twinge of jealousy washed over him. Cailen had never experienced such an emotion before and it took him a moment to name it. If anyone but Evan, he probably would've sought the hapless man out and crushed him. Mariah released a defeated sigh.

"Look, I promise I'll come out to the pub one evening this week, but not today. The painting is in a critical spot right now, and I can't let the oils set without finishing what I'm doing," she said.

"All right then," Evan conceded. "But if I dinnae see you by th' end of th' week—"

"I promise, you will. Let's leave it at that, all right?"

Cailen didn't wait around for the goodbyes. He didn't go down to the hall either. Instead, he wandered out to the secluded bridge Mariah had drawn with such astonishing accuracy. As he gazed out over the rushing water, he contemplated the foreign emotion the mere sound of Evan's voice inspired.

Throughout his entire existence, he had never once lacked for female companionship when he so desired it. Though, something he admittedly enjoyed, none of the women he knew ever invoked feelings of possessiveness or jealousy. No one except Mariah Jennings. He wondered what would come at the end of this experience if he traveled the uncertain path he now walked. Where could such a course possibly lead him anyway? She had just a little over five months before she packed up and left this place. If he had any sense about him, he would distance himself from her now. He would no longer seek her out, but remain cordial whenever their paths crossed—

A broad smile stole across his face over the

preposterous notion. Just as surely as the sun rose each morning, he would continue to walk this precarious path. He had no will to do otherwise regardless of where it led, nor the heartache it might cause. Regret, for lack of action on his part, had never been part of his temperament.

Perhaps at the end of it—just as he witnessed between the spirit of Mathias McGregor and his mortal woman—he and Mariah would discover a love that transcended time. He would have to win her heart, of course, but perhaps he could conquer that battle in the allotted time. After all, she did say his physical stature impressed her, did she not?

****

Later that night, after enjoying a rather hilarious evening with Cailen and his knights, Mariah readied herself for bed. She sat down in front of her desk and turned on her computer. During their conversation today, Cailen said he died at a place called Dupplin. She wondered then if she could find something on the Internet concerning his final battle.

She typed the key words into the search engine, pressed enter, and instantly received over nine thousand hits. History obviously knew the conflict well enough, even if she didn't. She selected the first entry and devoured the first couple of paragraphs. Yet, as time passed, she found the task more difficult than she first imagined. How could she find it otherwise? She now knew fifty-three knights personally, who fought and died in that horrendous battle. If not for the narrow valley, perhaps her knights might have reigned victorious. At the very least, some of them might have survived. She hoped that neither Cailen nor his knights suffered a slow, painful death, as did so many warriors on that bloody battlefield.

Her thoughts wandered to the conversation they shared this morning and to all the things she didn't get the chance to say. She didn't tell him that whenever he stood in the same room she occupied, her ability to take a normal breath ceased altogether or that her insides churned. She didn't get to tell him the man she had come to know stood far superior to the one her mind created and in every possible way. And what would he think of the anguish that consumed her whenever she contemplated the day of their final farewell? For such a day would come.

As she exited out of the Internet and shut down her computer, she said aloud to no one in particular, "He'd probably think you were crazy, Mariah, that's what he'd think. And no one would blame him for that."

She rose from her seat and closed the lid of her laptop. A yawn accompanied a sumptuous stretch as she turned toward the bed with every intention of climbing into it. But in that same moment, she spied a flash of red hair from the corner of her eye.

She whirled around for a better look. Mariah gasped as the ghostly presence drifted toward the same wall she went through once before. The vision couldn't possibly be a figment of her imagination or the product of shadows. Not this time.

"No, wait!" she whispered.

The entity paid her no heed. Mariah rushed out of the doorway, hoping to find the ghost in the hall. Her eyes darted in all directions, yet she didn't see anything out of the ordinary.

Suddenly then, the heavy scent of heather

permeated the air around her. She turned and followed it down the hallway. As the aroma drifted toward the stairs, Mariah continued to pursue it, grateful now, that shortly after her arrival, the knights insisted on keeping the wall torches lit at night for her benefit.

Her heart pounded inside her chest as she sought to follow the same path the ghostly woman traversed, and she wondered if the knights down inside the great hall could hear the sound of her bare footsteps pattering against the stone. Would they come and investigate the reason for it? She could only hope they would. They needed to see this ghost too. Once she stepped onto the landing, the scent disappeared as quickly as it had arrived. She didn't know whether to descend the stairs or try another hallway.

"Come on," she murmured. "Where did you go?" Just then, the distinctive click of a metal door latch echoed down the corridor of the east hall. She peered into the darkness, took a deep breath, and followed the sound. The creaking of the chapel doors, now standing slightly ajar, begged her attention. She opened them wider and stepped inside.

The light of the moon filtered into the room through the stained glass window. The colors cast eerie shadows on the wall. Her eyes struggled to adjust to the darkness as she made her way down the center aisle. She shivered against the sudden drop in temperature and right now, she could literally see the condensation of her breath. Her heartbeat accelerated and just as she thought to flee to the safety of the great hall, a low mournful cry resonated from behind the sacramental cupboard. Heart-wrenching sobs followed the ghostly wail.

She backed away from the anguished sound, yet never once took her eyes off the wall.

"Cailen!" she cried out. His name no more than passed her lips, before he appeared instantly at her side and so did more than half the knights. They filled the chapel and some even stood out in the hallway. Cailen's hand slipped around her waist as his eyes searched her face. The moment he appeared, the crying ceased.

"Are ye all right?" he asked.

"I heard something behind the wall," she said, pointing at the shelves. "It sounded like a woman crying—"

Duncan glanced at Cailen and shrugged. "I'll see to it. A beastie likely got itself stuck again," he said.

Cailen nodded and then Duncan disappeared. Mariah gazed into his eyes. "A beastie?"

"Aye. At times a hapless cat or squirrel will find its way inside th' castle, squeeze through th' cracks, get inside and cannae find its way out," he said.

She drew her brows together. "What's in there?"

"A small oratory," he replied.

A few minutes later, Duncan reappeared inside the chapel. He wore a broad smile on his face, and carried a small mewling kitten in his hand. He placed the creature gently into her hands. "I think it needs to eat."

Chapter 6

Mariah dipped her brushes inside and swirled them around the jar of turpentine atop the table. Once she had them cleaned, she dried them with a linen cloth and placed them in the top drawer of her cart. All without saying a word.

"You're cleanin' up early," Cailen finally said.

A guilty flush appeared on her face. "I know, but this is a good place to stop for the day and fulfill my obligation to Evan."

"Your obligation to Evan?" he asked, feigning ignorance.

"Yes, I promised I'd have dinner at the pub sometime this week and I'm just about to run out of time," she replied. "He's the man who brought me lunch several weeks ago. I'm sure you must remember his visit."

"Aye, I remember his visit. But since ye said that ye had just arrived from Wales, I've been meaning to ask ye where ye might have met him."

"Oh. Well, I met him at a local pub called the Water Cuddie. I happened across the place while on my way out here, actually," she said. "Hunger gnawed at my backbone and so when I saw the place off the side of the road, I thought I'd stop and get a bite to eat. Evan told me his regular help didn't come in that day because of the storm, so he waited on me himself. Once he discovered my purpose here in the Highlands, he decided to introduce himself. Then after he served my meal, he sat down at my table while I ate, and we chatted for a bit. He told me he managed the pub and invited me to return whenever I so desired to mingle with the locals."

"Is that all he told ye aboot himself—that he managed th' pub?" he asked, keeping his tone casual.

She shot a glance heavenward, paused for a moment, and then shrugged. "Hmm. Yeah, I guess that's about it, other than the fact he's lived his entire life in the general area of the village, knows everyone intimately, and didn't mind sharing personal information about the various residents. I think he likes to ask the questions, though."

Why didn't Evan tell her that he grew up right here on the castle grounds? The laddie must not have given Mariah his full name either. If he had, she would've surely questioned his kinship to George and Sybil.

"Well," Mariah said as her gaze meandered about the room. "That about does it for now, I guess."

"So it appears," he replied.

She checked the room a final time. "All right then, I guess I'll go change my clothes and get this little chore over with. I'll see you all when I get back, all right?"

He merely nodded in response and hoped she didn't detect his inner turmoil over her impending evening in Evan's company. The intensity of that turmoil did naught but increase as she entered her car and drove away without a backward glance.

"Is she goin' to meet up with Evan, then?" asked Duncan as he joined him there on the turret.

Cailen nodded, but said nothing in return.

Duncan tsked in response. "Why do ye suppose th' laddie doesna tell her who he is? He's had ample opportunity."

"I dinnae know," answered Cailen. "Sooner or later she'll find out on her own. I'm sure that come that day, she'll wonder aboot th' deception, for a deception it is."

Duncan let loose a derisive snort. "I wonder aboot it myself, for I see no logical reason for it."

****

Mariah took in a deep breath and held it as she entered the crowded pub. If not for her desire to extract some information from the locals, she would've found an excuse not to come at all, promise or no promise.

"Hey, Mariah," Evan hollered out above the chatter. "We were just talking aboot you."

She returned his broad smile with a pleasant one of her own. "You were?"

"Indeed we were." Evan shifted his attention to the man sitting upon the bar stool in front of him and backhanded his shoulder. "See? I told you."

"Told him what?" she asked as she slipped into a chair at an empty table close to the bar.

"I told him you braved th' horrors of Laird MacNaughton's castle and emerged from th' experience unscathed," he joked.

The man turned to face her, gave her a wink, and laughed. "You must have th' ghosties eating out of your hand then, lassie. Of course, I can't blame them for that," he said, bouncing his eyebrows. "Given th' chance—"

Evan shook his head as he cast his gaze heavenward. "Watch th' blatant flirting, Jeremy.

71

Katherine won't approve and you know it."

Mariah tilted her head to the side as she returned Jeremy's gaze. "What ghosts?" she asked.

The occupants of the pub roared with laughter over the question. All the while, she maintained a stoic expression and simply shrugged.

"Och, come on, now." The man sitting next to Jeremy said. "You can't tell me you haven't seen th' fearsome ghosts that haunt th' castle."

"Sorry, I haven't seen the ghosts you speak of. But, tell me, have you seen any of them at the castle yourself? Or, is this all just legend and hearsay?" she asked.

"I have seen them." His gaze wandered over the patrons in the room. Each of them nodded in turn to bolster his claim. "In fact, we have all seen them at one time or another."

"Really? What did you all see?" She leaned against the back of her chair and smiled her thanks as Evan set a glass of ice water in front of her. She picked it up and took a sip.

"Want th' special of th' day? We have roast lamb," he cut in.

"That'll be fine, thank you," she replied and then returned her attention to the men seated at the bar.

The man who last spoke had trouble meeting her eyes. His lips trembled a bit and then after he gave his head a shake, he fixed his gaze with hers and said, "Hundreds of medieval knights haunt MacNaughton's castle and they don't like trespassers."

Jeremy nodded. He downed the contents of his mug and then wiped his sleeve across his mouth. "Believe what Sebastian tells you," he said. "We have all seen them for ourselves."

"*Hundreds* of knights you say?" Mariah tilted her head to the side. "And you felt they all threatened you in some way or other?"

One of the burly patrons left his stool and joined her at her table. Jeremy and Sebastian followed suit. Though he never took his eyes off her, the man held his empty glass toward the pretty blue-eyed, brown-haired waitress and bellowed, "Another one, Linda."

"Coming right up, Jerry," she sang in return.

Jerry waited until Linda refreshed his beverage and set Mariah's dinner in front of her before he continued his tale. "We've all grown up here, and heard all th' scary stories from our parents and grandparents countless times through the years."

"Scary stories?" she repeated with a slight shake of her head.

"Th' scary stories that make bairns behave," Jerry said. "For more than a hundred years nobody has owned th' castle longer than it took to sell it again. They stayed there even less time than that—until Laird MacNaughton that is. But he only bought it in order to keep it out of th' hands of th' developers, you ken? He never lived there himself, nor did he ever intend to."

Mariah nodded.

"Anyway, we always heard th' knights didn't accept any strangers invading their home, regardless of the duration of time. While we were growing up, our parents forbid us to go anywhere near th' place. They had their own stories, of course. But we didn't believe them at the time."

Sebastian took a swig from his glass and chuckled. "No, unfortunately, we didn't."

"Anyway, one night, a crew of us decided to go out there and see th' place. We were all young teenagers at th' time and full of ourselves." He paused for several moments and then shrugged. "We learned that night that you dinnae provoke th' dead."

"You have to remember, lassie," Jeremy cut in, "That Jerry has a big mouth and doesn't know when to shut it."

The comment caused another round of laughter. Jerry shook his head and smirked.

"So, what happened?" she asked as she took another bite of her mouth-watering roast and followed it with sip of water.

"Well, after Jerry got cheeky, this very tall and very brawny knight appeared near th' bottom of th' stairway. He was just th' first, mind you. More knights appeared right behind him, and they all held these wicked-looking swords or axes in their hands," Jeremy said.

Sebastian nodded. "And th' first knight—th' one that led th' others—had a murderous expression in his eyes. He never looked away as he walked down th' last three steps."

At that point in his narrative, Mariah's gaze lit upon an older woman. She sat alone at a table near the back of the room with eyes cast downward. Yet as Sebastian's tale unfolded, the woman repeatedly balled her hands into fists, as if what he said filled her with either distaste or distress. Mariah wondered then if she had a story of her own. Her eyes wandered away from the woman and finally rested upon Evan. He gazed at her intently, seeking something she couldn't quite identify. Did he think their story frightened her? Once again, she focused her attention on Sebastian.

"I think we were all dumbfounded, for not one of us moved from th' spot upon which we stood, at least, not until th' knights raised their swords and suddenly, rushed at us," he said.

"After they let loose with their bloody war cries I dinnae mind telling you that we screamed like women and raced for th' door," Jerry said. "Several of th' lads even soiled themselves along th' way. We won't mention any names, however."

"Why not?" Jeremy raised a mischievous brow and smirked. "Afraid your name will be counted among them?"

Laughter filled the room and Mariah waited for it to die down before she asked the question his comments prompted. "Is that the one and only time you've seen the ghosts?"

Jeremy shook his head. "No, unfortunately, there are moments our local brew renders us senseless and makes us brave enough to try again. Especially if we hope to earn th' admiration and favor of th' lassies."

Mariah took another drink of her water. All the while she struggled to find the words that would provide the answer she sought without appearing to fish for it. She set her glass down. As she dabbed at the corner of her mouth with her napkin, Linda hurried over to refill her glass.

"You've told me that hundreds of terrifying knights inhabit MacNaughton's castle. But I have found, in the various castles I've painted, there are ghosts from many different eras," Mariah said. "For example, a very sweet Victorian spirit shared a castle in Wales with an insidious fifteenth century monk. So, do you think *all* the ghosts of MacNaughton's castle hail from the same time? Or do you think there might be one or two that might've—"

"I didn't get close enough to ask them," Sebastian cut in.

The crowd howled with laughter and Jerry slapped his knee repeatedly over the comment his companion made in jest, but stated in truth. Once he got hold of himself, he wiped his eyes. "They were all dressed in similar manner, Mariah. If not from th' same time, then very close to it, I would say."

No one said a word about the female ghost she both saw and heard. She masked her disappointment as the conversation drifted away from spiritual entities and onto other topics. The patrons had all the usual questions about her career, the castle project, and life in America. All the while, the elderly lady in the corner cast furtive glances in her direction. An hour or so later, Linda made her way to the woman while carrying a pitcher of water in her hand. She filled her glass and gave her an apologetic shrug.

"I'm sorry, Mum, but it looks like I'm going to have to work late," she said. "I can take you home when I get a break, that's th' best I can do."

Mariah offered silent thanks to the mercy of heaven as the opportunity to excuse herself landed right in her lap. She pushed away from the table and vacated her chair. Despite the protests, she scooped her keys off the table. "Linda, I really need to get back to the castle anyway, so if you'd like, I can take your mother home."

Linda looked surprised, yet at the same time she appeared grateful for the offer. "You dinnae mind?"

She shook her head. "No, I don't mind at all."

"Then I'd be grateful to you. I can see th' poor dear's getting tired, and I dinnae want to make her wait," Linda replied.

Evan expressed his disappointment as he walked them out to her car. He hoped he could have spent a little more time with her this evening, he said.

"I'm sorry about that," she replied. "But it's getting late and I need to get up extra early for the next phase of the paintings. In case you've forgotten, I do have a deadline to meet."

He said he understood—though he didn't—and waved them off with a sort of petulant look marring his face. Even so, she sighed with relief as she, and the woman Linda introduced as Hester, headed down the road. They made small talk during the drive to the house she shared with Linda. But then as she pulled up in front of the gate, Hester made no move to exit the car. Instead, the woman turned to face her and searched her eyes for several seconds before she spoke.

"You've met th' knights, haven't you," she said matter-of-factly.

Mariah paused for a moment. "Well, I can honestly say that I haven't met the terrifying knights the men spoke of tonight."

Hester leaned a little closer. She flashed an impish smile that erased years from her face. "I never thought Sir Cailen was terrifying, either."

The comment made Mariah laugh outright as she nodded. "No, he isn't."

"In fact, I must admit, there was a time I had a huge crush on th' man," Hester said. "I even asked him to marry me, as I recall."

"Well, I can't blame you for that, either. Cailen is

very charming and incredibly handsome. So tell me, when did you meet him?"

"When I was just a wee girl, during the time of World War II," she replied.

Mariah drew in a sharp breath and whirled her head toward her. "You were one of the children that stayed in the castle during the war?"

"Yes." Her eyes took on a faraway expression. "Although my family came from Scotland, my father's job took him to London aboot a year afore th' war began. We were there when th' bombs started to fall from the sky. Now in my opinion, th' sound of all th' explosions terrified me far more than living in th' castle. Anyway, during that time they sent th' bairns off to various remote places around th' U.K. to keep us safe. As one of th' lucky ones, I ended up at th' castle right here."

"And you met Cailen," she said.

"Yes, I met Cailen and Duncan, Edmund, Malcolm, Robin, Steven, and—well, you know all their names, I'm sure." Hester sighed, shifted her gaze to the scene outside her window, and shook her head. "'Twas a long time ago, but I have never forgotten how good they were to us, or how safe they made us feel during that turbulent time."

"I think Cailen and his knights could make anyone feel safe as long as you aren't the ones facing them in battle—or crossing the line of their hospitality."

Hester laughed and said, "You have that right."

They both grew quiet and for a time, each of them wandered in the thoughts of their own making. But then, just as Hester gripped the door handle, Mariah put a hand on her arm to detain her.

"Wait a minute," she said. "If you don't mind, I have a question I'd like to ask before you go inside."

"No, I dinnae mind."

Mariah rubbed her hands up and down the steering wheel. She gazed out at the darkness as she struggled for the right words. "Did you ever—I guess what I'm asking is, if you, um—"

"What is it, dear?" she asked. "Dinnae be afraid to ask your question."

"All right. Besides the knights, did you ever see any other ghosts in the castle?" she asked as she shifted her gaze to her companion.

"Other ghosts?" she repeated.

Mariah returned a slow nod. "You see, I've…seen someone other than the knights. I know I'm not crazy and I know she's not a shadow or a figment of my imagination. She can't be."

"You saw a woman out there?" asked Hester as she kept her eyes fixed on hers.

"Yes," Mariah said. "I did."

"Only one?" she prodded.

Mariah did a double take over the odd question and then nodded.

"What did she look like?" she asked.

"Red hair, slender—I would say that she's probably about my height, maybe a little taller. I can't give you a description of her face because each time I've caught a glimpse of her spirit she's retreating through the wall."

"Does th' scent of heather surround her being?" she asked.

Mariah narrowed her eyes and shook a pointed finger. "You've seen her too!"

Hester took in a deep breath and nodded. "But she's not th' only woman there, you know."

The comment surprised her. "She's not?"

"No she isn't. I have seen others. One here, one there. At times I've seen as many as five of them together down by th' moat." Hester shrugged in casual manner.

"What are their names?" she asked. "Why are they there? Did you ever speak with any of them?"

"I dinnae know their names. Although both gentle and kind, they never said a word to any of us," Hester said. "I'm not so sure they could speak."

"Did you ever see them talking or interacting with any of the knights?" she asked.

Hester focused her gaze upward for a moment. She shook her head and said, "No, not that I can recall. They seemed to keep to themselves most of th' time."

Mariah gave her hand a gentle squeeze. "Thanks, Hester. You've finally given me peace of mind. And you know what? It's nice to know I'm not crazy after all."

"Och, I think we're all a wee bit crazy in our own way," she replied. "Well, thanks for th' ride, Mariah. Drive safely and perhaps I'll see you again."

"I hope so," Mariah, returning her smile. "Good night, Hester. Sleep well."

Mariah waited until Hester safely entered her home before she turned the car around and made her way back to the castle. All during the drive home, she thought about Cailen's inability to see the female spirit though she and Hester could.

Cailen said that after he left his body, he saw only the knights from his fiefdom. Yet surely other spirits simultaneously occupied that same field. His death experience just seemed so far off everything she had ever heard or read concerning the subject. Did that mean something? But then again, perhaps for some unknown reason, Cailen and his men simply couldn't see other spirits. If that proved the case, then surely an explanation for such an oddity existed. And for whatever the reason, she felt a burning need to discover it before she left MacNaughton's castle.

Chapter 7

Mariah finally got around to naming the scrawny kitten. She called her Tatters for obvious reasons. From the moment the bedraggled gray-and-white tabby filled her little belly, she followed her around the castle. At times, she even slept on her bed. Contrary to information found in books and documentaries, the kitten didn't have a problem interacting with the ghostly residents, either. In fact, she thrived on the attention they begrudgingly gave when she demanded it from them. The sight of her brawny, ferocious knights attempting to amuse the tiny creature with bits of string or the small furry toys she bought during a recent shopping trip made her laugh.

Even though Duncan had discovered the kitty trapped inside the cleric's room, she didn't believe the sounds of the sobbing woman emitted from the cat. However, Cailen seemed convinced, as did Duncan and the rest of her ethereal companions. She didn't argue the point, but they didn't hear what she heard. A cat simply could not replicate the mournful cry of a broken heart. Surely, the ghostly woman who twice visited her room created the sound. Did she do it for her benefit? More important, what made her so sad?

Once Tatters finished her breakfast, Mariah lifted her off the table and placed her on the floor of the great hall. She followed her movements for a time as the cat set off to explore.

"Is somethin' troublin' ye this morn?" Cailen asked.

She turned to face him and gazed into his eyes. Did the expression on her face give her away or did he simply feel her mood as she could so often feel his? She took in a breath and lowered her lashes. Yes, something did trouble her. Something like a castle filled with ghostly women the ghostly men couldn't see. For the umpteenth time, she called to mind the conversation she had with Hester.

"What's wrong?" he asked, calling her away from her thoughts.

"Cailen, are you able to see other ghosts besides the knights that live here?" she blurted out.

"Aye," he said. "We see many spirits that reside here in th' Highlands. They even visit us from time to time, and there are times we visit them at th' places they dwell. If ye would like, next time they happen by, and if they feel so inclined, I'll introduce them to ye."

So much for that theory, she mused. Unless— "When? When is the very last time you encountered a ghost you didn't already know. Shortly after your death? Perhaps even centuries ago?"

He shrugged as he lifted a hand to his beard. "Nay, 'twasn't that long ago. In fact, 'twas just early spring when a spirit by th' name of Mathias McGregor came to see th' castle with his mortal woman. He introduced her to us as Jolena Michaelsson. Another spirit, Samuel Fraser, tagged along with them as well. Mathias told us they came from a place he called Pennsylvania, far over th' sea. Why do ye ask?"

Mariah drew in a sharp breath, and for the moment,

all previous thought and questions fled her mind. "Jolena Michaelsson, the master violinist?"

"Aye, I believe so. Jolena said they were here for somethin' she called a 'concert.' She was to play her instrument for th' event. Have ye met her as well?"

"No, not personally. I'd really love too, though. I've seen her in concert many times and truly, she's just—"

Mariah stopped short as the impact of Cailen's revelation finally sank into her brain. "You spoke to her? She actually saw you?"

"Aye. Like I said, she came to see th' castle, and so I decided to show it to her. I felt it th' courteous thing to do at th' time," he said.

A twinge of envy took hold as she envisioned Cailen showing the very lovely Jolena Leigh Michaelsson around the castle, just as he proudly showed it to her. Did he keep a hand at her waist while he pointed out the various architectural details? But, wait—back up just a minute.

"Did you mean to say Jolena Michaelsson *knowingly* accompanied two ghosts all the way from the States?" she asked.

"From Pennsylvania, aye," he said. "Mathias and Samuel were from a time they referred to as th' American Revolution. A time when their country fought against England for their independence, much as we did in earlier times. They both died in battle as well."

"I see," said Mariah. Her gaze wandered over to the stairway where she visualized Cailen walking alongside the famous violinist.

"And just like ye, Mathias's woman had no fear of

th' ghosts when first they met," he added.

The odd comment returned her attention to her companion and as their eyes met, she said, "Why do you refer to Jolena as Mathias's woman?"

Cailen smiled broadly. Her question pleased him somehow. "Because she *is* his woman, and by his own admission. Th' luv they feel for each other is an obvious and wondrous thing to behold. I've never seen anythin' quite like it afore."

"Oh," she said, somewhat surprised over the declaration. But then really, how many mortals fell in love with ghosts?

"Ye have th' same manner of speech as Jolena. Do ye hail from Pennsylvania as well?" he asked.

She shook her head. "No, I was born and raised in the state of West Virginia. However, West Virginia and Pennsylvania share a common border, so we're not that far apart."

"Is that where ye keep this closet full of sketchbooks ye told me aboot?" he asked.

Mariah lifted her brows a tad and nodded. "Yes. My parents refused to throw any of them away over the years so it's a literal museum of all my efforts."

"I think that mayhap one day, I would like to see th' pages of those books," he said.

"You would?" she asked.

He nodded. "Aye, I would."

"Do you think you could board a plane with me and travel all the way to the little town of Romney?" she asked.

Cailen shrugged. "I dinnae see why not. Mathias McGregor traveled here from Pennsylvania, aye?"

Mariah's smile broadened over the improbable

prospect of showing her knight around her hometown. The poor man would probably feel so out of place. But then again, maybe not. Perhaps he might feel at home once he saw the green, hilly terrain. "You're right. He did manage to come all the way out here, didn't he? Maybe when I'm finished with this assignment, you could come home with me for a while then?" she asked.

He winked. "Mayhap. So, are ye workin' this morn?"

She glanced down at her watch, shook her head, and said, "Not for a couple more hours. The paintings need a bit more drying time before I add the next layer. It's probably a good thing, too. I'm not sure I'm fully awake, yet. If not for Tatters, I would probably have slept a while longer."

"Then would ye like to take a walk with me?" he asked.

"Yes, I would *love* to take a walk with you," she replied.

Humor filled his eyes. He cocked his head toward the main door. "Shall we?"

He led her around to the back of the castle, and then headed for the forest. Once they entered the woodland, they spent a bit of time cutting a path through the trees.

"This area is so beautiful," she said as her hands swept along the branches. "The first day I arrived and looked out my window, I thought I'd died and gone to heaven, if you'll pardon the expression."

He laughed. "Mayhap this *is* heaven, and that's th' reason for the lack of light around us at the time of our death."

She lifted her chin and took a deep breath of the

fresh, crisp air. "You know, maybe you're right about that."

While they strolled ever nearer the river, Cailen entertained her with stories from his youth. In return, she related stories of her own. Though life in his century differed greatly from hers, she discovered they were very much alike in the things they enjoyed and the way they saw the world.

"We need to go through those trees," he said, pointing a little to the right.

She turned to look. "We do?"

"Aye, we do."

Just as they approached the banks of the river, her mouth dropped. She drew in a sharp breath and for several long moments, she took in the sight that filled her with absolute wonder. Finally, she turned around to face him. He seemed quite pleased with her reaction.

"You never said a single word about this when you looked at the sketches," she said. "I can't believe the bridge really exists. Is it safe to walk on?"

"Aye," he replied as he followed her onto the stone walkway and over to the center of the arch. "This bridge is far older than th' castle and yet it looks th' same as it did when I was a wee bairn. There are no signs of weakness or damage."

Mariah leaned way over, rested her arms atop the stone barrier, and gazed out over the rushing waters of the river. The scene made one feel at peace. She closed her eyes, took in a deep breath, and held it a moment before she slowly let it go.

"Careful now, ye dinnae want to attract th' attention of th' kelpie," Cailen warned.

Mariah returned his playful smile. "Kelpie?" she

repeated.

"Aye, the ghostly shape-shiftin' water horse that haunts th' rivers and lochs," he said. "Haven't ye ever heard of them? Th' males find bonny human women irresistible and will try to carry them off to their watery realm if they catch one."

Did he find her "bonny" then? A blush stole across her cheeks as she shook her head. "I don't think I've ever heard of the creatures."

"Kelpie are water horses that are uncommonly strong. Their shiny coat comes in colors of both black and white. They have a mane and tail that never dries. No matter how long they remain on dry ground, th' hair will drip water constantly from th' ends. Although their skin shines like silk in th' sun, it feels cold as stone when ye touch it no matter how warm th' day. These ghostly horses use trickery to keep themselves hidden from your eyes or they simply transform into any normal creature, includin' th' shape of a comely man or woman. 'Tis in this way they lure ye to them. And, 'tis also said that once they take ye captive, they might never let ye go back to the surface."

"That's a very interesting story. Have you ever seen a kelpie yourself?" she asked.

Cailen chuckled as he shook his head. "Nay, I cannae, in all honesty, tell ye that I have."

"So then you don't really know if these ghostly creatures carry women off or not," she challenged.

The look he gave her quite literally stole away her breath. He turned his body fully toward her then and moved closer still. His eyes bore into hers. "Nay, but th' danger still exists of other ghostly creatures that might."

Mariah held perfectly still as Cailen placed a gentle hand underneath her chin and tipped her face upward to fit with his. She anticipated the kiss he leaned in to give and held her breath as he drew ever nearer. Yet, just before his lips touched hers, Duncan suddenly popped in beside them. Cailen shook his head, shot a glance skyward, and conjured a sigh.

"What is it, Duncan?" he asked and none too kindly.

Duncan didn't remove the smirk from his face as he said, "Laird MacNaughton is here. He's quite frantic that he cannae find Murriah or get her to answer her phone. I thought ye should know."

"Oh no! I left my phone inside the castle." Mariah patted her empty pockets, and then as she considered his visit, she added, "I wonder why he came out here anyway."

Cailen placed a hand at her back as he escorted her off the bridge and headed for the trees. "I dinnae know. He doesna come verra oft. Mayhap he just wanted to see ye or take a look at your work."

"I suppose that's possible. But tell me, has he ever seen you or the knights?" she asked.

"No. I never found a need to show ourselves to him," he replied. "Laird MacNaughton had only th' best interests of th' castle in mind when he purchased th' place. For that, he earned our respect and good will."

They finished the walk to the castle in silence and just as Mariah made her way to the front entrance, Laird MacNaughton caught sight of her. Relief washed over his face and the moment their eyes met, he waved a hand in greeting.

She waved back and as she and Cailen approached

him she called out, "Hello, Laird MacNaughton. Are you looking for me?"

"Yes," he said. "I tried to call you first, but got no answer."

"I'm sorry about that. I was just out for a walk while the oils dried a bit, and I guess I forgot to take my phone along with me," she said.

"No need for an apology. I just wanted to check on you and see if you needed anything while I visited th' area. I wondered how your food and supplies were holding out as well," he replied.

"Everything is still good. I don't think I've even made a respectable dent in the food that George and Sybil left behind."

"Good. That makes my mind rest a bit easier then. We dinnae want you to go hungry."

He followed her through the doors and into the castle. His gaze took in every nook and cranny of the great hall and Mariah wondered if he searched for a glimpse of the legendary knights. Would he bolt from the castle if he could see them all but surrounding him at this very moment? "Would you like to come up and take a look at my progress while you're here?"

The question prompted a smile. "I would love to see your progress, if you dinnae mind."

"I don't mind."

As he followed her up the stairs, he cleared his throat. "So, have you been staying inside the castle then?"

The tone of his question and his sideways glance made her laugh. She shot a glance at Cailen, who shrugged in return. What he really wanted to know is if she had seen the castle ghosts.

"Yes," she replied. "You know, I've really come to love this place and I hope that feeling is reflected in my paintings. Of course, you'll have to judge that for yourself."

Cailen stood back as she opened the door and allowed Laird MacNaughton to walk inside first. A broad smile appeared on MacNaughton's face as he took in the sight of the primary portrait. Though far from complete, he could see enough to form an opinion.

"I never expected anything quite so grand," he said as he halted his steps directly in front of it. "I really like th' setting you've chosen."

The compliment pleased her. She tilted her head to the side as she regarded the portrait herself. "This is what the castle looked like upon my arrival. The structure appeared so majestic surrounded by the mist and the clouds. I just had to paint it the way I saw it at that moment."

"I have seen it look this way myself a time or two and if my opinion counts for anything, then I think you've chosen well. This painting is exceptionally beautiful," he said.

"Thank you."

"These others are just as impressive, though," he said as he approached each for a closer look. "I'm happy now that giclée copies are part of my contract."

"There are several paintings that I haven't even started yet," she said. "I plan to paint a total of seven portraits of your castle."

"I won't complain aboot that." He wandered over to her table and pointed to her stack of sketchbooks. "May I have a look at your sketches as well?"

"Certainly," she said. "Help yourself."

Laird MacNaughton picked up the book closest to his position and turned the cover. He studied each sketch in depth and every now and again, he made complimentary comments. Finally, he pointed to the drawing of Cailen's face, in which he wore his chain mail coif. She had drawn him with his head turned slightly to the right, his expression, reflective.

"I especially like this particular sketch of your knight," he said. "'Tis almost like you can feel what he must have felt at th' end of a battle once he surveyed th' cost in lives."

Mariah glanced at Cailen as MacNaughton made the remark. He winked in response. She returned her attention to the Scottish laird and said, "Evan liked that same sketch as well."

The revelation startled Cailen, but she didn't have time to ponder the reason for it.

"Evan?" asked Laird MacNaughton

"Yes, the manager of the Water Cuddie," she said, suddenly realizing she had no surname to give him. Nevertheless, the laird must surely know the man since Evan spoke so familiarly of him.

"Och, Evan MacGilroy, of course. Having lived most of his life right here on th' castle grounds, he would probably appreciate such a sketch. I remember George telling me how much he liked to pretend he was a knight in shining armor when he was just a wee lad. I think he favored that game most of all. George made him countless wooden swords over th' years as I recall, and he broke each and every one of them." MacNaughton chuckled as he closed the cover and replaced her sketchbook.

Mariah wondered if her face revealed her shock.

Evan had numerous opportunities to divulge that information. Yet he didn't. Why? Why would he keep something so inconsequential away from her? She and Cailen looked at each other for a brief moment. He confirmed the revelation with a single nod.

"I didn't know Evan lived out here," she stammered. "He never mentioned it."

The laird nodded. "Until he arrived at the grand old age of eighteen, if I remember correctly. Then he wanted to venture out on his own as most young people do. Fine lad. Fine lad, indeed."

Mariah could hardly wait for the Scottish laird to finish his visit and leave the premises. The minute the door shut behind him, she whirled around to face the knights. "Does Evan know who you are?" she asked, directing the question to Cailen.

He nodded. "Aye."

"And I'm assuming he knows the rest of the knights as well?" she asked as she included them all with a sweep of her hand.

"Aye, Murriah, he knows," he replied.

"I just don't understand then," she said. "He looked at all my sketches before I even stepped foot on the grounds. He never said a word. If nothing else, you'd think he would've wanted to prepare me for meeting you so it wasn't such a shock. Why didn't he tell me about your existence?"

"I dinnae have an answer for ye," he replied.

She shook her head as she lifted her gaze to the ceiling and tsked. "Every conversation we've ever had indicated he knew no more concerning this castle than any of the other locals. Why? Why would he want to give me that impression?"

"That's a verra good question," Duncan said. "We've all wondered that ourselves."

Cailen dropped an arm around her shoulder and gently propelled her forward. He led her to the bench and settled her onto it. He then took a seat beside her, radiating warmth and the assurance she sought.

"We thought mayhap 'twas their argument," Malcolm said.

"Argument?" she asked. "What argument?"

"Th' one between Evan and his father," Duncan answered. "We dinnae know what they argued aboot, but 'twas verra fierce. That night Evan moved out of th' cottage."

"Over th' years he's never come back. Never come back, that is, until th' day he presented your supper," Edmund added.

Alongside the almost imperceptible shake of her head, Mariah covered her lips with the tips of her fingers. "I don't see where that situation would have anything to do with his dishonesty about intimately knowing this place. Surely he had to know I would meet all of you eventually."

"Are ye goin' to confront him with it?" asked Duncan.

She took a deep breath and slowly released it. "No. I think I'll wait and see how long it takes for him to tell me himself."

"Well, I dinnae know aboot that," he replied. "But seems to me ye might be waitin' a verra long time. It stands to reason that th' more time passes, th' further away from tellin' ye, he'll get."

Chapter 8

"Do ye think it would do any good for one or two of us to scout out th' pub for a while?" Duncan waited until well after Mariah retired to bed for the night before he raised the subject. "If we take turns, mayhap we could discover what, if anythin', he's up to."

"Och, I dinnae know." Cailen raked his fingers through his hair. "That seems just a mite excessive."

"Ye have to admit th' laddie's actions are a wee bit chary. I mean, he shows up out here for th' first time in how many years? He tells Murriah that he's leavin', but then sneaks over to th' cottage and removes somethin' that likely belongs to his parents. I feel that if th' item belonged to him, he would have come after it long ago, do ye ken?" asked Alan.

"In my opinion, he's no better than a common thief," Steven added.

"Aye, and why all th' pretenses?" Malcolm rose to his feet and approached the circle of men surrounding Cailen. "Somethin' is not right. I can feel it."

"There could be a verra simple explanation for his behavior," Cailen said. "One that's not as dark as you're makin' out. Ye have to remember this is Evan you're talkin' aboot and not some stranger."

"I might agree if not for th' deliberate deceit." Duncan turned his head to the side. "We dinnae really know how much is left of th' wee lad we once knew.

95

Time and th' experiences one has change people. We've seen such time and again."

"It wouldn't hurt just to see, Cailen," Malcolm urged. "Dinnae forget we now have Murriah to consider in all this. Ye have to wonder why he would feel th' necessity to lie to her."

"I suppose you're right; mayhap we could go out on occasion and see if there is anythin' we need to—"

A sudden sorrowful wail interrupted the remainder of Cailen's comment. All eyes turned in the direction of the heart-wrenching sound that emanated from Mariah's bedchamber upstairs and echoed down the spiral steps. "I'll see to her," he said and with that, he disappeared from the great hall.

He appeared by her bedside a split second later. Although she sat upright in her bed, Cailen couldn't tell if sleep still claimed her. Her eyes remained closed, yet trembling hands cupped her mouth and nose while tears cascaded down her cheeks.

"Murriah," he whispered. He sat down on the edge of her bed and brushed the tousled hair away from her face.

Her eyes opened wide once he spoke and just as she would have thrown herself into his arms, it seemed she remembered she couldn't. Would that he had the power to overcome that obstacle—

"Cailen—"

His name sounded a bit ragged around the edges, and he could feel the anguish of her soul. He scooted a bit closer.

"What's wrong, my lady," he asked as he repeatedly combed his fingers through the length of her hair.

She shook her head slightly, gulped a small breath, and said, "I'm sorry. It's really nothing. I just had a…a nightmare. I'm fine now…really, I am…"

"Ye dinnae look fine," he replied. "Now, dry those beautiful eyes and move over a wee bit."

He waited until she complied before he swung his legs up on the bed and settled his back against the headboard. The expression on her face as he made himself comfortable almost made him laugh, probably would have, if not for her obvious torment over her nightmare. He placed his hand on top of hers and gently gripped her fingers. "All right, my lady, I want ye to tell me aboot this dream."

Mariah swallowed past the lump in her throat as she stared down at Cailen's large hand that all but dwarfed her own. An amazing amount of comfort passed through his hand and into her body. She welcomed the warmth. "I don't know where to begin."

"I would think at th' beginnin'," he teased.

Mariah managed a bit of a smile between sniffs as she regained control of her emotions. She dabbed at the corner of her eyes.

He gave her a gentle nudge with his shoulder and said, "Dinnae be afraid to speak. You're safe now. I will not let anythin' happen to ye."

She released a slow, uneven breath. "I…" She gulped a couple of times and paused for a moment, seeking order to her words. "Well, the night seemed very dark…I don't remember seeing the light of the moon or even the stars. For some unknown reason, I traversed the grounds from the back of the castle. I walked through the forest and over the bridge. *All* the way over the bridge to the other side." She fixed her gaze upward while she took a deep breath and slowly blew it out.

"Do ye know where ye were goin' and why?" he asked.

"No, not really. I think I wanted to look for something or someone. I don't know. In my dream I knew, but now…" She shrugged as she lifted a hand, and then let it fall into her lap. "I remember looking down at the ground as I walked through the trees. The walk seemed very long, and as I walked, whispers converged upon me from all directions at once. They said things I didn't understand and the voices scared me half to death."

"Could ye see anyone out there?" he asked.

Mariah shook her head. "No, I couldn't and I really tried to find the source because I didn't know which way to go or which way to turn to get away from them. I peered through the darkness, and I sensed something vicious and evil in every shadow that moved. And that evil grew in both strength and size." She shuddered as she recalled the feeling and at once, she could feel Cailen's fingers tighten. Instinct alone bade her curl her fingers lightly around his in return.

"Finally, I stepped into a clearing. I could see large piles of natural rock formations scattered across the ground and under the bushes. Then, in the midst of those rocky mounds, I spied purple flowers," she said.

"Purple flowers?" He brushed a hand across his whiskers. "So ye suppose ye saw heather or mayhap even thistle?"

"No, not heather. I don't know the name of it…it wasn't thistle either. In fact, I don't recall ever seeing this particular flower before. But despite the evil presence that surrounded me, I had the most overwhelming desire to pick some. That desire felt like an obsession. I just *had* to have it, no matter the cost to me personally. Isn't that a crazy thing to dream?"

"No. I dinnae think dreams are meant to make sense," he said.

As her eyes filled with tears, she made every effort to keep them from falling. She paused. "This next part is so hard for me to say," she said, pushing the words past the lump in her throat.

"'Tis all right, Murriah, I'm here," Cailen crooned softly.

While fighting for control over her emotions, she placed her other hand very lightly atop his and ran her fingers gently across the top of his spiritual form. Funny. She could feel the difference in formation when she traveled from the top of his wrist, over his knuckles, and along the length of his fingers. She thought spiritual matter would all feel the same—kind of like gliding over ice. Although she didn't look into his face while she made this discovery, she could feel the intensity of his gaze as he watched the play of her fingertips.

She sniffed and raised her hand to her nose before she dropped it again. After a deep breath, she forced herself to go on.

"No matter how hard I tried to get the flowers, I couldn't collect them. The gusty wind that encircled me tore them out of my hand. And then…and then from out of the shadows, this hideous old woman flew at me with tremendous agility. Most of her face stayed hidden beneath the black cloak she wore. Her sharp teeth looked rotted and she snarled and shrieked at me as if I somehow caused her rage…"

She stopped and closed her eyes against the vivid image that leaped into her mind. Her throat tightened yet again. Hot tears poured down her cheeks. She took in several small breaths as she leaned forward and buried her face in her hands.

"Murriah?" Cailen whispered tenderly as his fingers gently caressed the length of her back. "Trust me, it will help if ye get it all out."

A small mournful moan escaped her lips and in response, Cailen placed a light feathery kiss against her temple.

"The old woman she...she kept shoving me forward until I passed the rocks and stumbled upon some of the larger bushes. I lost my balance and fell to my knees. She laughed an ugly, awful triumphant laugh and I..." She choked on the words that tasted so bitter in her mouth. "I saw your lifeless body on the ground, Cailen. And I couldn't do anything to save you."

Cailen dropped an arm around her shoulder and he moved his body even closer to hers. She could feel the soothing pressure of his touch even if she couldn't bury herself in his chest in return. He whispered words of comfort until at long last, her tears ceased to fall.

Cailen spoke then, "Ye know, it sounds to me like your old woman was a banshee."

Although he spoke the words in jest, she shook her head and said, "No. Please don't say that. Don't ever say that again."

"Och, ye neednae worry, I'm already dead," he said. "She cannae take me now."

She closed her eyes against the pain. "Then why did it feel as if I had lost you? Why did it hurt so badly?"

The heartfelt question both surprised and delighted him. "Shh, 'tis all right, my lady. I vow you're not goin' to lose me."

His promise prompted fresh tears, for how could he ever keep it? She dabbed at the corners of her eyes.

"I'm sorry. Normally I don't fall apart over a dream, not even the occasional nightmare. It's just that the sight of your body..." She paused. "I need to talk about something else, please."

"What would ye like to talk aboot then?" he asked.

"I don't know—anything," she replied. "Tell me about Evan."

"Evan?"

She detected a slight edge to his voice as he repeated the name. "Yes."

"What would ye like to know?"

"Well, I'm still trying to understand the reason he failed to mention that he lived here—or that he knew you. His silence just doesn't make sense. Unless—"

"Unless what?"

"Unless he only saw you a handful of times and during those times he didn't get a good look at your face—"

Cailen shook his head. "No. Evan could see us from th' time he was a wee bairn. We never intentionally showed ourselves to him over th' years; he just saw us. But as time went on and he grew older, th' laddie didna choose to seek us out every day as he had previously. His ability to see us declined. Then, once he entered manhood, he never gave any indication that he saw us at all."

"I take it then, at that point in his life, you didn't purposefully show yourselves to him either?" she asked. "Sort of give him a reminder?"

"Nay. I didna see th' need for it," he said.

The comment made her smile. "So, what you're telling me then, is that you only bother to show yourselves to the living when you want to scare the petunias out of them?"

Cailen drew his brows together. "Petunias?"

His consternation over the phrase prompted a bit of a laugh. "A more modern phrase for scaring the devil out of someone," she said.

He shrugged away the comment. "I didna intend any such thing when I showed myself to ye."

The look he gave her caused her heart to flutter. A blush splashed onto her cheeks in response to the heat of his gaze. Before she made a complete fool of herself, she made all haste back to the subject of Evan.

"So despite the years in between, you don't believe Evan could've forgotten your face then."

Cailen shook his head. "Nay, I believe he remembers us well enough. I'm surprised he didna tell ye when he found out that ye had seen us yourself."

"He doesn't know that I've seen you."

"Ye didna tell him?" He seemed surprised.

"No, nor have I told anyone else for that matter. Well—except for Hester and somehow she already knew and confronted me with it. So, I had to confess."

"Hester?" he asked.

"The sweet old woman who once stayed here as child during World War II. She had a crush on you, did you know? In fact, she said she asked you to marry her at that time."

Cailen turned his gaze upward for a moment. "I think I remember the lassie now. As I recall, she followed us around like a wee pup whenever she had th' chance."

"I'm sure the dear little thing couldn't help but follow you around," she said. "You—and your men—are all very compelling you know. Although everyone should have the opportunity to meet you, I think it's up to you, to decide whom you wish to show yourself to—and when."

"Ye are an amazin' woman, Murriah Jennin's, do ye ken?" The intensity of his gaze caused the heat to stir inside her belly yet again.

"And you have the most wonderful bedside manner I've ever seen, Sir Cailen. I can only assume you must have gained a lot of experience rescuing females from their nightmares."

Cailen chuckled. "Only one other."

"Who?" She held her breath as she smoothed the duvet. Although she asked the question, she wasn't at all certain she wanted to know the answer.

"My younger sister, Mairwen," he said.

Mariah detected his affection for his sister in the tone of his voice. "Did she have nightmares often?"

He shrugged. "She didna have them all th' time, but mayhap more often than most when naught but a wee lass. I thought they deviled her because she was so young when her mother died."

"Oh, poor little thing. Do you mind telling me about her?" she asked.

"There isn't much to tell. She was a good woman, kind, gentle and compassionate. I think that's why she took to th' art of midwifery. Folk called on her skills from th' time of her youth. She seemed happiest while tendin' to others," he said.

"She sounds like a wonderful person," Mariah said and suddenly she could feel her eyelids getting heavy. She smothered a yawn.

"Aye, she was." After a lengthy pause, he added with a bit of sadness and regret to his tone, "She and Duncan announced their betrothal just days afore the battle."

The comment gave her pause. Since arriving at the castle and meeting her knights, she never once thought about their mortal lives. It never occurred to her to consider who or what they may have left behind on the battlefield of Dupplin Moor.

Duncan always seemed so cheerful, as did most of the other men. Yet, a goodly portion of them never saw their twentieth-fifth year while in mortality and most certainly, none of them saw forty. Vibrant lives cut short before they had an opportunity to experience all the wonders life could offer.

"I'm so sorry to hear that, Cailen," she whispered. "I wish things could've turned out better for Duncan and your sister. I'm sure they would've been happy together—if given the chance."

In response to her comment, he returned a single nod.

"What about the other knights?" she asked. "Did any of them leave wives or children behind?"

"Aye, some of them did. Steven had a bonny wife called Alison. Ian's wife, Aveline, was expectin' their first bairn, and Robert had four strappin' lads. His eldest son had just been made a squire at th' time of our death. Malcolm's wife died givin' birth a few months afore th' battle, though," he said.

Cailen talked of the other knights as well, and she

tried to pay attention to what he said about each of them, but the need for sleep conquered the desire. She settled a little deeper into her covers and turned to her side in order to face him while he spoke. Finally, his quiet chuckles entered into her waning consciousness.

"Go ahead and close your eyes, my lady," he whispered. "Ye need your rest. We'll continue our conversation later."

Panic set in and though she battled fatigue, she leaned up on her elbow and pried open her eyes. "Don't go yet, Cailen. Could you just stay until I fall asleep, please?" she begged as unbidden, the entirety of her nightmare crashed into her consciousness and she could see his lifeless, broken body—

"I will not leave your side, I swear. Just close your eyes and go to sleep." Once she settled into the softness of her mattress, he took hold of the hand resting on her pillow.

"Thank you," she whispered. Her eyelids fluttered and then closed. She curled her fingers ever so lightly around his and drifted toward sleep. But not before his lips pressed softly against her mouth. A pleasant shiver coursed through her body.

"Good night, my lady," he said. "Sleep well."

She fell asleep wondering what a more meaningful kiss might feel like. If not for the interruption at the bridge, she would already know.

****

Cailen remained at her side all throughout the night. She could still feel the pressure of his hand upon hers even as awareness crept into her consciousness. Her eyelashes fluttered. A deep intake of breath followed. She willed her eyes to open. Cailen met her sleepy gaze with a wink.

"Good morn," he said.

She inched herself into a seated position while combing her fingers through her hair. "Good morning, Cailen."

"You're up much earlier than I expected," he said.

She glanced at the clock and while smothering a yawn, she nodded. "So it seems. Thank you, for staying with me all night. I didn't expect it."

"I know, but 'twas my pleasure to look after ye," he replied as he brushed his fingers against her cheek. "I'll leave ye now, so that ye can start your morn. I will not be far if ye need me."

"All right," she said as she tossed the duvet to the side. "I'll be down in just a little while."

Once he disappeared, Mariah retrieved her clothes. She hurried through her morning shower, knowing Cailen awaited her inside the hall. But first, she wanted to make some quick sketches of the flower she saw in her dream while the details remained vivid in her mind. Something about that dream made it important, though for the life of her, she couldn't say why.

She changed her mind about the sketches once she walked into her studio and glanced at her laptop. Maybe she could find the flower she sought on the internet faster than she could sketch it. She typed "purple flowers, United Kingdom" and hit enter. The result box showed over two million images. She tried the search again using the term Scotland and still found over one hundred thousand pictures. Despite the daunting task, she pored over several pages. Nothing even came close to the flower she sought despite the twenty minutes she spent looking for it.

Finally, she gave in and took hold of her pencil and sketchbook. She flipped through each of the pages seeking the first blank sheet. But a little more than halfway through the book, she stared down at the page as horror engulfed her. For she had already drawn the flower. She had also sketched a couple of other plants that, to her recollection, she had never laid eyes on.

To top it all off, the shadowed face of the old hag taunted her from off the final page. She gasped with fright as she slammed the book shut, pushed it to the top of the table, and fled the room.

Chapter 9

Cailen gazed at Mariah as she sat atop the table with a sketchbook on her lap and her feet propped up on the bench. A week had now passed since she experienced her nightmare. Although at times he could see the dream still haunted her, she didn't speak of it again and neither did he. Instead, she placed all of her efforts and concentration on her paintings. He shifted his attention to her current drawing and it amazed him to see her bring the dais to life on the page. She sketched it exactly as he remembered it.

"All right," she said as she turned the book around. "Do I have an accurate depiction of the furnishings?"

"Aye, down to th' smallest detail," he replied.

"Then show me exactly where you knelt, and where King Robert stood," she said.

"I knelt right here." He pointed to the center of the dais. "And th' king stood just so."

"Did you kneel on anything, like a cushion or rug, or did you just kneel on the bare floor?" she asked.

"I used a cushion made of skins laced together with leather strips," he replied.

"How big?" she pressed.

He raised his hands to about the breadth of his shoulders and extended them about a foot and half. "Aboot this wide and aboot this long."

Mariah nodded and sketched the rectangular

outline, just as he indicated. "Is that about right?"

"Perfect," he replied.

When first she presented the idea of this particular painting, he wanted no part of it. In his opinion, such portraits depicted men of royalty or men of great magnitude. As an ordinary knight, he met neither description. She gaped at him, and then in an irritated huff, "begged to differ" with his ridiculous comment. He found her fit of pique most amusing. In fact, her indignation caused him to laugh out right, which in turn, ruffled her feathers even further.

But, in the end he couldn't deny her simple request. Besides, just as she pointed out, most people viewing the painting would focus on King Robert. She also argued that since this castle belonged to his family and that during the period he served as leader to his boisterous rowdy knights, he remained the likely choice.

"Now that I have Cailen sketched in, where did everyone else stand?" she asked, directing the question to his knights.

An excited clamor of voices filled the hall. He found it obvious that she couldn't make out a single word anyone said. As her hand lifted skyward, she shook her head and laughed. "Okay, okay! I think we're going to have to do this one at a time. Who stood nearest Cailen while King Robert knighted him?"

Duncan stepped forward. "That would be me, of course. I stood right here," he said pointing to the exact spot on her sheet of paper.

"And I stood here," Steven said as he peered over Duncan's shoulder and indicated his position.

One by one, each of the knights in attendance at his

accolade aided her quest to depict the event accurately. If she didn't get their stance or position right on the sketch, they pointed out the flaws. Finally, everyone agreed that her drawing faithfully reflected the scene. She closed her book and released a sigh. Then as she tapped the sketchbook with her pencil, she fixed her gaze to his.

"Well, I think I can get started on this come the morning," she said. "The canvas is already prepared. In the meantime, there are some portraits of Robert the Bruce hanging in a museum or two in Edinburgh that I'd like to study. I also want to see Edinburgh Castle while I'm in the city."

Cailen glanced at the floor and nodded. "When do ye think ye might go?"

"Today—now," she replied. "But the thing is—I want you to come with me. I'd like to know how close the paintings resemble King Robert, if at all. And, who better to ask than someone who knew him?"

Though her words took him by surprise, the request pleased him. He returned a single nod and said, "'Twould please me to act as your escort, my lady."

Squeezing his spiritual form inside the small car proved a bit difficult. In order to keep his head from popping through the roof, a portion of his backside ended up behind the seat even though she shoved the bloody thing just as far back as it could go. Nonetheless, once Mariah drove down the gravel road and away from the castle, he put the ordeal behind him and just enjoyed her undivided attention. Since the eve of her nightmare, the opportunity for a private moment had eluded them and he craved one.

They traveled a goodly distance with naught but

pleasant conversation passing between them. After a while, she gave him a quick glance and said, "Have you been to Edinburgh since—well, since before your last battle?"

He shook his head. "Nay, I haven't."

"No? Why not?" she asked.

"I didna find a need for such a journey," he replied.

"What about just for the adventure of it all?" she said. "I mean, haven't you ever been curious as to the modern changes that have taken place over the centuries?"

"Curiosity aboot such things ended a long time ago. We've seen our fair share of th' changes that have taken place durin' the passage of time. Many of th' forests are now gone, farmland has been cleared in favor of buildin' bigger cities and paved roads. I dinnae think people ken what they've traded away in th' name of your so-called modern technology," he said.

Mariah's lips curved into a slight smile as she tilted her head to the side. "You know what, Cailen? I think you're right about that. But then again, if not for modern technology, I would never have had the chance or even a reason to come to Scotland. Ryan Maitland more than likely would never have fulfilled his dream of seeing the world's castles. In turn, they would never have offered me the job his quest inspired. Therefore, I would never have met you—or your knights." She glanced at him. "What a tragedy that would have been for me."

As they arrived at the fork in the road, she stepped on her brake and turned to look at him. In that very instant, a powerful magnetic current bound them together with a strength he'd never experienced before.

And judging from her expression, neither had she. She released a shuddered breath and eased the car forward.

But just as he opened his mouth to speak, to tell her that he too would have mourned the loss, a befogging force of shadowy darkness settled over his form. She screamed his name, but he couldn't respond to her terror. The power that seized him gripped his spiritual body with a strength he couldn't fight. The force yanked him out of Mariah's presence and propelled him through time and space. Centuries of personal experiences stormed through his mind with blinding speed. All at once, he sat on the field of Dupplin Moor, resting beneath an ancient tree—just as he had centuries earlier, on a warm night in August, in the year 1332.

Someone grabbed hold of his shoulder and shook it. He opened his eyes with a start.

"Cailen—"

He turned his gaze upward. Duncan and Steven hovered over him. Cailen rubbed a hand across his eyes, grabbed hold of his sword, and rose to his feet. "Aye?"

Duncan shook his head and with a look of contempt said, "We've just learned that Murray of Tullibardine has willfully betrayed us to th' enemy."

This news didn't surprise him. Everyone knew the disinherited Scotsmen who chose the side of Edward Balliol sought their destruction by fair means or foul. If the traitors should reign victorious over the coming battle, they intended to place their pretended king on the throne. In return for their treasonous support, they expected to regain the property they forfeited when they chose betrayal instead of allegiance to their own country. He, the men from his fiefdom, and all those loyal to their late king, would bleed the fields red before they allowed such an atrocity to occur.

"What happened?" he asked, shaking away the final vestiges of strange dreams and sleep.

"Well, aboot midnight, Murray led Sir Alexander Mowbray and his men across th' ford. 'Twas his intention to give away our position at that time rather than wait for th' morn. Instead of our forces, Mowbray slaughtered naught but th' camp followers that slept there. All th' while he thought he fell upon th' army commanded by th' Earl of Mar, or so he claims," he replied.

"Laird Bruce wants us to use this blunder to our advantage. He says we now have ample time to cross th' river and position ourselves on th' high ground," Steven added.

"Have ye gathered th' men?" he asked.

"Aye," Duncan replied. "They're waitin' for ye now."

Cailen motioned for them to follow as he headed for the men of his fiefdom. Once gathered, they strode forward to join with Bruce's force. All the while, Balliol's army moved to outflank them. Then, once The Bruce settled into his desired position, he and his men turned around. Mowbray and Henry de Beaumont had gathered their opposing forces together ahead in the distance. Their opponents made all haste to form a half moon circle consisting of highly skilled English archers. They wasted no time in readying their lethal weapons in the hope of protecting their own army and decimating as many loyal Scotsmen as they could manage.

Lord Robert Bruce, enraged over the simple

maneuver, accused Donald, Earl of Mar, of treachery or incompetence. Donald vehemently denied the charges. Under a string of curses, both men vowed to enter the battle first and conquer their enemy.

"We dinnae need to start fightin' amongst ourselves," Duncan whispered in disgust.

"Aye, you're right aboot that," Cailen said. "There is no place for such here and now."

Nevertheless, he and the battle-hardened men of his fiefdom lined up directly behind The Bruce, illegitimate son of their late king, and awaited his order. Their commander's horse danced his impatience as he looked down at the disinherited and their small force of English soldiers and archers. He turned sideways to face his army with a look that bespoke confidence and determination. Their leader's self-assurance filled them with the same.

At that moment, Bruce raised an arm to the heavens and shouted, "For honor, for Scotland, to victory! Crush th' pretender!"

A surge of adrenaline coursed throughout Cailen's body as Lord Robert turned and charged forward. He and his garrison followed Bruce's lead. Battle cries abounded as they raced toward Balliol's army with swords drawn, intent on winning this battle as they had won so many others. Despite the unrelenting storm of arrows raining down around their heads, his battalion charged forward, causing their enemy to give precious ground.

Just then, an English arrow pierced his bicep. He broke it off, flung it aside and rushed forward, leaving a trail of men in his wake. More arrows pierced through his armor, they continued to pierce him until he could no longer feel them enter his body. Still, he fought on with the intent of sending to the devil himself, as many archers as he could. An enemy rushed straight at him. Cailen pivoted and raised his sword for the kill. But just as he thrust his weapon into his opponent's heart, the man raced straight through his body as though he didn't exist. His intended victim somehow ended up right behind him to engage another.

Stunned over the occurrence, he whipped around. Naught but death and devastation littered the grassy field. Most of his battalion lay dead on the bloodied soil, Lord Robert Bruce and the Earl of Mar among them. He noticed the strangeness then.

Something didn't feel right. He touched his body in various places. The muscles, skin, and bone felt solid enough beneath his fingers. Yet, just as he placed his hand against his chest seeking the beat of his heart, he spied his mortal body prone at his feet. Eyes, which no longer blinked, stared up at the morning sky. A hand, which would never again engage an enemy, clung to his sword. He knelt next to his mortal remains in quiet despair. A steady hand aimed for the arrow that pierced his heart and ended his mortal life. He couldn't grasp it, no matter how hard he tried.

"Cailen…"

He hesitated for a moment and then turned to face a bewildered Duncan. His friend of many years placed a hand of comfort upon his shoulder. Unable to speak, he gazed into his eyes and shook his head.

"I think we're dead," Duncan whispered.

A group of men filtered toward him, seeking his leadership as they had always sought it. All of them, men from his own fiefdom. In fact, *every* man from his fiefdom now gathered around him. Each face reflected the same astonishment and confusion that engulfed him.

"What do we do now?" asked Duncan.

Cailen rose to his feet, nodded northward and replied, "We go home."

We go home. We go home. Those same three words echoed and swirled around inside his head. The memory of his final day of mortality flew in and out of focus too many times to count. He shook his head to clear away the clutter and found it a useless exercise.

Despite his uncertainty, he turned north, leading his men back to the castle. Somehow, they traversed the distance at great speed. He observed the pace of his feet. They moved as they always moved, yet one stride covered far more ground than what seemed possible for a man to cover. Bits and pieces of memory spanning the centuries filtered into his mind. And then as he neared the castle, all the recollections of his entire existence pelted his mind until at last, the images settled upon Mariah. He recalled everything now, including the tremendous fear in her voice as she screamed out his name. Did something take hold of her in the same moment the wraithlike force surrounded and caged his being? He glanced at Duncan.

"We must hurry," he said. "I have to get to Murriah."

"Ye have to get to whom?" Duncan looked puzzled. The name meant nothing to him.

Cailen said no more as he continued his march to their fiefdom. Just as his gaze settled upon the towers rising above the trees in the distance, he looked over his shoulder to check the progress of his knights. He stopped dead in his tracks and stared at the alarming manifestation. For amidst a sudden and unexpected black storm of hail, raging lightning and exploding thunder, each of his men eerily dissipated, until at last he stood alone on the grassy fields. The skies cleared just as quickly as they darkened, and then the wind grew still.

Apprehension inundated his being, for the last time he entered the castle after the battle of Dupplin, he found it void of life. Would such an event transpire again? Would that unearthly presence force him to walk the halls of his castle alone? And what of Mariah? Had he forever lost her as well? Despite the outcome, he had to know. The castle doors loomed before him. He walked straight through them. Fifty-two men turned to face him. All conversation stopped as each one gaped in his direction. He found all just as he had left it.

"What happened to ye, man?" Duncan creased his brow and looked him over from head to toe. "Ye look as if ye've been to hell and back again.

Cailen waved him off as he strode toward the stairway. "I feel like I've been there and back. But never mind that right now. Where's Murriah?"

"Where's Murriah?" echoed Alan. "Th' two of ye left together, so ye should know her whereabouts better than anyone else."

"Cailen, stop!" Duncan stood just in front of him now, halting his progress. "Ye cannae just walk out. Tell me what's goin' on."

"I dinnae know, Duncan," Cailen replied as he stepped to the side to go around him. "And right now, I dinnae want to talk aboot it."

"Do we need to go out and look for her?" asked Steven.

Cailen shook his head. "I wouldn't even know where to tell ye start lookin'."

"Have ye checked th' pub?"

He whirled around to face Alan and for a brief moment, he considered the possibility before he dismissed it altogether. "Nay, I haven't. But I dinnae think she's there."

"I dinnae think it would hurt to look anyway," Roger said.

"Please yourself." The moment he said it, six of his knights disappeared. He spared Duncan a quick glance. "I'm goin' up to th' tower to wait for her. I think she'll return to th' castle afore she goes anywhere else." If she can, he silently added, for he had no idea what that powerful force did to her.

Duncan insisted on keeping him company despite his desire to the contrary. He braced himself for the onslaught of questions that would surely follow, for it had never been in Duncan's nature to leave well enough alone.

"Did ye quarrel with Murriah?" Duncan asked, coming straight to the point.

"Dinnae be daft," he scoffed.

"Then what happened?" he persisted.

"That's a verra good question, and I'm afraid that I dinnae have th' answer for ye," Cailen said.

"What do ye mean?"

Cailen turned his eyes away from the road to gaze at his friend. "'Twas th' strangest thing, Duncan. One minute Murriah and I were talkin' and th' next, I found myself on th' battlefield of Dupplin relivin' th' last day of my mortal life."

While they waited there on the turret for the first

sign of Mariah's car, he shared his experience just as it transpired. His companions down inside the hall grew quiet as they too listened to the incredible tale. Once he finished the narrative, Duncan stared at him, his mouth agape.

"I wonder what would cause such a thing to happen to ye?" he asked.

"I dinnae know." Just as the words left his mouth, Mariah's car turned down the gravel road and sped toward the gate. He glanced at Duncan. Yet, before he could say a word, Duncan raised a hand to stop his words.

"I know, I know. Ye dinnae have to say it," he said. "I'll just go and fetch th' lads from th' pub and tell them what happened. I'll let them know Murriah's home. But dinnae expect me to hold back their questions once they get here."

They both vacated the tower the same instant. While Duncan set about his self-appointed task, Cailen appeared just to the side of Mariah's car as she skidded to a halt. Relief filled her eyes as they looked at each other through the car door window. He could see the telltale sign of her tears. He cursed under his breath for causing her sorrow. She yanked on her handle, opened the door, and then bounded out of the car.

"Cailen." His name came out in a breathless rush as she gripped the car door. "Where have you been? I have looked everywhere for you. What happened back there? Are you all right? I've been so worried—"

In the totality of his existence, he had never wanted to take a woman in his arms as badly as he wanted to take Mariah right now. The woman needed the strength and comfort of a solid pair of arms. Would that he could give it. He settled for cupping her face with his hands and pressing a gentle kiss against her forehead.

"Dinnae worry aboot any of that right now. Th' question is, are ye all right?" he asked.

She closed her eyes, took a deep breath, and then nodded. "Yes, I'm fine. But, please, Cailen, I need you to tell me what happened to you," she said as she let go of the door and closed it with a thrust of her hip.

"Then, come with me," he replied. "Where we can have a bit of uninterrupted privacy while I try to explain."

Chapter 10

Cailen slipped a hand about her waist and keeping a leisurely pace, led her to the bridge and the solitude it promised. While they walked along, he filled her in on the details of his experience. Once they made their way midpoint of the walkway, she turned to face the rushing water and rested her arms atop the ancient stone barrier. As she gazed out over the river, she pondered his bizarre tale. What would prompt such a horrendous event? And that…that *thing* that yanked him out of the car—where did it come from? What kind of otherworldly force or creature was it? And why did it take only Cailen?

"Where have your ponderin's taken ye, my lady?" he asked, cutting into her thoughts.

She rubbed a hand across her forehead and sighed. "I'm just trying to understand all of this. This experience—well, all of your experiences, actually, are just so far off the mark of everything I have ever heard or read, and none of them make any sense to me."

"Mayhap it's just as ye said afore. Ye've not experienced them for yourself. 'Tis quite possible then, that everythin' ye've heard is naught but distorted misconceptions of what is truth," he replied.

"I suppose that's possible, but I really don't think it's probable," she said.

"Why not?" he asked. "What would trouble ye

aboot acceptin' such an explanation?"

She rolled her eyes heavenward and huffed out a breath. "Well, how about the fact that you were sucked out of a moving car today? Let's start with that one, shall we?"

"Mayhap such is normal for a man who is naught but spirit when inside a movin' car," he said.

"You were inside that car for over an hour, Cailen, and without any undue hardship until the moment you—" She clamped down on her mouth, unwilling to go any further.

"Th' amount of time afore th' occurrence could be normal as well," he replied.

"Then tell me, how did Mathias McGregor and Jolena Michaelsson manage to get here all the way from Pennsylvania without mishap? I can promise you their journey took far more than one hour."

He said nothing in response. But then again, she didn't expect him to.

"What aboot ye?" he asked after a lengthy silence passed between them.

She drew her brow together. "Me?"

"A considerable amount of time passed durin' th' time of our separation. What took ye so long to come home? I worried when I didna find ye here upon my return," he said. "I thought mayhap th' dark mist took ye as well."

"No, I went looking for you." She paused as she sought for the words to explain the mystifying event from her point of view. "You—somehow that thing encased your form in some kind of swirling vortex made of mist and hellish flame, and—it actually looked as if it sought you out personally. I could do nothing but watch as the whirlwind pulled you through the car and took you out into the fields. Words cannot express my terror at that moment. I tried to follow, but it didn't take long for me to lose sight of you. At that point, I didn't know what to do or where to go." She finished the last of her words in a voice just above a whisper, closed her eyes against the haunting vision she wanted to forget, and breathed out a slow, ragged sigh.

Cailen's arm dropped around her shoulders and he cuddled her just as close he could without having her penetrate his form. Just as in all previous times, she could feel warmth radiating from his touch, and as always, that warmth surprised her. She associated ghosts with frigid temperatures. For such had been her experience with other spirits in all the other castles she painted. Did that mean something?

"I'm so sorry," he murmured against her cheek. "I didna mean to put ye through it."

"But *you* didn't." She stepped away just enough to gaze into his eyes. "Something extraordinary happened to you out there today, Cailen, and whatever it is, I'm telling you, it just isn't normal. Nothing about your death or the centuries following it is in any way normal."

"'Tis all I know, Murriah," he said. "This life seems normal enough to me and to my men."

"You can't say that about this morning's experience," she argued.

Her comment elicited a quiet chuckle. He shook his head. "I'll have to give ye that one. But then again, I have never been inside a car afore, either."

As she recalled her own experience inside the car, the pain of his perceived loss washed over her anew.

She remembered experiencing that same pain during her nightmare and suddenly, it made her wonder if a connection existed between the two events. Perhaps they occurred as some kind of warning, or a clue to a puzzle she and Cailen needed to solve. But a warning or clue regarding what? The more she thought about such a possibility, the more sense it made.

Her gaze meandered over the unexplored area on the other side of the bridge. If she followed the same path outlined by her nightmare, would she find her mysterious purple flower? Such would give credence to her theory, wouldn't it? Suddenly, she had an overwhelming need to find out if both the path and the flower existed.

"Cailen, I need you to come with me, please," she said.

He followed the direction of her gaze and stiffened as comprehension dawned. "Nay, Murriah—"

"Please don't make me go out there alone," she begged.

Cailen dropped his shoulders in defeat. He then faced her desired destination and with a bit of reluctance took hold of her hand. "I dinnae think this is a good idea."

"I know you don't. But I have to know," she said. He merely nodded in return. Together they walked to the end of the bridge. The beat of her heart accelerated the moment she stepped onto the grass.

"Which way?" he asked.

She pointed to the right. "Over there. Straight through those trees."

Mariah gave no thought to conversation as she focused instead on each step of the path ahead. She didn't have any trouble following it exactly as she walked it in her nightmare. And then in the same moment she expected to see it, she entered the small glade. The bushes and rock formations were identical to those in her nightmare. She turned to face Cailen and for a brief moment, they looked at each other. The man appeared so troubled. Yet, a compelling force drove her onward. He let go of her hand as she rounded the second set of boulders, and just as in the dream, she veered off to her left. Cailen shadowed her every step. At last, she moved to the other side of the hill, knelt down, and took hold of the purple flower growing between the rocks. She pinched it off at the base of its long stem, and studied the bell-shaped petals that mirrored the ones in her dream. She held it aloft for his inspection.

"Do you know what it's called?" she asked.

"Nay, I dinnae think th' flower is common."

"That makes this all the more puzzling then," she said as she picked a few more.

"How so?" he asked.

"Well, if this flower grew in great abundance all over Scotland then I would have to consider the possibility that I had actually seen it before—that my subconscious noted it, and then the image worked its way into my nightmare." She rose to her feet and turned in the direction of the bridge, having no desire to follow the path of the dream any farther. "But since this is an uncommon flower I don't ever remember seeing before, I have to believe that for some reason, something is happening to us. Something fate intended—because something vital needs our attention."

"Happenin' to us?" Cailen drew his brows together

as they made their way back inside the forest. "I dinnae ken what ye mean."

"A while back you said our destinies were entwined—that the fates had decreed it." She halted her steps and gazed into his eyes. "Did you really mean that or were you just trying to make me feel better about my sketches?"

He stared down at her for several long moments and all the while, she held her breath awaiting his answer.

"Aye, I meant it," he finally said.

"Then surely there's a reason behind it, don't you think?" she asked as they resumed their journey back to the castle. "Why else would your image be my constant companion all throughout my life? I believe it's more than mere coincidence that of all the castles they could have assigned me to paint, they chose me to paint this one. For this is the one and only place we could ever have met. I mean logically, it would have made more sense to keep me in Wales, or even England," she pointed out.

"I do believe destiny sent ye to me, Murriah," Cailen said. "As for the reason?" He shrugged away his inability to explain it.

"Well, I'm sure we don't have all the pieces to this puzzle yet. So of course it's not going to make sense right now," Mariah murmured, more to herself than to him. "Perhaps we can build from the pieces we have though and figure it out."

"What pieces?" he asked. "Ye have only a nightmare that showed ye th' location of a flower."

"But it's a flower that truly exists, found in a place I'd yet to see except in that dream," she reminded him.

"And besides, that's not the only piece I have to offer."

"What else do ye have?" he asked.

She fell silent as she turned around and made her way to the center of the bridge. Cailen didn't press her for an answer as they walked. Yet, all the while, she debated her reply. He already thought her a bit bonkers when she mentioned the ghostly woman with red hair. But now she had another witness as to her existence and he couldn't refute that. What would he think of the drawings she had no knowledge of sketching? Perhaps if she showed him the drawings, he could help identify the plants and find meaning behind them.

At their customary spot, she stopped and turned to face him. He leaned back against the barrier, propped his elbows atop the stone, and waited for her to speak. She made the decision then to tell him everything. Let him think what he may. She cleared her throat and said, "Do you remember when I asked you about the female spirit with red hair?" she asked.

"Aye," he replied.

"I know you thought I saw shadows that night. But I *know* I didn't," she said. "You see, I saw her again the night we found Tatters."

He cocked his head to the side, but said nothing in return.

"I had just shut down my computer with the intent of getting into bed. When I turned around, I saw her go through the very same wall she passed through once before." She held up her hand to halt his reply.

"I know what you're thinking," she said. "But this time I followed her. I didn't see her out in the hallway, but I did smell the strong scent of heather that follows her. So, I chased after the scent. The aroma led me into the chapel. Once I entered the room, I could hear her heart-wrenching sobs. I know you're going to tell me the sound came from Tatters, because that's where Duncan found her. But it didn't. I know what I heard Cailen, and those sobs didn't come from a mewling cat."

Cailen maintained his silence and at the very least, it appeared he considered what she said rather than dismissing it outright.

"The night I went to the pub, I went for one reason alone," she said.

"To fulfill your obligation to Evan, I know," he murmured.

"Partly, yes. But there was more to it than just that." She brushed the hair away from her face as she faced the river and called Hester to mind. "I also wanted to know if any of the locals had seen my female ghost."

"And had they?" he asked.

Mariah shook her head. "Nope and I gave them every opportunity to reveal it if they had. A few minutes after I finished my dinner, the option to take Hester home landed in my lap. Offering her a ride seemed a good enough excuse to leave at that point. Once we arrived at her house, she raised the subject of you and your men. She guessed that I'd already met you and stated as much. I didn't feel inclined to deny it. So, we talked about all of you for a while and then just before she got out of the car, I asked her about my female ghost."

"I take it then, that she saw her as well," Cailen said.

"Many times," Mariah replied. "But the interesting

thing is—she told me my ghost didn't live at the castle alone. Hester said several female entities lived there. She told me that she saw as many as five different women gathered by the moat at one time."

Cailen narrowed his eyes and for several long moments, he simply regarded her without saying a word. Finally, he shook his head. "That's just not possible."

She lifted her brows and shrugged. "I don't know about the other women. I've only seen the woman with red hair, myself. But I *have* seen her. Hester corroborated that by simply asking me if the scent of heather accompanied her spiritual form. How else would she know that, since I didn't reveal that tidbit during the course of our conversation?"

He paused. "Did she tell ye her name and what period of time she hailed from?" he asked. "As ye might guess, we've had plenty of women with red hair livin' here over th' centuries."

"I'm sure you did, but unfortunately, she didn't give me her name." She shook her head. "Hester said she never heard her or any of the other women speak. She didn't know if they could. However, guessing by her style of clothing, I'd say my ghost lived during the middle ages. She wore a linen léine very similar to yours, only much longer of course."

"Verra interestin'," he replied.

"Yes it is—and then," she continued, "there are my sketches to consider."

"Your sketches?" he asked.

She nodded. "I'll show them to you when we get back to the castle. Twice now, I have found impossible drawings inside my sketchbooks."

"Why do ye say impossible?" he asked as he turned to face her and then rested an elbow atop the barrier.

"Because that's what they are. I've no doubt I made them, but the weird thing is—I don't have any memory of drawing them. I discovered the first of the drawings right after you finished our tour of the castle. If you recall, we ended that tour down in the secret passageway."

"Aye," he replied. "I remember."

"When I entered my studio afterward, I found my sketchbooks scattered across the top of the table, and as you might already have noticed, I never leave my books in disarray. When I went to put them away I discovered several new drawings. Those drawings depicted various scenes inside the secret passageway."

"I find that a wee bit disconcertin'," he said.

"To say the least. The second incident took place the morning following my nightmare. I wanted to draw this flower while the details were fresh in my mind," she said as she twirled the blossoms she clutched in her hand. "I don't know why, nor can I explain it, but I feel like this flower means something. Anyway, I thought I'd record the image on paper. But, once again, I discovered I'd already sketched it—along with a few other plants I cannot identify. And to top it all off, I already sketched the hag as well. Now, unless you watched me get up during the night, walk into the studio and draw those things in my sleep—"

Cailen shook his head. "Ye didna."

"Then I would have to have sketched them well before my nightmare," she said. "When you take all of these things together, then it's obvious they must mean something."

****

Mariah's words plagued him long after she retired to her bed. She'd yet to show him her drawings, for the instant they returned to the castle, his men quizzed them over a vast array of insignificant details concerning their shared experience. They did so for hours on end, and that tested his patience. For right now, the potential presence of ghostly females inside his castle troubled him far more than his experience did this morning. If the women truly existed, then why couldn't he or his knights see them? Such seemed impossible and he entertained the notion that Mariah and Hester simply fed off each other's tales and built them into something they weren't. Still, a simple method existed wherein he could put the matter to rest once and for all.

"Where are ye goin'?" asked Duncan the moment he noted his intention.

"I'm goin' to see Dugald," he replied.

"Not without me," he said. Several other voices echoed the statement. He chose to ignore them.

Once he appeared inside Sir Dugald's hall, Cailen discovered that most all his knights had accompanied him. No matter. They'd find plenty to keep themselves occupied while he chatted with his friend. Almost as many spirits resided inside this castle as did his own. The only difference being that Dugald hosted both men and women from various centuries and by the looks of things, he had a few visitors tonight as well.

Amidst the music and laughter, his knights settled in for an evening of fun among the revelers of Sir Dugald's castle. Short of tolerance for such an affair, he seized the first private moment he could find to speak with the fifteenth-century knight. They chatted amiably for a while before he broached his intended subject.

"I have a question for ye," he said as he wiped his ale away from his mouth and sat the tankard down on the table.

"Mayhap I might have an answer," Dugald jested as a pair of dancers very nearly collided with him. "Watch it now, afore ye trample us underfoot," he warned.

The couple merely laughed as they spun away.

Dugald shook his head as he rolled his eyes heavenward. "Ye were sayin'?"

"I just wanted to know if ye' have ever taken th' opportunity to speak with th' lassies that reside at my castle," he said.

"No." Dugald shook his head. "Not that I haven't tried, mind ye," he said.

Cailen hoped his shock hadn't manifested itself in his expression. Truly, he didn't expect that particular answer. "Why not? Is there one in particular ye were hopin' to chat with?" he asked, keeping his tone casual.

"Aye." Dugald wiggled his brows up and down. "I had my eye on th' well-rounded lassie with th' dark brown hair. Do ye know which one I'm talkin' aboot? I was hopin' they'd come and join us for our wee parties."

Cailen merely shrugged off the comment.

"Skittish hens." Dugald took a healthy drink of his ale. "They all just seem to disappear whenever we tried to approach. I can only assume that's your doin', Cailen Braithnoch. Archibald says ye just want all of them to yourself."

"Ye can rest assured that they dinnae speak to me either. Apparently they like to keep to themselves," he muttered.

Dugald returned a slow nod. "Betimes 'tis better to leave that type alone. Besides, there are women a plenty to go around."

Just as Dugald made the comment, Cailen heard the sound of his name. He turned around, dipped his head in acknowledgement and said, "Good eve, Beth."

"Come on Cailen, come and dance th' night away with me," she said as she raised a coquettish brow and smiled.

"Och," Duncan said, coming at once to his rescue. "I'm afraid that Cailen has guard duty tonight."

"Surely someone else can fill in for him," she whined.

"Not so; a man's word is his bond, my lady." Duncan took hold of her outstretched hand. "And Cailen pledged to relieve John."

"All right, then," Beth said as Duncan gave her hand a tug. "But I'll expect to see ye soon and dinnae forget."

Cailen chose not to respond. Instead, he bid Dugald a good evening and disappeared. Minutes later, he appeared inside his own hall, now void of all knights. He made his way to the bench and sat down, grateful for the solitude.

Dugald's confirmation as to Mariah's claims weighed heavy on his mind. Several female entities lived right here at this castle, and all this time he and his knights remained unaware of their presence. Yet, other ghosts, children, and now Mariah had seen them. Why couldn't he and his men see them too? Could they have anything to do with the events that had recently taken place?

Mariah believed they were all connected. Yet, even if this assessment proved accurate, what could it possibly have to do with the two of them collectively? Though he didn't know the answer now, he would soon enough.

Chapter 11

Cailen availed himself of the opportunity to study Murriah's mysterious sketches while she met with Humphries in Edinburgh. Other than the purple flower, the other plants seemed common enough. Yet the effort to name them fled his mind as he turned the page and gazed at the image of the hideous old hag that beset her dreams. He could understand the terror he saw within her eyes now. The image would set even the most battle-hardened warrior back on his heels. For reasons he couldn't name, the banshee looked vaguely familiar even though most her face remained hidden in shadow. Mayhap he envisioned such a creature in his youth while listening to tales meant to frighten wee bairns.

"Ye owe me for Beth," Duncan announced as he suddenly popped into the room beside him.

"You're a good man, Duncan," Cailen replied without taking his eyes off the sketch. "I will not forget your sacrifice."

Duncan tilted his head to the side and shuddered. "That woman's endless chatter could rattle th' patience of a saint. I'm beginnin' to think her unfaithfulness had nothin' to do with her husband wallin' her up alive. Th' more likely reason for the punishment is that he simply wanted to silence her tongue."

"Ye might be right at that." Cailen pulled his eyes away from the book and gave his full attention to

Duncan.

"Did Murriah say how long she'd be in Edinburgh?" asked Duncan. "She's been gone quite a while now, and darkness is beginnin' to set in."

Cailen shook his head. "She only said she and Humphries had to discuss th' frames for her paintin's. She took photographs of her progress along with her so they could choose th' proper wood and tones."

Duncan approached the table then and peered over his shoulder. "What's that?" he asked, nodding at the sketchbook

"Somethin' ghastly from out of Murriah's recent nightmare," Cailen answered.

"Somethin' ghastly, indeed. Almost makes me happy I dinnae need to sleep."

Cailen simply nodded, closed the sketchbook, returned it to its proper place, and said, "Murriah thinks her nightmare and my experience at Dupplin are connected."

"How so?" he asked.

Cailen heaved a sigh and glanced at the ceiling. After a few moments of indecision he said, "Come on, we might as well discuss this downstairs where everyone can gather, should they choose to listen. I dinnae want to repeat it."

Once they appeared inside the crowded hall, Cailen took a seat on the bench. With the undivided attention of his men, he launched into a full explanation of all that had transpired. He left nothing unsaid, and ended his narrative by revealing the presence of female ghosts they couldn't see though others could. A lengthy silence followed the revelation. The account even left Duncan speechless. Any other time, he might have taken a moment to enjoy the amazing achievement.

Finally, Steven looked up and said, "How many women did ye say were here?"

"I dinnae know," Cailen replied. "I didna ask Dugald outright, but Hester mentioned seein' as many as five at one time down by th' moat. I dinnae know if that includes Murriah's redhead or not."

"Could it be they come and go from other places—that they dinnae actually bide here?" asked Duncan.

Cailen shrugged. "'Tis possible I suppose. But th' fact remains, we dinnae have th' ability to see them whether they dwell here or not."

"Then mayhap Murriah's right aboot everythin' else as well," Duncan replied. "Mayhap somethin' strange is goin' on and either we, or the castle itself, is at th' center of it."

Just as he made the comment, Mariah burst through the entry doors and into the room. Her cheeks appeared flushed, and she looked both agitated and excited at the same time. Her eyes darted around the hall until at last they fell upon him.

"Is somethin' wrong?" he asked as she approached him.

"Cailen, do you remember feeling anything— anything out of the ordinary, *before* that force snatched you from the car?" she asked as she came to a halt just two feet in front of him.

He shook his head as he shrugged away the question. "I had no warnin'. Why do ye ask?"

She waved an impatient hand and hurried on. "You told me that after your death you returned to the castle and found it empty. You said you and the knights traveled quite a distance in search of your kinfolk. How far did you go? Where did you go? What directions did you search?"

"Slow down, Murriah," he said. "What's this all aboot?"

"Just answer the questions, Cailen, please. Did you ever go south toward the battlefield? Better yet, did you ever go beyond it?" she asked.

"Nay, we didna," Duncan cut in. "We felt we would have encountered our folk along th' way, if they had moved south."

Cailen nodded. "So we concentrated our searches in all other directions. We traveled east all th' way to Aberdeen, west to Skye, and north to St. Peter's Kirk."

"And you never encountered any problems of any kind during your quest?" she ventured further.

"Nothin' out of th' ordinary happened to any of us." Cailen took hold of her hand and gave it a little tug. Once he had her seated next to him he said, "Now, tell me, what is all this aboot?"

"I noticed it on my way home," she said. "Did you know that the battlefield of Dupplin lay just to the west of where we were when—when you left the car? In fact, we had just barely passed its borders."

Cailen combed his fingers through his beard as he considered that fact. He shook his head and said, "Nay, I didna realize that."

"So, it made me wonder if the place you met your death is a boundary you cannot cross," she said as she drilled her eyes into his.

"But why?" asked Alan. "Why should th' place we fell make a difference as to where we can go?"

"Especially since th' other spirits we know have no such boundary," Malcolm added.

"I don't know," she said as she glanced into each of their faces before returning her attention to Cailen. "Yet, surely it can't be mere coincidence alone. Nothing happened to you *until* I passed the boundaries of Dupplin."

The knights continued to discuss various possibilities for the malady long after Mariah retired to her bed. Still, they had to admit her theory held merit.

"If Murriah is right aboot this boundary," Duncan said to Cailen, "then I wonder if th' phenomenon only effects ye for some unknown reason or if it affects us all."

He merely shrugged in response.

"There is only one way to find out for certain," Steven said as he stood up.

"Aye," said Roger, "but there is danger in what you're suggestin' with so many of us at one time, ye ken?"

Duncan snorted and shook his head as he too, rose to his feet. "As if that's anything new for us," he said. "Let's see to it, then."

"No one need feel compelled to go," Cailen called out. He gave Duncan a nod and at once, all fifty-three knights disappeared from the castle.

****

Within a dense swirling fog, Mariah, along with her company, walked all throughout the night in order to arrive at the battle site by dawn. She could feel the somber mood intensify the moment their pitiful group approached the bloody field of Dupplin. She gazed upon the grief-stricken faces of all her companions—mostly women and boys—as they led the empty wagons onto the battlefield. Her throat tightened and tears cascaded down her cheeks as they looked upon the lifeless bodies strewn about the moor. Other people from other fiefdoms already walked the field, searching for their dead and wounded as well. The sorrow that settled over her being threatened to shatter her soul.

This task needed doing, yet if she could find a way to escape it, she would gladly take it. She inhaled a deep breath as she traipsed the field, searching for the men of their fiefdom, hoping to find some of them alive. The mass of mangled bodies made the task most difficult. They spent hours amidst the carnage gathering the bodies of their knights. As impossible as it seemed, none of them survived the battle. Not one. Finally, only one remained missing. Cailen—

Despite her fatigue, she picked her way to a group of fallen men. Mariah carefully stepped over one body, and then two. She passed yet another before she saw him. A small moan escaped her lips as she located her beloved knight. She sank to her knees in despair. Many English arrows pierced his body before death claimed him. Her tears fell freely as she yanked them out or broke them off. She would not have him return to the castle so displayed. After wiping as much blood off his body as she could manage with just her sash and a bit of water, she called out for Bernard. Several squires hurried to her side and lifted Cailen onto the wagon. Then with heavy hearts, they turned for home.

Mariah tossed and turned restlessly in her bed as she fought the disturbing images that continually assaulted her mind throughout the night. She could see the wagons, now laden with bodies, entering through the gates of the castle walls. The elderly cleric conducted a solemn mass funeral soon thereafter. She accompanied the procession of knights as they laid them to rest within a chamber below the castle foundation.

At the end of his service, the cleric approached an older version of Cailen. This man grieved the loss of his beloved son, his kin, and the courageous knights of his fiefdom.

As the priest rested a comforting hand on his shoulder, he said, "Ye've had to endure so much recently, and I'm so sorry for your losses, my laird."

Laird Braithnoch nodded, but said nothing in return. Unshed tears moistened his eyes. His throat bobbed up and down as he swallowed past the lump born of intense anguish and sorrow.

"What are we goin' to do now?" the cleric asked as he gazed upon the host of lifeless bodies that filled the cavern.

"We'll do as we have always done, Edgar. We'll survive," whispered the laird. "I have already sent for Ethan. He should be along soon."

Mariah followed the somber cleric out of the chamber and into the secret passageway. She accompanied him as he entered the castle and climbed the steps to the second floor. Once he entered the chapel, she stood back as he pulled away the massive cupboard, revealing the door behind it. He grabbed some of the sacramental wine from off the shelf and took a generous swig before he entered the room. Edgar sat at his desk, picked up a quill, and dabbed it into the ink well. A heavy sigh escaped his lips as he paused and then added the names of the knights to his list of recent burials. He began with Cailen—

Mariah's eyes flew open as she vaulted upright in

her bed. She placed a trembling hand against her mouth while she sought to banish the awful dream from her mind. Tears slid down her cheeks. Then, just as she leaned in the direction of the tissue box, she caught sight of long red hair from the corner of her eye. She swung her head toward the ethereal presence to ensure she actually saw her. Her female ghost stood by the door and steadily gazed in her direction for several seconds. Mariah could hear her heart pounding inside her chest as she stared back.

The transparent woman looked out of focus. Mariah couldn't see any of her features clearly, though she struggled to do so. Yet it seemed as though she looked through hazy distorted glass. The woman lifted her chin and turned her head and shoulders slightly to the right.

"No, please don't go," Mariah whispered. The ghost paid her no heed. As the spirit slowly turned away and dissipated, she called out for Cailen, hoping he could see the ghost at last. He didn't come. No one responded. The castle seemed far too quiet.

She glanced over at the table. The clock confirmed that dawn had yet to break across the horizon. Yet, she didn't want or need any more sleep, for she didn't want to risk a continuation of that horrendous dream. A dream surely produced by the conversation she had with Cailen and the knights prior to retiring for the night. She settled back into her pillows and stared up at the ceiling, willing herself to forget. Despite her wishes, and all attempts to replace the images with something else, the dream remained at the forefront of her mind. A host of questions nagged. Whispers continued to swirl in and out of her mind. They said she experienced no ordinary dream if she would but look for a deeper meaning behind it.

The unnerving voices finally compelled her to leave the bed and explore the possibility. She made her way down the stairs in search of Cailen and for the first time she found the hall empty. Strange. Where would all the knights have gone?

"Courage, Mariah," she whispered. "You can do this alone." She headed for the kitchen then and made it as far as the buttery. Images of Cailen's body entering the passageway bombarded her mind as she faced the door behind the shelves. She didn't have the heart to go any farther. Not now. Not even to see if the cave truly existed. Exploring the chapel, however, didn't seem as daunting a task.

Mariah climbed the stairs, turned down the hallway, and made her way inside the chapel. She approached the heavy cupboard, grabbed hold of the middle shelf, and tugged with all her might. Sliding it away from the wall took a great deal of effort, but at last she succeeded. The small cathedral shaped door behind the cupboard looked identical to the one in her dream, save the presence of the now missing latch. She shoved against the door hoping she could open it without the handle, but found she couldn't budge it. Perhaps when Cailen returned, he could assist the endeavor.

She wandered outside then, where the light and warmth of the sun called her to the river. Despite the invitation, the sound of the rippling water did little to erase the jumble from her restless mind. She lifted her face to the warmth of the summer sun and closed her eyes. A scant moment later, muscular arms encircled her body from behind. For a brief moment, she stiffened against the unexpected contact.

"What brings ye outdoors so early this morn, Murriah?" whispered Cailen as he nuzzled playfully against her ear.

Despite the warmth his form exuded, a shiver of delight passed through her body. Keeping her movements tight, she turned around to face him and gazed into his eyes. Those incredible eyes bore into her own with an unhurried thoroughness that left her breathless. "Cailen," she murmured. "Where—"

"Shh," he said as his finger rested lightly against her mouth. "Just hold still, my lady. Verra still—"

Mariah's anticipation escalated as Cailen's lips drew ever closer to hers. The moment they connected, a roaring blaze erupted somewhere inside the far recesses of her body and burst forth like the rushing waters of a mighty river. As Cailen deepened his kiss, she found it most difficult not to move. Unbidden, one hand slid upward and using great care, she rested it against the breadth of his chest while she placed the other very lightly upon the side of his face.

Of course, someone would choose that monumental moment to call her. As the phone rang inside her pocket, Cailen broke the kiss and muttered, "I swear by all th' saints, I'm goin' to murder that contrivance."

Mariah breathed out a small laugh as she withdrew her phone and glanced down at the screen before lifting her eyes to meet with his. "Why would Evan call me at this hour?" she asked as she raised the phone to her ear.

"I dinnae know, but ye'd better answer th' bloody thing afore he thinks th' ghosts have done away with ye and races to your rescue," he replied in an irritated huff.

A smile accompanied the slight shake of her head. "Hello, Evan."

"Good morning, Mariah," he sang out. "I'm calling to see if you'd like me to bring you out some lunch. I have th' day off, so I thought it would be th' perfect opportunity to pay you a visit. 'Tis such a lovely day, I thought we could picnic outside if you're not opposed to th' idea."

"That's very kind of you, Evan," she said. "But I really don't have the time today. I went to Edinburgh yesterday and met with Mr. Humphries. He's expecting the first of the smaller paintings in just a few weeks and I'm going to need every waking minute to get them done in time."

"You still have to eat," he argued.

"I know, but you needn't worry, I won't go hungry." Cailen's fingers brushed a wayward strand of hair away from her face and she found it impossible to concentrate on anything other than his touch and the effects of his stirring kiss. "I'm sorry, Evan. Perhaps another time."

"All right," he conceded. "I'll hold you to that."

"I've got to go now, but thank you for calling," she said.

Mariah's desire to end the conversation matched Cailen's. Evan knew a dismissal when he heard one and therefore, didn't prolong the call. That suited him fine. In fact, it would suit him if he never called her again. "Ye didna answer my question," he said.

She looked a bit puzzled. "Your question?"

"Aye, I wondered what brought ye outside so early this morn," he reminded her.

An attractive blush stole across her cheeks as she peeked up at him through lowered lashes. "As I recall, you didn't give me time to answer."

He shrugged away the comment. In truth, he hadn't meant to kiss her at that moment. Yet, when he saw her standing by the river, bathed in glorious sunlight, she looked so very lovely. He didn't have the strength or will to deny himself the experience any longer. She didn't seem to mind the intrusion and that meant she could feel his kiss as he intended her to feel it. He no longer needed to concern himself over that particular quandary.

"I offer no apology for my actions, my lady, nor will I give ye an oath that it will not happen again. However, I do vow to let ye answer th' question now."

His words brought a haunted look into her eyes that troubled him. "What's wrong?" he asked.

She stepped away from him then and gazed out over the river. "I had another dream last night," she finally said.

"Another nightmare?" he asked.

She returned an almost imperceptible nod and he cursed under his breath for not being here when she needed him. "Th' same one?" he asked.

"No."

"Tell me aboot it," he said.

She turned and gazed into his eyes for what seemed a very long time. "I'd like to ask you a few questions first, if you don't mind," she said.

"I dinnae mind."

"Do you know someone from your fiefdom named Ethan?" she asked.

"Aye, Ethan is th' name of my oldest brother," he

replied.

"Was Ethan away when you went off to your final battle?"

"Aye, he sailed to Ireland along with a few of th' knights," he said.

"And what about the names Bernard and Edgar? Do they mean anything to you?"

He wondered if the surprise that assaulted him registered on his face. "Bernard is Roger's oldest son. Edgar is th' name of th' cleric that bided here during my mortality," he said.

She said nothing for several moments, but remained thoughtful. Finally, she said, "You look just like your father, don't you."

"Such has been said many times afore, Murriah," he replied. "Do these questions have somethin' to do with your dream?"

"Yes," she replied.

He took hold of her hand then and led her to the old fallen log. "Tell me aboot it," he said once they were seated.

He listened without interruption as she related the details of her nightmare. All the while, he held her hand, offering what comfort his touch could give. Her account amazed him. She described many of the people she saw in her dream so vividly that he could put a name to each of them.

"So, I don't suppose you know if they buried you inside the cavern, do you?" she asked at the end of her tale.

He shook his head. "Nay, I didna witness our burial."

"But is it possible they might've put you down

147

there," she persisted.

"Aye, with so many to bury at once, and given th' outcome of th' battle, 'tis quite possible. They wouldn't have wanted any delay."

She took a deep breath. "Then I'd like you to accompany me down there. I need to know if the place I saw really exists."

"If ye wish," he said, for he too desired to know.

"And I also want you to help me open the door behind the sacramental cupboard," she said. "Just to see if it looks the same as it did in my dream."

"I can already tell you that it will not look th' same. All th' furnishin's were removed a long time ago. 'Tis empty now."

"Still," she said as she rose to her feet, "I'd like to see it anyway. I can't explain it. The task just seems like something I need to do."

He took hold of her hand and as they made their way to the castle she added, "I went looking for you when I first woke up. I wanted you to come along with me as I searched for the cavern, but I couldn't find you or anyone else for that matter. What happened to you? Where did all of you go?"

Cailen met the question with a great deal of reluctance. He had hoped to avoid that question altogether.

Chapter 12

"Is something wrong with the question?" she asked.

"We went out to th' field of Dupplin."

Mariah halted her steps, drew in a breath, and turned to face him. Her rounded eyes and incredulous expression filled him with humor. A slight grin emerged in response.

"There is no need to look at me like that," he said. "Th' lads just wanted to see if th' aberration would affect them th' same way it affected me. That way they would know if they were involved or if this situation has somethin' to do with just me."

"And did it affect them as well?" she asked as they resumed their trek.

"Aye," he replied. "They experienced th' same events I did, down to th' smallest detail. We found that we couldn't go any farther south than th' battlefield, just as ye surmised."

"I wonder why not?" she mused.

"I wished I could tell ye, but I dinnae have th' answer ye seek," he said.

Once they entered the castle, she found the hall still void of its residents. Their absence caused a moment of alarm. "Where are the knights?" she asked. "Are they all right? I mean, everyone returned home with you, didn't they?"

"Aye, everyone is fine, Murriah," he said. "Ye dinnae need to worry. They just decided to go out and see if they could find your ghost or her companions. 'Tis their thinkin' that mayhap, for reasons known only to them, they only visit here from time to time."

"Oh. I suppose that's a possibility." She dropped her gaze as she brought her ghost to mind. "I saw her again, this morning."

"Where?" he asked.

"Standing by my bedroom door just as I awoke from the dream," she replied. "I know this might sound crazy, but her presence at that precise moment made me wonder if she's responsible for the nightmares and perhaps even for my drawings. I mean, how else could I see faces of people I've never met before and know some of their names unless somehow she showed them to me while I slept? How else could I draw things I'd yet to see?"

"Could ye finally see what she looked like?" he asked.

She shook her head. "No, I couldn't see any of her features clearly. The only way I can describe her image is to say that when I looked at her, it seemed I peered through a slow moving fog. No matter how hard I tried, I couldn't bring her face into focus."

Cailen said nothing in return, but his expression told her he considered everything she said. She headed for the castle kitchen then and together they made their way to the buttery. Mariah waited as he opened the door and lit the torch before she descended the stairway.

Once she had the torch in hand, he stepped to the side and said, "Ye lead th' way and I'll follow. And dinnae worry, I will not let ye fall."

She walked all the way down the steps and then turned to the left, just as she had in her dream. They passed two junctions before she stopped at the first passageway off to her right.

"All the way down to the end," she said, pointing the way.

Cailen nodded and said, "There is a large chamber down that way as I recall. Come on."

She followed him to the end of the broad corridor. The natural cavity now had rows of block stones sealing the entrance. She took a quick breath and said, "I think you're all inside there."

"Wait right here, and I'll have a look around," he replied.

An apprehensive shiver coursed through her body as she waited for Cailen to reappear. The wait seemed longer that what she thought it should. But then, just as trepidation set in, he walked straight through the stones.

"You're right," he said. "We're all inside the chamber together and amazingly well preserved."

"You are?" she asked.

"Aye," he replied. "We look as though we have just recently been laid to rest. 'Twas still obvious they buried us in our surcoats and hauberks. I could even see that my father buried me in my black-and-red surcoat Mairwen made me shortly afore my death. They also laid us out with our—"

Mariah held up a hand to stay further comment and gulped. She knew the image well enough. "I know. I saw. You don't need to go into detail."

She took a moment to study the large stones used to seal the entrance. "Is that limestone rock?" she asked.

"Aye, th' walls and caverns down here are all limestone," he replied.

"Well then, that probably explains your high state of preservation," she said. "Limestone is known for absorbing the moisture that decomposes bodies. Archeologists have found what they term 'accidental mummies' in such places before."

Cailen dipped his head in the direction of the chamber. "Some of th' more valuable things we had in th' castle prior to my death are stored inside th' cavern as well."

"Why would they put stuff like that in there?" she asked.

"I dinnae rightly know," he replied. "Mayhap my father decided to hide them away in th' event Balliol tried to lay claim to th' castle after our defeat. 'Twas a common practice with those that conquered in battle."

"I suppose that makes sense," Mariah replied. "Did you ever learn what happened to the castle between the time of your death and the time you could finally observe people living here?"

"Nay, no one ever discussed such in our hearin'," he replied. "Like I told ye earlier, Nathan's son, Alasdair ruled over th' castle at that time. But it also wouldn't have been uncommon for the castle to change hands many times in between."

"Yes, I know, I have read some of those accounts in Scottish history," she said. "But since a member of your family governed this castle for several centuries after Alasdair died, I wonder why no one ever retrieved the property inside the cavern."

"Mayhap the knowledge of it became lost, just like

these passageways," he said.

"I suppose you could be right." She took a deep breath and gave it a slow release. "So, off to the oratory then. Are you ready?"

"Aye, just dinnae expect to see much when ye get there."

Just as Cailen said, the cleric's oratory sat empty of the furnishings she saw in her dream. Still, as she walked into the center of the room and slowly turned a full circle, she envisioned the small cubicle just as it looked at the time of Cailen's death. She could see the priest sitting at his little wooden desk, the candle situated near the top right hand corner, and the parchment he stared at for so long before he picked up the quill and recorded names of the dead. She could see his small bed at the back and his personal things crowded haphazardly around it. The vision prompted a bit of curiosity about the fate of the priest.

"I don't suppose you know what happened to Edgar, do you?" she asked.

"Nay, but I would assume he died here, even if Balliol took control of th' castle. Th' man was gettin' up there in years. I dinnae think he had any desire to go anywhere else, even if given th' opportunity," he said. "Why do ye ask?"

"Oh, I don't know. He just seemed so sad after your death. He had this look of helplessness and inadequacy when he offered comfort to your father." She shrugged. "I felt sorry for him."

He nodded. "Knowin' th' man th' way I do, he would likely have appreciated your concern."

"Thank you, Cailen, for coming with me while I verified the things I saw in my dream. I found the chore much easier with your company."

"You're welcome, my lady," he replied. "Is there anything else I can do for ye while we're aboot?"

"No," she said. "I have another half an hour or so before I can work on the paintings. So, I thought I might use that time to sketch the faces of the people I saw in my dream. I want to have a record of them just in case we need them later for one reason or another."

"Mind if I come along and watch?" he asked.

"You know I don't mind. I love having you with me."

The comment solicited a small grin, yet he said nothing in return. Once she collected her sketchbook from off the table, she sat down on her stool and flipped through the pages. A small gasp escaped her lips, and her eyes widened the moment she turned to the final sketch inside the book. Yet again, she created an image she had no memory of making. This time, she had drawn the backside of her ghost, crouched down on the floor of the oratory. One hand rested on her knee, while the other hand touched the floor. The angle of her head indicated a pointed look at something specific, though her hair completely covered her face.

"Ye have another one," Cailen said matter-of-factly as he approached her.

She nodded and turned the drawing around to face him. He rested a hand atop her shoulder as he studied the image. "My ghost," she said. "And for some reason, I have sketched her kneeling inside the oratory where I heard her crying."

"What's she lookin' at?" he asked.

"I don't know. It looks like nothing more than a portion of the floor. I'm not sure why or what it might mean."

"Mayhap she wants ye to find somethin' in that area," he suggested.

The comment drew Mariah's startled gaze to his, and for a moment, they simply looked at each other. "Come on," she said. "Let's go have a look and see if something is there."

Cailen led the way back inside the chapel and into the cleric's room. He made his way to the exact spot the ghost knelt in her sketch and thoroughly searched the area. "I dinnae see anything out of th' ordinary."

"I don't either," she replied. Yet, she continued her study of the floor.

She tapped against the surrounding stones with the tip of her foot. One of them moved under the pressure. "This one is loose," she said as she dropped to her knees. She inched her fingers inside the cracks and tugged.

Cailen knelt beside her and assisted her effort to haul the loose stone away from the flooring. Her heart hammered a slow beat as she dropped a hand inside the small oblong cavity. She withdrew the tightly wrapped leather bundle that had occupied the entire space.

"I wonder what this is," she murmured as she turned the parcel over and brushed against the skin.

"I dinnae know," he replied. "Open it up and see."

She rose to her feet and nodded. "All right, but let's do this at my table. I don't want to chance dropping something important here on the floor."

Once they placed the bundle on the table, Mariah untied the leather strips that held the contents bound. Then, as if made of the most fragile glass, she swept away the leather skin that covered the contents. Inside the protective wrapper, lay a three-inch stack of parchment pages. Considering the age of the Latin texts, they were very well preserved. The pages looked identical to the ones Edgar used in her dream.

"What's all that aboot?" asked Cailen pointing at the stack.

"My Latin is pretty rusty, so give me a minute," Mariah said.

Cailen chuckled. "Ye know Latin?"

She spared him a glance and said, "I'm certainly not fluent by any means, but I did take a couple years of the tedious language in college. Hopefully I can remember enough to figure some of this out."

"Now tell me," said Cailen. "What would cause an artist to study Latin?"

"Because for some reason, the artist in question thought it easier to learn than French." She lifted a single shoulder and then added, "And she needed two years of foreign language to earn her Bachelor's degree. Now let's see here—"

Cailen peered over her shoulder as she attempted to decipher the words. "I think I'm going to need a dictionary or an online translator to get this exact, but this first page looks like terms set forth for an impending marriage. I believe the contract is between a man named William Ross, acting on behalf of his daughter, and Sir Neil Moore. Obvious by omission alone, they didn't feel the need to mention the name of the bride. Such is an unimportant detail in these matters, I suppose," she quipped.

Cailen chuckled as he ran his fingers through the length of her hair. "'Tis only because her father was th' one payin' her dowry. I can also tell ye that Neil accompanied my brother to Ireland while th' rest of us were called to Dupplin. At th' time, th' man had no plans for marriage if that helps ye in your quest," Cailen said. "Is there a date on that piece of parchment?"

"Well, let's see," she said as her eyes traveled over the document. "We have the year 1335 right here, and the month of May, here—"

"Almost three years from th' date of our death," he mused. "I'm sure this is all verra interestin', but I dinnae see what it has to do with any of us."

"Perhaps not this page," she said. "But there has to be something in this stack of documents that'll help unravel whatever it is we're supposed to unravel. Otherwise my ghost wouldn't have shown me where this lay hidden. I'll work on them whenever I can and in time, we'll see what they might reveal."

After Mariah secured the leather wrapping around the parchment pages, she took up her book and sketched the faces she recalled in her dream. Each time she completed a drawing, Cailen gave her the name of the person she sketched.

"I guess that about does it," she said as she closed the book and placed it between her bookends. "At least for now."

"Ye've drawn everyone ye remember from your dream?" he asked.

"Yes," she said and then as she took in his puzzled expression she added, "Why? Is something wrong with the sketches?"

He shrugged and said, "I just dinnae see faces I would have expected to see."

"Like whom?" she asked.

"Like my sister, Mairwen, for one. Steven's goodwife, Alison. Ye have no sketches of Margery or Aveline to name a few others," he replied.

"Who does Margery belong to?" she asked.

"Robert is her husband," he said. "I know her verra well. Nothin' would have kept her at home once news of th' battle arrived at th' castle. More likely, she would have led th' company."

"Well, maybe they *were* there and I just didn't see them for one reason or another. Nothing says my dreams are a complete representation of what actually transpired. Perhaps I'm only given pieces of what we need to know."

"I suppose ye could be right aboot that," he said, "And for now, that will suffice. Aye?"

She gave him a smile and nodded. "Aye."

The knights returned to the castle well after Mariah finished her work for the day. She and Cailen sat talking downstairs inside the great hall when they suddenly burst through the walls, as did the host of spirits that accompanied them. Cailen conjured a deep sigh, shook his head, and fixed his gaze heavenward.

At once otherworldly musicians began playing their ghostly instruments. Couples danced amidst the laughter and an abundance of conversation filled the hall. Mariah dropped her mouth and sucked in a breath, but truly, she couldn't help doing otherwise. She had never seen such a sight before. Ghosts from almost every era filled every corner of the room. And what's more, bounteous representations of food and drink covered the tables.

Duncan approached her with a broad smile covering his face. He leaned close to her ear and whispered, "Do ye see your ghost in attendance?"

She looked all about the room. Her gaze lingered on each of the female spirits with long red hair. Finally, she shook her head and said, "No, she's not here."

"Well, keep your eyes open," he said, "More women are bound to show up afore th' evenin' ends. We sent out an open invitation."

Just then, a lovely woman dressed in fashionable seventeenth-century attire approached the table where they sat. The ghost, ignoring her presence completely, raised a dainty brow. She gave Cailen a dazzling smile, and extended her hand in invitation. "I've come to collect on your promise, Cailen," she cooed. "Come dance with me."

Mariah's heart dropped somewhere into the pit of her stomach and landed with a sickening thud. This type of social event had never occurred to her before. Therefore, she never once considered that ghostly women would be part of Cailen's life now. But then, why wouldn't they be. The woman gazed at him with a familiarity that filled her with distress. Suddenly, she didn't know whether to stay put or excuse herself.

Cailen focused his irritation upon Duncan, who shrugged sheepishly in return. And then, as if he sensed her disquiet, Cailen took hold of her hand. He gave it a gentle squeeze, and settled it onto his lap despite the woman's presence. Her watchful eyes narrowed in response to the blatant display of affection.

"I've noticed that social events have a way of confusin' things," Duncan said, using an amiable tone and smile. "But if ye recall when last we met, Cailen made ye no such vow afore he left to relieve John. And he has already pledged this eve to Murriah. Therefore,

I'm afraid I will have to step in as your first dance partner unless, of course, ye prefer another."

The woman inclined her head but said nothing in return.

"Och," continued Duncan. "Where are my manners? Beth this is Murriah Jennin's, and Murriah this is Beth Ogilvie."

Mariah murmured a hello, or at least something close to it. In response, Beth merely produced a smile that didn't look the least bit genuine.

In that same instant, Cailen drew her to feet while Duncan ushered Beth onto the dance floor. The woman turned her head and looked over her shoulder one last time. "But she's just a mortal, Duncan! What can she possibly offer any of us? She shouldn't even be here and ye know it."

"Put your claws away, Beth," Duncan said. "Murriah is our guest and is just as welcome here as anyone else."

Mariah gazed up at Cailen who held her close to his chest as they danced. Beth was not the only woman in the crowd shooting daggers in her direction and it made her very uncomfortable. She shouldn't be here. "Maybe I should excuse myself now," she whispered. "I am a little tired."

Cailen shook his head. "I have a better idea. Just as soon as all of the guests arrive, we'll both leave this tedious gatherin'. 'Twas Duncan's good intention to give ye the opportunity to see all of th' spirits that reside in th' Highlands. Mayhap ye might find your mysterious ghost amongst th' crowd if we stay for a wee bit longer."

Mariah gave him a single nod. Once they finished

the dance, Cailen propelled her toward an attractive man dressed in elegant fifteenth-century apparel. His dark blond hair accented his blue eyes and devilish smile. He looked as if he might have just approached his forties at the time of his death.

The moment they approached, he took hold of her hand and lifted it to his lips. The fact that spirits could touch or hold a mortal body without going through them, amazed her. She couldn't find a logical answer for the manifestation. When she asked Cailen about it, he simply shrugged. She sighed. If only mortals could reciprocate—

"Where have ye been hidin' this delectable creature, Braithnoch?" he roared over the chatter of the crowd.

"Where she's spared from th' likes of ye," he bantered in return. "Murriah, may I present my good friend, Sir Dugald Carnegie, and Dugald, this is Murriah Jennin's."

Dugald leaned close to her ear and said, "When ye tire of havin' a mere lad at your side and would rather have a real man, you're welcome to come reside at my castle. We have room aplenty."

Mariah dropped her gaze and smiled, but said nothing in response.

"Good try, Dugald, and I commend ye for it," Cailen countered. "But th' lassie is already spoken for."

Dugald shot a glance at his pointed shoes, and shook his head. "Mores th' pity."

Despite the playful repartee that passed between them, Mariah remained thoughtful. She found so many things to occupy her mind, from the presence of Beth and the other women who craved Cailen's attention, to the comment he just made about her availability. What did he mean by that remark?

Between their dances, she and Cailen chatted with Sir Dugald and as the hour grew ever later, her ghostly redhead remained elusive. Finally, Cailen placed an arm about her waist and said, "I dinnae think your ghost is goin' to make an appearance. So, come on, my lady, let's get ye upstairs and off to your bed. Ye look dead on your feet, if ye'll pardon th' expression."

Mariah shot a quick glance at Beth Ogilvie. "You don't have to escort me to bed, Cailen. You can remain here with your guests."

Completely ignoring her comment, Cailen extended a hand to Dugald. "'Tis always a pleasure to see ye, my friend, but if ye'll excuse us I think I'll escort Murriah to her bedchamber."

Dugald grinned as he once again took hold of her hand and kissed it. "'Twas a pleasure meeting ye, Murriah Jennin's. I hope ye'll accept th' invitation to visit my castle verra soon, and ye best see that she does, Cailen or I'll come lookin' for ye both."

"Dinnae worry, we will," Cailen replied.

Troubling thoughts plagued her mind as they climbed the stairs. Once they stepped inside her bedroom, she turned to face Cailen and opened her mouth to speak. He put a finger to her lips to stay the comment.

"I'll wait just here while ye change into your bed clothes," he said.

Mariah swallowed past the knot in her throat as she made her way to the bureau, retrieved a nightshirt, and put it on. She said nothing as she opened the door to allow him entrance. Just as she would turn to her bed, he took hold of her waist and gathered her into his arms. She stood very still as his eyes bore into hers.

"Just go ahead and ask th' question I know ye have," he said.

She didn't quite know what to say to that, so many different questions begged an answer. After several silent seconds passed between them, she shrugged. "I'm sorry if I kept you from enjoying Beth's company tonight. Truly, you didn't have to spend all of your time with—"

He ended the rest of her needless apology with a ghostly kiss even more incredible and powerful than the first. That single kiss left her breathless and emptied her mind of all coherent thought. She could feel love, in its purest, most magnificent form passing between them like a blazing bolt of lightning and it left her without doubt as to the meaning of his comment to Sir Dugald. Cailen had claimed her as his.

Chapter 13

At long last, she found it. Mariah dropped to her knees, took hold of the plant's base with both hands, and yanked it out of the ground. She clutched the grubby root to her chest and with a sense of satisfaction, rose to her feet. The back of one dirty hand wiped across her cheek as she glanced at the distant castle towers, now silhouetted in sunset's shadow. She closed her eyes, took a deep breath, and quashed the feelings of guilt that accompanied her errand. If she could find any other way to accomplish her goal she would take it. But another way didn't exist.

She tucked the root inside her bag, along with everything else she had gathered this evening, and turned for home. Her path would take her through the ancient trees and across the river. She could hear the howling of wolves in the distance and the familiar sounds of insects and birds. That she expected. However, she didn't expect to hear the crunching of twigs coming up behind her. Several times she halted her tracks and turned her head in the direction of the noise. Two possibilities leaped into her mind and neither gave her any comfort. Either a wild animal or a person followed her footsteps. Each time she stopped, so did the sound.

The rate of her heartbeat accelerated as the unknown menace mocked her fear. She swallowed past the dryness in her throat and once again turned in the direction of the castle. With each hurried step another echoed while closing the distance between them. Then, as she stepped onto the bridge, a terrifying shriek erupted just behind her. She whirled around as a flaming pair of large red eyes flew at her. Her heart thudded inside her chest as she faced the shadowed wraithlike form of the hideous banshee.

The old woman extended a wrinkled hand, palm up, in expectation. She hovered inches above the ground. Her grotesque teeth gleamed in the moonlight. A bizarre mix of tremendous fear, shame, and unavoidable resignation engulfed her at that moment. She removed the bag from around her shoulder and handed it to the shrouded figure. The woman snatched it from her grasp. Her gleeful cackle caused her to cry out in sudden panic. Yet, only a whimper escaped her lips.

"Shh, Murriah—" The tender voice, along with a series of gentle strokes through the length of her hair, called her away from her hellish nightmare. She stirred. Cailen pressed a kiss against her forehead then and whispered, "I'm here. You're safe, everythin' is all right now."

She drew in a deep breath and slowly exhaled it as she opened her eyes. Cailen reclined on the bed alongside her. He gazed at her with such tenderness and concern. Her hand traveled to the side of his face and for a moment, her fingers traced the length of his beard before she dropped her hand atop the pillow. "Cailen," she sighed. "You're still here—"

"Aye," he replied. "Ye appear surprised."

"I thought you would return to your guests once I

fell asleep," she said and then hoping she hadn't made a silly spectacle of herself by crying out, added, "Is everyone still downstairs?"

He glanced at the door and nodded. "For th' moment, but they're gettin' ready to quit the place now. Dawn is approachin'."

Quiet laughter accompanied the shake of her head. She lifted a hand to her brow and said, "What? Does everyone turn into a pumpkin if they don't make it home before sunrise?"

Cailen chuckled as he brushed the tangled hair away from her face. "Nay, 'tis just th' courteous thing for them to do. Now tell me what made ye tremble and cry out in such fear."

She adjusted the height of her pillows, turned onto her side, and offered her hand. He immediately took hold of it as he waited for her to speak. She took in a breath. "Just another weird dream," she said.

He said nothing in return, but waited for her to continue. She dropped her gaze and took a moment to gather her scattered thoughts. "This dream seemed different from the others. Scary—but not in the same way. I'm beginning to think I'm not me in these dreams, if that makes sense to you."

"How so?" he asked.

She lifted her brows and shrugged. "Well—we know now through our own discoveries that the previous dream I had revealed actual events. That made me wonder if someone is showing me these past events as seen through their eyes and interpretation."

He cocked his head to the side as he regarded her. "I suppose that's possible. What did ye see in your dream this time?"

"I saw the old hag again. But her presence didn't affect me the same way it did the first time I saw her. In this dream, I stood on the other side of the bridge in the opposite direction of where we discovered the purple flower. I collected bits of plants here and there along the way. Then, at the end of the dream, I yanked this huge root out of the ground. I placed everything I collected inside a pouch I carried around my shoulder. As I began walking back to the castle, I could hear footsteps behind me. Each time I turned around the footsteps stopped. Yet, once I stepped onto the bridge, the hag revealed herself. She shrieked her anger, her agitation, or her impatience—I don't know. Maybe all three of them rolled into one. I turned around to face her. She extended a gnarly hand, and somehow I knew she wanted the pouch. I suddenly understood I collected everything inside the bag at her request. Guilt overwhelmed me the moment I handed it to her."

"Ye weren't frightened of her presence?" he asked.

"Yes, scared to death in fact," she said. "But her presence didn't hinder me from doing what I had to do."

"And ye needed to give her what ye collected in completion of this task?" he asked.

Mariah touched a finger to her lip and nodded. "The intriguing thing is that I also understood she needed the contents of the pouch for something important to *me*."

"That's a verra interestin' twist," he said.

"And bizarre," she added.

He chuckled and said, "That too."

Cailen traced light, gentle patterns atop her hand as they both fell silent. The path of her tangled thoughts danced around and then landed atop an intriguing notion. "Cailen?"

"Aye?"

"Do you think it's possible that one of the women you expected to see on the battlefield and didn't, is responsible for the dreams?" Before he could answer she said, "The thing is, if I'm looking through someone else's eyes, it would make sense that I'm looking through one of theirs. You said nothing would keep Margery home once she heard the outcome of the battle. Maybe she, or one of the other women you mentioned, is trying to tell us something."

"'Tis possible I suppose, but I cannae imagine any of them havin' a reason to deal with a banshee. That part of your dreams makes no sense to me."

"Other than the fact a banshee is a bringer of death," she said.

"Our mortal lives have already ended," he countered. "Nothin' will change that now, banshee, or no banshee."

Before she could remind him the creature could be a recollection of the woman's experience, Cailen shifted his attention to the door. Something caught his attention.

"Is something wrong?" she asked, gazing in that direction herself.

He shook his head. "Nay, 'tis just everyone clearin' out of th' castle."

"Oh." She cast her gaze downward and nodded. "Do you think you ought to go downstairs and tell them goodbye?"

"I see no need for it," he said.

She drew her brows together. "But you're the

host," she argued.

"Such matters not. Duncan can see them off well enough since he's the one that did th' invitin' in th' first place. I'm quite comfortable right where I am, my lady."

The way he looked at her as he said the last created a burning inside.

She glanced down at her bedding, self-consciously picked at the little fuzz balls on her blanket, and rolled them into a tight little ball.

"So, do you have that type of gathering often?" she asked, saying the first thing that entered her mind.

"Depends upon what ye mean by oft," he replied. "We dinnae get together every eve, but mayhap once or twice in a moon."

"I'm curious, can you really taste the food you eat and the ale you drink?" she asked. "Or are you just going through the motions of what you did in mortality?"

Humor filled his eyes. "Aye, we can both eat and drink if we choose. Everythin' has its spiritual form, ye know. Is such hard for ye to accept?"

"No, I guess not, it's just that I never stopped to consider the possibility before. Until I met you, I had limited experiences with ghosts. They were more like the common stories one hears. You know—a partial apparition here and there, disembodied voices, balls of light floating about, cold chills, and some of the things we talked about when first we met.

"I never truly believed in ghosts until I saw one at the first castle I painted in England. After that, they became familiar enough. But I never once witnessed a party with dancing, music—or food and drink on the tables. I never considered the possibility that such a large number of ghosts would exist in a given area to warrant a party, either."

"I suppose we exist in numbers th' livin' might find surprisin'. We also have time aplenty on our hands, and with that time we do many of th' things we did in our mortal life, just in a much different way," he said.

She took a moment to think about all the various activities those "things" might entail. Her gaze dropped to the big hand that still caressed her own. "So, tell me, does Beth participate in most of your activities as well?"

Cailen cupped her chin and tilted her head upward, forcing her gaze to meet with his. He shook his head. "Ye dinnae need to worry aboot Beth. She has never captured my attention, much less my heart," he whispered huskily. "In truth, my lady, you're th' first woman that has accomplished both."

They gazed into each other's eyes for several long moments, before he added, "Do I dare allow myself to believe that I have captured your heart as well?"

Mariah shook her head ever so slightly as a breathy laugh escaped her lips. "Cailen, you took possession of my heart the moment my childish fingers sketched your face for the very first time. Surely you already know this."

His eyes filled with triumph. "Aye, but I needed to hear ye declare it," he said as he grazed his lips against hers.

Then just before he deepened his kiss, Duncan called out from the bottom of the stairs. Cailen dropped his forehead against hers and sighed in frustration. "What is it?"

"We could hear voices from down in th' hall. Is Murriah awake then?" he asked.

"Aye." The word no more than left Cailen's mouth before Duncan appeared inside her bedroom—along with Steven, Malcolm, and Edmund.

"Did ye ever catch sight of your ghost?" asked Duncan, his anticipation of her forthcoming answer evident in the gleam of his eyes.

Mariah lifted a shoulder as she shook her head. "No, she never showed up."

Each of the knights exchanged baffled glances.

Duncan plopped himself at the end of her bed. "Ye know, I'm beginnin' to feel as if we're in th' middle of a nightmare ourselves. Somethin' unnatural is happenin' around here," he muttered.

The comment made her smile. "Now that's an interesting statement coming from a ghost," she said.

"Aye," said Steven, nodding his agreement.

"I take it then, every female ghost you know showed up at your party?" she asked.

Duncan nodded. "We accounted for every lassie we know."

"Are ye sure that ye didna see her, Murriah?" asked Malcolm. "I only ask because Cailen told us ye've never seen her face clearly."

"That's right," said Edmond. "Mayhap ye just couldn't pick her out."

Mariah lifted a hand and then dropped it. "I suppose that's always possible. But, I have seen the frame of her body, and the length and color of her hair in detail, several times, now. Last night I just didn't see anyone that fit with what I've seen."

"Murriah is an artist and a good one," Cailen

reminded them. "She will not be mistaken in the details she sees."

"Aye," Duncan said. "That's true enough."

"But where could these women be hidin', especially here at this castle?" asked Steven. "Better yet, how are we ever goin' to find out?"

Cailen shook his head. "I dinnae know, Steven. Mayhap such will manifest itself in one of Murriah's dreams in th' days ahead."

"Speakin' of those dreams," said Steven, shifting his attention to Mariah, "As ye know, Cailen is a man of few words. Gettin' details out of him is nigh on impossible at times. Would ye mind tellin' us aboot th' dreams ye've had, yourself? Mayhap one of us could learn somethin' new that might help us figure this thing out once and for all."

"I'm all for that," she replied.

Cailen sighed in obvious displeasure, shook his head, and focused his gaze heavenward. The knights paid his agitation no heed.

****

After the breakfast Cailen insisted she have first, Mariah met the knights in the hall with sketchbook in hand. They gave her their undivided attention as she related the dreams exactly as she remembered them and in the order in which they came. At the end of her narrative she picked up her sketchbook and exhibited each of the pages.

Duncan shuddered when she revealed the face of the hag. "I've seen it afore and Cailen's right. Th' old crone looks just like a banshee."

Edmund nodded. "Did ye ever see her face?" he asked.

Mariah shook her head as she pressed her lips together. "No, I'm afraid this is as good as it gets. In my dreams she wears the hooded cloak, pulled down over her forehead. Her face remains hidden in shadow. When I saw her eyes in my last dream they in no way resembled anything human. They looked more animalistic and filled with raging fire."

Not wanting to dwell on that portion of her nightmares, she moved past the ominous hag and focused instead on the array of plants she had sketched. To her disappointment, none of the knights could identify her purple flower, or the yellow one that looked similar to a dandelion, but far larger and more robust. She turned the page.

Roger moved a little closer to study the current sketch. "I cannae be certain, but I think I remember my goodwife callin' that coriander. I'm not sure, mind ye," he warned.

"Coriander," Mariah murmured as she wrote the word underneath the sketch. "That gives us one possibility. I suppose I should be grateful for that—"

"What did ye expect? We're knights, Murriah," Steven hollered out good-naturedly. "Not a bunch of mewlin', milk-livered poets with naught but time on their hands to study th' foliage."

Despite the declaration, the knights identified two more of her sketches—the willow and guelder rose. Only two left to go.

"All right, how about this one then?" she asked, not really expecting an answer. The simple, green-leafed plant could be just about anything.

"I dinnae know its name, Murriah," said Cailen. "But there is one of those plants sittin' atop th' counter, inside Sybil's kitchen."

Mariah fastened her gaze to his as she sought to bring Sybil's plants to mind. "She does?"

He nodded and said, "Aye."

"Evan might know what it's called then. In all likelihood, Sybil has always maintained such a plant to keep her herbs well stocked," she mused aloud. "Perhaps I could ask him."

Cailen said nothing in return. However, she didn't miss the look of annoyance that passed over his face. On the other hand, Duncan shook his head over her suggestion. "Nay, Murriah, we cannae trust Evan right now."

"Oh come on, Duncan," she said. "I'd only be asking for the name of a plant, not giving him a history."

"And what will ye tell him if he asks ye why ye want to know?" he challenged.

Mariah shrugged and said, "Simple curiosity and nothing more. I'm sure he'd think nothing of it, especially if I ask about all the other plants at the same time."

"I dinnae think 'tis a good idea to invite him out here," said Edmund.

"All right," she conceded as she turned the page. "I'll see if I can figure it out myself. This drawing here is the last of the plants. Any ideas?"

Steven moved a bit closer and stared at the tiny white flowers surrounded by much larger six-pronged leaves and a long slender stem.

"I dinnae know what it's called," he said. "But I remember that Alison sewed a wee sprig of those blossoms into my layna th' day afore we left for battle.

When I asked her what she thought she was doin', she told me th' weedy thing was for luck and to just humor her. So, I humored her."

The comment set off a round of boisterous laughter as well as excitement. Many of the knights revealed then, that their sweethearts, wives, or mothers had sewn a sprig of the flower into the sleeve of their léines as well and for the same reason.

Mariah and Cailen looked at each other. "Did someone sew of sprig of this flower into your léine?" she asked.

"If someone did,' he said, "they did it without my knowledge."

"I'm wonderin' if we all carried a piece of th' flower into battle," said Duncan as he rubbed against the stubble on his chin. "Such would stand to reason, with so many others carryin' th' thing."

"I only know of one way to find out," Cailen replied as he rose to his feet.

Less than a second later, the knights disappeared from the room. Mariah let out a sigh as she closed her sketchbook and climbed down from the table.

It didn't take a rocket scientist to know the boys had gone down to the passageways and into the cavern in which their bodies lay interred. They had wanted to explore it the moment Cailen mentioned it. Now they had a reason.

In that same moment, Tatters twined her body around her leg, thereby startling her out of her wits. Quiet laughter accompanied the shake of her head.

She leaned down and scooped her up into her arms. "Aww—did those mean old knights abandon you too? Well, come on, you can come with me and watch me paint for a while."

She made her way upstairs. After she put her sketchbooks away, she retrieved her paints and brushes. This morning, she wanted to focus her attention on the painting of Cailen's accolade. She would finish the intricate detail of his hauberk and surcoat first, and then perhaps work a bit on the attire of Robert the Bruce.

She had just finished the chain mail across the breadth of Cailen's broad shoulders when she felt his arms about her waist.

He planted a gentle kiss on her cheek and said, "How's th' paintin' comin' along?"

Once he released his hold, she stood back and surveyed the portrait with a critical eye. "I guess it's coming along all right," she said. "I'm hoping to complete your armor early this afternoon."

"Appears close to finished, now," he replied. "So, I'm sure ye'll meet your goal."

"So, what did you find?"

"Duncan's suggestion proved accurate," he said. "We all have a bit of the weedy thing sewn into our sleeves."

Though she clung to her brush, Mariah dropped her arm to the side of her body. As their eyes met and held she said, "What does all of this mean, Cailen? How are we ever going to put it all together in time?"

He lifted a brow in consternation. "In time? I dinnae know what ye mean."

"Well, before I have to leave the castle," she said.

Cailen stared at her for several long moments. A host of emotions flashed across his features as he regarded her.

Finally, he dropped his gaze and said, "Those, my

lady, are some verra good questions. Right now, I dinnae have any of th' answers for ye."

"My ghost has the answers," she said. "I just wish she could find a more simple way to tell us."

Chapter 14

Cailen paused for a moment outside Mariah's bedroom doorway. She had yet to notice his presence and that gave him a moment to indulge the pleasure it gave him just to look at her. All throughout the week she'd used every free moment searching for the identity of her unknown plants, even to the point of setting aside the parchment. Right now, she sat cross-legged on her bed, a pencil in her mouth and her computer open as she compared the various images on her screen to those she had sketched.

Throughout all the centuries of his existence, he'd never met another woman like her. In fact, no other woman had even come close. Despite the long centuries he awaited their destined meeting, he didn't intend to question the wisdom of the fates or demand to know the reasons for their tardiness. But, by heaven, he did expect them to supply a way for them to remain together.

The reminder of her impending deadline did naught but fill him with a growing fear he couldn't banish. As if she sensed his presence then, she looked up from her task and blessed him with a captivating smile. Cailen answered with a wink as he entered the room. He took a seat on the edge of the bed near to where she sat. "Ye look pleased aboot somethin'," he said.

"I found the identity of the large yellow flower,"

she said. "Coltsfoot, according to this article, is a plant that is mostly used to control coughs."

Cailen shook his head and let loose a snort. "I'm sorry, but I dinnae see th' connection any of th' plants have to each other, much less to me and my garrison of knights."

"Right now, neither do I," she said. "Still, we now have six out of nine names for these plants, thanks in part to your astute observation of the plants inside Sybil's kitchen."

He shrugged his indifference. "'Twas ye that found th' dried leaf in her jars."

"Yes, well—I would never have identified it as basil without you noticing the plant in the first place," she argued. "Now we have much more than what we started with."

"Aye, but ye have two cookin' spices among th' medicinal remedies. And dinnae forget that one of those remedies only applies to th' maladies of women," he reminded her. "A man would have no such need for your guelder rose."

"I know that. But I must've sketched these particular images for a reason. Therefore, an explanation has to exist. We just need to find it. Once we find it, I'm sure we'll understand the connection."

"So, what are ye still lookin' for then?" he asked as he peered at the notebook filled with words he didn't understand.

"I still need to find the name of that root thingy I pulled out of the ground in my last dream. The purple flower still remains a mystery, and of course, the white flower sewn into everyone's léine," she replied.

"I can give ye th' answer to that," Duncan said as

he popped into the room, looking very pleased with himself.

Mariah drew in a sharp breath and looked up at him with hope shining in her widened eyes. "You can?"

"Aye, 'tis called woodruff," he replied with a firm nod of his head.

"How do ye know?" asked Cailen.

"Because Phoebe told me," he said. "We came across a verra large vine filled to over flowing with blossoms as we strolled along th' river bank. She said she favored th' flower above all others, even during her mortality. I asked her if she could name it, and she said 'twas called woodruff. She said she used to wear them in her hair during her mortal life."

"Who's Phoebe?" asked Mariah.

"Th' woman that followed me around like a lost pup th' other night, do ye recall such?" He flashed a roguish grin as he bounced his brows.

"Oh, the pretty brunette." She nodded, returning his smile. "You're right. As I recall she did follow you around and I must say you didn't seem to mind a bit."

"Nay, I dinnae. She adores me," he said casually. "Such is expected, though. I generally have that effect on th' lassies."

"In your dreams, mayhap," Cailen countered.

The bemused smile remained on Mariah's face as her fingers raced across her keyboard. She nodded then as she turned the screen toward them. The photographic image matched her sketch in every detail. "Woodruff is exactly what the flower is. But how strange—" her voice trailed off as her eyes traveled down the page.

"What's strange?" asked Cailen.

"Woodruff is neither a spice, nor does it have any

medicinal value attached to it. Because of its potent scent, they mainly use it in potpourri," she said.

Duncan looked as confused as he felt. "What's potpourri?" he asked.

The corners of her mouth curved upward as she said, "A concoction of dried flower petals and spices used solely to make a room smell nice."

Cailen shook his head. "Are ye sayin' that our women wanted us to smell good while goin' into battle?" he huffed.

Mariah burst out laughing and said, "Maybe—"

Duncan stared long and hard over her continued mirth. "I dinnae think 'tis funny," he finally said.

"You, of all people, can't see the humor in this, Duncan? Oh come on," she said. "Can't you just imagine the looks on the faces of your enemies as they approach and get a whiff of the heady scent? The potent fragrance would surely distract them long enough to give you the edge, especially if you added a little twinkle-toed dance step along with it."

Laughter consumed her again. In fact, she held her stomach and rolled with it. Did her laughter arise from some ridiculous image her mind conjured of him and his knights tiptoeing on the field with a sword in their hands? If so, he didn't think it funny either.

"We dinnae need an edge," Duncan retorted. "And now if ye'll excuse me, I need to get back to Phoebe. I left her pinin' away for me down by th' river, and I dinnae want her to wait overly long."

Mariah stared in the direction he vacated for several seconds before she gave him her full attention. She smiled broadly, and lifted a brow. "Do you suppose he disappeared because of something I said?"

"Mayhap ye might have went a wee bit far with your twinkle-toed dance step." He winked.

She took a deep breath as he captured her gaze. "Come here, my lady," he whispered.

"Oh, I don't know," she said as her eyes filled with mischief. "Do you think it's safe to move any closer to such a fearsome knight?"

He returned a slow shake of his head as she closed the lid of her laptop, pushed it aside, and inched her way to his side. "Nay, I cannae, in all good conscious assure ye of such."

"You're a dangerous man, Cailen Braithnoch, do you know that?" she murmured.

"Aye," he replied as he twined his fingers through her hair and joined his lips with hers. Cailen had kissed many women during his mortal lifetime, and ghostly women aplenty over the centuries that followed, but none of them affected his soul as did the intoxicating kisses of Mariah Jennings. The profound love and affection he had for this woman filled him to overflowing. Judging by the response she gave in return, she surely harbored the same depth of love and passion for him. The knowledge humbled him, for surely he didn't deserve her heart. That fact notwithstanding, he intended to guard it with ferocity throughout all the eons ahead.

"Mariah?"

Evan entered the castle, calling out her name and the mere sound of his voice irritated him no end. He broke away from the kiss and fused his gaze to hers.

"I wonder what he's doing here?" she asked in a breathless whisper.

"I dinnae know, but I suppose ye ought to go see

what we wants afore he comes lookin' for ye," he grumbled.

At least for now, he could do naught but stand aside as she removed herself from his arms and walked out of the door. Despite his charitable act, Evan sorely tested the limits of his good graces. He wouldn't receive much more.

Just as Mariah stepped onto the landing, Steven said in passing, "Looks like he's brought ye somethin' to eat, again."

"Oh, for pity's sake," she muttered under her breath as she stomped down the stairs.

Steven peered inside the room then and looked him over. "Ye dinnae need to look so grumpy," he said. "I think we've just been handed a gift."

"What are ye talkin' aboot?" he asked.

"Me and Alan have found somethin' inside Evan's rooms behind th' pub—and we think ye should see it," Steven said. "Now would be th' perfect time since th' man is otherwise occupied with your woman."

The look in Steven's eye bespoke the importance of their discovery. He called for Edmund and Malcolm who instantly appeared inside the room. "Watch over Murriah while I'm out," he said. "And dinnae let anythin' happen to her. Be especially wary of Evan. She didna invite him to th' castle."

"Certainly, Cailen," said Edmund. "Ye can count on us."

"All right, Steven, lead the way," Cailen said.

Several minutes later, they entered Evan's private domain. Cailen took a moment to look around the cluttered mess Evan now called home. Stacks of books and papers lay scattered across two small rooms. The man left his bed rumpled and dirty clothes on the floor. Food and drink still sat atop the kitchen table.

"How could ye find anything of value in here?" he asked.

"We didna have to find it," said Alan. "Th' laddie opened it up right in front of us."

"We felt certain then, he could no longer sense our presence," Steven added.

Cailen nodded. Shortly after Evan's first visit to the castle, he and the knights discussed the possibility the lad still possessed the ability to feel them, but chose not to reveal it.

"This morn, we decided to pay Evan a visit. After we arrived, we watched him pull a book out from underneath his mattress," Steven said.

"We thought it a wee bit strange as no one lives here with him, so we wondered just who he is tryin' to hide it from and why. And Cailen—I cannae be sure, mind ye, but 'tis possible th' book is what Evan carried out of th' cottage durin' his first visit to th' castle," Alan said. "For 'tis th' same color and size."

"Once he had it out, we positioned ourselves behind him to have a look. And well—come and see for yourself," said Steven as he withdrew the book from its hiding place and placed it atop the table. "Ye need to start at th' beginnin' and turn each of th' pages."

Cailen approached the table and opened the black leather cover with faded gold embellishments. The well-worn book creaked a bit under the strain. He turned the first page over. "By all the saints—what is all this?" he asked, not really expecting an answer, nor did they offer any.

A vast array of strange, wicked-looking symbols

appeared on the open pages. Words, such as those Mariah created, lay underneath the symbols. What's more, it appeared that Evan drew those symbols himself. Each subsequent page revealed more of the same until at last his eyes fell upon sketches of various plants. Evan didn't possess the artistic hand that Mariah owned, but one could identify them easily enough.

He turned another page and stared at the drawing for several long moments before he drew his gaze to the knights. Steven nodded, and said, "Aye."

"'Tis th' yellow flower along with th' coriander, for certain," Alan said. "And as ye turn th' pages ye'll find all of Murriah's sketches somewhere in th' book. Some of them used multiple times, in multiple combinations."

Cailen took the time to locate the pages that contained the plants Mariah still needed to find. Once he found them, he memorized the letters and the order that comprised their names.

He also memorized as many symbols as he could, especially those Evan used most often. Perhaps if he could describe them to Mariah, she might understand their meaning.

"I dinnae ken th' reason for it," Steven said, "but that book gives me th' screamers."

"Och, now why would ye say somethin' like that?" scoffed Alan. "Is it because of th' bloody daggers, th' vials of poison, or th' wormy skulls th' lad seems fond of drawin' along th' sides?"

"Well, I think those foul lookin' symbols are proof enough th' laddie is involved in some type of sorcery of th' blackest kind."

The very thought of such a notion sickened

Cailen's soul. "Exactly what did Evan do with this book?"

"Nothin', he simply looked through all of th' pages, one at a time, and then put it away," said Steven.

"Did he study any one page, longer than th' others?" he asked.

Steven and Alan exchanged glances and shrugged. "Aye," Steven said, "But, I'm sorry, Cailen, we dinnae remember which ones grabbed his attention."

Cailen raised a hand to his chin as he considered the implications of the disturbing book. For the first time he gave credence to the idea that very little—if anything at all—remained of the pleasant, inquisitive wee boy they once knew. He also found it troubling Evan didn't retrieve the book until after Mariah's arrival. Mayhap it might be coincidence. On the other hand— "I think we better keep a closer eye on Evan from here on out," he said.

"Dinnae worry," Steven said. "We'll take care of it."

As Cailen headed for the castle, he debated how much, if anything, to tell Mariah. He didn't want to add to the burden she already carried. Yes, he saw wisdom in giving her all of the known facts. Knowledge provided one with the ability to prepare for all situations one might face.

On the other hand, he and his knights could protect her well enough if the need arose.

He arrived at the castle in the middle of the great hall. Mariah stood near the entrance with eyes cast downward. Although Evan had his hand upon the latch of the door, the boy gazed at Mariah as if loathed to leave her.

Neither of them looked very happy.

"What's goin' on?" he asked as he looked from Malcolm to Edmund and then fixed his gaze upon Mariah.

Edmund shrugged. "Well, shortly after they finished their lunch, Evan tried to give Murriah a kiss. She refused his advances even though he sought to change her mind and with steely resolve. I thought we might have to step in and help her out, but she told him in no uncertain terms that she had no interest in that type of relationship with him. She also told him that it would be best, if he didna come back to th' castle while she remained in residence."

"As ye can see," said Malcolm, "Evan is not happy aboot that."

Cailen didn't feel the least bit happy about the situation either. Nonetheless, he shook away his feelings of anger. "Malcolm, I need ye to fetch that notebook Murriah has in her bedchamber along with her computer. Bring somethin' for her to write with, ye ken?"

Malcolm disappeared as Mariah turned to face him. He arrived at her side just as Evan crossed the threshold and closed the door behind him.

"Cailen," she said.

"My lady," he replied as his fingers brushed lightly against her cheek. "Are ye all right?"

She glanced at the door and nodded. "The whole thing just left me feeling a bit awkward, that's all."

"I'm sorry I was not here for ye when ye needed me," he replied. "Mayhap I could have prevented it."

"You left the castle?" she asked. "Where did you go?"

"An errand needed my attention." He took hold of her hand the instant Malcolm appeared near the table with the things he requested. As he escorted her over to the bench, he said, "I think I can help ye name th' last of your plants."

A puzzled look entered her eyes but she said nothing as they sat down. Malcolm opened the lid of her computer, handed her the pencil and slid the notebook to the right of her machine.

"Okay, what do you want me to do?" she asked as Malcolm gave them a friendly salute and disappeared from the hall.

Cailen studied the keyboard until he found the letter he sought. "That one there begins th' name of your purple flower." He waited until she copied it on the page of her notebook. "This one here comes next, followed by that one, right there."

Each time he pointed out a letter, she copied it on the paper. Once he finished the word, he nodded. "That's it."

"Betony," she said as she typed the word on her computer. Moments later, she found a picture that matched the one in her sketchbook. She scrolled through the words underneath the photograph.

"What does it say?" he asked.

"Well, it's an herb, which probably explains why I couldn't find it when I searched for 'purple flower.' One can use this herb as an antiseptic and it also has antibacterial properties." She turned to face him and shrugged. "I suppose, we can list this one under the medicines."

"All right, th' bulky root ye pulled out of th' ground begins with th' same letter as th' betony," he said, touching the key. "'Tis followed by this one right here and then that one." Four more letters followed. Once complete, the word looked exactly like the one written in Evan's book. "Good. Now, there's another word beside it and it begins with this letter here, copy this one twice and then this one finishes it."

"Burdock root," she said as she typed the words and then located one of the many photographed images. She placed her elbow on the table and nibbled at a nail while she read the words beneath the picture. "This one is odd—"

"How so?" he asked.

"Well, it says right here that at one time people commonly ate the root, which is considered a vegetable. However, as we speak, it's fallen out of favor in Europe but remains popular in Asia. The plant has a few medicinal uses as well—a blood purifier for one. However, it seems people also use it as a scalp treatment."

"Scalp treatment," he repeated.

She laughed. "Yes, you know for dandruff and to prevent hair loss."

"Hair loss," he repeated her words again with a tone of disdain. He shook his head. "I dinnae see what that would have to do with anythin'."

"No, not now," she agreed, bringing her mirth under control, "but perhaps during the fourteenth century your healers used it exclusively to purify the blood. Whether it had the desired effect is anyone's guess."

"Mayhap, I dinnae pay much attention to such," he said. "Mairwen could have told ye aboot all this stuff. 'Tis a pity she's not around to ask."

She placed a gentle hand atop his arm and nodded. "Yes it is. Still, we have them all identified now and that's progress. We have betony, burdock, coltsfoot, golden gorse, and willow, all possibly used for medicinal purposes. The basil and coriander are simple cooking spices as far as we know, and we have one flower that simply smells good." She tapped her pencil on the notebook as she stared down at the words.

Cailen still couldn't see the connection, but perhaps if one existed, the explanation lay within the pages of Evan's book. Yet, for many reasons, he didn't want her to know of the book's existence. At least, not yet.

"Cailen?"

She said his name as if awaiting his response.

"I'm sorry," he said. "Did ye ask me somethin'?"

"I wanted to know where you found the names of the plants," she said.

With a bit of reluctance he said, "In th' pages of a book."

"A book?" Curiosity lit up her eyes. That made him instantly wary. "What book? Where did you see it? Is it here in the castle?"

"Nay, th' book is not here," he replied, hoping she would leave it alone.

"You saw it on your errand then. Can you take me to see it?" she asked.

"Th' book doesna belong to me, Murriah and I dinnae think it's a good idea to ask th' person to whom it belongs to show it to ye either," he said.

"Why not?"

"This person wouldn't feel comfortable showin' it to ye, trust me on that."

She looked him over for several seconds before she dropped her gaze and nodded. "All right, I suppose we'll just leave it at that, then."

"If ye dinnae mind, I want ye to draw a triangle on your paper." Without saying a word, she did as he asked.

"Now, draw another one next to it, and this time draw a line aboot a third of th' way down from th' top. On th' right side of th' line, draw another small line goin' upward, but dinnae pass th' top of the triangle."

"Like this?" she asked, her curiosity returning.

He rubbed a hand across his beard and nodded. "Draw another triangle, but this one upside down. Put a line through th' bottom third, like ye did th' other one. Draw a small line goin' in both directions on th' left side of th' line, like a straight-edged ax. Aye, just like that—"

She drew her gaze upward as she completed the drawing and tilted her head to the side. "Where did you see this?" she asked.

"While on my errand," he said.

"You saw it in the same book, didn't you," she said as if she already knew the answer.

He would not lie and risk losing her trust. Not for any reason. "Aye, I did."

"That's interesting," she said.

"Why do ye say that?" he asked. "Do ye know what they mean?"

"They are symbols of alchemy," she replied. "I had to learn several such symbols for a class I took in college. This first one is the element for fire, this one is for air also called wind, and the last one is the symbol for earth." She took a moment to create another symbol

191

and then slanted the book toward him. "Did you see this one as well?"

"Aye."

"Water," she replied matter-of-factly. "The four elements."

Chapter 15

Several days after they identified the remaining plants, Mariah put the finishing touches on the two smaller paintings. She took a step back, surveyed her work, and deemed it complete. Cailen's accolade turned out better than what she hoped. This time a painting of her knight depicted a real piece of his history and exactly as the event had occurred.

"All right, Mariah," she murmured. "These two are finally finished."

Just as the words left her mouth, a round of applause, hoots, and cheers erupted behind her. She turned around to find all the knights crowding into the room and out to the hallway.

"Now those are some amazin' portraits," Duncan said with a firm nod of his head.

"Finer than any I have ever laid eyes on. Especially th' paintin' of Cailen's accolade. Just look at that dashin' figure standin' right there," Steven said, pointing to his own image. "One's eyes cannae help but gravitate to him, do ye ken?"

"Och, in your dreams, ye dingy maggot," Duncan said as he gave him a shove in the direction of the door.

Steven merely laughed good-naturedly. "Try not to be jealous, Duncan. 'Tis unbecomin' of a knight."

Edmund cocked his head to the side while he studied the portraits. "Ye know, I think 'tis an abomination that we cannae have them all hangin' right here where they rightfully belong."

"That's a true statement, Edmund. I agree with ye wholeheartedly," said Malcolm. "Mayhap we ought to filch them at th' end of th' tour."

"Well, I'm partial to th' paintin' of th' joustin' tournament," Roger said. "Ye notice how easily I have unseated my opponent. Poor man is stretched out on th' ground lookin' all dazed."

"Aye," said Edmund. "'Tis a cryin' shame ye couldn't have done it with th' same refinement while in your mortal frame. Ye ought to get down on your knees and thank her for allowin' ye to appear with such dignity."

"Never mind all th' silly banter, Murriah," Malcolm said shaking his head. "Your paintin's are a wondrous thing to behold and ye have honored us by makin' us part of them."

"Aw, you're all too kind," Mariah replied as she dabbed her brush into the turpentine on the table.

Cailen shook his head. "Kindness has nothin' to do with it. You're one talented woman, Murriah Jennin's, and th' lads are just tellin' it like they see it."

"Well, I'm happy you all think so," she replied. "Let's just hope it meets with Humphries' approval as well."

"They cannae help but meet with his approval," Duncan replied. "Th' man will be dancin' with delight when he sees your work, ye can trust me on that."

"Is th' large castle paintin' just aboot finished as well?" asked Edmund. "I dinnae see where ye need to do much more."

"Almost—I still need to add a little more detail to

the turrets and outer fences. I'm hoping by the end of the week I'll have it finished."

"All right," Cailen said. "Everyone out and give Murriah some space to work. She has other paintin's to attend to afore th' sun sets, and she cannae get it done with all your chatter."

Once the knights cleared the room, she gave him her full attention. "Finished your training for the day?" she asked.

"Aye," he said.

"Pity," she countered. "I do so enjoy watching you wield your sword."

"Is that right, my lady?" He propped a booted foot against the wall while a slight grin curved the corners of his mouth.

"Mm-hmm."

He paused for a moment as he gazed at her. "Do ye really have to work, or can we go for a walk?"

"Oh. I'd like nothing better than to go for a walk with you, Cailen. But—I'm afraid I really do have to work on the paintings. Gordon Humphries is supposed to come to the castle tomorrow morning and he'll want to see my progress. I'll need something to show him."

Cailen didn't argue the point, but perhaps if he had, he might've talked her into taking a break. Instead, she made her way to her stock of canvases and selected one a size smaller than the primary painting. On this canvas, she would paint the castle as it looked shortly after completion.

"Murriah," said Cailen as he watched her cover the dampened canvas with gesso. "Do ye think ye'd have th' time to teach me how to read?"

The question caught her off guard and with brush

in hand, she turned around to face him.

"You want to learn how to read?"

"Aye," he replied. "I have always thought such might be useful. And ye do have to admit it would have come in handy when I saw th' book with th' plants. Mayhap I could have told ye more than I did."

"I would love to teach you how to read," she said. "When would you like to get started?"

He shrugged. "Any time that's convenient for ye. Ye'll find I can learn things rather quickly."

"All right. We'll get started right after I finish work for the day and get a little something to eat."

"Will such interfere with th' readin' of your parchment?" he asked. "I know ye want to get started on th' task, and I dinnae want to keep ye from it."

She shook her head. "No, I can only muddle through so many words before the Latin and poor handwriting will drive me up the wall. So, don't worry. I'll have plenty of time for both."

Throughout the rest of her day, Mariah sought a motive for Cailen's unexpected request. Did his desire to read have anything to do with the mysterious book he mentioned? Curiosity over its contents troubled her mind. Who owned that book? Who authored it and better yet, when did he or she write it? This century, last century? She had so many questions that demanded an answer. But unfortunately, Cailen didn't want to discuss the subject with her. Therefore, she couldn't help but believe the book belonged to Beth Ogilvie. Why else would he be so reluctant to talk about it with her? And the premise fit well with his comment regarding the owner of the volume. Beth wouldn't have any desire to share such a book with her. More likely,

Miz Ogilvie would just as soon she fell off the face of the earth. Thus, she would leave Cailen to her vile clutches without undue interference.

****

As promised, she sat at the table with Cailen later that evening. Several of the knights crowded around behind them in anticipation of the forthcoming lesson. They too, wanted to learn how to read. "So, is everyone ready?" she asked.

"Aye," replied several voices in unison.

"Not knowin' what th' symbols mean has deviled us throughout th' last couple of centuries," added Duncan.

"From th' time readin' became a common thing among th' residents of this castle, we could feel th' lack," said Edmund.

"Especially since th' wee bairns could make sense of the letters, while we couldn't," said Malcolm. "That dinnae do much for our self-image."

Mariah opened her notebook to the first blank page. "Well, we're about to fix that. First, reading is not so very difficult once you can recognize each of the letters and the sounds they make. The rest is just putting them all together using a host of ridiculous rules that always have a multitude of exceptions. In my humble opinion, I think those who wanted nothing more than to vex the populace put them in place. At least when it comes to the English language. Anyway, we call the letters the alphabet and the alphabet contains both consonants and vowels. Together, they total twenty-six distinct symbols."

Cailen had informed her of his ability to learn quickly. She just didn't realize how quickly he would absorb what she taught. The aptitude of the knights didn't linger far behind his, either. When she asked him about the amazing skill, he simply said it was part of their spiritual nature to learn and retain things swiftly. By the end of the first lesson, all the men could read simple sentences and although she wanted to continue, Cailen put an end to the exercise.

"Ye dinnae need to wear yourself out," he said. "We have time aplenty stretchin' afore us."

"But I'm not really tired yet," she argued.

He flashed a flirty grin and winked. "Good, then ye will finally consent to take a walk with me, aye? I swear ye'll enjoy th' time ye spend in my company."

She returned his smile and rose from the bench. "Now, how could I possibly refuse an offer like that?"

He took hold of her hand, escorted her out of the castle, and led her to the river. They talked of small inconsequential things and experiences from their past. Many of the memories he shared made her laugh and he seemed to find humor in a few of her own. Once they approached the banks, they stopped to watch the water play against the rocky bottom for a time, and then they moseyed toward the bridge.

"It's such a beautiful evening," she said as they strolled along at a leisurely pace. "The stars look absolutely brilliant, don't they?"

He drew his gaze heavenward and searched the sky. "'Tis always such after th' rain though."

"I'm so glad you don't have big city lights marring the view. All that artificial light interferes with the night sky, you know. Sometimes those glaring lights make it difficult to see the stars at all."

"Such would be a tragedy, I think," he replied.

"Believe me, it is."

They walked along in silence for a time before she gathered enough courage to ask the one question she needed him to answer.

"Cailen—"

"Aye?"

"I wonder if you'd mind answering a question for me and you don't have to elaborate. A simple yes or no will suffice."

"What's your question?" he asked.

A small sigh accompanied the shake of her head. His well-phrased reply didn't guarantee her an answer at all. Nonetheless, she forged ahead. "Does the book containing the names of the plants and symbols belong to Beth?"

Cailen slipped a hand around her waist, turned her body around, and drew her just as close to his chest as he could get her. He cocked his head to the side for a moment and studied her eyes. After a moment he said, "Nay, th' book doesna belong to Beth. But I have to tell ye, th' same emotion I see in your eyes right this minute, is th' same emotion I feel when Evan calls ye on your phone or stops by th' castle to see ye. 'Tis th' same emotion that overtook me when I heard he took ye into his arms intendin' to kiss ye."

She dropped her gaze and said nothing in return. He placed a hand underneath her chin, and tilted her face upward.

"Beth is not a threat to ye, my lady, nor could she ever be," he said as once again, their gazes met and held. "I've said such afore and I meant what I said. I luv ye, Murriah Jennin's, and ye need to know that I would never say th' word casually. While still in my mortal state, I vowed never to say th' word unless I truly meant it. I have kept that vow. Ye are th' only woman that has ever heard me speak it. Ye will be th' only woman that will ever hear me speak it. Do ye ken?"

Mariah could feel her throat tighten over the huskily whispered declaration.

She swallowed past the lump in her throat and sniffed. "And I love you, Cailen Braithnoch, with every fiber of my being. There's no room for Evan or anyone else, not when you have filled me so completely," she replied.

A slight smile tugged at the corners of his mouth just before he kissed her with a slow, unhurried thoroughness that thrilled her all the way down to her toes. She still found it a challenge to hold still when he kissed her, especially when he kissed her with the passion he did right now. But the strong desire to remain in his arms and not penetrate his spiritual form, aided her effort.

Another such kiss followed the first. Soon she lost track of the number as well as the time. Did the midnight bell already sound? She didn't know nor did she care. She only knew she didn't want the evening to end. Not ever. If only she had a way to stop the clock from moving forward. But move forward it did and at an alarming pace.

"Oh Cailen," she whispered raggedly once he released her. "What am I going to do?"

He put just enough space between them to meet her troubled gaze. "Do? Aboot what?" he asked.

"About this impossible situation in which I find myself," she replied.

"I dinnae ken what ye mean," he said, and it truly

seemed he didn't.

She shook her head ever so slightly. "I can't stay at the castle forever. This place doesn't belong to me, and I doubt very seriously that Kyle MacNaughton would allow me to stay here for the remainder of my life. That means in just a little over three months, I'm going to have to go. We already know that for some reason, you can't leave the Highlands and I don't know how long I can possibly stay."

****

Her words and the torment that filled her eyes haunted him throughout the duration of the night. Surely, the fates that smiled upon them at this moment wouldn't have done so just to rip them apart. A way for them to remain eternally together had to exist. They just needed to discover it.

Cailen gazed down upon her sleeping form and gently brushed the tangled hair away from her face. From all appearances, she slept peacefully. The terrifying dreams hadn't plagued her for several nights now. He hoped they wouldn't return. Nonetheless, he remained at her side, just in case.

His ponderings led him to the door of her bizarre nightmares. Mayhap they did hold all the clues to the solution he sought, just as Mariah suggested. Such would make sense. They simply needed to solve what providence had already given them. And he would solve it, because nothing in the realm of heaven or hell could tear him away from Mariah Jennings. He wouldn't allow it.

That resolve drew him to his feet and after placing a gentle kiss upon her cheek, he exited her bedchamber. He appeared inside the great hall where most the knights congregated. Those who missed Mariah's reading lesson now learned from those who hadn't.

"Who's standin' watch over Evan?" he asked.

"Right now, 'tis Duncan and Roger," said Ian. "They should return shortly and then Robin will go with me."

Cailen turned his gaze in the direction of the village and nodded. "We need to keep an eye on that book at all times," he said. "I want to know which pages he studies when he has it out. Ye each need to memorize th' order of letters of that which ye cannae read. Ye need to do it from this moment forward. Do ye ken?"

At that moment, Roger popped into the room. Relief etched his features the moment their gazes met.

"Cailen," he said. "I'm glad to see ye here. I didna want to disturb ye if ye kept company with Murriah. But right now, Evan is here at th' castle. He went straight over to th' cottage. Duncan is there with him now."

"What's he doin here this time of night?" asked Cailen.

"Up to no good, for certain," Malcolm said.

Roger spared the man a glance. "We dinnae know. After he finished workin' his shift, he just got into his car and drove out here. He didna even go home, first. I can tell ye that all th' way here he appeared ill at ease. Sweat trickled down his face. He had to keep moppin' it away. We didna find his heavy breathin' in any way normal either."

Cailen didn't wait to hear any more. He disappeared from the great hall and reappeared inside th' cottage. He found both Duncan and Evan inside the kitchen.

"Have ye discovered what he's aboot?" asked Cailen.

"Nay, but just as afore he came in th' back way," Duncan replied. "Th' way he looked around afore he slipped in, made me laugh. Who did he think would follow him out here this time of night?"

"Mayhap he's hopin' to avoid th' perturbed knights," Cailen spat.

"It might do him some good if he did," Duncan countered.

"No." Cailen shook his head. "'Tis more important to see what he's up to, and if needs be, stop him from doin' somethin' that might bring harm. Especially if his actions have anythin' to do with Murriah."

"Aye, I agree with that," Duncan replied.

They observed as Evan made his way to the spice jars above the stove. The lad perused each label on the shelf. During that perusal, he selected three jars, and placed them atop the counter. He then dropped his hand into his pocket and withdrew three small vials. Once he removed each of the lids, he filled his vials with the contents he pilfered from Sybil.

Cailen didn't want to risk giving away their presence should Evan have retained a small portion of his early ability to detect them. 'Twas far more important to discover what he wanted and why. Therefore, he and Duncan maintained their distance. As Evan replaced the jars, Cailen noted their position on the shelves.

"I'll just go fetch Ian and William, and let them know th' laddie is gettin' ready to go. I'm sure they'll want to accompany him on th' way home in case he stops somewhere else afore he gets there," Duncan said.

Cailen nodded but said nothing in return. He waited as Evan withdrew a pen from his shirt pocket and wrote words on his vials. After he named each one, he shoved them back inside his pocket. Evan shifted his attention to the stairs and glanced upward. He hesitated for only a moment before he climbed them. Once he stepped onto the landing, he approached his bedroom door and opened it. He switched on the light but did naught but look around his empty room from the doorframe.

While Evan occupied himself with peeping, Cailen made his way to the jars. He studied each name of the filched ingredients. Ian and Robin arrived just as he finished his task. He could only read the word rosemary. However, he memorized the order of the letters contained in the other two. They both began with the letter *V*.

"Where's Evan?" asked Robin.

"Upstairs," just as he said the word, Evan turned around and commenced his descent. "The man has taken some of Sybil's herbs that she keeps inside those jars," he said pointing at the shelf.

"What's he want with them?" asked Ian.

"I dinnae know," he replied. "But that's what we need to find out. He put some of th' weedy bits inside three small vials, which he now has inside his pocket. Keep watch for what he does with those vials. At th' same time, keep a close eye on that book, for surely they have a connection."

"Dinnae worry, Cailen," said Robin. "We'll shadow every move he makes. I vow he'll not get close enough to ever harm Murriah or anyone else."

Chapter 16

A very pleased Gordon Humphries made his promised appearance and vacated the premises with the two completed paintings tucked safely inside his car. A van, he said, would come for the primary painting at the first of next week. The framing of those paintings would take place shortly thereafter. Once they had them framed, they would lock them inside the vault alongside all the others until the public opening.

After his departure, Mariah placed the first layer on the secondary painting and provided backgrounds for the rest of the smaller portraits. Now they all needed some drying time and that gave her the opportunity to work on Edgar's parchments.

She made her way into the chapel and retrieved the Latin texts from their hiding place beneath the flooring. Once she had them cradled safely in her arms, she descended the steps and entered the great hall.

The thick stack of documents looked rather intimidating. Nonetheless, something of importance lay hidden within them. The marriage record she and Cailen discovered earlier proved the final document recorded in the hand of the same cleric. Everything else preceded that record. Cailen believed that Edgar penned them all. Therefore, he too had knowledge of what her ghost wanted them to find.

After putting the records in order by type and date,

Mariah picked up the earliest piece of parchment and studied the heading. If she translated the words accurately, the cleric collected tithes as his first duty in the year 1318. He met the people of Cailen's fiefdom and prepared for his first Sabbath. The next paragraph contained words she didn't recognize and would therefore require an online translator. She turned her gaze toward the stairs. Just as she rose to her feet, Cailen appeared at her side with computer in hand.

"I thought ye might need this." He gave her a wink as he set the computer on the table.

"Yes, in fact you just saved me a trip," she said as she opened the lid, and powered it up. "Thank you."

"You're welcome." He took a seat beside her, sitting backward on the bench and then settled his back against the table. "Afore ye begin, I wondered if ye could help me out."

"Of course, what would you like me to do?" she asked.

"Well, I tried to decipher some of th' words I found in Sybil's kitchen. There are a few on some of th' jars that I had trouble readin'," he said.

"Do you remember the order of the letters?"

"Aye," he said. "They both begin with th' letter *V*."

"Go ahead and sing them out." Mariah wrote the letters as he gave them to her. Once finished, she turned the notebook to face him. "The first word is valerian and the second is vervain."

He looked befuddled. "I never heard of them. What are they used for?" he asked.

"I don't know. In all honesty, I've never heard of them either. Hang on a minute and I'll look them up. I'm kind of curious, myself," she murmured as she turned her attention to her keyboard. After locating both terms, she scanned through the articles and said, "Vervain and valerian are commonly used as herbal teas."

"Ye look puzzled," Cailen said.

She raised her brows a tad and shrugged. "Well, I'm sure if I studied the herbs in depth I might find other uses for them. Who knows why Sybil has them in her stock of herbs and spices right now. But, it says right here in this paragraph the vervain herb is widely used among folk herbalist to prevent pregnancies. Going in the opposite direction, it can also aid a woman's milk production." She looked up from the computer screen and fastened her gaze to his. "Seems a strange herb to grow since I'm assuming Sybil is well past the child bearing years and therefore, doesn't need to worry about pregnancy or nursing a baby. Unless—"

"Unless what?" he nudged.

"Unless she uses her knowledge of herbs to look after the people living in this community. Do any of the local women visit Sybil on a regular basis? Or—does she go out and visit them?"

"Nay, she doesna," he replied. "Sybil rarely leaves th' property except of course to go on holiday. And visitors to th' castle are rare. We have never seen anyone seekin' her help."

Mariah lifted her shoulders as she shook her head. "Then only she would know why she keeps them. Maybe she truly uses it as a spice."

"And what aboot th' other?" Cailen's voice had a slight edge to it as he asked the question.

"Um—let's see," she said. "Valerian is used to help people sleep. Perhaps Sybil or George has insomnia." When he didn't respond, she glanced up from her computer. He looked past her, focusing his gaze upon the stairway. Something troubled him. She could see it his eyes. She turned in the direction of his gaze, but saw nothing that would cause concern.

"Cailen?"

He shook himself a bit as if coming out of his reverie and said, "Aye?"

"Are you all right?" she asked.

He nodded and replaced the troubled look with a slight grin. "Sorry—just thinkin'. So what does that piece of parchment tell ye?" he asked, pointing to her stack of pages.

"What?" she teased. "You can't read it for yourself?"

"Might I remind ye that we're learnin' to read English, Murriah, not Latin," he countered.

"Well, maybe we ought to tackle Latin next," she said. "And to answer your question, this piece of parchment deals with the collection of tithes and here near the bottom, he recorded some of the names of his little flock."

Mariah read off several of the names Edgar mentioned on the document. A wistful smile stole across his face as she did so. "I take it you know these people."

He nodded. "Most of them, and some I have not thought aboot for a long time now."

"Is it difficult for you, Cailen?" she asked.

"Is what difficult?"

"Your present life—I guess I'm asking if it's hard for you to remain here at the castle while those you loved and interacted with during your mortality have all gone on."

He shook his head. "Not so much anymore. We have carved out a good life here, Murriah. We are happy enough. My men are still here with me, and we have made many friends over th' centuries."

"Yes, and that's something that also puzzles me."

"What would puzzle ye aboot that?" he asked. "I dinnae ken what ye mean."

"The fact that there are no other ghosts living here inside your castle. Well, besides you, your men, and at least one woman I'm sure all of you know."

"Why would such trouble ye?" he asked, ignoring her comment about her female ghost.

"Well, it's just that in every other castle I've lived in, the resident ghosts come from various ages. Take Sir Dugald's castle, for example, as one you're familiar with yourself. He has spiritual entities from many different centuries residing with him. I'm sure everyone else does too. It's a fact that not everyone who dies moves on to their spiritual realm. So why, of all the people who have died at this castle over the many centuries of its existence, did no one else ever choose to stay here with you?"

Cailen rubbed a hand across his chin and shook his head. "I have to admit I never gave it much thought afore. But ye do have a point. Mayhap no one else wanted to bide amongst a bunch of unruly knights."

Mariah laughed outright. "Please remember that you're the one that admitted to that, I did nothing to solicit or coerce the confession."

Cailen only chuckled in return.

With the aid of an online translator, she breezed through the rest of the document without difficulty.

Though interesting to read, she found nothing to further their quest. The next two records documented gifts of barley for use in the brewing of ale, which task the cleric seemed fond of performing. Cailen revealed that in turn, the cleric would sell *most* of his freshly made ale, and the proceeds would furnish the funds for the upkeep of his church.

"Did he also use a portion of the funds for replenishing his sacramental wine?" she asked and all the while she worked at keeping any telltale signs of humor off her face.

Before he had the chance to reply, Duncan popped into the room wearing a broad grin on his face.

"Dugald is here," he said. His eyes gleamed with anticipation. "He said he needed somethin' to combat his boredom and therefore, decided to gather some knights from all over th' Highlands for a bit of sport. We're assemblin' out on th' fields now."

Cailen gazed at her for a moment before speaking. "Do ye want to come out and watch for a while or would ye rather stay here and work on your dusty old parchments all by yourself?"

She answered his question by standing up while closing the lid on her computer. "You can go on ahead if you'd like. I'll be there just as soon as I put the records away. I don't want to chance leaving them on the table unattended. Tatters might get into them if I do."

"I'd rather go outside with ye on my arm, my lady." Cailen winked. "That way th' other knights will know to keep their distance."

Mariah rewrapped the stack of parchment records, placing the completed records on the bottom. A brief smile emerged as she glanced at the heading for the next record in line. The document contained names of the couples Edgar united in marriage beginning in the year 1318. Perhaps Cailen would remember those couples and the children they may have had. Not that such would aid their quest—

After they returned the cleric's records to the chapel, they made their way outside, and over to the fields on the west side of the castle. As she gazed over the grassy meadow, she estimated that at least fifty other knights had congregated "for a bit of sport." Many of them she recognized from Duncan's party, but some she had never seen before. The knights brought along a vast array of weapons. They carried swords, daggers, maces, and some scary-looking spears. Good thing no one could actually get hurt during their fun and games.

Cailen settled her onto a large rock to the right side of the field before he joined his knights. Each man selected a partner in a game of sparring. They battled each other with their weapon or weapons of choice. Though concentrating mostly on Cailen, every now and again Mariah's gaze wandered over the field. If she understood this activity correctly, each winner of each individual contest chose another winner to spar against in an ongoing process of elimination. Those who lost, battled each other, but more for the practice and pleasure it gave them, rather than advancement. And just as she expected, a host of friendly insults and ancient swear words flew as they viciously hacked at each other. The combination of the antiquated words made her laugh. Finally, it came down to a battle between Cailen and a brawny knight that used both ax and sword.

Mariah glanced at Steven and Duncan who had come to keep her company after they lost their own battle against the same knight. "Who is that?" she asked.

"Kenneth Armstrong," said Duncan.

"Aye." Steven dipped his head toward the knight. "He tells us he earned th' surname two centuries afore we were even born. His king gave it to him for his prowess on th' battlefield. He slew many enemies, in many different conflicts afore his mortal life ended. And as ye might guess, he didna die in battle. He died from poisonin' of th' blood from a wound suffered durin' his final conflict."

The burly knight turned to face her then, and all eyes seemed to follow the direction of his gaze. He looked her over for several moments before he spoke. She could feel heat rising into her cheeks over the unwanted attention.

"I intend to collect a kiss from th' bonny lassie on yonder rock, should I win th' contest, Cailen Braithnoch," Kenneth bellowed out before the crowd. "'Tis a fittin' prize for such a contest, aye?"

A host of whistles and cheers erupted from the knights, who now turned their undivided attention to the final contestants. Cailen merely shook his head as if unconcerned. "Ye will never succeed despite your greatest effort, so th' prize is already mine."

In response to Cailen's cockiness, Kenneth swung his ax at Cailen's head. He sidestepped it at the last possible moment, pivoted, and slashed his sword across the knight's chest. Armstrong countered by grazing Cailen's arm with the blade of his sword. A scant moment later, Cailen effectively relieved Kenneth of his ax and sent it flying across the field.

The battle continued in earnest and lasted well over an hour. The unmistakable sound of metal clanging against metal reverberated all around them. Nonetheless, at the end of the battle, game, or whatever they chose to call this particular "sport," the weaponless knight lay prostrate on the ground with Cailen's sword piercing through his throat. One foot rested atop his chest to keep the knight confined.

Kenneth laughed good-naturedly and nodded. "I concede to ye this time, but one of these days, Cailen, I'll best ye, yet," he said.

"Ye'll have to keep hold of your weapons, first!" hollered Duncan. In response to the jibe, the crowd roared with boisterous laughter.

As the knight rose to his feet, Cailen shook his hair away from his face, turned and strode toward her. He took hold of her hand and tugged her to her feet. Once he had an arm about her waist, he drew her close to his chest. "Now, Kenneth," he hollered out as he maintained eye contact with her. "Ye can watch as th' victor collects th' designated prize."

Mariah could hear the boisterous laughter as Cailen leaned down and joined his lips to hers in a kiss that solicited a host of whistles and cheers. As he backed a way, he gave her a wink and grinned before he once again turned his attention to the rowdy men on the field.

More games followed the first, and all of them fascinated her no end. Then just as the sun dipped below the horizon, the games finally arrived at their logical conclusion. The knights dispersed a few at a time, until only the residents of the castle remained. She wondered then if they had indulged in such ferocious activities during their mortality.

"So—" She swept a hand across the now vacant fields as Cailen approached. "Is that something all knights participated in while they lived?"

His lips twitched as he extended her his hand. "We're still livin', my lady, just not in' th' mortal sense of th' word. But, if you're askin' aboot our mortal existence, then aye. Only, we had to be more careful with th' force we put behind th' blow and watch our aim. After all, we didna want to maim our fellow knights."

She considered that as they headed for the castle. "At what age does the training for knighthood begin, anyway?"

Cailen lifted his brows and shrugged. "A man who is to become a knight can start his trainin' as early as seven."

Mariah dropped her mouth as she stared into his eyes. "Oh surely they didn't put a sword in the hand of a seven-year-old boy!"

He gave her hand a gentle squeeze as humor filled his eyes. "Aye, they did. But 'tis just a small wooden one with rounded edges. Leaves naught but a bruise or two along th' way. Pages, as they are called, learn archery as well as how to handle a sword. Some of the wealthier fiefdoms will also teach horsemanship if horses are to be had. Then when a page arrives at th' age of fourteen, he advances to squire. However, if a laddie shows exceptional skill, he can become a squire at th' age of ten."

Mariah tilted her head to the side. "Just like you did?"

"Aye." He chuckled and shook his head over her astute comment. "Just like I did. A squire's trainin' focuses on gainin' strength and acquirin' skill with all kinds of different weapons. Then somewhere around th' age of twenty a squire who has proved himself will become a knight."

"What does that particular rite involve?" she asked. "I know you get a tap from a sword on either shoulder, but is that all there is to it?"

"Nay," Cailen replied. "On the eve afore th' ceremony we are required to have a bath to symbolize our purification. We make confession, and seek solace in th' chapel to pray for guidance and th' ability to carry out our duties. These rituals last all throughout th' night. Then come th' morn we are duly knighted."

"Does anyone say anything during the ceremony, or do they just tap your shoulder and say something like 'Arise, sir knight'?"

"Generally, th' knight is given charge to mind his oaths and obligations."

"What oaths?"

"Och, things like loyalty, honor, justice, protection of th' weak, just to name a few," he said. "Depends on who's doin' th' knightin'. Some can prattle on for what seems a verra long time. Others make their speeches short and sweet."

"Thereafter then, in order to keep in shape while honing your skills, knights engage in the type of sport I saw out there today?" she asked.

He nodded. "Among other types of weapon practice designed to build muscle and increase our ability. But now, since we are void of our mortal frame, we dinnae have to be as careful when we spar as we once did. Other than that—" His voice trailed off as he let the rest of his sentence hang.

She took in a breath and gave it a slow release. "Well, I found it an impressive sight, nonetheless."

"Did ye now?" he asked.

"Aye," she said using her best Scottish accent. "That I did, Sir Cailen."

As he chuckled in response to her pathetic attempt, a sudden movement caught her attention. She halted her steps, stood very still, and gazed in the direction of the moat.

Cailen followed the direction of her gaze yet saw nothing to cause the wide-eyed stare or her mouth to drop. "What do ye see?" he asked.

Her body retained its rigidity as she gave a very slight, single nod at the portcullis. "Do you see them?" she asked in a voice barely audible.

He peered into the shadows caused by the setting sun, yet he didn't see a single soul. He shook his head. "I dinnae see anyone, Murriah."

Her eyes never strayed away from her focal point. "Right there, just this side of the castle," she whispered.

Cailen wondered for a moment if she saw naught but the tall grass moving in the wind. But as he took great care in searching the area, he realized the wind didn't blow. "Tell me what ye see," he said.

"Ghosts," she replied. "I see four of them, all women—just like Hester said." He could hear the genuine surprise in her voice as she slowly uttered the final words. She didn't expect to see them.

"Can ye tell me what they look like?" he asked, bringing Dugald's well-rounded brunette to mind.

"These women look more like the other ghosts I've

seen in the past. They are all—milky-looking and transparent, void of color. I can't see any of them head on. I either see their back, or side profile," she murmured. "They are all wearing linen léines, just like my redheaded ghost. One of the women has her hair hanging loose, while the three have their hair tied back."

"Is your redhead among them?" he asked.

"No, and that means we do, in fact, have at least five women here," she replied.

"What are they doin'?" he asked as he searched the landscape hoping for a glimpse. Why couldn't he see them? Why?

"This is going to sound strange, because I can't see any of their mouths moving, but for whatever reason, it looks to me like they're talking to each other," she said. "I think it's the way they're moving their bodies—their necks, their hands, their heads."

Although he knew it pointless to ask— "Are ye sure ye don't just see shadows, Murriah?"

"I see them Cailen, just as clearly as I see you and—" She gasped and offered him her hand. Once he took hold, he twined his fingers around hers. "Oh! They're heading for the castle now. Come on. Let's see where they're going," she said.

Cailen followed along as she led him stealthily toward the portcullis. She made every effort to keep her movements small in order to shield their presence from the ghosts. He didn't have the heart to tell her she wasted her efforts. If her ghosts were out there, they knew they followed them.

"They just went through the bars," she said, "And into the passageway. Hurry!"

Her pace quickened as they made their way to the iron doorway. She took hold of the bars and tugged, but they refused to budge.

"Here," he said. "Let me do it for ye."

Once the door gave way, she rushed through the opening, halted her steps, and rocked back on her heels.

"Do ye still see them?" he asked.

"Wait," she whispered. "My eyes are trying to adjust to the darkness."

She peered straight ahead and nodded. "Yes. They're just up ahead and right now they look as if they are—oh no!" Mariah shook her head and released a sigh.

"They're gone?" he guessed.

"Yes," she replied. "They just sort of evaporated right where they stood."

He took hold of her hand. "Show me where."

She led him down the passageway, halted her steps at the first junction, and made a large circle with her hand. "Right in this area here."

Cailen turned and gazed down the corridor.

Yet he saw nothing.

He didn't feel anything either. Why? Why couldn't he or any of his men see these women? Why couldn't they feel their presence as they did other spiritual entities when in close proximity? Nothing made sense and it vexed him no end.

"Cailen?"

"Aye."

"Do you think the women have chosen to live down here?" she asked.

"I suppose 'tis possible, but I dinnae know why they would choose to live in such a place when th' castle rests just above them."

She took in a breath, lifted her shoulders, and said, "Maybe for reasons known only to them, they stand watch over your tomb."

Chapter 17

The gloomy sky matched his mood. Dark-gray clouds stretched across the horizon and cloaked the brilliance of the morning sun. Though rain had yet to fall upon the castle grounds, before long it would come down in torrents. Not a good day for traveling. Nonetheless, Cailen escorted Mariah to the door of her car. As she turned around to face him, he used just the tips of his fingers to brush the windblown stands of hair away from her face.

"I wished ye didna have to go," he said as their eyes met and held.

"Well—at the very least, I wish you could come with me." She dropped her gaze for a brief moment. "I know this is just an overnight trip, but I'll miss you, Cailen."

"As I will miss ye, my lady." He cuddled her into his arms, tilted her chin upward, and leaned down to give her a farewell kiss. And he made sure she wouldn't forget this kiss anytime soon. "Make your journey a safe one, mind th' rain when it comes, and hurry home," he said.

"Don't worry, I will. See you tomorrow morning."

Cailen stood his ground until he could no longer see her car on the road. Though far from happy over this impromptu meeting called by Gordon Humphries, it provided him the opportunity to spend the day observing Evan.

"Are ye ready to go, then?" asked Duncan who appeared standing just to his right.

He gave him a nod as he conjured a heavy sigh. "Aye, I'm ready." Minutes later, they entered the center of the pub where Edmund and Malcolm awaited their arrival.

"Evan is alone for th' moment," said Malcolm aiming a thumb at their target. "He's done nothin' out of th' ordinary durin' th' time we have monitored his actions."

"Th' man just watched a bit of telly afore he went to bed," said Edmond. "He slept soundly through th' night, although I dinnae ken how he can sleep through all his thunderous snorin'. 'Tis enough to wake th' dead."

"We are dead, ye swag-bellied miscreant!" Malcolm backhanded Edmund's shoulder and rolled his eyes.

"Aye," Edmund said without missing a beat, "and as ye can plainly see, we're still wide awake."

"Did he ever retrieve th' book?" asked Cailen, altogether ignoring their mirth.

"Nay," Malcolm replied. "He didna."

"All right," Cailen said. "We'll take it from here."

The twins no more than disappeared when a young female entered the establishment. Evan glanced up from his cooking pots and smiled in greeting.

"Good morning, Evan," she said in singsong fashion.

"Good morning, Linda," he replied. "How are you today?"

"Fine, how aboot yourself?" she asked as she

walked behind the bar and placed her bag underneath the counter.

"I'm facing th' world with a song in my heart and a smile on my face." The girl met his ridiculous comment with laughter.

"So you are. Tell me, does Mariah Jennings have anything to do with your song and that smile?" she asked as she tied her apron around her waist.

Evan grinned as he bounced his brows, but said nothing in return.

"I take it things are progressing between th' two of you then?" she prodded.

He wagged his head from side to side. "Depends on what you mean by progressing."

"Och, you dinnae need to play coy with me, Evan MacGilroy! Your face says it all anyway." Linda fumbled around inside the cupboard, withdrew a stack of plates, and set them on the shelf next to the stove. "Well, I'm happy for you. You deserve to have someone in your life, and she seems like a sweet girl."

"She's a wonderful woman, I can attest to that," replied Evan.

Cailen exchanged an incredulous glance with Duncan. His companion shrugged in response.

"There is just one thing I feel th' need to mention. What are you going to do when she has to leave MacNaughton's castle and Scotland altogether?" asked Linda. "She cannae stay here forever, and as I recall, she has three months or so left to finish her paintings."

"Who says she cannae stay?" countered Evan. "We live in a global world where people are free to travel and live where they will. So what would keep her from staying right here with me should she choose to do so?

On th' other hand, perhaps I might feel inclined to go with her to th' States for a time. 'Tis hard to say right now."

"I prefer th' former solution if ye dinnae mind, and so would all your friends," Linda replied.

Evan chuckled and said, "In all honesty, so would I. Therefore, I'll just have to convince her that my wee flat is cozy enough for th' two of us."

He took a step forward and in that same instant, Duncan grabbed hold of his arm to stay his position.

"Calm down, Cailen," he said. "Dinnae do anythin' to give us away. We still have more to discover here, and we'll never learn it if he knows we're aboot. Besides, th' man is only yappin' his jaw. His words dinnae mean anythin' to anybody."

Duncan had a valid point and he knew it. Nonetheless, it infuriated him to stand by and do nothing while Evan touted his untruths concerning the relationship he had with Mariah. Especially when he wanted nothing more than to shove his fist into his lying mouth. He pulled his arm away from Duncan's grasp and said, "Ye dinnae need to worry."

"Well, while Evan is busy here at th' pub," Duncan said, keeping his tone casual, "why dinnae ye go over to his home and take another look at that book? See if ye can find out if he has pictures of th' herbs he took from Sybil. Mayhap we can determine th' reason for his theft. I'll give ye plenty of notice afore he goes home. If he says or does anythin' of great import, I'll let ye know right away."

Cailen returned a curt nod, knowing that just as Duncan perceived, it was best for all concerned if he exited the pub now. "All right. I'll see ye at closin' time."

Once inside Evan's private domain, Cailen made his way to the disheveled bed, stuffed his hand under the mattress, and extracted the book. He placed it atop the table, sat down, and opened the cover. Though he'd seen the macabre images before, this time as he studied them he would memorize every detail of each symbol. If he could just describe them to Mariah, she could decipher their meaning by using that wondrous computer of hers. The only difficulty would come in leading her toward the idea of sorcery, for thus far, she focused solely on medicine or the proper use of alchemy. The pictures Evan sketched stated otherwise.

Cailen studied each page with the same thoroughness he did the first. In so doing, a pattern revealed itself. Coriander, coltsfoot, and the guelder rose often appeared together on the same page. More often than not, Evan combined pictures of basil, betony, golden gorse, and burdock. Willow could appear with almost any combination of plants. However, drawings of the sprig of woodruff he and his knights carried into battle occurred only a single time inside Evan's book. Despite his wish to the contrary, nothing inside the volume listed all the ingredients of Mariah's dream together.

The vervain, valerian, and rosemary appeared together but once, along with drawings of a birch tree, heather, and one other flower with the word "yarrow" written underneath. He couldn't discern the concoction's use.

Once he returned the book to its hiding place, he wandered into Evan's kitchen in search of the vials. They didn't take long to locate. He had placed them just inside a small corner cupboard, along with other such flasks. Cailen removed them one at a time in order to read the labels. The names written on the vials matched many, if not all, the flowers, plants, and herbs, inside his book. Just as he put the last of the jars away, Duncan popped into the room.

"Evan is finished for th' night," he said. "He'll be along soon."

Cailen turned away from the cupboard and nodded.

"Did ye make any significant discoveries inside th' book?" asked Duncan.

"Just a bit of speculation on my part," he replied. "But we can discuss all that when Murriah returns to th' castle. For now, we're just goin' to have to keep our ears and our eyes open."

Duncan shrugged. "At least it gives th' lads somethin' different to do with their time and provides somethin' new to talk aboot. They seem to be enjoyin' th' assignment well enough."

The sound of a jauntily whistled tune alerted them to Evan's approach. Seconds later, they could hear the jangling of keys. The lad then shoved one of them inside the lock and twisted the handle. Cailen and Duncan backed well away from the entrance just as Evan entered the room. He tossed his keys on the table, opened his refrigerator, and pulled out a bottle of water.

Evan didn't drink from the bottle as expected, but merely poured the contents into the teapot on the stove and that puzzled him. Once the lad lit the fire, he made his way to his bed, and retrieved the book. He flipped through the pages as he carried the volume to the counter and set the thing atop it. He opened the corner cupboard, sifted through his vials, and selected various flasks from his stores.

Duncan turned toward him. The expression on his face surely matched his. "What's he doin'?"

"Makin' up one of his concoctions," Cailen replied.

Duncan shook his head and snorted, "I know that—but which one? Can ye see from where ye are standin'?"

"Nay," Cailen said, "I'll try to get closer."

"Mayhap ye ought to wait until he steps away from th' kitchen," Duncan said. "Just to be on th' safe side."

They didn't have to wait long, for once Evan completed his task he vacated the kitchen to make use of his bathroom. Cailen didn't waste any time in getting to the book. Duncan peered over his shoulder as they studied the open page.

"I dinnae know what it is, but he used th' herbs he stole from Sybil's kitchen to make his potion," said Cailen.

"I wonder what it's for?" asked Duncan.

Duncan didn't expect him to give an answer, nor did he attempt one. Yet, as the evening progressed Evan's actions grew progressively more bizarre. He methodically stirred the contents of his kettle several times, which might not have concerned him, if not for the fact that he chanted the same unknown words each time he did so.

Finally then, just before he went to bed, he took the teapot, and poured some of the steaming hot liquid into a cup. He chugged it down, rinsed his cup, and put it inside the sink. A short while later, he lapsed into a deep sleep. Cailen remembered then Mariah said valerian could help people sleep. Perhaps his brew did no more than that. Yet, why the need for the strange incantation then?

He and Duncan returned to the castle just as Mariah drove her car through the castle gates. A moment later, she exited her car and blessed him with one of her dazzling smiles.

"I didna expect ye so early," he said as he took hold of her hand and escorted her to the open doors of the castle. "Ye must not have had much sleep."

She dismissed his concern with a wave of her hand as they entered the hall. "I just wanted to come home. Besides, the roads aren't cluttered with travelers this early and that makes for an easier commute."

"I suppose that's true enough. How did th' meetin' go?" he asked.

Mariah shot a glance heavenward, and sighed. "Long, boring, and unnecessary," she said.

"Unnecessary?" he asked. "How so?"

"Well, a few of the artists have not completed a satisfactory number of paintings. Mr. Humphries is worried they won't have them done in time for the opening," she said. "I suppose that by having all of us there and speaking to us as a group, he felt no one would take undue offense. Artists are notoriously temperamental, and I'm sure he didn't want to suffer through anyone's temper tantrums."

"'Twould seem Humphries took th' coward's way out then, aye?" he said.

She laughed and said, "I guess you could say that."

"Do ye think ye ought to take a wee rest afore ye begin your day?" he asked as they ascended the steps. "Ye look like ye could use it."

"No, I don't need any sleep right now," she replied, "I might look tired, but really, I'm wide awake. So, I think I'll just go ahead and paint for a while. Humphries inspired me—"

He chuckled in response to her derisive comment.

****

Throughout the morning hours, Mariah worked on each of the remaining paintings. All the while Cailen kept her company. Their topics of conversation varied, yet she sensed they never quite arrived at the subject he really wished to broach. He wanted to discuss something with her, something important—she could see it in his eyes. Finally, she wiped the excess paint onto her palette and dipped her brushes into the jar of turpentine.

"That's about all I can do for now," she said. "So if you want to come with me while I get some lunch, maybe we can talk about whatever it is that's bothering you while I eat."

"What makes ye think somethin' is botherin' me?" he asked.

Mariah said nothing in response. She merely tilted her head, raised a brow, and simply waited for him to speak.

He shook his head and shot a glance skyward. "All right," he said. "Let's go find ye somethin' to eat and we'll discuss it."

Just as they descended the stairway, Ian appeared inside the great hall. He looked both alarmed and concerned. At once, he connected his gaze with Cailen's and strode toward him. "Evan is just aboot to th' castle. Roger is still with him in his car. Th' man has brought along some lunch for Murriah, and Cailen—he also brought her a cup of that tea ye watched him make last night." At the end of his announcement, each of the knights appeared inside the castle. No one said a word.

"What aboot th' food?" asked Cailen.

"Harmless enough," Ian replied. "Th' lassie in th' pub made it."

Mariah shifted her attention from Cailen to Ian and then back again. Ian appeared anxious while she could quite literally feel Cailen's rage. "What's going on?" she asked.

Cailen gazed at her then and placed a hand atop her shoulder. "We dinnae have th' time to discuss this right now, or give ye my reasons. Just dinnae drink what Evan gives ye, Murriah," he said. "Have an accident, knock it onto th' floor, or spill it on th' table, but dinnae drink it. I give ye my word we'll discuss it later. Will ye do that for me?"

She only had time for a single nod as Evan chose that moment to enter the castle. He seemed surprised to see her standing by the stairway.

"Mariah," he said as he licked his lips and shut the door behind him. "I had hoped to find you free from your painting long enough to share some lunch with me and there you are."

Mariah returned an almost imperceptible shake of her head, clasped her hands, and brought them to her chin. She closed her eyes and sighed. "Evan—"

"Please, wait." He extended his hand toward her. "Just hear me out. I have come to apologize for my boorish behavior last time we met. You must allow me to make amends. I'll not stay long, I promise."

Cailen slipped his hand around her waist, leaned down close to her ear, and whispered, "Go ahead and have somethin' to eat with him, just dinnae drink th' tea. I'll remain right here, so ye'll not be alone with him."

She released a breath and gestured at the table. "All right, but I can only give you half an hour, Evan. I'm really busy today."

Evan twitched a smile as he approached her. "I'm to tell you that Linda made you her specialty. She said she hopes it meets with your approval."

Mariah made her way over to the table and waited as he spread his offerings atop it. Once he divided the food between them, he dug around inside his bag and withdrew two disposable cups, capped with plastic lids. Two straws followed.

"This is an herbal tea, made with mint and cinnamon among other things," he said as he handed her the larger cup. "I think you'll like it fine, most folks do. This is my way of telling you how sorry I am for my behavior when last we met."

"I've already accepted your apology, Evan, you know this," she said.

"I know, but I just wanted to drive th' message home."

Ignoring the offered straw, Mariah removed the lid and inhaled the aroma. "Hmm, I can detect both the mint and cinnamon, but it also smells kind of flowery. The tea does smell good," she said as she took a seat just opposite him, put the cup on the table close to the edge, and picked up her sandwich. She peeked over at Cailen who stood against the wall at the bottom of the stairs. As their eyes met, he bobbed his head and winked.

"Th' tea is my own special brew," Evan said nodding at her cup, urging her to taste it.

"I'm not surprised to hear that," she replied,

ignoring his subtle invitation. She bit into her sandwich and swallowed a bite. "You are a pretty good cook."

Evan smiled over the praise, but said nothing in return.

"The sandwich is really good too, give Linda my compliments," she added.

"I will for sure." A few minutes of silence followed the comment. "Tell me something, Mariah, have you ever thought aboot making Scotland your permanent home?"

She gazed at him for several seconds and then said, "Why would you ask something like that?"

"Och, I dinnae know." He lifted his shoulders as he took another bite of his sandwich. "Curiosity I suppose. I mean, you have mentioned how much you love it here a time or two."

"I said that I loved living here *at the castle*," she replied. "But unfortunately, this castle doesn't belong to me. Now, if Kyle MacNaughton wants to give it to me—" She let the rest of her sentence take him wherever it might as she dabbed at the corner of her mouth.

During the long, nerve-wracking minutes that followed, Evan chattered on about the various people she'd met at the pub. They were asking about her and wanted to know when they might expect to see her again. While he spoke, his eyes darted between her and the untouched tea.

"Oh, I don't know, Evan," she said as she glanced at her watch. "You see, right now I'm really busy and when last I talked with Gordon Humphries—" She chose that moment to swing her hand outward and tip over her cup. The contents spilled across the table, into her lap, and onto the floor.

She gasped as she leaped to her feet and brushed at the liquid staining her clothes. "Oh no! Look what I've done. I'm so sorry, Evan, but I'm going to need to change my clothes and clean this mess up."

A look of dismay filled his eyes as he gaped at the mess. "Well, here, let me help you," he offered.

"No," she said, "No thank you. I'm going to clean myself up before I tackle the floor, so if you don't mind?"

"Oh, of course." He cleared his throat. "You need to get out of those wet clothes—" Evan paused as he shoved his hands inside his pockets and looked about the hall. "Well, perhaps you'll allow me to come out again?"

"Oh I don't know—we'll have to wait and see. As I already told you, I'm really busy right now. My deadline is looming, and I have to get these paintings done in time for the grand opening. So please, Evan, please call me before you come out again?"

A sullen expression marred his features for a split second before he replaced it with something akin to a smile. He nodded and said, "Of course, but you might also consider coming out to th' pub when you have a bit of time. I know everyone would like to see you once or twice before you leave th' Highlands."

"I'll try," she said. "That's the best I can do. Thank you for the sandwich. It was a thoughtful thing for you to do and I really appreciate it."

"You're welcome." He cast his gaze upon the door, rocked back and forth on his feet, and then said, "All right, I guess I'll let you get cleaned up."

"Thank you." Mariah waited where she stood as he

approached the door and took hold of the latch. Once he had the door open, he turned and waved. She returned the gesture.

The moment the door closed, Cailen looked over at Robin. "'Tis your watch, aye?"

Robin nodded. "Aye, 'tis me and John. Dinnae worry, Cailen, we'll not let him out of our sight."

"Let me know if he doesna leave th' property right away," he said.

"I will," he replied and then with a bit of a salute, he disappeared from the hall.

"Cailen," Mariah said as she made her way to his side. "Please tell me what's going on here. What's all this about?"

Cailen gazed pointedly at her soiled clothes. "Ye need to get cleaned up first, my lady. Then we'll talk, and while we're talkin', you're goin' to need your sketchbook."

Chapter 18

Mariah entered the great hall with some dampened towels, her sketchbook, and a notebook in hand. Several knights still filled the room, talking amongst themselves. She could see Cailen awaited her at the table and that he had fetched her computer from the studio. He had already powered it up. A thing that only served to fuel her curiosity and growing sense of disquiet. She tossed the towels atop the spilled tea and placed her books next to the computer.

"Dinnae worry aboot th' floor, right now," Cailen said. "There is not that much that needs cleanin'. Most of th' tea landed in your lap."

She shook her head. "I would rather clean it now. The chore will only take a minute and the mess is easier to clean when it's fresh. Besides, I don't want it to leave a stain on the stone."

She ignored Cailen's sigh. Once she mopped the floor, she sat down on the bench next to him. "Okay, I'm ready," she said as she opened her notebook and picked up her pencil.

He dropped his gaze to the notebook and gave it a nod. "First, I need ye to draw a circle and then a smaller circle inside of that, but leave a bit of space in between for some words. I dinnae know what they say, so I'll just have to give ye th' letters."

"No, what I meant is that I'm ready to hear your

explanation. After that, we'll work on whatever it is you want me to sketch."

"Fair enough," he replied. "I suppose I should start by tellin' ye that we've been watchin' Evan for some time, now."

"What would compel you to do something like that?" she asked.

Duncan took a seat just across from her. "Several things, Murriah. His strange behavior and his deceit to begin with. We wanted to discover th' reason for it."

"Aye," Steven added. "Then a while ago he entered his parents' cottage and came out with somethin' that didna belong to him. We felt then that we needed to keep a closer eye on him."

"When did he go inside the cottage?" she asked.

"'Twas durin' his first visit, right after he left th' castle," Alan replied. "I watched him do it, though unfortunately, I didna follow him inside. He went in a second time as well, just a few days ago. 'Twas late. In fact, he snuck into th' place while ye slept. Both times he entered in through th' back way. We have to assume he wanted to avoid detection by either ye or us."

"Well, I'm not trying to defend him, mind you, but how do you all know that whatever he took didn't belong to him in the first place. He grew up here, for goodness sake. For all you know, he might've left a whole plethora of things behind. Perhaps he just wanted to retrieve some of the things without running into his parents."

"As it turns out, you're right on one account, but not th' other," Cailen said. "Ye have to remember that we witnessed what took place th' night he argued with his father. That night he packed all his things and put them in his car, or so he said. Just afore he left, Evan told his parents that he would never come back. That as far as he was concerned, he no longer had parents. So when Alan saw him sneak into th' cottage and carry somethin' out durin' his first visit, we could only assume he took what didna belong to him."

Mariah gazed into his eyes for several long moments while she considered what he said. "Do you know what he took?" she finally asked.

He nodded. "Aye, 'twas a book of his own makin'."

Mariah drew in a sharp breath. "Are you talking about the book that contained the alchemic symbols and names of the plants?" she asked.

"Aye," he said as he met and steadily held her gaze.

"Why couldn't you tell me the book belonged to Evan when I asked you?"

"Because at th' time, I didna know what he used it for. I didna ken its purpose and I didna want ye to worry unnecessarily if it proved naught but harmless."

"I see." She paused for moment. "And now you think the book has something to do with the tea he brought me today?"

"I know it does," he replied. "While ye were away to your meetin' with Humphries, me and Duncan observed as he took th' book from underneath his mattress where he keeps it hidden away."

"Strange thing that, as well," Duncan pointed out. "Evan lives alone, so why does he feel th' need to hide it?"

Mariah had no logical answer and didn't try to give one.

"Nonetheless, he opened it to a specific page and followed th' directions to make th' tea," Cailen said. "All th' while he chanted some strange words as he stirred his concoction, and then afterward he—"

"Wait a minute," she said as she held up a hand to halt the progress of his explanation. "You don't really think Evan tried to poison me today, do you?"

He placed a hand against her cheek as he shook his head. "Nay, Murriah, I didna say that, nor do I believe he intended such. Ye see, Evan drank th' same tea afore he went to sleep."

"Then what are you suggesting?" She gazed into his eyes, seeking an answer. Yet, he said nothing. He simply waited for her to draw her own conclusion. But in which direction did he want her to go? Several thoughts flashed through her mind and for one reason or another, she rejected each one. And then all of a sudden, a single notion took root—a ridiculous notion at best. Nonetheless, with the strange incantations Evan spouted, Cailen might entertain such a thing, especially living out his mortal life in the fourteenth century in a place where superstition abounded.

"You can't be serious," she said aloud. "You're not suggesting some sort of *magic* potion, are you?"

"What would trouble ye aboot such a thought?" he asked.

"Well—because—there's no such thing as real magic, spells, incantations, or curses," she replied. "I'm not saying that people don't pretend to use them, I'm just saying they have no actual effect. That's why we call magicians illusionists in this day and age. Magic, in the real sense of the word, simply doesn't exist."

He returned a slow nod. "Aye, just as there is no

such thing as ghosts. They dinnae exist either, do they."

His reminder silenced all further argument.

"Oh, all right," she finally conceded. "Let's just say for a moment that you're right about the contents of his book. Can you tell me what he put into the tea?" Her thoughts immediately went to nauseating things like "eye of newt"—"toe of frog"—"blood of raven's beak" or some other such nonsense. In which case she'd be thrilled to pieces that she didn't drink it.

"He used what I watched him steal from Sybil's kitchen durin' his second visit—vervain, valerian, and rosemary. To those, he added heather, yarrow, and birch."

"Really?" Mariah drew her brows together as she turned her notebook on a slant and wrote down the harmless ingredients. "But for what possible purpose?"

"I dinnae know. Mayhap ye can find th' answer with your computer," he said, giving the machine a nod.

She shook her head and released a sigh as she turned to her laptop and searched for the "magical" properties of each ingredient in Evan's tea. Though she truly didn't expect to find anything magical about any of the plants, her research proved otherwise. Within the world of supernatural dabblers, each ingredient shared a common use—physical attraction and love. She gazed into Cailen's eyes and found them filled with rage. Never once had she seen him look so fierce.

She put the pencil on the table, and gently touched the side of his face. "Cailen," she said, "Even should it have worked the way Evan intended, which I seriously doubt, I didn't drink it."

"I know. But he wanted ye to drink it nonetheless. He wanted to cloud your mind and take ye against your will," he said, ignoring her skepticism altogether. "'Tis a thing Evan had no right to seek or attempt."

"I agree. But you're here and you wouldn't have let him harm me," she said.

"Ye can count on that, my lady, I will never allow him to touch ye," he declared.

She took in a breath and once again retrieved her pencil. In the hope of distracting him away from his present mood, she said, "Now, you said something about two circles with words in between?"

During the next few hours, Cailen described the chilling symbols he found in Evan's book while she sketched them. Once they finished the task, they searched out their meaning. The discoveries disturbed her far more than she cared to admit. And, whether real or imagined, she couldn't deny a link to sorcery any longer. Evan filled his book with all forms of magic rituals. Some far darker than others and the knowledge made her feel sick to her stomach.

"I noticed somethin' else while I studied his book," said Cailen.

"What did you notice?" she asked.

"More oft than not, he put coriander, coltsfoot, and guelder rose on the same page," he said. "Th' same holds true for basil, betony, golden gorse, and burdock."

"Surely you don't think Evan has anything to do with what's going here, do you?" she asked.

"I dinnae see how he could," he replied. "But whether by coincidence or not, Evan has th' same plants inside his book that ye have sketched in your sleep. That got me wonderin' if for some reason, a form of dark magic figures into this puzzle as well. Dinnae forget th' banshee that terrorized ye in your dreams. Believe me when I tell ye, she is no friend to humankind. Therefore, I think it prudent we discover all uses of your plants, whatever they might be. That includes cookin', medicine, and th' dark side of witchcraft."

"Dark magic," she repeated the words aloud that sounded so ridiculous to her ears. "Tell me something, Cailen, did people commonly use magic in this fiefdom during your mortal lifetime?"

"Not openly, for 'twas considered pagan and not in line with Christian belief," he replied. "Still, whispers abounded that said folk could be found who had retained such knowledge from their predecessors."

"Anyone from around here?" she pressed.

"No one that ever came to my attention," he said. "My father forbade its use and would banish any such practitioners."

"All right then, what about the woodruff?" she asked. "Did you find that in Evan's book, as well?"

"Aye, but I only found it once. Th' laddie didna seem to require th' use of it in the spells he concocted."

"And the willow?" she asked.

"Regularly scattered throughout th' pages," he said.

"Well," she replied, "let's find the magical properties for each, shall we?"

After an exhaustive search of each individual plant, they arrived at an interesting conclusion. "Although they have other uses, the common application for coriander, coltsfoot, and the guelder rose is to bind or unite something," she said, giving him her full attention.

"On the other hand, the common use for basil, betony, burdock, and the golden gorse is protection. Woodruff can bring victory, balance, or ensure justice. While willow gives us inspiration, the gift of prophecy, eloquence, or a heartfelt desire."

"I'm sorry, Murriah, but none of this makes any sense to me."

"If it makes you feel better, it doesn't make any sense to me either. Except for the woodruff in your sleeve. Perhaps the women of your fiefdom wanted to ensure more than just luck. Maybe they wanted to ensure a victory."

"That's assumin' they involved themselves in th' use of magic, which I dinnae think they had th' proper knowledge of," he replied.

She tapped her pencil on her notebook. "Still, my ghost is trying to tell us something, whether magic or medicine. I know that whatever it is, it's important to her and therefore, it must also be important to us."

"Mayhap it doesna involve us directly at all," he said. "Mayhap she just needs someone to help her set somethin' aright."

Mariah considered that scenario for a moment and then dismissed it. "No, I don't think so. You are somehow involved in this, Cailen," she replied. "Don't forget you're a central part in each of the dreams I've had, and let's not overlook your recent experience at Dupplin. In some way, you're involved in all of this, even if at the end of the day, my only purpose here is to help understand and resolve the problem."

"Nay, Murriah." Cailen brushed his fingers against her cheek. "Ye serve a far greater purpose than just that. Th' fates have finally presented ye to me and after centuries of waitin' for the one woman destined to win my heart. Though indeed, we might have to help your ghost in exchange for this gift, 'tis only a small part of why ye have come here and now. Surely ye feel this as well."

Cailen's convictions echoed inside her mind throughout the remainder of the day. She took them into the shower with her that evening. Yet, did fate really intend for them to have some kind of future together— odd though it might be—or did they just arrange one incredible moment in passing? Her time inside this castle grew shorter with each passing sunrise and nothing would stop the moment of reckoning. Nothing.

She released a heavy sigh as she turned off the water and exited the shower. Once dressed, she gathered her belongings and stepped into the hallway. In that very instant, four ghostly women traveled down the darkened corridor themselves. She didn't know if they were the same ethereal phantoms she spied at the moat or not. Right now, it didn't matter. Her mouth dropped, as did the towels and clothing she clutched in her hand. Without giving it another thought, she pursued the vision. If only she could get them to speak to her—

She chased them past the chapel and all the way down to the end of the hall. From there, they glided up the stairs to the third floor. Once they made the landing, they turned left and moved down the hallway. Despite the fact these women looked furtively over their shoulders many times during the journey, they refused to acknowledge her presence in any way.

They swept into the room at the end of the hall. Mariah approached the open doorway and peeked inside the chamber that now contained a complete array of furnishings. The women huddled together in a tight semi-circle. They gazed at something, but she couldn't see past them well enough to identify the object of their attention. They whispered amongst themselves, and although she could discern the serious tones, she couldn't make out a single word they said. Finally, she took a deep breath, walked through the open doorway, and approached them.

"Excuse me—" The women still didn't acknowledge her presence. Bewildered at best, she tried again. "I don't mean to intrude upon your conversation, but I'm hoping you can help me—" She clamped down on her teeth as the scene melted into wispy swirls that slowly dissipated right before her eyes. She blinked several times as the room shifted in and out of focus. And then at last, the chamber reverted to its original state. She backed out of the deserted, empty solar and try as she might, she couldn't make sense of what had just occurred.

"Cailen!" she called out.

A scant moment later, he stood at her side and slipped a hand about her waist. "Are ye all right, Murriah?" he asked as he fixed his gaze to hers.

She shifted her gaze to the inside of the room and said, "I just saw four of the ghostly women again, they went in there, and it looked—"

"Ye saw th' same ones from th' passageway?" he cut in.

"I'm not sure." She took in a breath and turned her head to the side as she studied the empty room. "Unfortunately, I could only see the back of their bodies while I followed them here. Then, once they passed over the threshold, they huddled together—right there in front of a bed. They stared at something while they spoke to each other. Yet, all the while, I just couldn't see their faces."

"When and where did ye first see them?" he asked.

"Just after I finished my shower," she said. "I walked out of the bathroom and saw them gliding down the hallway. So, I followed them up the stairs, then down the corridor and into this room. They didn't pay any attention to me at all. In fact, I had the impression they didn't even see me."

The comment clearly puzzled him. "And then what happened?" he asked.

"Like I said, they simply entered the solar and clustered around something. I couldn't see what they looked at. Although I could hear them whispering amongst themselves, I couldn't make out what they said. I tried speaking to them, but either they ignored me or they just—didn't hear me." The last of her words trailed off as a sudden thought entered into her mind. She placed a finger against her lips.

"Residual haunting," she mused aloud.

"What did ye just say?" he asked.

"Residual haunting. According to paranormal scientists, the term refers to a traumatic event of the past that's imprinted on time itself. This event can replay itself repeatedly and indefinitely. They say the ghosts are not actually present so it's useless to try to speak to them or gain their attention," she said. "The spectacle is like watching something on the television George has inside the cottage. The actors who made the film are long gone."

"I dinnae ken," he said, shaking his head. "I have

never witnessed such a thing afore."

"Neither have I," she replied. "In truth, I never gave the idea much credibility, but now I'm not so sure. Maybe those scientists are right, after all."

"What makes ye think this is a—a residual hauntin'?" he asked.

"Well, for one, I saw this room completely furnished with medieval style furnishings. Yet, the scene only lasted a few minutes," she said.

Cailen looked at her for several long moments before he said, "Can ye describe it to me?"

She pointed to the left hand side of the room. "I saw a bed, positioned at the center of that wall. The bed was large and constructed from heavy timbers. Ivory-colored curtains hung from the canopy frame. Braided cords tied them back at each of the four posts. A light-brown quilt covered the mattress and I believe I saw a fur coverlet on top the quilt."

"Did ye see anythin' over there?" he asked pointing straight ahead.

Mariah called the scene to mind and in doing so, peeked past the women in the circle. "I'm not sure, the women stood just in front of the bed blocking my view. However, I think I simply saw a chest. A big one. The top of it would probably stand about the height of my hip."

"Could ye see anythin' else concernin' th' chest, such as th' color or th' material used—"

"Umm," she said as she struggled to remember. "The wood looked chestnut. The metal clasp and the lock were...black, I think. And—I saw carving across the front of the lid—a string of ivy perhaps?"

She glanced up from her task and found Cailen

staring at her with something akin to disbelief. "What is it?" she asked.

"What else did ye see?" he countered.

She rubbed her lips together and shrugged. "Oh, I don't know. There might have been a smaller chest in front of the bed, which the women surrounded. I think whatever they looked at sat atop it. A few clothes pegs were situated over there—"

"Could ye give me a description of th' women? By that, I mean, th' color of their hair or th' clothes they wore?"

"No," she said. "Just as in the passageway, these ghosts were void of all color. They all had long hair, obviously, which they tied with a ribbon behind their neck. Just as before, they all wore the linen léines common to your era."

Cailen took hold of her hand and stepped inside the room. His troubled gaze swept every nook and cranny of the entire area.

"Cailen, what is it?" she asked. "Please tell me what's wrong."

He gave her hand a gentle squeeze and as he locked his gaze with hers, he said, "Ye have just described this solar with astonishin' accuracy, my lady."

"Who did this bedroom belong to?" She swallowed past the knot in her throat as she awaited his answer.

"Durin' my lifetime, this particular chamber belonged to my sister—Mairwen," he replied.

Chapter 19

Mariah smothered a yawn as she placed her pencil on the table and rubbed a finger across the top of her aching forehead. "I think I need to take a break, Cailen."

"Aye, and 'tis long past due," he replied. "Ye've been workin' on th' parchment all morn."

"I know, and the names are starting to run together or worse yet, look alike. If I keep going, I'll miss something. I have to tell you, it doesn't help that Edgar has such terrible handwriting."

"I'm not surprised to hear that," he said. "The man was old and more oft than naught, a wee bit into his cups. Made him fair tottery most of th' time."

"And that's puttin' it courteously," Duncan added. "'Twas common enough to see him without th' full possession of his mind as well. As I remember, we deviled him aboot that verra thing quite oft. Ye know, now that I think on it, that's probably why he didna like us so much."

A breath of laughter accompanied a nod as Mariah dropped the lid of her computer. "No doubt," she replied.

"Well, come on then." Cailen got to his feet and offered her his hand. "Let's go for a walk, so ye can take in a bit of th' fresh air and sunshine."

"That sounds really good right now." She swung

her legs over the bench and rose to her feet. "Just let me put this stuff away before we leave."

"Are ye goin' to work on it when ye get back?" asked Steven.

"Yes, I am. I still have to wait a few more hours before I can put a brush to any of the paintings."

"Then dinnae worry aboot leavin' it right where it it sits," he said. "I'll watch over it and make sure Tatters doesna get close to it."

"Thanks, Steven, I appreciate that. We won't be gone long," she said as Cailen took hold of her hand and led her to the door.

"Has it occurred to ye," Cailen began as they made their way outside and then to the back of the castle. "That ye wouldn't feel so muddled if ye didna try to read everythin' that Edgar wrote on th' parchment?"

"No. I might miss something important if I don't read everything Edgar left behind."

"I dinnae see any value in searchin' through th' marriage records or th' names of all th' bairns he christened. Surely, none of that would have anythin' to do with me or my knights," he countered.

"It's not so much the names as what he sometimes writes underneath or next to them in the margins of the parchment. Every now and again, he leaves some fascinating information," she replied. "For instance, if not for his notes, we wouldn't know that your family retained possession of the castle all throughout his tenure. Balliol, nor any of his cronies, never touched it."

"That's true enough, but none of that information has helped to further our cause," he pointed out. "'Tis just given us a bit of insight as to th' day-to-day doin's of th' castle folk."

"So far," she added. "But that doesn't mean there still isn't something there for us to find. You have to remember my ghost hasn't seen fit to point out the page or pages she wants us to find, and I don't know if she ever will. After all, I haven't sketched anything in my sleep, or had an informative nightmare for quite some time, now."

"Mayhap th' reason for that is because I have remained at your side while ye sleep. My presence doesna give your ghost much opportunity to interact with ye should she wish to do so."

"I suppose that's always a possibility. But then again, she could show herself when I'm by myself in the castle studio, or when I get ready for bed. After all, she has appeared inside my bedroom on three different occasions already."

"That brings me around to another question I've wanted to ask ye."

"Another question?" she repeated as she sidestepped one of the larger bushes.

"Aye. Th' other night ye seemed quite convinced th' ghosts ye saw down by th' moat and again in Mairwen's room were naught but a residual hauntin'," he said. "Images from th' past that repeat like a movie on th' telly, ye said."

Mariah nodded. "At least I'm beginning to think so, but I suppose there's always room for doubt. I'm certainly not an expert in the field of ghosts, but why do you ask?"

"Well, it got me thinkin'. Wouldn't it also stand to reason then, that your redhead might be part of th' same phenomenon?" he asked. "Such would explain why we cannae see her or the others for ourselves. Mayhap we've just never been around when these images repeat."

"No, I don't think that's it," she replied. "There is a distinct difference between the two sightings."

"Th' difference is?" he prodded.

"Well, the ghosts who went from the moat to the passageway and those in Mairwen's bedroom looked very different from my redhead in both appearance and demeanor. Although transparent, I see my redhead in the colors of her mortality. I can see the color of her skin, her hair, and léine, just as clearly as I see you and the knights. The other ghosts are void of color. My redhead also gives off the scent of heather and I really don't think odor is associated with a residual haunting.

"To top it off, the last time I saw my ghost she *looked* at me as if well aware of my presence," she said. "Even though her face remained out of focus, I know we made eye contact with each other. I truly feel that in her own way, she attempted to communicate with me that morning. I'm as sure as I can be, that she's responsible for the dreams and everything we've discovered this far. There is no other explanation for it that I can see."

"Mayhap," Cailen replied as his only concession to her rationale.

"That brings *me* to a question of my own," she said.

"All right," he said, "I'm listenin'."

"Why can't she speak to me? All of the other spirits I've met here in the Highlands can speak well enough," she said, bringing Beth's nasty little comments to mind.

Cailen shrugged. "She might never have had th' desire to gain th' ability. A spirit doesna have to speak aloud to communicate with each other, ye know."

Mariah drew her brows together. "No, I didn't know that. How do you talk to each other if not aloud?"

"Through our minds, my lady. 'Tis as simple as payin' attention to each other's thoughts. Remember 'tis an acquired skill to project ourselves in such a way for mortals to both see and hear us. This is likely th' reason ye cannae see your ghost clearly, as well. She might not have gained th' full ability of projection."

Her mouth dropped as she gazed up at him wide-eyed. "Are you telling me that you can just read each other's thoughts at will? You have no privacy from each other?" she asked, ignoring the rest of what he just said.

Cailen burst out laughing and touched a gentle finger to her nose. "Are ye scandalized over th' thought of such a thing?" he asked.

"Well, it's just that you and—" She stopped mid-sentence and swallowed the rest of her words as she considered the personal conversations they had shared. All those conversations began with thoughts. She shook her head and said, "Just answer the question, please."

"In th' beginnin' of our post-mortal existence, aye. But over time, we have acquired th' skill to keep private, those thoughts we wish to remain private. Ye dinnae need to worry aboot th' knights peepin' into my personal ponderin's."

Although his explanation gave her a small measure of relief, she said nothing in return. In fact, they continued their journey in silence until they stepped onto the bridge. She strolled over to the center, turned to face him, and smiled. "Funny thing about our walks together—most of the time, we always end up right here," she said.

Cailen brushed a hand through her wind-tangled hair and nodded. "I have always been fond of this place, but ye made it even more special when ye drew it without havin' th' foreknowledge of its existence," he replied. "Since th' day ye showed me th' sketch, I have oft wondered how ye knew aboot it."

Her gaze drifted over to the clear, rippling water as it traversed the twists and turns of its borders.

"I dreamed of it," she finally said as she propped her elbows atop the barrier and rested her chin on her hands. "Many times. The first time I saw the bridge in my dreams, you stood here alone as if contemplating the problems of the day, or seeking answers to some weighty dilemma. Then at times, in other dreams as I grew older, I stood right here beside you."

"And what were we doin'?" he asked.

"Most of the time we just talked," she replied as she lowered her hands and toyed with her fingers. "I never remembered what we talked about, though. The topic always seemed to disappear when I woke up."

"'Tis a pity," he said as he took hold of her hand, and twined his fingers around hers.

She looked up and fixed her gaze to his. "Why? I'm sure more often than not we talked about stuff and nonsense. Most dreams are made up of such things, you know."

"But not th' ones between us, I should think," he said as he tilted his head to the side. "Now then, ye said most of th' time we stood here talkin' to each other. What aboot th' rest of th' time?"

She lifted a single shoulder. "I'm not sure I should divulge that information."

"Why not?" he asked.

"Well, because—some things should just remain a mystery, don't you think? From what I've heard, it's supposed to make a relationship far more interesting."

Cailen's eyes filled with humor. So much for the mystery. Somehow, the man already knew. He leaned down, and proceeded to kiss her quite senseless just to show her that he did know. By far, this live version of her dreams surpassed the ones created by her mind. And as usual, she lost all track of time and sense of responsibility.

Once he allowed her a moment to breathe, he said, "I think that aboot settles it then."

"What settles what?" she asked as she sought a return to some small semblance of normalcy.

"I cannae let ye go, Murriah Jennin's," he replied. "I will not let ye go. Ye belong right here with me throughout all th' ages of time. And ye can trust me when I tell ye, 'tis our great fortune that the ages of time go on forever."

"Well, I suppose we'll just have to figure out a way to accomplish that then, won't we. Maybe we can convince Kyle MacNaughton to sell me the castle for a pittance, or perhaps he would give it to me in exchange for a houseful of paintings."

"Ye would trade away your possessions to stay here with me?" he asked.

"Every last one of them."

Cailen flashed one of his flirty grins that always made her weak in the knees. Well, that and the fact that he inched closer yet and tipped her chin upward.

"Interestin' thought that, but dinnae worry, my lady. I vow to make such a reality without ye havin' to make th' sacrifice," he whispered against her lips.

Sometime later, and she had absolutely no idea how much time passed, they made their way back to the castle. Steven folded his arms against his chest and lifted a brow as they entered through the doorway. The smirk he wore on his face let her know they were gone much longer than her last comment suggested. She merely returned his smile and shrugged in return.

Nonetheless, feeling invigorated after her outing, Mariah focused her attention on the parchment. In short order, she finished the document that had given her such fits earlier. Once completed, she placed it atop her completed stack and focused on the next record.

The Latin terms for "Death and Burial" headed the page. Her heart dropped into the pit of her stomach, for without doubt, she would find Cailen's name listed somewhere in this grouping of records. She took a quick peek through the stack of parchment to see how many such pages existed and counted four. The dates on the last page exceeded the death of the knights.

She glanced at page three and knowing just where to find it, her eyes traveled down the page to where the cleric recorded Cailen's death. Duncan's name followed and then she saw Steven's, Edmund's, and Malcolm's in turn. The first hint of dewy liquid formed in her eyes as she recalled her dream with perfect clarity. In that moment, she relived her grief on the battlefield as she knelt over Cailen's body, the sorrow of his father, and Edgar's despair. Although she tried to hold them at bay, the first wayward tear escaped. She wiped it away, sniffed a couple of times, and placed a hand underneath her nose.

"What's wrong, Murriah?" asked Cailen. She noted the concern in his voice, and sought to dismiss it with a casual wave of her hand.

"Nothing—I mean, surely you know by now that women can get all weepy at the drop of a hat." She breathed in a laugh and then gulped. "And, I've just found where Edgar recorded your death. It brought my dream, as well as the sorrow of that dream, to mind—that's all."

He sat backward on the bench next to her and leaned his back against the table. With a touch of cockiness to his tone, he said, "Och, dinnae let th' words bother ye. Edgar was just deep in his cups when he penned my name there. As ye can see, I'm still here, safe and sound and so are all my knights."

His comment solicited a smile as their eyes connected and held. "So, where did th' cleric make his preposterous error?" he asked as he shifted his gaze to the document.

Mariah looked down at the parchment and just as she pointed a finger at his name, she gasped and stared in horror at the entry written just above it.

"Is somethin' wrong?" he asked.

She wanted to ignore the question altogether. Yes, very wrong, she mused as her eyes slowly traveled upward on the page. Several other names accompanied the first. She found them all listed under the same date. "Something terrible must have happened here."

"What are ye talkin' aboot?" he asked.

Did she make that comment out loud? Truly, she didn't mean to. She fastened her gaze to his, lifted a hand to the side of his face, and gently combed her fingers against his beard. "I'm so sorry, Cailen."

"Why are ye sorry? I dinnae ken what ye mean," he said. "Th' parchment is naught but words, hundreds of years old. They have no power to hurt me or anyone else."

She didn't know what to say to that, except to come right out and tell him. "Mairwen," she whispered as she dropped her hand to the table. "Her name is recorded just above yours. Do you see right here?" She pointed to the name she referenced. "This says she died August ninth, just two days before you died yourself."

He said nothing for several moments. "'Twas th' day after we left for battle then," he finally replied.

"There's more," she said, swallowing past the lump forming in her throat.

"Just go ahead and say it, Murriah. I swear 'twill not be painful." He took hold of her hand, gave it a gentle squeeze, and nodded his encouragement. "Everythin' on that parchment happened centuries ago. All th' folk we once knew have been gone for a verra long time now, and we reconciled ourselves to that fact shortly after our death."

"I know that, but—well, it says here, ten other people died the same day as Mairwen, all of them women." Her comment drew the attention of all the knights. Those who had not been in the room moments earlier, now crowded around the table. She shook her head and lifted her brows. "No wonder Edgar seemed so filled with grief and despair when he offered comfort to your father. The poor man still grieved the loss of his daughter and I'm sure, the women who died alongside her as well."

"What other names do ye see written there,

Murriah?" asked Steven as he ambled over to the table.

Mariah raised her shoulders together, took a deep breath, and slowly exhaled it. "Margery, Alison, Glenna, Aveline, Lillias, Rhona, Joan, Helena, Ruth, and Adeliza," she said.

Steven first broke the lengthy silence that followed. "Did Edgar say what happened to them?" he murmured.

"I wonder if th' castle suffered an attack?" said Duncan.

Before she had the chance to answer, Edmund said, "'Tis possible that Murray of Tullibardine had a hand in this, just like he did at Dupplin. Ye have to remember his betrayal there. Mayhap he and Balliol conspired to take control of th' castle in our absence. Such could have been th' price of his treachery. And our women would have done all in their power to defend th' place."

Cailen shook his head. "I dinnae think Murray would have an interest in this castle, the place is too far away from his clansmen. And even if he or Balliol wanted to take it, why would th' opposin' forces slaughter eleven women and leave all of th' men alive?"

"Besides," Edmund said, "th' battle had yet to take place. Murriah said they died two days prior, do ye ken?"

"And no one would have dared come here without knowin' th' outcome," said Malcolm.

"The castle was not under siege," Mariah cut in.

Once again, silence fell over the hall. Each of the knights turned to face her and waited for her to speak.

She pointed to the note written on the side of the page. "Edgar said they found and recovered their bodies from the passageway, underneath the castle."

"What were they doin' down there?" asked Steven.

"He didn't say. The only thing this note says is that once they retrieved the bodies, they laid them to rest in the cemetery behind the castle." She looked up at Cailen and said, "I don't remember seeing a cemetery out there."

"Aye, 'tis still there," he said. "But no one has used it for burial for well over a century. All of th' markers are long gone."

She said nothing in return.

"Ye know," said Cailen, "that could explain why ye didna see any of these women on th' battlefield in your dream. None of them were alive at th' time we met our death."

"Then who is showing me everything I have seen so far?" she asked. "It made sense before when you thought it might be Margery, Alison, your sister or one of these other women. All of them had a strong connection to you and your men."

Cailen shrugged and as he swept his hand over the mound of documents, he said, "Mayhap you're right aboot Edgar's records after all. It just might be that ye'll find th' answers ye seek, somewhere in that parchment."

Chapter 20

Cailen rose from the edge of Mariah's bed and made his way to the window. He gazed out at the cloudless sky, yet paid no heed to its brilliance. Instead, he focused his thoughts on Mairwen, and the companions that perished alongside his sister on that fateful day. But, what would cause such a horrendous event to occur? A plausible explanation eluded him. Disease surely couldn't take them all at once. He considered noxious fumes within the passageways. Yet, such a thing had never happened during his mortal sojourn, or in the centuries that followed. What were they all doing down there anyway? He couldn't find a logical reason for their presence. They didn't store anything of importance down there. In all but a few instances, they used the corridors and chambers solely to keep their women and children safe during times of siege and war—

A small, tiny whimper escaped Mariah's lips at that moment, and silenced all further thought. As his gaze traveled over her face, she stirred. Her movements seemed restless and agitated. The fluttering of her lashes followed. She turned onto her side and faced the door. In the same instant, her eyes fully opened. She sat up, and while resting her weight on her elbows, she stared at the outer wall. He saw nothing amiss.

"What is it, Murriah?" he asked.

She didn't answer. Instead, she tossed the covers off to the side, slid off the bed, and crammed her feet into her slippers. In just two quick steps, she turned the handle, and yanked open the door. Notwithstanding his confusion, Cailen followed her hasty advance down the hallway and over to the landing. She turned down the east hall, made her way to the rear staircase, and descended the steps.

"Murriah," he tried again as they arrived at ground level.

"Shh, Cailen," she whispered in return.

Despite her call for silence, she offered him her hand in unspoken invitation to tag along beside her. Once he had taken a firm enough hold, she towed him over to the back door, and together they stepped outside. She made straight for the river, turning in a northerly direction as if she had done so a thousand times before. They followed along the bank for several minutes before she halted her steps, put a finger to her lips requesting continued silence, and gazed straight ahead.

Without doubt, they followed the ghost or ghosts he couldn't see. Yet he couldn't fathom where they led her or understand their reasons. Mariah tugged on his hand again as she moved through the thickening foliage. Suddenly, she made an abrupt turn to the right, swept away the tall grass, and passed through a slender opening that looked no more than a crumbling fissure in the rocky wall. A fissure he could never have passed through during his mortality. The full moon filtered light into the mouth of a small cave he had never once explored.

Mariah made her way to the darkened passageway

just up ahead, but stopped at the edge of visibility. She shivered, rubbed her arms against the frigid temperature, and released a dejected sigh.

"I've lost sight of her again," she said in a voice barely audible.

"Who did ye see this time?" he asked.

"My redhead," she murmured. "She went down there and disappeared. I wished I would have thought to grab my flashlight before I left my room."

He gazed at her for several moments in indecision. "Wait right, here. Dinnae move, do ye ken? I will not be gone long, I swear."

In less than a heartbeat, he appeared inside the castle and grabbed the first torch he encountered. Mere seconds later, he reappeared inside the cave. Once he lit the thing, he handed it off. Her smile bespoke her gratitude. He winked in return.

"Whatever would I do without you?" she whispered.

"Murriah, ye dinnae need to keep whisperin'," he finally said. Though difficult to control his laughter, he somehow accomplished it and without a trace of humor showing on his face. "Your ghost can hear th' smallest of sounds from quite a distance. She knows ye followed her, and if she's still around, she knows we're standin' here right at this verra moment."

"Oh—of course." She gave her head a little shake and shrugged. "I guess the shot of adrenaline made me forget." She stood still for several seconds. "But then, that means she *wants* us to follow her, doesn't it? So, come on, let's see if I can find her again."

He again took hold of her hand as she turned down the darkened passageway. Together they moved through the visible mist that filled the narrow corridor. Damp, rocky pebbles crunched beneath her footsteps and more often than not, she had to evade the massive roots that protruded through the walls like bony fingers ensnaring unsuspecting prey. Finally, they arrived in front of a T-junction. She turned slightly to the left and holding the torch aloft, peered into the darkness. A finger touched her lips as she shifted her gaze to the broader path off to her right.

"I don't know which way to go," she said.

"Ye dinnae see any trace of her then?" he asked, referring to her ghost.

"No, I don't." Her gaze darted between the two passageways. "Well, let's go right. If we don't see anything down that way, we can come back and try the left side."

"All right," he said. "Ye lead, and I'll follow your steps."

They traversed the corridor for a time before it curved east. The path finally led them to familiar ground underneath the castle. "If we keep walkin', said Cailen, "we'll see the stairs that lead to the buttery."

Mariah nodded as she covered her mouth and smothered a yawn. "Yes, I know. I recognize it now. We should've turned left instead."

"Mayhap," he replied. "But you're exhausted, Murriah. I can see it in your eyes. Let's get ye back to th' castle. Ye need to get some sleep afore th' sun rises."

"I know you're right and truly, I don't want fatigue ruining the paintings." She paused and then cast her gaze behind her. "But on the other hand, I want so much to know what's down the left pathway."

"Ye will not see a thing when you're so tired," he replied. "Th' passageway isn't goin' anywhere and we can fully explore it later."

"Are you familiar with that particular passage?"

He shook his head. "I've never explored that paricular area afore."

"So you don't know where it leads then."

"Nay, I dinnae. We'll find out soon enough," he said. "But only after ye've had some sleep."

She turned and fixed her gaze with his. "Oh come on, Cailen. How long could it take, after all?"

"Much longer than ye might think, my lady," he said, "since I will not let ye pass. That is a pledge ye can count on, for 'tis one I intend to keep. Now, if ye so desire, I can go down there and see where it leads after we get ye off to bed."

"You can't go down there without me," she huffed. "That's not fair."

"Then its exploration will have to wait." He almost laughed outright over her sullen expression and exasperated sigh. Nonetheless, she accepted his judgment without further fuss. He escorted her back to the castle and assisted her into her bed. A small grin stole across his face, for it didn't take any time at all for her to fall into peaceful sleep with her fingers curled lightly around his.

****

Thick clouds prevented the sunlight from invading her bedroom. Therefore, Mariah slept far later than she intended. She hurried through breakfast in order to make up for time lost. Yet, the moment she applied the last possible dab of paint to the last canvas, the roaring boom of crashing thunder sounded directly overhead.

The torrential clatter of furious raindrops, pounding atop the castle roof, immediately followed. Within minutes, the passageways underneath the castle would fill with impassable mud, muck, and water, most especially those pathways near the river. She dropped her arm to the side and looked heavenward.

"Oh, not now!" she wailed.

The moment she uttered the words, Cailen appeared inside the room. He chuckled as he ambled toward her. "Aye, 'tis a fact th' rain in th' Highlands can be just as obstinate and unpredictable as her people."

"I knew we should've explored the cave and passageway when I first woke up," she said, ignoring his mirth.

"'Tis not as important as th' paintin's are right now," he replied. "They must come first."

"I know, I know," she muttered. "But I really wanted to go down there today and see whatever it is my ghost wants me to see or to find."

"Dinnae worry, we'll get there," he replied. "Just not today."

A ragged sigh of defeat passed through her lips as she made her way to the table, cleaned off her brushes, and put them away. After she tidied the room she said, "I think I'll console myself by working a bit on the parchment. Maybe we'll get lucky and find something we need. Heaven knows I'll have plenty of time since the humidity is going to prolong the drying of the paint."

Cailen chuckled and offered her his hand. "Mayhap ye will."

Her comment proved prophetic. Several hours

later, Mariah stared at the final words Edgar recorded on the parchment she clutched in her hand. She had no idea how much time had passed since she made the spine-chilling discovery in the records following Cailen's death. Time and again, along the way, she wanted to blurt out each sentence she deciphered in Latin, but copied down in English. She studied the words several times to ensure accuracy. All the while, the knights conversed amongst themselves, leaving her free from interruption. She needed it. Now, at the end of Edgar's horrific tale, she had to tell the knights what she'd learned, for the cleric offered nothing more concerning the subject matter.

She turned around on the bench with notebook in hand, and rested her back against the bench. Her gaze wandered around the hall in search of Cailen. Once she located him standing next to Duncan near the dais, she called out his name. She could hear the trepidation in her voice as she did so.

"Aye, my lady." He locked his gaze to hers as he approached.

"I found something you all need to hear."

He settled himself next to her on the bench and dropped an arm around her shoulder. The comment silenced all conversation as each of the knights turned to face her. Perhaps the expression she wore bade them gather a bit closer, for suddenly, the knights had her surrounded.

"First, who is Elspetha MacShymes?" she asked. "For she is our subject."

"'Tis th' goodwife of Ewen MacShymes," he said. "Th' man which George MacGilroy descends from, ye ken?"

"Oh—yes. I remember you telling me about that now," she murmured. "You said you all thought his wife 'dunderheaded,' if I remember correctly."

"Aye," Duncan quickly responded, smiling broadly. "And for good reason."

She returned a slow nod as she dropped her gaze to the notebook. Good reason, indeed, yet how to begin?

"What did ye find out aboot Elspetha?" prodded Cailen.

She took a deep breath and closed her eyes. "They burned her at the stake for murdering your sister and the other women they found down inside the passageway."

The comment caused an immediate stir as the knights discussed this disturbing information. Cailen raised a hand to silence his men, an order they obeyed in the same instant.

"Go on, Murriah," he said.

"Let me read the very first part exactly as Edgar wrote it," she replied. "I don't want any of my own impressions sneaking into this inaccurately."

"All right," said Cailen. "Ye have our attention."

Mariah lifted the notebook from off her lap and took a deep breath. " '*Be it known on this the eighteenth day of August, in the year of our Lord, one thousand, three hundred and thirty-two, the sentence of Elspetha MacShymes, (that of death by fire) for the atrocity of murder and witchcraft, was duly executed, by order of Laird Braithnoch. Let all men know further, that Elspetha MacShymes, niece of Louis de Brienne, cousin of Henry de Beaumont, did willfully confess to said crimes, and to the end of life remained unrepentant before men and God. She met her death defiant, with a curse on her lips. I could not, in good conscience, beg mercy for her soul.'* "

Steven gaped at her with widened eyes. "Elspetha was Henry de Beaumont's cousin?"

Mariah nodded as she glanced at the parchment. "That's what it says here, and he further states that because of her lifelong allegiance to the supporters of Balliol, she willfully committed these acts."

"But that doesna make sense, Murriah," Duncan said, drawing his brows together. "What possible good would it do to murder innocent women?"

"Edgar doesn't give us all of the details. Perhaps he didn't have them," she said. "Elspetha admitted her guilt. Yet, she refused to say anything in her defense. According to Edgar, the inquest began with a confession of a young girl by the name of Anne. She said Mairwen approached her well before you all rode off to battle."

Cailen nodded. "We all knew Anne, quite well. I thought her a timid lassie."

"Scared of her own shadow," Steven added. "Never looked ye full in th' eye."

"I suppose that makes sense with what I've read. You see, during the course of their conversation, Mairwen told Anne that Elspetha possessed the ancient skills to ensure victory, as well as the life of every knight going into battle. In order to accomplish this goal, Mairwen said Elspetha needed the participation of eleven women. Anne feared these skills, considering them evil, and didn't want to participate. Mairwen didn't press her. The girl said she didn't know Mairwen proceeded with her plans until after the discovery of the women's bodies.

"Shortly thereafter, she sought out the cleric and

made her confession," Mariah said. "Edgar didn't waste any time in relating the details to your father. At that point, your father ordered Elspetha arrested and thrown into the dungeon. Her trial waited until after your burial and the return of your brother from Ireland.

"Elspetha remained haughty and insolent throughout her imprisonment. She quite readily admitted her desire to bring about the demise of all those in support of King Robert the Bruce and his 'wretched' descendants. However, she refused to confess the details of what transpired down in the passageway or reveal whether or not anyone else conspired alongside her.

"Edgar added just one other frightening detail. A guard reported that upon hearing of your deaths, a fit of demonic laughter possessed her. He said the unholy sound of it would make the bravest of men cower." Once Mariah finished her narration, she closed the notebook, placed it on the table, and met Cailen's troubled gaze.

"I didna know of her hatred for us," he said, shaking his head. "It never crossed my mind that she would try to harm anyone in this fiefdom."

"Nay," said Duncan. "Th' old woman never let on. In fact, as I recall, she never had so much as a bad word to say aboot th' Bruce. At least, not in my presence. Most surprisin' is knowin' that not only was she a witch, but that she would use this skill to harm Mairwen."

"Why do you say that?" asked Mariah.

"Because she always seemed so fond of her," Duncan replied. "Elspetha taught Mairwen th' skill of midwifery and how to use th' various plants to aid sufferin' women throughout th' ordeal of childbirth."

"Aye, that she did," Cailen added. "From th' time she was just a wee lassie, Elspetha took her under her wing and taught her all she knew aboot medicines and th' birthin' process."

"Do you think she might've taught Mairwen the use of magic as well?" she asked.

"Nay, I dinnae think so," Cailen said. "It was not in Mairwen's nature to go against her Christian beliefs. That much is certain. Therefore, Elspetha wouldn't have wanted to chance being found out until Mairwen gave her a good enough reason to divulge it."

"Aye," Duncan agreed. "I can tell ye that Mairwen was verra frightened when she learned of th' upcomin' battle. We talked aboot it at length. She said she had a bad feelin' and that she couldn't bear to lose any more of her clansmen, especially ye, Cailen, for she was closer to ye than any other."

"'Twould stand to reason then," said Steven, "that Mairwen would confide these same fears to Elspetha. Th' woman could use those fears to her advantage without fear of being found out. In turn, Mairwen would keep her secret if she thought it would keep us safe."

"And Elspetha used Mairwen's concern to conjure a spell of death on us," Malcolm spat. "Dinnae forget all our women sewed woodruff into th' sleeves of our léines. 'Tis th' one thing we all had in common and for this we all died."

"But that doesn't make sense," Mariah replied. "Woodruff is supposed to bring victory, balance, or ensure justice, not injury and death."

"Unless Elspetha's idea of justice is to seat Balliol

on th' throne," Malcolm argued.

"Ye might have a point at that," Duncan said. "She could see that both as victory as well as justice."

"After all," Malcolm added, "we dinnae have a single clue as to what transpired down there in th' passageway."

"Perhaps we haven't discovered all th' uses of woodruff, either," Cailen suggested.

"Cailen," Mariah cut in when a thought suddenly struck her.

"Aye?"

"Would Anne have accompanied the women to the battlefield at Dupplin, to collect your bodies?" she asked.

"'Tis likely she could have, especially given the circumstances here at th' castle durin' that time," he replied.

"Was she thin, about my height with long red hair?" she asked.

He nodded. "Aye, though a bit taller, I would say."

"Did she have flaming red hair, like Donald's?" she ventured further.

Cailen cocked his head to the side and locked his gaze with hers. "Ye think Anne is your ghost?"

"I don't know—maybe," she said. "I mean, we're looking for a woman who fits that description, aren't we? We also need a woman who knew firsthand what happened on the battlefield. A woman who knew where they buried your bodies. Anne fits that scenario. And, she is the one who exposed Elspetha."

"But she didna participate in th' intrigue with th' other lassies," Cailen replied. "Therefore, she wouldn't have a speck of knowledge of what took place down in th' passageway, do ye agree?"

"Well, yes, but—"

"If she didna participate, how would she know aboot th' plants ye sketched?" he asked.

"I don't know. Do you think Mairwen could possibly have discussed that information with her beforehand?"

"As ye have said many times afore, all things are possible, Murriah, but I dinnae think 'tis probable," he said.

"Why not?"

"Because I know th' character of both women. Once Anne said she didna wish to be involved with Elspetha, Mairwen wouldn't have pressed her any further. Anne even said as much to Edgar. On th' other hand, Anne would have fled th' boundaries of th' fiefdom screamin' bloody murder if Mairwen had attempted such a thing, do ye ken?"

"Then who else?" she asked. "We need a slender woman with long red hair, around my height with knowledge of plants and Elspetha's schemes. Who else in your fiefdom would fit that description?"

"'Twould fit Mairwen for certain," said Duncan with a casual shrug of his shoulders. "Except she didna survive long enough to get out to th' battlefield or witness our burial."

Chapter 21

"Cailen?" whispered Mariah. Sleep should've claimed her hours ago. Yet, she stared up at the ceiling of her bedroom, wide awake. The chaotic thoughts swirling through her mind simply refused to quiet themselves without providing an outlet.

"Aye?"

"What if my redheaded ghost *is* Mairwen?" she asked. In turn, he rolled onto his side, took hold of her hand, and steadily met her gaze.

He remained quiet for several minutes before he spoke. "Is that where your thoughts have taken ye, my lady?"

"Yes," she answered.

"What would lead ye to that conclusion?" he asked.

She lifted her brows and shrugged. "Well, to begin with, Duncan said the physical description fits."

"'Twould fit at least a dozen other lassies in th' fiefdom, as well," he said.

"I'm sure that's true. But of everyone in your entire fiefdom, she also had the most knowledge concerning Elspetha's abilities, right?"

"Only as far as we know," he replied. "'Tis clear now, that Elspetha could have conspired with any number of folk and without our full knowledge or even theirs. Obviously, none of us knew her true nature, not even her own husband. I can tell ye, Ewen would never have stood for it. I dinnae mind tellin' ye that if he knew his goodwife practiced witchcraft, he would have locked her in th' dungeon himself and left her there to starve."

Mariah shuddered as she considered the slow agonizing torture of such a sentence. Nonetheless, she ventured forward. "Still, wouldn't you have to agree, that of all the women in your fiefdom, Mairwen is the most likely person responsible for my dreams?"

"Mayhap some of them. But not all. Mairwen lost her life afore th' battle. How then, could she possibly know what took place on the field followin' our deaths, witness our burial, and then show those things to ye with such clarity?"

"Perhaps she witnessed it after she died and in her spiritual form. Maybe because of the way she met her death, she didn't choose to move on to her spiritual destination," she said. "Surely the possibility exists that just as your spirit traveled from Dupplin to the castle after the battle, she could accomplish the same feat going in the opposite direction. Maybe she wanted, even needed to see what Elspetha's deeds had wrought. I think once she did, she would feel compelled to take responsibility for the result."

"For what purpose?" he asked. "There is nothin' that can change th' outcome of what happened on th' battlefield. 'Tis all in th' past. Not Mairwen or any other spirit on this earth can take back what happened centuries ago."

"True, but what if she just wants you to know what happened and how and why it transpired? Perhaps her spirit can't rest until she completely unfolds all of the events that led to your deaths. Only then, can she seek

273

your understanding and forgiveness."

"If your ghost is Mairwen, she doesna need to seek my forgiveness, Murriah," he replied. "I dinnae lay th' blame at her or anyone else's feet for that matter."

"I know you don't, and I'm sure that whoever our ghost is, she must know it too. Nevertheless, she still might want to ask your pardon, anyway." And then, after just managing to suppress a grin, she added, "After all, she might think it's the *courteous* thing to do."

"Mayhap."

Several minutes later, while she drifted toward sleep, she whispered, "Cailen?"

"Aye?" he answered.

"I still think my ghost is Mairwen." He merely chuckled in response and leaned over to give her a wee kiss.

In truth, the same notion had plagued him for quite some time now. Especially when he cast his gaze on Mariah's sketch of the ghost in the oratory. The woman's form looked very similar to that of his sister's. Yet, he still found plenty of room for doubt. He and Mairwen were very close during their mortality. He had been her confidant, her protector, and advisor. 'Twas the trust his sister had in him that fed his uncertainty now. The Mairwen he knew in mortality would not feel the need to stay hidden from his view, regardless of perceived guilt. More likely, she would have awaited his death on the battlefield and begged his pardon the moment his spirit left his body.

"Cailen?" called Duncan from the great hall. "Dugald and some of his men have come seekin' a bit of respite, and th' hospitality of our hall."

The announcement didn't surprise him, for such had happened countless times before. His eyes swept over Mariah's sleeping form, looking for any telltale signs of discomfort. She slept peacefully enough. Should she cry out in fear, he would hear the smallest whimper, for he had now attuned himself to her soul. After placing a gentle kiss against her cheek, he disappeared from the room and entered the hall.

Dugald sat at the table appearing quite miserable as he clutched his half-downed tankard of ale. Cailen chuckled as he approached him. "Trouble with th' lassies again?" he asked as he placed a hand on his shoulder and gave it a consoling pat.

"Bunch of ill-nurtured, folly-fallen harpies...th' lot of them," Dugald snarled. "I would give them all th' boot if I thought they'd go somewhere else. But, sadly, they would just turn their prickly talons onto me instead of each other. So, if ye dinnae mind, me and my men will just hide out here for a while."

"Nay, we dinnae mind," Cailen replied as he settled himself on the bench just opposite his friend.

"Who started it this time? Beth or Cecilia?" asked Duncan.

"I dinnae know and truly, I dinnae care," Dugald said. "I don't have any interest in th' petty squabbles of th' women folk nor do I want to take up sides. Just be grateful that ye dinnae have to put up with such around here."

"Amen to that!" said several voices at once. Following the outburst, they each raised their tankards to the toast.

"And ye can also be thankful that neither of th' lassies has a twin residin' at your castle!" bellowed

Steven.

"Hear, hear!" the voices rang out yet again.

"Och, such would be th' death of me, yet again, I'm afraid," said Dugald before he downed the contents of his mug.

As the evening wore on, the toasts grew ever more fanciful, shouted out more often, and the boisterous laughter rose ever louder. Yet, thus far, nothing disturbed Mariah's peaceful slumber.

****

At length, a clamor downstairs called Mariah to awareness. She turned her face in the direction of the doorway, hugged the pillow to her cheek, and slowly opened her eyes to make sense of the commotion. In the same instant, two things bolted into her mind with absolute certainty. One—Cailen no longer occupied the space next to her and two—her redheaded ghost stood against the wall, next to the door. This time, however, she could see her lovely face with absolute clarity.

Mariah inched her body upward into a seated position as she maintained eye contact with her visitor.

"Mairwen?" she whispered.

In response, the presence curved one side of her lip into the slightest smile, but said nothing in return. What did that mean? Did she have her identity right or did she not?

"Please don't go," Mariah barely whispered as she extended her hand. Yet even as she made the request, she received the distinct impression the ghost didn't intend to leave this time. "You've got to help me understand all of this, please—"

As the woman approached, Mariah's heartbeat accelerated. Her heart thumped so loudly that surely, every ghost in the Highlands could hear it. The ethereal being settled herself next to her on the edge of the bed and took hold of her extended hand. The instant they made contact with each other, images flooded into her mind.

No, not images.

She saw more than mere pictures—she witnessed a *memory* as it unfolded. And the moment she understood that, she and the ghost became as one person inside the memory, sharing the same thoughts and feelings. In every way possible, she lived the memory as if she experienced it firsthand.

The midnight hour approached. Ten women accompanied her steps through the small opening next to the riverbank. They followed her into the passageways under the castle and into the innermost hollow of an ancient cave. She carried the only torch to light the path along the damp and rocky terrain. Their mission held the deepest sense of urgency, and she prayed they didn't come too late. For soon, their beloved husbands, sweethearts, sons, and brothers, would face Balliol's army. An army strengthened by the aid of the detested English king, Edward the Third.

Death had already claimed so many of their men in battles both won and lost. She couldn't bear to lose any more, not if she could help by using powers better left alone. But desperate situations called for desperate measures. Therefore, she and some of her more willing companions had secretly called upon Elspetha.

The potent stench of stagnant water filled her nostrils as they rounded the final turn. She could now hear the sound of the constant drips of water that splashed into the small murky pool at the end of the cave. So focused on her destination and purpose, she didn't notice the meager bundle of rare betony herbs, falling away from the lefthand pouch she carried. Or see the ten sets of footsteps that trampled over and mashed them beneath their feet.

Mariah let out a gasp as the hideous embodiment of her dreams and sketches glanced up from her simmering cauldron while the women entered the chamber single file. The witch stood to her feet and stepped back to allow them entrance. Her heart skipped a beat as she approached the old crone. She secured her torch between two large rocks, and then handed the woman the bag she carried over her right shoulder.

"Th' fruit and leaves of th' coriander with th' leaves and flowers of th' coltsfoot," she said by way of explanation.

"Th' guelder rose bark?" asked Elspetha as she raised a gnarly brow.

"Right here, along with th' seeds of th' golden gorse," she replied. She scooped her hand into the folds of her sash and placed the herbs in Elspetha's outstretched hand. Then, she gave the woman the second pouch, which hung over her left shoulder. "This one has th' root of th' burdock and th' betony, along with th' basil, just as ye have asked."

"Good." The witch nodded. "And ye have made sure that each man has a sprig of woodruff sewn into th' sleeve of his léine?"

"Aye, each man wears it now."

"Then gather in a circle around th' fire, and hold hands," Elspetha instructed.

Mariah exchanged surreptitious glances with each of her companions as they took their first good look at their surroundings. Elspetha's cauldron, encircled by smooth round stones hung on an iron brace over the fire. To the left, the witch had built a makeshift altar that housed a dagger, a goblet, a stack of long willow shoots and a few leather strips. She could see that everything Elspetha needed to complete the complex spell now rested inside this cave. A shiver coursed through her body in response to the gravity of their errand.

Once they did as she asked, Elspetha turned to face the fire. The old woman paused for several moments, closed her eyes, and mumbled something in a language she didn't understand. Nonetheless, it caused a shiver to race down her spine.

The witch turned to face them. "Afore we begin, ye must forever swear a vow of silence as to the ritual I'm aboot to perform, ye so swear?"

Eleven voices in perfect unison replied, "Aye, we so swear."

Elspetha tossed the guelder rose bark into the fire, and extended her arms toward the heavens. "Th' mighty power of water and earth, and th' wind that fans the flame. We entreat thy presence here tonight, for a blessing we seek in thy name."

The women gaped in silent wonder as blue flames blasted upward. They shot through the large crack in the high domed ceiling in response to the witch's words. The flames belched red and yellow embers as they spiraled downward. Elspetha closed her eyes and took in a deep breath of smoke before she added the golden gorse to the blaze. Once again, the fire shot upward, this time in flaming hues of purple and green. At that very moment, an unholy wail erupted forth from the fire. An unnamed dread caused Mariah, and each of the women within the circle, to shudder. They gripped each other's hands all the tighter. Despite their fear, they remained silent and still.

"Through earth and fire, bind our men, bind them together as one. Keep them ever in thy presence, that no man be left alone." Elspetha poured the herbs from the right bag into the cauldron, stirred, and inhaled deeply of the fragrance.

Once she seemed satisfied with the scent of the potion, the old hag retrieved the remaining pouch, spilled the contents into the cauldron, and stirred. Once again, the eerie moan accompanied a burst of flame. "By th' almighty power of water and wind, encircle each soul in thy care," she said. Then as she bent over the pot and breathed deeply of the scent, she paused, and inhaled again. Elspetha drew her brows tight together and fixed her piercing gaze upon hers.

"Ye brought everythin' I requested and in proper amounts?" asked Elspetha

Mariah gulped. "Aye, I made sure."

Elspetha shook her head slightly and took another whiff of the brew. She picked up each bag and peeked inside them to ensure she emptied all the contents. Then she followed another whiff by a slight shrug of her shoulders.

Despite her obvious misgivings, she moved forward. "Upon the field of battle, seek each heart by the woodruff they wear."

Elspetha leaned to the right of the cauldron and retrieved an armful of tender willow shoots along with the leather strips that rested atop the altar. She dipped the leather into the cauldron four times, one for each element, and then tied them in a knot around the willow. To the left of the seething brew, she picked up a dagger, dipped it into the pot, and then sliced it across the palm of her hand. She dripped the oozing blood across the willow, and then passed both bundle and knife to her, so she could do the same.

Each of the women followed her example. Once the bundle completed the circle, Elspetha dunked the bloodied dagger into the pot once more and stirred four times, counterclockwise. She then gazed into each of their bewildered faces. "For th' time being, our life's blood ties us to th' ritual, as well as to our men. Such is necessary."

She then hid away the willow into a cavity of the northern cave wall. Afterward, she retrieved the goblet, filled it with the potion brewing inside the cauldron, and took a sip. The witch then handed the goblet to her. She lifted the cup to her lips and then passed it to the woman on her left, who passed it to the woman on her left. Each woman in the circle followed this same pattern. Finally, the metal container found its way back to Elspetha's waiting hands.

Elspetha set the goblet on the altar, retrieved her torch, and nodded. "'Tis finished for now. Off to your beds afore you're missed. Once th' battle is over, I'll come back, and leave a gift of gratitude. This will complete and secure th' spell."

As each of the women filtered out of the chamber with Elspetha at the lead, Mairwen stood firm.

"If ye dinnae mind, I'll stay behind for a wee moment," she said.

Elspeth stared hard at her for several seconds and then bobbed her head. "Dinnae stay long and dinnae disturb anythin'," she warned.

"I won't, I swear," she replied. Once the others vacated the cavern, she sat down and gazed upon the fire until only embers remained beneath the cauldron. Mariah didn't really know why she stayed behind or what she hoped to see in her solitude. Yet, nothing manifested itself, nor did she receive any comfort or assurance that what they did here tonight even mattered. She released a slow sigh, grabbed the remaining torch, and abandoned her rock. At once, the action made her feel dizzy, nauseated, and drained of all natural strength. Her hand pressed against a brow as she sought to steady her feet.

She turned her gaze to the ground and made her way to the entrance. All the while, her nausea increased. So did the pounding in her head. And then as she kicked one of the larger rocks out of her pathway, her heart sank deep into her chest and landed with a sickening thud. Surely, it couldn't be, her mind begged. She stared at the ruined remnants strewn about the ground. "Please, anythin' but this—" she whispered aloud.

She stooped down to get a closer look, for she had to know one way or the other. Her fingers trembled as she gathered the thin ragged pieces of twine with which she had bound the betony. She squeezed her eyes shut as she pressed the braided thread to her lips. Despair overtook her soul. The precious herb needed to provide a protective barrier around the knights of her fiefdom, never made it inside the cauldron. She rose to her feet—she had to get to Elspetha. They needed to do the ritual again. Elspetha could gather the women while she sought more betony. She knew just where to find it now. Traversing the passageway grew ever more difficult. Her skin now burned and the nausea rose to her throat.

Then just as she made the turn, she saw the lifeless bodies of all her companions scattered about the dank corridor. Her hands flew to her mouth to stifle her cry. She turned in each direction, seeking the reason for the malady. Elspetha stepped from the shadows then, wagged her head back and forth, and calmly met her gaze. A smug, evil little smile pulled at the corners of her mouth.

Disbelief engulfed her, and despite the intensity of the pain that now ravaged her body, she used the last of her life's breath to ask one question.

"Why did ye do it, Elspetha? Why?"

Elspetha cackled gleefully in return as suffocating blackness overtook her senses.

The memory drained Mariah of all strength, but no more so than her ghostly companion. The lovely woman placed a hand to her chest. She shot her an apologetic look as both head and shoulders slumped forward. An instant later, her form faded away like mist in the breeze.

Mariah had no idea had long she sat there staring at nothing, before she finally retrieved her sketchbook. While she recorded the faces and images pertaining to the memory, she could hear the knights downstairs in the hall. From the sheer volume alone, it appeared they had company. She had no desire to intrude on their social gathering or speak to anyone other than Cailen. Once she completed her sketches, she lay back against her pillows and closed her eyes. Her unsettled thoughts took her in a thousand different directions, for the shared memory produced far more questions than it provided answers.

****

Sometime later, Cailen's gentle caress awakened her. The late morning sun streamed through her window. She took in a deep breath and slowly released it. "Cailen."

"Good morn, my lady," he said as he sat down next to her on the bed. His eyes then fell upon the sketchbook she clutched in her hand. He took possession of it. "What's this? Did ye draw again in your sleep?"

"No."

Various emotions accompanied his perusal of the sketches. Among them, she detected consternation and anguish. Finally, he turned back the pages to the first sketch pertaining to the memory Mairwen shared and held it aloft for her inspection.

"Your ghost?" he asked in a low voice.

She nodded. "Yes—she visited me last night while you were down in the hall."

"I see." He paused. "Did she speak to ye this time?"

"No."

"Ye dinnae know her name?"

She shook her head. "Not for certain."

Pain marred his features. "'Tis Mairwen."

She closed her eyes and released a breath. "I thought so. She shared a memory with me."

"Would ye care to share this memory with me, as well?" he asked.

The tone in Cailen's voice reflected his anguish. She could tell his sister's refusal to reveal herself throughout the centuries following their deaths both hurt and bewildered him. She hoped the explanation she might offer would give him the comfort he sorely needed. "I'll tell you all about it while we explore the left side of that passageway," she replied as she rose from the bed. "I think you'll find it's pertinent."

Chapter 22

The penciled faces of the ten women in Mariah's sketchbook matched the names of the dead found inside the passageway. Now that she had also completed the face of her banshee, Cailen didn't find it at all difficult to see Elspetha behind the shadows of the cloak. He berated himself for not seeing it earlier, for it seemed so obvious now. The difficulty occurred in finding understanding to all this insanity concerning death, witchcraft, and his sister's inexplicable behavior over the centuries that followed. But why did Mairwen's visit with Mariah elude his notice, for surely Mariah spoke to her. Yet, he'd heard nothing.

"Are you ready?" asked Mariah once she retrieved and checked the batteries of her flashlight.

Cailen placed the sketchbook on her desk and nodded. "Aye."

"If you don't mind, I think it'll be easier for me to get to the passageway from the riverbank," she said.

"I dinnae mind, Murriah." He took hold of the hand she offered him as they descended the stairs together. "I take it th' memory Mairwen shared with ye has somethin' to do with what happened in th' passageway, and that's why we're goin' down there?"

"Yes, it does," she replied. "But I don't need the tunnel to tell you what happened inside it, Cailen. We're going down there because I have this burning need to see the cavern for myself."

"Why?" he asked.

"I want to see if everything is as Mairwen left it, or if your father or someone else in the fiefdom discovered it and then emptied it of its contents."

"Why do ye say as Mairwen left it?" he asked.

"The night the event took place, Mairwen remained behind after everyone else vacated the chamber," she replied. "According to Edgar's account, Elspetha wouldn't have had the opportunity to revisit the place herself at a later date, so unless someone in the fiefdom found it, remnants of everything I witnessed within the memory should still be there."

He shrugged away the notion. "Would it make any difference if someone emptied it out after their deaths?"

"I don't know—maybe." She fell silent while they journeyed away from the castle and toward the river. He didn't wish to disturb her thoughts. Once they approached the small opening, she turned on her torch. "Mairwen began her memory from here. She led her friends through the fissure. All along the way, I never once heard anyone speak. I could only hear the sound of their footsteps."

He followed her into the cave. Even though she seemed sure of her path, he wouldn't break her concentration by asking questions. The answers he sought could all come later. Without warning, she halted her steps and aimed the flashlight upon the walls. After she swept the light in a complete circle around the area, she pointed the beam of light onto the ground.

"Mairwen didn't realize it on the way inside, but the betony she collected fell out of her pouch, right here," she said. "The women trampled over it, crushing the petals beyond all recognition. I don't see any remaining evidence of that now, though. Of course, I didn't really think I would after the passing of so many centuries."

"How did she come to know aboot th' lost betony?" he asked.

"On her way back out she saw the twine she wrapped it with here on the ground. She stooped down, picked it up, and looked at it to make sure."

"What happened to them, Murriah?" he asked. "How did they come to die?"

"I'm not sure, but I think Elspetha poisoned them," she said. "Come on, our destination is not much farther. Once we get there, I'll share all of the details as I saw them. Hopefully, I won't leave anything out."

The sound of dripping water grew ever louder, and when they made the final turn he could see a stagnant pool at the center of the chamber. He could only imagine the foul stench Mariah now endured as she set about exploring the area. The cavern contained an old rusted cauldron attached to a corroded metal brace. Evidence of an ancient fire lay beneath it. A crude altar sat to the left. The altar held a putrid pewter cup and a rusty dagger.

"'Tis one thing to hear aboot it, and quite another to actually see th' evidence of it," he said, pointing to the artifacts. "Th' use of witchcraft, I mean."

"And unlike those who use the craft to benefit others, Elspetha unleased the darkest form of magic to suit her malicious purposes."

Mariah rubbed an arm to ward off the chill. She turned her gaze upon the large rock off to the right of the cauldron, made her way to it, and sat down. She took a deep breath and slowly released it as her gaze wandered about the chamber.

"I could feel Mairwen's desperation as if it were my own," she said. "Without her showing me the actual images, I somehow knew she spent hours praying inside the chapel before she escorted her friends down here. Not only did she pray for the safety of you and your knights, she also sought forgiveness for turning to Elspetha's dark craft.

"You have to understand that she couldn't bear the sorrow of even one more death, for she loved you all so much. She truly thought Elspetha's expertise in the ancient ways, could prevent it, for such was her claim. The old woman convinced her that she used only white magic, and the things the witch asked her to collect seemed harmless enough. No one had to offer or give their soul in return—"

"Only their lives," Cailen whispered.

"Such a thing never entered her mind," she replied. "She trusted Elspetha and had no reason to doubt her sincere offer to use her magic to protect you and the knights."

"Why has she never come to me with this, Murriah?" he asked. "I'm her brother. She shouldn't fear to speak with me."

She shook her head and extended her hand. He took the offered hand and sat down next to her. She gazed into his eyes. "She doesn't fear you. I believe she would give anything if she could appear before you right now and tell you all of this herself. The problem is—I don't think she can."

The comment took him by surprise. "What do ye mean?"

"Elspetha made them swear a vow of silence before the ritual even began. I think the power of the spell binds them to that promise. It's the only reasonable explanation for her lack of personal contact. Just think about it for a moment. None of the children sheltered here during the war ever heard the women speak. I have never heard Mairwen speak. However, *nothing* in the spell prevents her from showing me her memories."

"By that reasonin' she could show her memories to me as well," he said.

"I thought about that too, but you told me that most of the time, a spirit speaks to another spirit through thought, isn't that right?" she asked.

"Aye."

"Then surely the power of the spell would prohibit this type of communication as well. What I know about magic you could put in a thimble, but perhaps the power of the spell will not allow these women to have any kind of contact with you or the knights because of this spiritual ability," she said. "Elspetha's magic connected the women to you. Therefore, you're all part of the same curse. Maybe this is why others can see the women while you cannot."

He returned a slow nod. "I suppose ye might have a valid point and for now, I'll accept that as fact. So, ye said that Elspetha swore them all to silence. Then what happened?"

"The witch babbled some kind of incantation—she used a dialect I have never heard before and I somehow knew that Mairwen didn't either. I wondered at the time if the words came from an ancient language long forgotten," Mariah said.

"'Tis quite possible for a dark witch," he said.

"The truly frightening thing about that is we have no idea what hideous things she might've said." Mariah tilted her head to the side and shrugged. "She used the bark of the guelder rose first, not by adding it to her cauldron, but by throwing in onto the flames. After that, she summoned the power of the elements and from what I saw—I truly believe they, or some sort of entity connected to them, accepted her invitation. Once these spirits made their presence known, she added the golden gorse to the fire. In so doing, an eerie, malevolent wail burst forth from the blaze itself." She shuddered as she called the scene to mind. In response, Cailen held her hand a little tighter but said nothing in return.

"Then she added the fruit and leaves from the coriander and the leaves and flowers from the coltsfoot to the cauldron. She did so to bind you and your men ever together as one unit. I thought about our trip to Edinburgh then and the boundary you couldn't pass. Surely that part of the spell is the cause."

"That would seem logical," Cailen said. "For none of us can pass the moor even though each of us have tried, as well ye know."

Mariah nodded. "After she stirred her pot for a time, she added the contents from the second bag. Mairwen told her that it had the basil, burdock, and betony. At that time, she didn't know the betony fell out of her pouch. Elspetha then asked the rulers of water and wind to encircle your souls, keeping them in their care. She further stated that these entities could discern you by the woodruff you wore in your sleeves. You know, the word ever seems so significant now, but I don't think Mairwen gave it a second thought when Elspetha uttered it."

"Nay, she probably didna."

"Anyway, Elspetha sensed something amiss when she inhaled her potion. She asked Mairwen if she collected everything she requested in the proper amounts, and your sister said she did. That seemed to pacify her and so she continued. She picked up a stack of willow shoots from the altar and bound them with leather strips. After she had them tied together, she picked up that dagger right there, sliced it across the palm of her hand, and let the blood drip onto the willow. She required each of the women to do the same. When the bundle completed the circle, Elspetha put it in the crevice over there," she said, pointing toward it.

Mariah stood up then and walked over to the northern wall. She bent down and peeked inside the limestone crevice. "Look, Cailen, the bundle is still in there."

"Dinnae touch it, Murriah," Cailen warned. "Just leave it alone. Ye dinnae know what evil might still be attached to it."

Heeding his advice, Mariah turned away from the wall to face him. "Elspetha told the women that their blood not only tied them to the ritual, it also tied them to you."

"Ye think th' spirits Elspeth conjured prevented us from seein' and enterin' th' light ye told me aboot?"

"Yes, at this point I do," she replied. "I believe those entities took possession of your souls the moment your mortal life ended on that battlefield."

He paused for a moment to consider the whole of it. "I suppose 'tis verra possible given the evil curse

Elspetha uttered. Then what happened?"

"Well, as disgusting as it sounds, she dipped the bloody dagger into the pot. She picked up that cup, filled it with her potion, and drank from it, or so it appeared. Each of the women did the same."

"Ye think this is when th' witch poisoned them?" he asked.

She nodded as she returned to his side. "Yes, I do. Elspetha could've simply pretended to drink the potion before she passed it on, or perhaps her brew didn't have the same effect on her. Once the cup made the circle, Elspetha placed it right where you see it now and said that after the battle, she'd come back and leave a gift of gratitude to secure the spell she conjured."

"Which she couldn't do," he said.

"No, she couldn't, could she," Mariah replied. "I wonder if that made any difference."

"It doesna appear that it did," he said. "We're still here and apparently still bound by the forces she invited to th' castle."

She let go of a sigh as she fixed her gaze to his. "Elspetha ushered everyone out except for Mairwen. Your sister asked if she could remain behind for a while."

"Why did she do that?"

"She just wanted to be alone with her thoughts. Mairwen agonized over whether or not she did the right thing. Then, once she stood up, sickness assaulted her. The farther she walked the more ill she became. She finally happened upon the remnants of the betony, which made her panic. Mairwen believed it necessary to redo the spell. Yet, as she hurried after Elspetha to confess the omission, she stumbled across the bodies of all her friends. Confusion set in until Elspetha stepped out from the shadows. Right before she died she questioned the old woman's betrayal. The last thing your sister heard in mortality was Elspetha's triumphant laughter."

At the end of her tale, Mariah lifted both brows in concert with her shoulders. "After she showed me her death, the memory ended. I felt drained of all energy after the experience, and I believe it had the same effect on Mairwen. She looked very weak before she faded away and I believe she apologized for it."

Cailen nodded, "Aye, such an experience could weaken her. Showin' ye a full memory like she did would take most all her energy. Especially if she never tried to attain th' full abilities she's capable of attainin'."

"What happens when a spirit uses all his or her energy?" she asked.

"Best way to explain it is to say we are just left to ourselves until we regain our strength. At such a time we dinnae see or hear anyone in th' vicinity," he said.

"How long does it take for you to regain your strength?" she asked.

"I dinnae rightly know, for we pay no mind to th' passin' of time," he replied. "Awhile. Why do ye ask?"

"I'd really like to see her again—if she'll comply. I have so many questions I'd like to ask her," she said. "*If* she can find a way to answer them, that is."

"What questions do ye have?"

"Showing me this memory can't be all there is to this puzzle. I truly feel that Mairwen wants me to do something with all of this information."

"Like what? Ye cannae change anythin' that

happened centuries ago, Murriah. I see naught that ye can do other than tell us what happened so that Mairwen can find her rest. Ye have done that. She has our forgiveness if this is what she needs to forgive herself."

"No, there's more to it," she said. "There just has to be. I can feel it."

Cailen shrugged, rose to his feet, and claimed her hand. "If there is, I'm sure we'll discover it in th' days to come. Now, let's quit this place afore the noxious smells overcome ye."

Just as they rounded the fields to the front of the castle, he spied a car just outside the gates. The driver switched off the engine. Mariah drew in a short breath as Gordon Humphries and his companion exited the car moments later.

"Oh! I completely forgot they were coming today," she said. "I guess it's a good thing you dragged me out of there when you did."

"What are they doin' here?" he asked.

"Making the rounds, checking everyone's progress," she said as she smiled at her visitor and returned his wave. "Time is growing short and I think panic is setting in."

"Hullo, Mariah!" Gordon called from the other side of the fence.

"How are you this morning?" she asked as she approached and opened the gate.

"Just fine, thank you for asking," he replied. "What aboot yourself?"

"I'm doing just fine."

"Have you met my assistant, Blaine Larsen?" he asked.

"No, I haven't," she turned to face him and smiled. "Hello, Mr. Larsen."

"Blaine, this is Mariah Jennings—"

The man offered his hand as he dipped his head. "Miss Jennings."

"Blaine is going to take some photos of your unfinished work if you dinnae mind," said Gordon.

"Not at all," she said. "Follow me."

Once they entered the castle and climbed the stairs, Mariah ushered her guests into her studio. Humphries and his companion exchanged broad smiles as they gazed at the paintings.

"Well done, Mariah. Well done." Gordon took in a deep breath and as he released it, he shook his head and tsked. "Th' paintings are exceptionally beautiful. I truly admire each of th' scenes you've chosen and because of that I'm not sure which ones to select."

"Which ones to select?" she repeated. "I'm afraid you've lost me."

"For th' upcoming photo shoot to promote th' project," he said. "This is one of th' reasons I wanted to make this visit and get th' photographs. Ryan Maitland has put together an advertising campaign. We'll start off with an article in th' newspaper, complete with pictures. Then when we get closer to th' grand opening, he'll purchase television spots throughout th' United Kingdom. In light of this fact, we'll require your presence in Edinburgh for a couple of days, beginning Tuesday next at ten in th' morning, if that is satisfactory."

A wave of dismay settled into Cailen's soul over the unexpected revelation. He exchanged a quick glance with Mariah. She didn't appear happy about the prospect either.

"Of course, but why do you need me?" she asked.

"We want to take photos of each artist alongside a few of their paintings. That's what I meant when I said it would be difficult to choose which of your paintings to use." He shook his head and sighed as he continued to study her canvases.

"Well, these are in no way finished, and it's impossible to have any of them done by next Tuesday," she said.

"Och, dinnae worry aboot that," he said. "Ryan said it would be quite acceptable, perhaps even preferable to see one or two of th' paintings in progress. He thinks an unfinished product might whet th' appetite of th' public even more than a finished one."

"Oh—I see."

Gordon chuckled and put a friendly hand on her shoulder. "You dinnae need to look so worried. I can promise you that should I select one of these, they will suffer no damage during th' journey to Edinburgh and back."

"When do you think you might decide? I'm only asking because if you choose one of these, I won't put any more fresh paint on them until after you have them photographed," she said.

"I have two days to submit my selections to Ryan. However, I'll let you know th' moment I make my decision."

"I'm afraid it's your own fault for doing such phenomenal work," Blaine said good-naturedly as he raised his camera to his eye. "You have some amazing portraits, both here and in th' vault in London. I'm sure I wouldn't know which ones to choose either."

Mariah dipped her head and said, "Thank you, you're both very kind."

Twenty minutes later, she bid her guests goodbye and secured the gates. Cailen's feeling of relief echoed hers.

"Well, let's hope they choose from the paintings they already have," she said as she met his gaze. "I really don't like the idea of the ones upstairs being jostled around before they're finished."

"Mayhap he'll come to see th' folly of that decision, and use that which he already has in his possession," he replied as they made their way back to the castle. "'Tis like he said, each paintin' is a tremendous work of art in its own right. He doesna need to use those ye have not completed."

"Either way, I still have to make another trip to Edinburgh."

"Aye, and it grieves me that I cannae go with ye," he said.

She presented him a smile. "Why does it grieve you?"

"For one, I dinnae like th' separation away from ye, and two, I dinnae like th' way Blaine Larsen ogled ye."

She laughed. "He didn't 'ogle' me."

Cailen slowly nodded as he cupped her face and just before he kissed her, he whispered, "Aye, my lady, ye can take my word for it, he ogled ye."

Chapter 23

"I wonder if I can find a subtle way to get Evan to answer some of my questions regarding the darker side of magic," Mariah mused as she lifted Tatters off the lid of her suitcase and onto the floor. She watched her scurry into the hall as she packed away the last of her things for the trip to Edinburgh. "Perhaps on my way home I could stop off at the pub and lead a conversation in that direction."

"Nay, Murriah," Cailen said. "We cannae trust Evan right now, especially not with somethin' like this."

"Well I certainly wouldn't reveal anything pertaining to Mairwen or you and the knights. I thought I could just ask some general questions—questions born of curiosity—nothing more." She closed her bag, zipped it shut, and turned to face him.

"Ye cannae forget what he tried to do to ye with his iniquitous magic. And ye need to remember that Elspetha is his ancestral grandmother. Her tainted blood flows through his veins. From what I can see, th' man inherited her disposition and attitude of inflictin' their will upon others. I dinnae think it wise to bring th' subject up, subtle or not, for I can assure ye Evan isn't stupid. He'll know there is more to your questions than what you're revealin'. Besides, it would bring me a great deal of pleasure if he didna come anywhere near ye ever again—for any reason."

"I forgot about his relationship to Elspetha," she said. "All right, I guess we'll just have to wait around for Mairwen to show herself and give me the next step."

"Ye might have to accept th' fact that she has nothin' left to tell ye and will not come back," he replied.

"No, there's more to all of this," she insisted.

Humor filled his eyes. "What makes ye so sure?"

"If she only wanted you to know what happened down in the cavern, she would've shared her memory the first time I saw her in my bedroom and left it at that. She wouldn't have provided all of the dreams, the sketches, and this feeling of unrest that refuses to leave. I don't think she would've withheld her identity as long as she did either. There's more, Cailen, much more. I just have to figure out what it is." Mariah shrugged and took hold of her bag. "And, I'll have plenty of time alone to do that over the next couple of days."

Cailen took the bag from her hand as they turned toward the doorway. "I wish ye didna have to go."

"No more so, than I. Surely you know I would give just about anything if I could skip the publicity part of this assignment altogether. Unfortunately, it's part of my contract."

"At least Humphries didna take your artwork from here," he replied as they descended the stairs. "That's one less thing for ye to worry aboot."

Mariah nodded in agreement. It pleased her that along with the primary portrait of her first English castle and a scene from one of the Welsh castles, Gordon had selected Cailen's accolade, admittedly, her personal favorite. But then again, she happened to love the subject of that painting, more than life itself.

Once they arrived at her car door, she turned to face him and gave him a half-hearted smile. "Well—I guess I'll see you in a few days, although I don't know exactly what time I'll return. I will, however, come home as quickly as I can."

Cailen shook his head very slightly as he drew her body close to his chest. He didn't say a word in return. He simply claimed her lips in a series of kisses that told her of his reluctance to part with her, and just how much he'd miss her. Surely, her responses conveyed the same message. Finally, she pulled back and took a much-needed breath. "Much more of this, and I'm afraid I won't go at all, contract or no contract."

"Do ye so swear?" he whispered before he kissed her witless yet again.

Ah, if only she could—

Nonetheless, Cailen's stirring kisses, and the huskily spoken "I luv ye" in his ancient Scottish brogue, made for good company all the way to Edinburgh. The man had her heart so firmly in his grasp that she wouldn't rest until she discovered a way for them to stay together—for surely a way existed.

She thought of little else during the intensive, twelve-hour photo shoot they required all the artists to endure. When the time arrived to put her in front of the camera, they demanded a perky smile so often her muscles ached from the effort.

At last, all parties seemed satisfied with the finished product for the newspaper advertisement and forthcoming commercials. The director called it a wrap. They all laughed when their collective sighs of relief echoed throughout the room. Gordon Humphries insisted on taking all of them to dinner then, to celebrate a job well done. Somehow, she managed to withhold a discouraged groan. For she wanted nothing more than to go back to her hotel room, get some sleep, rise early, and go home.

At the restaurant, they seated her next to a lovely middle-aged Scottish native, named Lorna. The women entertained her with her amiable chatter. As the dinner meandered to dessert, the woman took hold of the chain around her neck and played with the pendant while she spoke. The exquisite jeweled pentagram not only captured her attention for its beauty, but also for its underlying meaning. Curiosity got the better of her.

"That's a gorgeous pendant," she said. "Do you mind if I ask of its personal significance to you?"

Lorna looked down at the piece and smiled. "Th' pendant is part of who I am. I'm Wiccan, Mariah."

Her mouth dropped. "Are you really?" Cailen's "fates" or perhaps even Mairwen must've had a hand in this meeting. She wouldn't waste the opportunity.

"Yes." The woman tilted her head to the side and scrutinized every inch of her face. "Does th' revelation disturb you?"

"The practice of benevolent white magic? Not at all," she replied. "It's my understanding that you use your craft for the good you can accomplish with it."

"'Tis nice to find someone that understands that outside our circle," she said. "Most of th' time we keep our religion to ourselves, but for some reason, I didn't have a problem blurting it out just now. I suppose you must have made me feel comfortable in speaking to you aboot it."

"I'm really glad to hear that because I have a few burning questions if you don't mind answering them," Mariah said.

"Ask away," Lorna replied as their waiter placed their apple butterscotch pie à la mode in front of them.

"Well, for starters, how long have you personally been involved with Wicca?" she asked.

Lorna laughed over the question. "My whole life, lovey. You see, I come from a long line of witches, dating back centuries."

"Really? I find that so fascinating."

She picked up her fork and nodded. "Most do when they find out aboot it."

"Well, since I first learned of the Wicca, I've often wondered how long it takes one to learn the spells and incantations and to do them properly."

"A considerable amount of time for most," she said after she swallowed the first bite of her pie. "Th' art takes a great deal of patience and discipline. That's th' thing that annoys us most, I think. So many young teenagers out there think th' craft is a lark. They find a few books, read a few pages, and think they can conquer th' world with their newfound knowledge. I can tell you it doesn't work like that. Th' dabblers out there can cause a lot of mischief for those of us who take our beliefs seriously. They give us all a bad name."

"Speaking of those kids," she said, "what happens if they conjure up a spell and say—inadvertently leave a key ingredient out of their potions or say the wrong thing?"

"Then th' spell must be done again, of course," she replied. "One simply cannot leave a spell in disarray."

"What if they didn't realize their mistake and

therefore, never returned to set it right?" asked Mariah.

"Then th' purpose of their spell just remains in a state of limbo, for lack of a better term. Do you see what I mean by th' dabblers giving us a bad name? So much can go wrong if you dinnae ken what you're doing."

"Yes, I can appreciate that," she said as her thoughts raced to Cailen and the knights. Did the improper spell put him and his men in some kind of limbo? Would that explain the oddity of their death experience and current spiritual existence?

"Why are you asking these questions, lovey?" asked Lorna as she probed deeply into her eyes. "Have you perchance meddled yourself and made a mistake? 'Tis all right if you have, I can help."

Mariah laughed as she waved a hand in dismissal. "Oh, heavens no. Trust me. I wouldn't have the heart to attempt something I know so little about. No, it's just that I've wondered about these things after hearing so many contrary reports regarding your ideology. I have heard stories of these young teenagers turning good magic into something entirely different and causing all sorts of havoc because of it. Magazine articles and newspapers have reported the sacrifice of innocent animals and all for the sake of evil charms and spells they're attempting to produce."

Lorna shuddered over the comment. "Th' parents of those kids ought to take a switch to their unruly offspring, for such is not th' way of a true Wiccan. Oftentimes when we hear of such things we try to quietly undue their mayhem afore it leaks out to public knowledge and serve us up another black eye. Sadly, we cannot reclaim th' sacrificed animal."

"I didn't know you could undo a spell," Mariah said as she sat a little more forward in her chair and tossed her napkin on her plate.

"There are times a spell can be reversed or at th' very least repaired," she said with a casual shrug of her shoulders. "We do what we can, when we can."

"Well, that's good to know," Mariah answered.

Lorna began asking questions of her own then, leaving the subject of magic behind. She seemed more interested in learning where she studied, under whom—and of course, the inevitable questions about her country. Still the woman provided her with much to think about. She wondered what would happen if they could reverse the magic enchantment to which Cailen and his knights were bound. Would they be free then, of the boundaries that imprisoned them? If so, Cailen could go with her anywhere he pleased, couldn't he?

All throughout the night, she toyed with the idea of calling Lorna and telling her about Elspetha and the spell she witnessed through Mairwen. Yet, she just couldn't reveal Cailen's presence and situation without his knowledge or consent. Despite the difficulty of waiting, she wouldn't proceed with that notion until she discussed it with him first.

****

Cailen settled down on the same rock he and Mariah shared when they first explored this cavern together. He looked about the chamber and envisioned the events in the order she related them. In truth, he found the task most difficult. To his recollection, Mairwen had remained more faithful and devoted to her Christian faith than any other person he knew. He just couldn't imagine her turning to the use of magic, even in desperation. But she did. And not only did she willingly participate, she instigated the intrigue amongst her friends. The proof of that lay before him. Nevertheless, the question remained. What did Mairwen want them to do with this information now, if anything at all?

Mariah did have a valid point. Why all the sketches and dreams if his sister only wanted him to know the circumstances surrounding their deaths. Could he harbor any hope at all that Mairwen perceived his love for Mariah and could assist his quest to remain forever at her side? Perhaps in this way she sought to give penance for her deed, even though he truly didn't require such penance. His sister had only the best intentions when she approached Elspetha and for that, she had his gratitude.

"What are ye doin' down here again?" asked Duncan as he appeared standing just next to the cauldron.

Cailen shook his head. "Just tryin' to find some understandin' and mayhap a few answers."

"I dinnae think ye'll discover a thing in this place." He picked up the dagger. Disgust filled his eyes as he studied the blade for a moment before dropping the weapon where he found it. "Whatever secrets Elspetha had, she carried them with her to th' grave."

"Murriah seems to think Mairwen has more to offer," he said.

Duncan let loose a snort and shook his head. "I cannae imagine what that would be. 'Tis not like anythin' can change what has already happened."

"Nay," he replied. "But mayhap somethin' could be done which might improve our current circumstances."

"What would give ye that impression?" asked Duncan.

"Th' fact that Murriah cannae leave th' situation alone. She feels certain Mairwen is tryin' to give us more information than just th' cause of our deaths."

"Well, Murriah has been right aboot everythin' else thus far."

Cailen returned a slow nod. "Aye, that she has."

Duncan looked him over for several moments. "Ye know, I must tell ye, that I envy your relationship with Murriah. Never afore in my entire existence have I seen a luv so strong."

Cailen met his gaze but said nothing in return.

"I possessed a deep fondness for your sister, Cailen," he said. "But I must confess, I dinnae luv her th' way ye luv Murriah, and truly, I dinnae think she luved me in such a way, either. At least, not in th' same way Murriah luvs ye. I think what we had was more of a mutual affection born of friendship and respect."

"Mayhap your affection for each other might have grown, if given th' chance," Cailen countered.

"I suppose 'tis possible," Duncan said. "But that brings us around to another quandary. What are ye goin' to do when Murriah grows old and—"

"When I look at Murriah, I see her spirit, Duncan," Cailen cut in. "Aye, 'tis a fact that she's comely on th' outside as well, but time will never fade th' beauty of her soul or make me luv her any less despite th' age that overtakes her face. Do ye ken?"

Duncan held a hand up in protest as he shook his head. "That's not what I was gettin' at. I was talkin' aboot th' time her mortality will end, and end it will.

What are ye goin' to do, if she cannae remain where we are? Not a single person that has died inside this castle has remained behind. What if perchance, that is part of th' spell that binds us together?"

"Know this, Duncan," Cailen countered as he rose to his feet and approached him. "There is no magic strong enough to take Murriah away from me. I will not allow such to happen. Ye can count on that."

Duncan grinned and smacked Cailen on the back. "Aye, and I am countin' on that verra thing, Cailen, now that I've brought th' problem to your attention. And whatever ye do, dinnae let me down, for I'll never forgive ye if ye do."

In the same moment Duncan finished his thought, Mariah called out his name from the great hall. Duncan grinned while making an outward sweep of his hand and inclined his head in the direction of the sound. Seconds later, Cailen appeared in front of the stairway, blocking her path. Mariah gasped and rocked back on her heels, just as she would've walked straight through him.

"Cailen!" She lifted a hand to her heart and returned his smile.

"My lady," he said before he leaned down and gave her the kiss that wouldn't wait for a better time. "How was your journey?"

"Now that I'm finally home, I can actually say it wasn't all that bad," she said.

"Did Blaine Larsen attend this event?" he asked as he took hold of her bag and walked alongside her up the stairs.

A breath of laughter accompanied a nod. "Yes, but perhaps it will please you to know that we only said hello to each other and nothing more."

"Aye, I can say that pleases me verra well," he said in jest.

"What about Beth," she countered, with mischief dancing in her eyes. "Did she take advantage of my absence and pay you a visit?"

"Nay." He shook his head and sniffed. "I dinnae think she likes me anymore."

Mariah laughed. "I can say that pleases me very well too." She closed her eyes and took in a deep breath before she opened them again. "It's so good to be home."

"And 'tis good to have ye home," he said. "Dare I hope there is nothin' further to take ye away from me?"

"We can at least hope," she replied as they stepped inside her room. "Truly, I can't think of anything else required by the board of directors. So, until MacNaughton kicks me out of here, I think we're good."

"Mayhap I can convince him to let ye stay on." He set her bag beside her bed and turned to face her.

"Perhaps you could at that. I have to admit your various powers of persuasion are quite effective."

"Would ye stay with me then, for always?" he asked, bringing Duncan's comment to mind. "Even after ye left your mortality behind?"

"You know I would," she said as he gathered her into his arms. "I've no desire to leave you, Cailen. Not even for a single day. But what if I told you there might be a way to reverse Elspetha's spell? And what if in reversing it, it would mean that you and the knights would be free to travel wherever you wanted to go? Would you take it?"

Cailen gazed into her eyes for several moments while he pondered on what she said. Such an event would guarantee them the ability to remain together, would it not? If his spirit became like any other spirit, then surely he could follow whatever path she chose during her mortality and after her mortality ended. If that decision entailed walking into the light she spoke so highly of, then surely he could enter alongside her, as well.

"Where did ye hear aboot this reversal?" he asked. "Have ye seen Mairwen?"

Mariah shook her head. "No, not yet."

"Then where?" he asked.

"Gordon Humphries took everyone to dinner last night and I ended up sitting next to a very lovely woman named Lorna. She's not only one of the artists for the Gallery project, she's also a witch that only practices white magic."

He lowered his chin a notch, but said nothing in response.

"She's a Wiccan, and by all reports they're a people who believe in using magic for good. For whatever actions they perform, the witch will receive it back threefold," she said.

"Is that what she told ye?"

"Yes, and during the course of the evening I asked a few general questions about things I've read concerning their ideologies. And then, as our conversation progressed I asked her what would happen if a person performed a spell incorrectly by saying the wrong thing or leaving out a key ingredient. She said in such a case, the spell needed redoing. I asked her what would happen if the person performing the spell didn't realize the mistake. Cailen, she said the subject of the spell would end up in limbo. *Limbo*—" She emphasized the word again. "And I think that's where you are right now."

"And that's when your witch said such a spell might be reversed?" he asked.

She nodded. "She said the spell could be reversed or repaired. I really wanted to tell her about the situation here, but I didn't. I didn't want to tell her anything until I discussed it with you first. But Cailen, I truly think she might be able to help us. What do you think?"

"I cannae tell ye that I'm not tempted," he said. "But ye dinnae really know this woman, Murriah. Just because she tells ye that she uses her magic to good purposes, doesna mean there is any truth to what she says. Ye must remember that Elspetha said th' same thing to Mairwen, And she believed it."

"Yes, but Elspetha had an agenda of her own," she reminded him. "Lorna doesn't know anything about what happened at this castle centuries ago. So she wouldn't have any kind of vendetta against you or the knights. Therefore, why would she do anything other than help us set things right?"

"Are ye no longer of a mind to believe Mairwen will come to ye then?" he countered.

"No, I didn't mean that at all." She shook her head. "I still believe, in one way or another, Mairwen will come."

"Then, at least for now, let's give her th' chance to tell us what she wants us to do next, without th' interference of an outside source," he said. "She's led ye this far already. If she doesna make an appearance in a reasonable amount of time, then we'll talk aboot your Lorna."

Mariah let go of a sigh and nodded. "You're right, Cailen. I'm sorry—I'm afraid I'm not a very patient person. I guess I'm just one of those people who want what they want, when they want it. It's a fault of mine."

Cailen cupped her face. "I think you're perfect and I would not want ye any different than what ye are. Now then, do ye have to work or would ye care to take a walk with me instead?" he asked as his lips playfully teased just above hers. "I vow to take your mind off all this fuss and worry."

"Cailen Braithnoch, I think you're a very bad influence on me. Do you know that?"

"Aye, my lady," he whispered, just before he kissed her.

Chapter 24

Mariah couldn't have asked for a more perfect afternoon or evening with her knight. They walked along the river and streams, visited the waterfall, squandered time on the bridge, and explored the surrounding forest, all at a leisurely pace. All the while, they avoided talk of magic spells, Elspetha, and Mairwen.

Memories of those enchanting moments lulled her into restful sleep that night, and somewhere along the way, she drifted in the direction of blue cloudless skies and the green grassy fields beside the castle. As she floated into the area, she could see Lorna sitting on an ornate wood-and-iron bench, inundated by sunlight. Though a bit surprised to see her there, she smiled at her friend and waved.

"Hello, Mariah," said Lorna, responding with a wave of her own.

"What are you doing out here?" she asked as she sat down next to her.

"Och, I have just come to enjoy th' sunlight on this beautiful morning. 'Tis more glorious than I have ever seen it before. You must have managed to reverse th' spell. That's th' only explanation for such brilliant light. I'm so proud of your accomplishment, lassie. How did you know th' proper words to speak without needing to call me?"

313

"The proper words?" repeated Mariah blankly.

"Yes," she said with a single nod of her head. "*The request begun in a moment of time, forgive, turn back, repeal. And those that wear the woodruff, release, set free, reveal.*"

Mariah drew her brows together, shook her head, and shot a glance at the castle. "No, I'm afraid I don't know what you're talking about. I haven't done anything special."

Suddenly she no longer sat next to Lorna. For as she shifted her gaze from the castle and back onto her companion, Mairwen sat on the bench in Lorna's place. Cailen's sister smiled, rose to her feet, and beckoned her to follow. They strolled to the back of the castle, through the corridor of the sleepy hollow trees and made their way inside Sybil's kitchen. None of this seemed out of the ordinary.

Mairwen approached the brick shelves that housed Sybil's spices. As she perused the contents, she removed a jar here and there, and placed them atop the counter. Mariah fastened her eyes upon the labels. Mairwen had selected chamomile, frankincense, sandalwood, klamath weed, and rue. She opened Sybil's cupboard then and selected a large ceramic bowl and pestle. To the bowl, she added just a pinch of each ingredient from the jars on the counter. She took hold of the bowl, turned to face her, and beckoned her to follow.

Mariah accompanied Mairwen outside. Her ghostly companion stopped beneath a pine tree and collected a handful of needles. She dropped them inside the bowl and made her way to the portcullis. They entered the passageways, headed straight to the tomb of the knights, and stepped into the chamber. Curiosity gave way to bewilderment as Mairwen ran her fingers through the hair of each knight. She dropped the hair she amassed into the pot alongside the other ingredients. What an odd thing to do—

Finally, they entered Elspetha's chamber, where ten other women awaited them. The colorless, wispy spirits she had seen in both the passageway and Mairwen's bedroom, seamlessly evolved into the women in her sketchbook. At once, they formed a circle around the altar. Mairwen sat the bowl upon the altar and using the pestle, ground all her contents together. She crumbled a few pieces of coal, added them to the bowl, and set them ablaze with the small torch she suddenly had in her hand. While the contents burned, Mairwen retrieved the willow from the cavity, cut the leather strips with the rusty dagger, and placed some of the dried shoots atop the fire. At that point, she mouthed the words that Lorna mentioned earlier multiple times. In response, the fire turned varying shades of green, purple, yellow, and red.

They all waited in silence until nothing but ash remained inside the bowl. Mairwen retrieved the crock and beckoned her to follow. They traversed the corridor and exited the passageway through the fissure alongside the riverbank. The sun shone bright as Mairwen lifted the bowl high above her head and while turning a complete circle, scattered the ashes into the wind.

A broad smile appeared upon her face the moment Cailen emerged from the passageway, followed by all the knights. Exuberant laughter accompanied their reunion. Mairwen rushed into Cailen's waiting arms. Mariah could feel their joy.

With a start, she sat straight up in her bed just as her alarm clock sounded. She turned to face Cailen. He gazed back with a look of wonder on his face. "Cailen," she began, "I just had this really amazing—"

He put a gentle finger to her lips and whispered, "I know, I saw it too."

"You did?" she asked. "But how?"

"I dinnae know," he answered. "Unless it's because we were holdin' hands and our souls somehow connected as one while ye dreamed."

"You saw Mairwen take me into Sybil's kitchen," she said, just to make sure they witnessed the same thing.

"Aye, and she extracted th' jars from th' shelf and placed some of th' contents of each one into a bowl," he said.

Mariah bounded out of bed and took hold of the notebook and pencil atop her desk. "We better write this down before we forget any of the details," she said as she returned to her bed. Cailen observed as she recorded each ingredient and each step Mairwen presented in the dream.

After they completed the task to both their satisfaction, she slid off the bed and stepped into her slippers. She extended her hand and said, "Come on, let's go take a look inside Sybil's kitchen and see if we can find what we need."

The walk to the cottage never took so long, but when at last they arrived at the door, Mariah all but burst through it. She rushed over to the shelves and studied each label in turn. Cailen stood just behind her to assist the effort. Yet, as they arrived at the last jar on the bottom shelf, disappointment engulfed her. Sybil didn't have a single thing Mairwen collected in the dream.

"What do you suppose this means?"

Cailen shrugged. "Mayhap Mairwen just wanted to show ye what ye needed, and in th' way ye would understand."

Mariah fastened her gaze to his and nodded. "You know, I think you're right. This way is much easier than having me sketch a bunch of plants that I have to spend hours identifying." Her thoughts raced ahead. "I wonder if there's an apothecary shop in Aberdeen where we can buy all the things we need."

"Why Aberdeen?" he asked.

"Because it's not so very far away all things considered, and more importantly, since you've already visited it yourself, I know you can come with me without mishap," she said.

A slight smile tugged at the corners of his mouth as he folded his arms against his chest. "I suppose we could go take a look at what Aberdeen has to offer then. When do ye want to go?"

"Just as soon as I finish work for the day," she said. "Unfortunately it's going to have to wait until then, because no matter how much I might want to leave this very minute, I really can't play hooky again today."

"Hooky?" he asked, sounding quite perplexed over her use of the word.

"Didn't you ever play hooky during your mortal life?" she countered.

"I dinnae ken what it means." He shrugged.

"Basically it means not showing up for an assigned duty, skipping knight's training when you're expected—that sort of thing."

Cailen dipped his head and chuckled. "Then by all means, my lady, finish th' work ye need to do, afore we go."

Mariah worked through both breakfast and lunch so they could arrive in Aberdeen before the shops closed. Once there, they located the quaint little shop she found listed on the Internet. The helpful shopkeeper scratched his head as he looked over the list she presented him.

"I'm afraid th' only things I have on your list is th' chamomile and sandalwood," he said.

Mariah drummed her fingers atop the counter and shifted her gaze upon the window facing the street. "Do you have any idea where I can get the frankincense, klamath weed, and rue?" she asked.

He shook his head. "Not around here, but if you're not in a big hurry I can order them for you."

"How long would it take you to get them here?"

"Aboot five business days—give or take a few," he said. "However, there's a chance it could take a wee bit longer than that."

"Just go ahead and make th' order, Murriah," Cailen whispered. "We are not in that big a hurry. At least this way we'll be certain to have what we need."

Mariah gave the shopkeeper a nod. "All right, I'll go ahead and let you make the order then. But, please keep in mind that I would like to have them as quickly as I can."

"Certainly. I require a small down payment, and then if you'll just leave me your name and phone number, I'll call you as soon as your order arrives," he said.

The transaction complete, they made their way

outside the shop.

"Are ye ready to go then?" asked Cailen.

"No, not yet. I want to see if I can find a small clay or cast iron pot and a pestle while we're here. I know Mairwen showed us Sybil's bowl, but I'd rather not start a fire in one of her lovely ceramic dishes. I don't want to ruin it or have to explain the burn stain upon her return."

After wandering in an out several of the surrounding shops, Mariah finally located the perfect pot and pestle to suit their needs. And then as they began the drive back to the castle, a thousand different thoughts flooded her mind. Her earlier satisfaction gave way to doubt as one notion landed with more force than all the rest.

"Cailen, what do you think Mairwen's instructions will accomplish?" she asked.

He paused for a moment as he sought a reply to the question he'd asked himself a hundred times since he shared Mariah's dream. "I dinnae rightly know. At th' verra least, it seems I'll be able to see my sister again. Mayhap it also means that I and all of my knights will be just like any other spirit—free from all boundaries and hindrances."

Mariah said nothing after he made the comment and for a while, they drove in silence. "Where have your thoughts taken ye my lady?" he asked.

She tried to produce a smile and didn't know how miserably she failed. Finally, she gulped and said, "Are you tired of the life you lead at the castle, Cailen?"

He shook his head. "I dinnae ken what ye mean?"

"Well, you've been in this limbo for centuries," she said. "You've done the same things every minute of every day for over seven hundred years. Does the routine of it ever wear thin?"

"'Tis all we know, Murriah," he replied. "I have told ye such afore. We are happy enough."

"I know that." She paused for several seconds before she went on. "But if a spell reversal is what Mairwen intends, then you'll have freedoms and choices you've never experienced or expected since your death. You'll have the ability to go anywhere you want to go—including walking into the light to join all the members of your family and friends who've passed on to wherever it is that spirits go. Once Mairwen feels she's set everything aright, she and her companions will probably want to enter this spiritual realm. Perhaps, when that time comes, you'll find you want to go with them."

She glanced in his direction and in that instant he could see a touch of fear and sorrow filling the depths of her beautiful eyes. He understood her inner turmoil, for he'd experienced it himself.

"Pull th' car over for a minute, Murriah," he said in a low, quiet voice. "I'd like to speak to ye without distractions." Once she complied with his request, he took hold of her hand and fused his gaze to hers.

Cailen found it difficult to find the proper words to express his thoughts and feelings. And because of that, he had refrained from ever speaking them aloud. Nonetheless, she needed to hear them now—regardless of the consequences.

"I dinnae know what my men will choose to do with their freedom, should such occur. As ye know, I can only speak for myself. But I want ye to know that I have no intention of forsakin' ye. Whether ye should will it or not, I will remain at your side until th' moment death takes away your mortality and every day thereafter."

She opened her mouth to speak. He shook his head and placed a finger against her lips to stay her comments until he finished saying what he needed to say.

"Th' moment I first laid eyes on ye, Murriah, somethin' stirred deep inside my soul. I dinnae have th' words to explain th' powerful feelin'. I just knew that I had to have ye for my own. And so I pursued ye with that goal in mind. I didna care aboot your mortal state or that ye deserved a man that could take ye into his arms and hold ye with a warm, physical body, and one ye could hold in return. I didna care that ye deserved a man that could make—"

"*I* don't care about any of that either, Cailen," she cut in. "Really, I don't."

He returned an almost imperceptible shake of his head. "'Tis no light thing choosin' to live out your mortal life with a spirit, Murriah. Have ye truly considered that? Mayhap th' day will come when ye realize your life is incomplete. I cannae give ye children, do ye ken?"

"No, Cailen. That day will never come because nothing is more important to me than you are. Nothing."

"Not right now, I know," he said. "But mayhap someday it will not be so. Nonetheless, I give ye fair warnin' that should that day ever come, I will do all in my power to keep ye with me regardless of your feelin's. That includes subjectin' my competition to more terror than what their weedy souls can endure. Do

321

ye ken? And if that doesna work, I have several other methods to accomplish th' same goal, for accomplish them I will."

She laughed over his oh-so-casually stated comments. "Oh, Cailen—you'll never have to worry about that. Not ever. I've loved you far too long and far too deeply."

He gave her a wink. "'Tis a good thing. For I luv ye, my lady, with my whole heart and soul and I will not lose ye. I intend to remain by your side throughout all th' ages of time and then some."

"Promise?"

"Aye, upon my honor, I so swear."

After a kiss that quite easily shook the foundations of the very earth, Mariah finally started the car and eased onto the road. The moment she could think rationally again, her thoughts wandered back to the complexity of the spell. "I have a few questions."

"And what would that would be?"

"The pine needles," she began. "I know Mairwen pulled them off the tree on the way to the passageway. But I wondered if fresh needles are difficult to burn."

"Ye have a point," he replied. "I would think that if ye let them dry for a time, they would burn easier."

"On the other hand, I wondered if fresh needles are required." She shrugged. "I don't want to do anything wrong. Lorna said one needed to do a spell correctly for it to have the proper effect."

Cailen considered that for a moment. He too, wanted the spell reversal done properly. "I dinnae know," he finally said. "Ye could experiment with th' needles. We have plenty of time while we wait for our order to arrive. If th' fresh needles dinnae burn, then we might need to gather some and let them dry out."

"That's a good idea," she said. "We'll throw some fresh ones into the pot once we arrive home, light them on fire, and see what happens."

"Ye said questions," he reminded her.

"Yes." She shot him a quick glance. "Your hair. A wall seals your bodies inside the cavern. How are we going to collect it?"

"Such will not be a problem," he replied. "We can get ye th' hair ye require."

The moment they arrived at the castle, Mariah gathered her things from inside the car and headed straight for the nearest pine tree. In his estimation, she collected more needles than what Mairwen required. Once inside, she placed her pot on the table and dropped a handful of the foliage inside.

"Do you want to get me the matches from my bedside table? You can do it much faster than I can," she said as the bemused knights gathered around them and wondered over their bizarre behavior.

"What are ye doin'?" Steven asked her as Cailen popped upstairs.

"We're going to see how easily these pine needles burn," she replied.

"All right," said Duncan, "I'll be th' first to ask th' obvious question. Why would ye do such a peculiar thing?"

"Because," said Cailen as he reappeared inside the hall and handed the matches to Mariah, "Mairwen has finally supplied us with th' next step in this intrigue. We believe it will free us from th' spell."

At once, the knights began asking question, yet Cailen raised a hand for silence as the needles burned.

"Dry needles would burn faster," he said, "but along with th' other ingredients, fresh will do just as well."

Mariah concurred with a nod. "I think you're right. Let's be safe and use fresh needles. Maybe there's something in the odor they give off, or—"

"Th' spirit of th' thing itself," Duncan offered.

"All right," Cailen said, giving his men his full attention. "We need to go down into our tomb and each man needs to collect a bit of hair from off his head, do ye ken? I will explain everythin' along th' way."

As the knights disappeared from the great hall and journeyed to the cavern that entombed their bodies, he shared the memory of Mariah's dream. Once they entered the chamber, each man made his way to his mortal remains.

"Ye know," Duncan said as he clutched his prize. "Th' condition of our bodies still amazes me. I would not think th' power of th' four elements, or any other entity could keep us from turnin' to dust."

"I wonder if we'll do just that once th' spell is reversed," mused Steven.

"I wouldn't doubt it," Malcolm said. "Might be interestin' to come down here and watch it happen."

"Ye know, it might at that," said Edmund. "Then just think, all that will be left is our armor, shields, swords and mayhap a few bones."

Cailen mulled the comments over as he looked about the cavern filled with their bodies and the most valuable possessions his father once owned. The collective contents inside this chamber were worth a king's ransom.

"Come on," he finally said. "We need to give th' hair to Murriah. Take care that ye dinnae drop any of it along th' way.

Mariah awaited their arrival next to her clay pot. Each of the knights took their turn dropping the hair inside. When his turn arrived, he looked inside the bowl and saw that she had already added her chamomile and sandalwood. After he added his own hair, she covered the contents with her lid with all haste.

"Now," she said. "Where do you suppose is the safest place to put this? I don't want to chance it falling over by keeping it up high, and I don't want Tatters messing with it if I put it on the floor."

"Why dinnae we put it inside Edgar's stone box on th' floor in th' oratory," Cailen suggested. "I think it will stay safe enough in there."

"All right," she said.

"I'll give ye one better than that," said Duncan. "We'll all take turns standin' watch over it, until such time as ye perform th' spell. Will that work to your satisfaction?"

Mariah smiled broadly over the suggestion. "Now that is one of the best ideas I've heard all day. However, I don't think we have to go quite that far."

Chapter 25

"Well, it's now quite obvious the apothecary shop is going to take every single minute of their allotted time," Mariah groused as she meticulously brushed a weathered pattern onto a single painted stone of the southwest turret.

Cailen shrugged away her comment. "Dinnae worry, Murriah, your order will get here afore ye know it."

"You're only saying that because they have until tomorrow at the latest," she pointed out. "I wished they would've just said so and left it at that. It's not right to toy with people's emotions, you know."

"Aye, but look at all th' work ye've accomplished while ye've waited. Despite th' torment it cost ye, you're well ahead of your schedule now," he replied, gesturing at her paintings. "For that ye can be grateful."

"And that's the only good thing about the wait." She dabbed her brush into the paint on her palette and then swabbed off the excess. "When it comes time to perform the spell, I don't want to worry about anything else."

"Well, now ye dinnae have to," he replied.

Duncan chose that moment to appear inside the studio. His eyes fell upon Mariah first before they landed on him. "I thought I would let ye know that MacNaughton is comin' in through th' gates," he informed them.

"Did he come alone?" he asked.

Duncan nodded. "Aye, he did."

Mariah held her brush mid-air as she turned to face him. "Really? I wonder what he's doing here?" she asked.

Cailen shrugged and said, "I dinnae have any idea."

Nonetheless, he had looked forward to, and anticipated, this hour. He turned his attention upon Duncan and connected his gaze to his. A gradual smile appeared on his lieutenant's face as Cailen conveyed his thoughts. The moment he finished, the knight disappeared from the room to gather a few men as instructed. A few minutes later, Laird MacNaughton's friendly "hullo" wafted up the stairs.

Mariah stepped into the hallway and made her way to the edge of the landing. "Up here," she called out. Cailen waited at her side as Kyle ascended the stairs and ambled toward her.

"Good morning, Mariah," he said. "I wanted to check on your supply of wood and petrol. With fall settling into th' Highlands, th' nights are beginning to get quite cold as I'm certain you're aware."

"Yes, I've noticed that," she replied. "But I think we're doing okay on both."

A nod accompanied a friendly smile. "I know I could've sent someone else to check on your supplies for me, but I couldn't resist taking another peek at th' paintings myself. I hope you dinnae mind."

"Of course I don't mind." Mariah invited him into her studio with a wave of her hand. "You're welcome to come anytime. After all, this castle belongs to you, does it not? So, feel free to stop by whenever you wish."

As he followed her into the room and cast his gaze upon the paintings, appreciation filled his eyes. "Och, you're almost finished."

"Actually, I have quite a ways to go yet. I still have to add all the details to each of the paintings. Those tiny little details can take far longer to apply than all the rest of the layers put together. But in the end, they make the portrait far more interesting. You'll see what I mean when I'm actually finished. At least—I hope you will."

"I'm sure you dinnae need to worry about that. I find all your works of art quite impressive," he said. "But, you know, I didn't realize so much went into a painting before. This has been a very interesting and rewarding experience for me."

"In turn, let me tell you that living here at your castle has been a most amazing experience for me," she replied. She turned her attention away from MacNaughton for a moment and gave it to Cailen. The expression she bestowed as she connected her gaze with his stirred the embers of his soul and set them ablaze.

"So tell me," she said, shifting her gaze to the laird. "Are you planning to attend the unveiling?"

"I wouldn't miss it," MacNaughton said. "I take it you'll be there as well?"

"With bows on my toes." Mariah spared him a glance, took in a deep breath, and cleared her throat. "That brings me around to something I'd like to discuss with you, if you have a minute."

"I can give you as much time as you need," he replied. "I'm in no hurry."

"I have a rather selfish request, which you can

refuse if you want to. If so, I promise I'll understand."

MacNaughton shook his head as he shrugged. "What's your request?" he asked.

"Even though I'll be quite finished with the paintings, if you don't mind, I'd like to stay here at the castle until the unveiling in January. It would just be so much easier than trying to find a hotel for such a lengthy period of time, and I'll gladly pay you rent and board, or whatever else you'd like to agree upon while I'm here—"

He held up a hand to halt her progress. "I will not hear a word of you payin' any rent," he said. "You're quite welcome to stay here as long as you want. I would consider it an honor to have you as my guest."

"Better be careful with that offer," she replied, sounding much relieved. "I might never leave this place."

He laughed and gave her shoulder a friendly pat. "All right then, it's settled. I will not allow ye to go to a hotel or anywhere else while you're here in Scotland. George and Sybil should return from holiday by mid-November and I know they'll be happy to look after you."

"What about a painting then?" she asked. "I would really like to do something nice for you in exchange for all of your many kindnesses."

A gleam appeared in Laird MacNaughton's eye as she made the suggestion. "'Tis not a requirement for you to stay here, lassie, but I certainly wouldn't refuse a gift comin' from you. And speaking of that, I've been meaning to compliment you on a particular painting I saw on your website titled *Winter in the Tundra*, which sadly, is already sold. I'm really drawn to paintings like that one." He winked. "One such as that would look great in my study. Even the colors are perfect."

Mariah laughed and bowed her head in understanding. "I'll keep that in mind," she said.

"All right then, I'll go ahead and let you get back to your work. Thank you for allowing me this interruption."

"You're welcome, and thank you so much for allowing me to stay awhile longer than planned," she replied.

"My pleasure." Kyle paused just before he stepped all the way through the doorway. "By th' way, have you had th' chance to see th' newspaper today?"

"No, I haven't," she replied.

"They have printed th' first article aboot th' Gallery opening, and have included some very nice photographs. Of course as you might guess, I'm especially fond of your accolade." He winked.

"Oh! I guess it is the fifteenth of the month already, isn't it," she said. "My, how time flies—"

"That it does, especially when you get my age." He gave her a single nod. "I'm really going this time. I'll check on you later, but until then if you have any needs, dinnae hesitate to call me."

"Thank you, I will," she replied.

The moment MacNaughton turned toward the stairway, Cailen stepped toward her. "I think I'm just goin' to dash out for a moment and find us a newspaper, Murriah. I would verra much like to see th' article myself. Dinnae worry, I'll hurry."

He disappeared from the room, without giving her any time to reply. Grateful for the excuse provided, he would truly get the newspaper as promised, but he had one other errand he needed to take care of first, and it would suit him well if Mariah didn't know about it.

Duncan awaited his presence in the great hall. As instructed, he had gathered Steven, Edmund, Malcolm, and Robin.

"Hurry along, Cailen," said Steven. "MacNaughton's already approachin' his car."

"Dinnae concern yourself," Cailen countered. "We'll catch him afore he passes through th' gate. Does everyone know what to do?"

"Aye," Duncan smiled broadly, as he held aloft his ghostly sword. "We all know just what ye want us to do."

"Then let's get it done."

****

Mariah sighed over her growing impatience as she awaited Cailen's return. Just how long did it take a ghost to fetch a newspaper anyway? If he had only waited a few extra minutes, he would know they could've purchased one in Aberdeen on the way to pick up her order. She looked at her watch again. If she didn't leave soon, she wouldn't make it to the shop before it closed. She could give him five more minutes. If he didn't make it back by then, she would just go ahead and make the trip herself. For she would not put this errand off another day.

Yet, now that she had the remaining ingredients all but in hand, apprehension and uncertainty engulfed her. Doubts about her ability to complete the spell correctly, tormented her mind. If she didn't do it right, would her feeble effort make the situation worse? But surely, Mairwen would attend her endeavor. Cailen's sister wouldn't allow her to do something wrong, would she?

She shuddered over the very notion of such an event as her conversation with Lorna, burst into the forefront of her mind. In that same moment, Cailen slipped his arms around her from behind. She spied the newspaper he clutched in his hand. He already had it turned to the page with the photograph of his accolade prominently displayed.

"What caused ye to shiver, my lady?" he asked.

She turned around to face him. "Stressing over the spell, I guess. The rest of the ingredients have arrived, so—once we get home with our treasures, I guess we can see about releasing you from limbo."

He brushed his fingers through the length of her hair. "Dinnae be afraid, Murriah. Everythin' is goin' to work out just fine, ye'll see."

Except for their brief conversation in regards to her extended stay at the castle, on the way to and from Aberdeen, their conversation focused solely on the complexity of the spell. Somewhere along the way, Cailen calmed her insecurities. By the time they returned to the castle, confidence replaced all doubt.

"Well," she said as she looked about the great hall, "let me go get my pot."

Cailen shook his head. "Nay, Murriah. More than half my men are gone right now as ye can see, and it would take quite some time to gather them all back to th' castle. Let's just do th' ritual in th' morn after ye've had some rest. Besides, it will give Mairwen one more opportunity to speak with ye, should she feel th' need."

Despite her newfound assurance, his words provided a small measure of relief. She returned a single nod. "You're right," she said. "I think I'd feel better about doing it in the morning anyway. For as I recall, in the dream, Mairwen released the ashes underneath a sunny sky."

****

Later that evening, Cailen sat at the edge of her bed. To take her mind off the spell she'd perform in the morning, he retrieved the newspaper they abandoned earlier, and placed it in her hands. Along with the other photographs, the story took up an entire page.

"Seems they favored your paintin' of King Robert," he said. "Ye'll notice it's much larger than all th' rest."

She shook her head. "I wished I could take the credit, but they planned for each newspaper company throughout the U.K. to feature a painting from their area. That way, they hope to whet the appetite of the locals."

Cailen scoffed, "I think they would have chosen it regardless. Just look at that handsome man th' Bruce is knightin'."

She gave him a slight smile. Her expression softened, and she locked her gaze with his. He could see the depth of her love reflecting in her eyes and it humbled him. "Yeah," she said. "Just look at him."

Surely, no one could expect him to resist giving her a kiss after that—now could one. He didn't even try.

Several hours later as she slumbered deeply, Malcolm called to him from the great hall. He'd rather not abandon Mariah right now, but something in the man's tone compelled him to leave her side.

Once he appeared downstairs, Malcolm strode toward him and said, "Evan is on his way out here right now. Edmond stayed inside th' car with him, but I thought ye should know he's in a terrible rage. I dinnae know what he has planned once he arrives."

"Why is he comin' out here this late at night?" he asked. "What happened?"

"'Tis th' picture in th' newspaper," he said. "Once he got home from th' pub he read th' thing while he sat at his table drinkin' his tea. Murriah's paintin' of your accolade screamed to him from off th' page, I wager. He turned all shades of purple as he raised th' page close to his face and looked at th' thing. Edmund thought he would likely pass out then and there. Instead, he started blatherin' aloud like some dunderheaded fool, for not another soul stood inside his kitchen to listen to his rant. He grabbed his keys and muttered a few more swear words, along with your name I might add, underneath his breath."

Comprehension dawned. His face alone wouldn't have perturbed the man, but seeing the unexpected faces of Duncan, Steven, Robert, and some of the other knights would tell him that Mariah did in fact, know them all. Since she'd never revealed her knowledge concerning them, he might feel a sense of betrayal over the omission, despite the fact he'd yet to admit knowing them himself.

"Dinnae let him through th' gate," Cailen ordered. "Mayhap he'll just go home if he cannae find a way in. I dinnae want Murriah's sleep disturbed, ye ken?"

"Aye," Malcolm replied just before he disappeared.

Despite his hopes, no more than twenty minutes passed before Evan repeatedly bellowed his name from outside the fence. The man proceeded to beat his fists upon the iron gate that refused to open despite his key. The annoying sound was enough to wake the dead if any of them actually slumbered. Evan's fit of temper put him in a foul mood.

Less than a second later, he appeared standing in front of the gates. Each of his knights stood just beside or behind him, with swords drawn. "What do ye want, Evan?" he ground out.

"What have you done to Mariah?" he asked between clenched teeth.

"I have done nothin' to Murriah," he replied. "Now, go home—there's a good laddie."

"Dinnae patronize me, Cailen. You have done something to her and you know it!" screamed Evan. "Somehow you've made her fall in love with you and you've done it against her will. Without a single doubt, no woman on this earth would choose a ghost over a man with a warm physical body and a heartbeat! Such a thing is ridiculous to even consider and you know it."

"Th' relationship I have with Murriah is none of your concern, Evan," he shot back. It took every ounce of self-control to refrain from mentioning his knowledge of the love potion the man tried to force upon Mariah himself. "Just go home and leave it alone."

"I will not, do you hear?" He rattled the gates yet again and yelled out, "I want to speak to Mariah, and I want to speak to her now! She deserves to know what you've been aboot. Mariah? Mariah!"

Cailen had enough of his annoying twaddle. He strode through the gate, took hold of Evan, lifted him off his feet, and slammed him hard against the iron bars. Evan's eyes bulged from their sockets. He exhaled short, shallow breaths over this unexpected turn of events, for they had never once laid a hand on the lad. He probably didn't know they could.

"Get into your car right now and go home," he spat out. "What's more, ye will stay away from Murriah and this castle from this day forward or suffer the consequences, do ye ken?"

"You cannot make me go," Evan retorted.

Cailen smiled then, a most terrible, wicked smile, and it made Evan tremble beneath his hands. His knights chuckled, and th' frightful, low, rumbling sound of the surrounding laughter made the lad squirm even more.

"Aye, Evan," he whispered using the most menacing tone he could muster. "I can make ye. Ye seem to forget that I have been around for over seven hundred years. Durin' those years I have acquired knowledge and abilities that ye cannae even begin to comprehend or compete with, no matter what skill ye think ye might possess. After all, ye have only existed a mere thirty years. So, dinnae test me, laddie. I can assure ye, ye will lose and then ye will come to regret makin' th' attempt more than ye did th' losin'."

Evan gulped several times. Cailen could feel the fight leave his body as it slumped forward. Finally then, the lad gave him a curt nod after which Cailen slowly slid his body down the iron bars and lowered him to his feet. Evan's legs seemed a little stiff as he returned to his car. Nonetheless, he turned to glare at them a final time before he opened his car door, climbed inside his vehicle, and took his frustrations out on the gravel road.

"Did anyone go with him?" asked Cailen.

"Aye," said Duncan. "Steven wanted to go and so did Robin."

"Good. He'll need to be watched even closer now," Cailen replied. "I'm goin' back up with Murriah, but let me know if th' weedy scut does anythin' else to cause alarm."

"Ye can count on that," Duncan stated with a firm nod.

Mariah occupied the same position she did before he vacated the room. That told him Evan's late night visit didn't wake her or intrude upon her sleep. He sat down next to her on the bed and placed his hand atop hers as he glanced at her clock. She would probably sleep another few hours at least and once she awoke, she would make the spell reversal her first priority.

As the night progressed, he wondered if the reversal would make them feel any different. If it didn't, they would have to travel to Dupplin and test their boundaries. Only in this way could they tell if the spell worked for each of them. Their absence would probably cause her a great deal of anguish, for she'd have to await their return.

The thought gave him pause. He didn't want to leave her unattended with the threat Evan still posed. One could *hope* his experience tonight would preclude him from doing anything stupid—but love had a way of causing a man to lose his head. And most unfortunately, Evan had fallen in love with his lady. Therefore, he and his men would need to visit Dupplin in shifts.

Steven's voice interrupted his personal thoughts. He looked heavenward and shook his head in renewed agitation. Steven's tone told him that Evan's stupidity clouded his judgment, just as he feared. He leaned over, kissed Mariah's cheek, and made his way down to the hall.

"Now what?" he asked as he strode toward him.

"Evan is makin' somethin' from his book, again,"

Steven informed him. "But not th' same potion he made afore. His absurd mutterin's are not makin' any sense either."

Cailen waved the comment aside. "Did ye read th' name of his concoction?"

Steven shook his head. "There weren't any words on th' page to label th' potion. I can only tell ye what's in it."

"We dinnae have time to figure it out," Cailen replied. "Go back to his room, draw away all his energy, and put th' man to sleep. That should give Murriah enough time to complete th' spell without any interference from Evan. Wait for th' dawn afore ye do it, though. And Steven, empty out his pot afore ye quit th' place. Such an event shouldn't surprise him now. Not after what happened tonight."

Steven's eyes lit up in anticipation of the assignment. He flashed a grin. "Dinnae worry, Cailen. We'll take care of it."

"All right, just dinnae be late gettin' back," said Cailen. "I know Murriah. She'll wake up about daybreak and want to get this done."

Cailen stood in the hall and waited until Steven disappeared. A moment later, Duncan grabbed hold of his shoulder in friendly camaraderie and gave it a shake.

"Well-thought-out plan, Cailen." He nodded, clearly amused with the situation. "And in my opinion, 'tis no more than th' man deserves. 'Tis a pity we cannae see th' look on his face when he finally awakes and finds his vile potion missin'."

Chapter 26

The first hint of dawn seeped through the curtains and into Mariah's bedroom. Along with it, awareness of the day and full clarity of the daunting task ahead. She took a deep breath, stretched her body from shoulder to toe, turned onto her side, and wrapped her arms around one of her pillows. In the same instant, she sensed Cailen sat next to her. As he brushed the tangled hair away from her face, she slowly opened her eyes, and greeted his smile with one of her own.

"Good morning, Cailen," she whispered. He took hold of her hand and gave it a gentle squeeze. And it made her wonder—would his form feel different after the completion of the spell? Instead of warmth, would he emit the same chill she experienced from other spirits? Would she feel his kisses? If she had to trade those things away in order for them to be together forever, then so be it.

"Good morn, my lady," he replied as his grin deepened. "Did ye sleep well?"

"Amazingly well," she said, turning onto her back. "Before going to sleep, I resigned myself to tossing and turning the night away, but I don't think I even budged. As a result I feel completely refreshed and ready to tackle my assignment."

"That's good to know," he replied.

"Why? Are you afraid the novice witch will mess

up the spell and turn you into a frog or some hideous-looking creature that only she will love?"

"No." He drew her hand to his lips and dropped a kiss. "I know ye'll do just fine."

His confidence in her ability helped calm her sense of unease. "Speaking of this morning's undertaking, have all the knights returned from their evening's entertainment?"

He nodded. "Aye, they are all gathered down in th' hall as we speak."

"Good," she said, smothering a yawn. "I'd like to get this done as early as possible."

"I know ye would. Did Mairwen give ye any further instructions durin' the night while ye slumbered?"

"Nope," she replied. "In fact, I don't remember having any dreams at all."

"Then mayhap she feels ye have all th' skill ye require."

"I hope so," she replied as she tossed the quilts away from her body and inched her body upward. "On that note, let's get to it, shall we? I so want you all free of Elspetha's enchantment. Just think, once you're free, you can come with me to the Gallery opening. From there, we can travel to West Virginia where you can see my pathetic pile of sketchbooks if you like. After that, we can go anywhere we choose."

Cailen shrugged and as he leaned down with his lips hovering just above hers, he said, "Aye, we'll go down to th' hall in just a minute—mayhap two would be a better assessment."

His two minutes stretched to at least five before he finally allowed her to rise—not that she had any complaints over the delay. A smile remained on her face as she approached her wardrobe closet. "It'll only take me a minute to get dressed. Then once we retrieve the pot, we can head for the passageway. What do you say to that?"

"Nay, we will not fetch your pot until after ye've had breakfast," he said as he rose from the bed.

She whirled around to face him and noted the stubborn set of his jaw. Perhaps she could win the battle anyway, because really— "I'm not hungry, yet. In fact, the thought of food makes me queasy. So, I think I'll wait and eat after I complete the reversal of the spell if you don't mind."

He shook his head. "I want ye to eat first, Murriah. We dinnae know how long this is goin' to take. Therefore, I want ye to have all your strength afore we begin."

She huffed out a breath as she rolled her eyes heavenward. "All right, if you insist, I'll have something to eat first."

"I'll await your presence down in th' hall," he replied before he disappeared from the room.

Mariah sighed as she opened the armoire. She selected her black button-up jeans and warm, royal blue sweater to ward off the chill of the passageway. She didn't know how long it would take the contents of the pot to turn to ash and she didn't want to freeze to death while she waited. Once ready for the task ahead, she hurried into her studio and looked through her sketchbooks just in case she found some last minute thing Mairwen wanted her to know. Nothing else appeared inside the pages. She took a breath to calm the growing swarm of butterflies that flitted about her belly, and descended the steps.

All the knights turned to face her as she entered the hall. They greeted her with smiles and nods of encouragement. They seemed just as anxious for the unfolding of the day's events, as she did. She returned their greeting in kind and all the while, hoped she didn't end up disappointing them in some way. Cailen offered his hand. She readily accepted it.

As he took firm hold, he turned to the knights and said, "We'll return as soon as Murriah finishes her breakfast. So dinnae go anywhere."

"As if—" one of the knights hollered back.

Once they stepped outside and headed for Sybil's kitchen, Mariah gazed up at the bright, cloudless sky. "The day couldn't be any more perfect," she breathed out.

He followed the direction of her gaze and nodded. "Aye. Seems it'll be just as Mairwen showed ye in th' dream."

"And let's hope everything goes just as well."

"Dinnae worry. It will."

Of course, she should've known Cailen wouldn't let her get by with a simple bowl of cereal. No, she had to have scrambled eggs and toast with her orange juice. She did have to put her foot down when it came to the bacon he tried to foist upon her, though. Just the thought of eating something that greasy made her even more nauseated. He only conceded when he saw her blanch.

After she cleaned the kitchen, she located a small paper bag. Mariah collected a few pieces of coal from the coal bin and slipped them inside the sack. She used Sybil's meat tenderizer to crumble them into manageable pieces that would burn easily.

"All right," she said. "I just need to get some pine needles on the way back to the castle, and then I think we're ready to go."

He opened the door, swept a hand in front of him, gave her a chivalrous bow, and said, "My lady—"

As they walked along the sleepy hollow corridor, she mentally recalled the dream to ensure she had each step firmly in mind. And as she did so, a question occurred.

"Cailen," she said as picked a handful of needles from the same pine tree Mairwen did in her dream.

"Aye?"

"Where are all of you supposed to wait while I perform the spell?" she asked.

He stared at her for a few moments. "I dinnae rightly know. Let me think on it."

"Well, during the dream, you weren't with me inside Elspetha's cavern," she reminded him. "In fact, I didn't see you or the knights at all until after Mairwen released the ashes."

He returned a slow nod. "You're right aboot that, we didna go inside th' chamber with ye, did we—"

"Oh, but Cailen, I don't know if I want to do this without you there. You would know if I made a mistake and could correct me."

They stopped in their tracks and turned to face each other. He cuddled her into his arms and at once, she could feel his warmth flooding into her being. For a moment, she savored the feeling just in case it disappeared after the completion of the spell.

"I know ye can do whatever it takes to get this done, and so does Mairwen," he whispered. "She wouldn't have come to ye, if she had any doubts as to th' ability ye possess. Ye must also remember that she'll be there to help ye along th' way. In light of that fact, I think Mairwen intends for us to await ye in th' passageway. In all likelihood, this is why she showed us comin' out through th' fissure. So, we'll go with ye as far as Elspetha's chamber, and then we'll stand guard in th' corridor. If ye find ye need me, all ye have to do is call and I vow, I will come, regardless of adherin' to th' rules of magical procedure."

She shook her head. "No, you mustn't do that. I'll be all right. Like you said, Mairwen will be there." She took a deep breath and gave it a slow release as they made their way to the castle.

After they retrieved the pot from the oratory, Mariah added the remaining ingredients and replaced the lid lest she should lose a single ingredient. That small action caused her heart to thud against her chest, knowing the next step would take place inside Elspetha's cavern. The need to throw up assailed her as she picked up the bowl, her pestle, the small sack of coal, and her box of matches. Once she had everything in hand, she fastened her gaze upon Cailen and gave him a nod. "All right, let's go."

As she headed for the door, Cailen raised a hand to halt her steps. "Dinnae forget ye need a torch to light th' way once your inside th' passageway." He fetched the closest one from the stairway wall.

"Oh, yes. That's right. Thank you." She pasted a reassuring smile on her face—or at least she tried. Did she come anywhere near to accomplishing the feat? Gauging from the expression on his face, probably not.

"Murriah," he said as he brushed his hand against

her cheek. "'Twill be all right, ye'll see."

She gulped past the lump in her throat and nodded. They turned toward the door, exited the castle, and made their way to the river. She followed the now familiar path along the bank. The presence of Cailen and the knights boosted her courage and resolve.

Once they entered through the fissure, Cailen lit the torch and handed it to her. She gazed into his eyes for a moment and then feeling the sudden, overwhelming need she said, "I love you, Cailen, with every fiber of my being."

A small grin appeared in response to her heartfelt declaration. He brushed both hands through the length her hair and just before he kissed her, he huskily replied, "As I luv ye, my lady. Dinnae forget it."

Once he released her, she closed her eyes and whispered. "I won't forget, not ever."

Another deep breath filled her lungs before she whirled around and headed for Elspetha's chamber. As she made the final turn, she sensed she walked alone. However, she refused to look over her shoulder in order to confirm that fact. Her apprehension increased with each step she took. She could now hear the slow drip of water falling into the murky pool up ahead. A shiver shot through her body as she entered the cavern, wedged the torch between the same rocks Mairwen used centuries ago, and approached the altar. She studied her pot for several moments before she sat it next to the rusted dagger. And then she lifted her gaze. She drew in a sharp breath as Mairwen entered and with all ten of her companions close behind. For some reason she didn't expect to see all of them.

The ghostly women appeared just as they did when

she saw them the first time down by the portcullis, and then again in Mairwen's bedroom. She fixed her gaze on the unfolding scene as their wispy translucent forms morphed into one of color and solid-looking mass, rivaling that of the knights.

Each of the ladies met her gaze with a mixture of excitement and anticipation. She took a moment to consider all they had endured over the seven hundred year span since Elspetha took away their men and their lives. Their hearts must have broken a million times over as they watched over their beloved knights from afar, always seeing, yet never touching—never speaking.

Mairwen nodded encouragement. Mariah dropped her gaze to the altar, removed the lid from her pot, and set it aside. Next, she picked up the pestle and mashed the contents of her bowl. The procedure took far longer than she expected. Nonetheless, once Mairwen gave her nod of approval, she retrieved the matchbox.

Her fingers shook as she removed a single match and struck the head against the box. She trembled so much that it took several tries and several matches before the small flame took hold of the fragments. Just how long it took the flames to rise, she couldn't say. The wait took forever. Despite the chill, the first droplets of perspiration formed around her hairline as she added the crumbled coal to the blaze.

Cailen's sister focused her gaze on the small cavity that held the willow. Mariah touched her fingers to her lips. "Oh! I'm sorry—I forgot."

She hurried to retrieve the shoots before the flame died away. The dagger sliced through the leather strips with efficiency and ease despite its deteriorated condition. But then again, the leather had deteriorated as well. As she pinched off a portion of the dried willow, the women formed a circle around her. Once they held hands in an unbroken line, she added the foliage to the fire.

Again, Mairwen nodded encouragement for the next step. The words—she needed to say the words. She swallowed a couple of times to overcome the dryness in her throat.

"The request begun in a moment of time, forgive, turn back, repeal. And those that wear the woodruff, release, set free, reveal." How many times did Mairwen repeat the phrases? She didn't know, nonetheless she slowly repeated each word again.

The fire inside the bowl shot upward, the flames turned green and then purple. She had to bite down hard on her lips to keep from crying out over the manifestation. In an exaggerated manner, Mairwen dipped her head twice. She understood then, she needed to repeat the words two more times. Once for each element perhaps? The moment she complied with the direction, the flame shot upward, this time in hues of yellow and red. An unholy wail emitted from the bowl as if the very contents suffered from some form of intense agony. Fear cemented her feet to the floor and her insides burned.

As her heart thumped wildly in her chest, it occurred to her that she saw the colors of flame in the reverse order she had witnessed them when Elspetha performed the spell. Did that mean she had completed this portion of the spell correctly? She hoped so. More than anything, she wanted this ordeal done and over with. She wanted to stand at the bridge with Cailen and hear him laugh over her silly fears.

Mairwen gazed steadily into her eyes. Seconds later, a smile appeared on her face. Mariah could literally feel the joy and relief of her companions. Mairwen dropped her eyes to the bowl. She followed suit. Together they waited for the fire to consume the contents. Her thoughts settled upon Cailen and the knights many times during the lengthy process. Did they feel any different right now?

At long last, only ash remained inside the bowl. The women broke the circle as she retrieved the pot, and then her torch. She carried them both out of the cavern. Her ghostly convoy followed her around the bend and into the corridor.

Cailen?

Her eyes meandered all about the passageway in anticipation of seeing him or one of the knights. Yet, she didn't see any of them during her journey toward the sun. Where could they all have gone? They said they would wait for her right here. Apprehension engulfed her as they made their way out of the fissure. She still didn't see Cailen—she drew her brows together as she shifted her gaze to Mairwen. The woman wore a brilliant smile that at once soothed and calmed her fears. That radiant smile told her that thus far, all had gone according to design.

Mairwen focused her attention upon the bowl and then raised her arms high as a reminder to give the contents to the breeze. She ran the tip of her tongue over the top of her lip and nodded. She set the torch against the rocks and made her way over to the grassy area by the river.

A sudden gust of wind converged around them as

Mariah lifted the bowl above her head and turned a full circle, just as Mairwen had demonstrated. The currents caught the ashes and carried them ever higher into the heavens.

And then in a single instant, dark, black clouds formed above them. They rolled, churned, and twisted in a frightful manner. She had never witnessed anything like it before. The roaring tempest grew in intensity, spreading the clouds from horizon to horizon with mercurial speed. Lightning bolts shot sideways across the sky with unparalleled voracity. Crashing thunder shook her very frame. Rain dropped from the sky and pelted the ground in raging torrents. All the while, the earth literally groaned beneath her feet. The eerie wailing erupted from somewhere deep within the earth itself.

Cailen and the knights emerged through the fissure at that precise moment. His gaze meandered about until he found her. She could see elation in his smile. He took a brief moment to acknowledge each of her ghostly companions. Then, just as he moved toward her, his spirit transformed, as did the forms of all the knights. They faded in and out of focus.

Mariah could see by expression alone Cailen experienced something strange and most unexpected. His hand traveled to his chest and a look of intense pain marred his features. Seconds later, he gazed at his arms and hands as if he had never seen either before. He mouthed words that for the first time, she couldn't hear. Each of the knights experienced something similar. Fear grabbed her heart as the terrifying manifestation unfolded beneath the raging storm.

Simultaneously, the image of Mairwen and all her

ghostly companions flickered in and out of existence. Mariah clamped wet hands over her mouth to stifle the wail that threatened to surface. Despite her bewilderment and fright, instinct moved her feet in Cailen's direction. The moment he invited her into his arms, a resounding crack, followed by a deafening roar reverberated all around her. Then, just before their fingers touched, a dark cloud encircled his form. A millisecond later, he vanished before her eyes, as did all the knights that stood alongside him.

She screamed his name as she sank to her knees in despair. Trembling hands covered her face. Hot, bitter tears streamed down her cheeks over the loss. Something had gone horribly wrong and she could lay the blame at her own feet. She must've missed a step or said the words incorrectly. Cailen and all his knights had disappeared and she didn't have a clue why or even where the gloomy mist had taken them. Intense pain assaulted her body and entered her soul.

"Get up, Murriah!" a feminine voice called out in sudden alarm. "Run!"

Confusion beset her as she whirled her head from side to side. Yet, she couldn't locate the owner of the voice. Then, from the corner of her eye, she caught sight of Mairwen's dissipating form waving a frantic hand. At the same time, her ghostly eyes widened in horror as they focused on something beyond her.

"Run!" she commanded yet again.

Mariah couldn't make sense of Mairwen's words or her bewildering actions. The ghostly specter wanted her to run? Just where did she want to her to go and why? Notwithstanding her confusion, she sprang to feet. Though she lurched forward, a pair of arms grabbed her roughly from behind and halted her flight. She struggled against the unknown assailant with all her might. He responded by crushing her back against his chest. A harsh, raspy voice demanded she stop fighting him.

Anger overrode her fear and she used it. She battled the arms that held her bound in spite of his odious demand. He lifted her feet off the ground and in retaliation, she flung her leg forward and then swung back against his groin just as forcefully as she could. He screamed out in pain, yet he still didn't release her. Instead, he covered her face with a gloved hand. A strange odor assailed her nostrils as she struggled to breathe. Then, despite all will to the contrary, she gave in to the blackness that engulfed her mind.

Chapter 27

Noises trickled into Mariah's consciousness far ahead of rational thought. She detected the sound of dripping water, the echo of the wind through narrow fissures, and the shifting of tiny pebbles somewhere in close proximity. Her head pounded in agony. The throbbing interfered with her struggle to make sense of her surroundings. Her eyelids wouldn't budge. She didn't have the strength to open them.

Her hand slid off her stomach and onto some form of thick padding. Most certainly, she didn't lie on her bed inside the castle. The rough blanket beneath her fingers felt far different from her soft, cozy quilt. A deep breath passed through her lips as she raised her hand to her forehead and rubbed at the pain.

Just then, something slithered across her face—an insect perhaps. She sprang into a seated position and wiped frantically at her cheeks as she forced her eyes open. Tatters climbed onto her lap then and curled into a tight little ball. The cat arched her back and brushed her furry cheeks against the bottom of her chin demanding attention. Relief replaced apprehension. Thank heaven the cat's whiskers assaulted her face instead of some revolting bug. She shuddered at the thought of a huge, hairy-legged spider creeping across her nose.

Yet, the moment her eyes drifted away from her

pet, the relief vanished. Corroded iron bars shot into focus, and they were no more than three feet in front of her. She whirled her head to the right, to the left and then looked behind her. Walls made of stone, returned her gaze. Her mouth dropped and she gasped. *How in the world did she end up inside a dungeon?* In the instant the question stormed her mind, she remembered.

Cailen! Her hands flew to her mouth as the entire memory, from beginning to terrifying end, burst into her mind. She bounded to her feet, grabbed hold of the rusty bars, and shook them until she wearied herself from the effort. They didn't budge. Who tossed her inside this terrible place and for what purpose? In spite of all effort, she couldn't place the owner of that gruff voice that demanded cooperation.

Mariah peeked through the bars of her prison. About twelve feet of floor space separated her cell from those across the aisle. But to which castle did this dungeon belong? She moved closer to the stones in order to examine them a little better in the diffused light. If not mistaken, this prison belonged to Cailen's castle, or at the very least, this structure used the same quarry during construction. In a twisted sort of way the thought provided some comfort. Yet at the same time, it also unleashed a great deal of despair. Her captivity meant that Cailen didn't, or perhaps even couldn't, detect her presence.

He had vanished before they touched, and the expression on his face in that moment haunted her now. He disappeared just as he did in the car when they crossed the Dupplin boundary. Both times the dark, ethereal force took him away against his will. Did the possibility exist, in completion of the reversal, the elements forced him to relive the last day of his mortal life again? Such an event would take several hours, wouldn't it? But just how long had this filthy cell imprisoned her? Mere minutes might've passed, or even hours for all she knew. Her cell phone could give her that information quick enough. She patted her pockets. To her dismay, she found them empty.

"Are you looking for this?"

She turned toward the sound of the unexpected voice. *Evan!* He stepped away from the shadows, holding her missing phone aloft. His smug expression filled her with revulsion. How long had he stood there, staring at her? Did it bring him pleasure to watch her struggle for a means to escape his vile prison?

"As a matter of fact, I am. Could you give it back to me now, please?" she asked, extending her open hand beyond the bars.

He chuckled and shook his head. "I can't do that, now can I? Stands to reason you would use it to call someone to assist your efforts to leave your wee nest. Surely you must understand I cannot let you do that just yet."

"Does that mean you'll allow me a phone call later?" she asked, raising a disdainful brow.

"Certainly, once you've taken th' special tea I'm brewing just for you." He tossed her a flirty smile and winked.

She rolled her eyes and huffed out a derisive breath. "Please don't tell me it's another ridiculous *love* potion."

He whipped his head to the side and locked his gaze to hers. The look in his eyes sent shivers down her spine. "So, th' knights were spying on me as far back as that, were they?"

Mariah clamped her lips together as she turned her face away and slammed her arms against her chest. She shouldn't have said that. Why did she always allow her temper to take control of her mouth?

"Is that why you so *clumsily* spilled it and refused even so much as a taste?" he asked.

She declined to answer his question, though he waited several long moments for her to do so.

He tilted his head to the side and shrugged. "It wouldn't have mattered. I didn't know when I brewed it that you had already given your heart away. And of all th' stupid, ridiculous things you could possibly do, you gave your heart to a ghost. I should have realized it from th' beginning when I first laid eyes on your sketches. Therefore, my potion wouldn't have had th' desired effect."

"And you think this new one will?"

"Och, without doubt." He nodded his confidence. "This one will make you forget any of th' knights ever existed. Do ye ken? All your memories of them will be gone in th' mere blink of an eye."

The arrogant tone roused her temper even further. "Just so you know—there's not an herb, potion, or magic incantation powerful enough to erase Cailen from my heart. He's possessed it far too long. You're wasting your time."

He shrugged. "We'll see."

Though she tried not to show it, Evan's calm assurance scared her half to death. Her thoughts drifted to Cailen. Surely when he returned to the castle, he would move heaven and earth to find her. If she called out to him periodically, he would hear her. He could find her simply by following the sound of her voice—

"If you're thinking your knight will rescue you, let me save you th' trouble of hoping," he said. "Cailen is not coming back."

Dread descended upon her. "What makes you think not?" she countered.

"Because th' man died on th' field of Dupplin centuries ago. Your spell managed to send him to where ever he should have gone in th' first place. Knowing him, 'twas probably th' deepest pit of hell."

"No, he wouldn't leave, not now."

"Oh, is that so? You've been here almost forty-eight hours, now. If your courageous knight had th' power to remain behind, he would have come for you already, do you ken?"

She'd been inside this filthy cell for two full days? If the reversal forced Cailen and his knights to relive their final hours at Dupplin, he would already have returned hours ago. Desperation provided a host of other reasons for the delay. Yet, she had to cast each impossible notion aside until none remained.

Her throat constricted as unbearable grief shattered her heart. She had lost Cailen, just as Evan said. She turned around, leaned her back against the bars, and closed her eyes against the onslaught of pain that assaulted her heart. Tears threatened to surface but somehow she held them at bay. She wouldn't let Evan see her cry.

"Well," said Evan as he strolled toward her cell. "I've got to get back to th' pub. You might like to know, I no longer feel th' need to keep you sedated now that you're back to yourself. So, as a special treat, I'll bring you something to eat after my shift."

"Don't bother," she whispered. "I won't eat it."

"Dinnae tell me what to do, witch! Now isn't th' time," he snarled.

She drew her brows together. "What?"

At once, he shifted his mood. He flashed a smile and waved a hand in dismissal. "Look—you dinnae need to worry, Mariah. I'm not going to put anything into your food, and I know you must be getting hungry by now. So that being said, is there anything special you'd like me to bring you?"

"Yes, you can bring me the key."

His laughter echoed as he tromped up the steps. She then heard the latch click and the door creak open. The moment it banged shut, she released the flood of tears. Memories of Cailen filled her mind then, one after the other. She recalled her first day at the castle when he spoke her name—the moment she saw him wielding his sword on the fields when she thought him an illusion. His flirty grin the instant he appeared in the tower and presented himself. The very first kiss that left her both amazed and breathless. Each wondrous kiss that followed the first. She relived every word they shared and clung to each "I luv ye" he whispered into her ear. They created a thousand precious memories together and she summoned them all, many times over, during the darkest hours she had ever endured. She would need those memories in the days, months, and years ahead. The instant the thought entered her mind, Evan's insidious plans stormed into the forefront of her mind.

"No!" She shook her head and clenched her teeth. "You'll not take him from me, Evan. I won't allow it."

Grim determination prompted a thorough study of

her environment. She had to find a way out of here before Evan's return. The remains of a rough-hewn table built from massive logs sat abandoned in the center of the aisle close to the stairs. The table supported the only artificial light inside the dungeon. She supposed she could muster a miniscule amount of gratitude for the propane-powered lantern Evan left behind.

The dripping water originated from small open windows at the top of the dungeon walls, as did the sound of the wind. Surely, these same windows allowed Tatters passage. But were they big enough to allow her escape if she could get to them? She could move the table against the wall. Once atop the thing, she could jump up, catch hold of the ledge, and hoist herself up. She could then ease herself through the opening.

She shifted her gaze to the ground in a desperate search for something she could use as a tool. Rocks in various shapes and sizes littered the floor. A large, sharp stone seized her attention first. She could do quite a bit of damage with that one, but try as she might, she just couldn't attain it. A further search located a palm-sized rock, just outside and to the right of her cell.

She stooped down, smashed her body against the bars, and stretched her arm to the limit in order to claim it. The tip of her fingers grazed along the edge. She shifted her body to give her shoulder a little more freedom and inched forward. This time, she rolled the stone toward her using just the tips of her fingers. Several attempts later, she succeeded in dragging it up against the bars. Yet, even as she grasped it, her hopes faltered. The rock didn't have sufficient weight to sever the iron.

Nevertheless, she bashed it against the rustiest bar, hoping to bend it far enough to allow her body passage. She hammered until her exhausted hand went numb from the effort. Yet, she didn't so much as put a dent in the thing. Her eyes closed as she rubbed her fingers over her brow. She drew in a deep breath and gave the rock an indifferent toss. Fresh out of ideas, she returned to the makeshift bed. Tatters, who miraculously remained at her side, climbed into her lap. She gathered her close, taking comfort in her presence. A lump formed in her throat as she called her knight to mind once again.

"Cailen," she whispered. "Can you hear me at all from wherever you are now? If you can, please know how very much I love you and that I'm sorry—so very, very sorry." Tears streamed down her cheeks as she relived the moment just before his disappearance. What did she do wrong and why didn't Mairwen stop her?

Mairwen. Her ghostly friend warned her of Evan's approach and tried to help in the only way she could at the time. Would she abandon her now, knowing Evan held her captive if she could choose otherwise? Surely, she wouldn't. Although the knights had vanished during that horrible instant, Mairwen and her companions remained behind at least long enough to witness her capture. Were they still here somewhere inside the castle or on the grounds? Did they stand by while Evan carried her down here, or perchance did he use one of his horrid spells to banish them from his presence?

She turned her gaze heavenward. The bizarre notion seemed so far-fetched, but then again, so did magic love potions, and evil spells that bind men's souls to a specific place and boundary. And, last but certainly not least, Evan wanted her to drink something that would make her forget Cailen existed.

What if he really could?

She sat up and brushed the tears away from her cheeks. After swallowing past the knot in her throat, she called out in a quiet voice, "Mairwen? Can you hear me? Evan has me locked inside this dungeon and I can't get out. Please, please, if you're anywhere near and can hear me, I need your help. I need to get out of here."

How long she awaited a response, she couldn't say. Yet nothing but silence met her desperate plea. Weariness beset her and she welcomed the fatigue with open arms. For while she slept, she wouldn't feel any torment. Painful thoughts couldn't afflict her mind. Mariah took a deep breath and slowly released it. She eased her body onto the mattress, cuddled Tatters close to her body, and closed her eyes.

****

A while later, and she didn't know how much time had passed, the sound of metal clicking against metal intruded into her dreams. The violent rattling of irons bars followed. Her heart thumped in response to a rising hope. Cailen! Her eyes flew open as she bolted upright and turned her head toward her prison gate.

"Cailen?" she called out. She rose from her mattress, took hold of the bars, and stood on tiptoes, trying to peek around them as best she could.

She waited for what seemed an eternity for some kind of response. Nothing but silence followed the sound of her voice. She must have dreamed it then. Disheartened, her fingers slid down the rusted metal as she placed her forehead against the door and battled a new wave of tears. Just then, the door at the top of the stairs groaned on its hinges and assisted her efforts. Footsteps followed. Evan stepped around the corner and entered her view. He bowed low at the waist in greeting and shifted the bag he carried into his other hand.

"You're up," he said jovially. "Since it's so late in th' evening, I would have thought you'd be fast asleep."

"Yes, well—it's difficult to know the time, down here in this dank little hole. All I can tell you," she said pointing to the windows, "is that it's night."

He halted his steps and looked all about as if inspecting the dungeon for the first time. "Och, I dinnae know, the place looks fairly large to me. You should be comfortable enough for th' time being."

She turned away from him and released a sigh of exasperation.

"Now there is no reason for th' surly attitude," he said as he approached her cell. "Look, I have brought you something to eat. That should cheer you up some."

"I told you," she spat, as she rose to her feet, "I will *not* eat anything *you* bring me."

Despite her rage, he shoved the bag between the bars and let it drop. "You will when you get hungry enough, I should think. In th' meantime, I have brought you something to drink. I know you must be very thirsty by now." He winked.

Evan stuck the paper cup between the bars. Mariah ignored his smug expression as she took hold of the container and removed the lid. She lifted a brow as she stepped to the back of her cell, turned the cup upside down and poured the foul-smelling drink onto the ground.

Anger filled his eyes and for just a moment, she thought he would strike her. And that's exactly what she hoped for by dumping out his vile potion. For then he would have to open the door. She could pick up that large sharp rock, smash him over the head with it, and make her escape.

"Let's be reasonable, Mariah," he said as he shifted his mood to one of casual humor. The instant change unnerved her. "We both know Cailen isn't coming back. That knowledge must bring you unnecessary pain and a powerful heap of suffering. I'm sure if you gave it some thought, you'd arrive at th' conclusion that forgetting would be th' most desirable course to take. Especially since you're directly responsible for his removal from this earth."

His comment intensified her pain.

He chuckled and lifted his eyes heavenward before he returned his gaze to her. "Th' storm you produced at th' conclusion of your spell was something to behold. Everyone in th' entire community talked aboot it. They all raced outside and watched it. 'Twas quite a miraculous event. They said they had never seen th' like before."

"What makes you think I'm responsible for the storm?" she murmured.

He laughed as he shook his head. "This might come as a surprise, but you are not th' only person to receive instruction from th' redheaded ghost that dwells here."

She used every shred of will power she possessed to maintain an indifferent expression. His comment *did* surprise her, but she refused to respond.

"Despite your obstinate silence, I know you must be curious, so I'll go ahead and tell you aboot my experience with th' ghostly lass. She began working on me when I was just a wee lad. Somehow she made pictures flash through my mind. At times, we would take walks. During those walks, she would show me where I could find some of those pictures inside my head. Any of this sound familiar to you yet?"

She smothered a yawn.

"'Twas all those lessons she gave me that got me interested in th' art of sorcery. Once I could read, I devoured every book I could find on th' subject. My little hobby distressed th' ghost something fierce, as it did my parents. They took away my book and hid it. Though it took quite awhile, I finally found it again—just after you arrived at the castle, in fact. Anyway, I digress.

"When I understood what th' lassie wanted me to do with th' plants and th' pictures, I decided that I didn't want to comply. I had grown quite fond of th' knights by then, and didn't want them to leave th' castle. They were my friends."

Mariah shot him a scathing look. "They were your friends, and yet you didn't want to help them?"

He paused for a moment and then shook his head. "No, I didn't. They told me often enough that they were happy here, so why chance sending them off to a place that would bring them misery?"

Like you did, the expression he assumed all but shouted. He might just as well have said the words aloud. Still, she didn't deign to reply.

"If you had told me from th' beginning that you met th' knights, I would have taken th' necessary steps to complete th' old woman's spell at that time, not th' redhead's."

He paused and for just an instant, his face morphed

into a hideous mask of revulsion that looked nothing like his own. He dropped his gaze as his entire body shuddered. And then at once, his triumphant smile returned. The scene unnerved her.

"You see, though the redhead never knew it, th' witch intended to cast th' knights into th' outer reaches of darkness from whence they could never escape. In her mind, supporters of King Robert and murderers of her clansmen deserved no less." Another lengthy pause followed the revelation.

She closed her eyes and leaned her head against the wall.

"You really had me going, you know," he goaded. "I didn't even suspect you knew th' knights until I saw th' picture of your painting in th' newspaper. You gave it all away with that one. If you had wanted to keep your precious secrets, you shouldn't have painted th' faces of th' other knights."

That cemented it. She turned her face to meet his gaze and glared.

"What you don't seem to understand is the relationship I have with other people is really none of your business," she hissed.

Evan chuckled. "That's just what Cailen said as well."

Cailen said that? When did he show himself to Evan? Although she had a burning desire to ask him about it, she refused the need.

After another lengthy silence, he shrugged. "You ought to eat while th' food is fresh. You dinnae want it to spoil."

She gave her head a little toss. "No. That would be a pity, wouldn't it?" Evan flashed a satisfied smile as she picked up and opened the bag. Tatters twirled around her legs while she withdrew the sandwich, piled high with meat and cheese. And although her stomach growled in hunger, she sat down on her makeshift bed and tore the meat into small pieces so Tatters could eat. The sneer that replaced Evan's smile gave *her* satisfaction.

His eyes narrowed and he balled his hands into fists. "Well, your time inside this prison is just about up, Mariah. Soon you'll be free of this place. Come th' morning, I'll once again, have my special brew ready for consumption. In th' meantime, think on what I said aboot th' blessing selective amnesia will bring you. I can promise, such a thing will free you from th' torment you feel right now. But know this—willing or not, I swear by everything I hold dear, this time, you will drink it."

Chapter 28

Cailen pondered the strange new feeling that plagued him. He felt—weighted. No matter how often he tried, he just couldn't move his form away from its current prison. Yet, he never once lost consciousness during this peculiar ordeal. His thoughts functioned as they always did, and he remained cognizant of everything going on about him.

He called out to the knights several times over. None of them responded. Such a thing had never happened to him before. At least, not in his spiritual state. Where did everyone go? Did they find the light and travel its path while someone confined him in this unknown place by himself? What power held him bound? Exactly what did the reversal of Elspetha's spell accomplish?

Strange noises surrounded his consciousness. He could hear rhythmic thumps and it sounded very much like someone continuously beat a drum somewhere in his vicinity. A ritual perhaps? The annoying noise, soft at first, grew louder as time passed and he wanted nothing more than to find the perpetrator, viciously throttle him, and banish him from his presence for all time, ritual or no ritual. He could also hear the sound of collective breathing. Did a host of living people surround his soul? Why would a multitude of mortals watch over his spirit anyway? For what purpose and how long did they intend to detain him in this dark place? He desperately wanted the answers because he needed to escape this confinement, return to his castle with all haste, and either find all well there, or do something about the mayhem.

The troubling, chaotic thoughts led him back to Mariah once again. Concern engulfed him as he recalled her total devastation when the powerful force yanked him from her presence. The same force, in fact, that took him out of the car on their way to Edinburgh. Therefore, he truly expected to find himself on the field of Dupplin. He didn't return. Instead, the forceful entity took him to a place of darkness he didn't understand. Did that force intend to keep him shrouded in shadows for all the ages of time? Did he deserve such a fate?

No. He refused to accept that. Somehow, he had to break free of this prison, and find Mariah. For the umpteenth time, he sought for the abundant energy that surrounds all living things and strained with all his might to gather a portion of it unto himself. Once again, he failed, just as he had each time before.

Up until the reversal of the spell, he could perform the action with ease. That energy gave him the skill to speak, to walk, to move things about and appear as if mortal to those who still breathed. Did the completion of the spell mean he would have to learn those abilities all over again? If such proved true, then he wouldn't have the necessary skill to communicate with Mariah right away. Would she think he abandoned her to the light—a light he still couldn't see—despite the promise to the contrary? A heavy sigh passed through his lips and as it did, he could feel—

Movement.

His thoughts abruptly ceased as he sought to understand the movement and its origin. Did it exude from his form or did it exude from some other source? It occurred to him then that the obnoxious thumping and sounds of breathing had ceased. For that, he offered his heartfelt gratitude.

"Cailen!"

A feminine voice, laden with desperation called out to him. Did the familiar voice belong to someone from Dugald's castle or the area roundabout perchance? No, wait a minute—

"Cailen, ye churlish, ill-headed wagtail! Wake up!"

Only Mairwen had ever called him that—and got away with it. Mairwen! He turned his head in the direction of her voice. Why couldn't he see her? Why indeed, he scoffed. He'd never been able to see her in his spiritual state. At least not until he walked out of the passageway. But then again, he'd never heard her speak, either—

"Open your eyes, ye great fool!" she shouted into his ears.

Open his eyes? What in bloody blazes did she mean by that? The lassie made no sense.

"Och, how thick can ye get? You're in your mortal body, ye misbegotten gudgeon," she screamed. "Evan has Murriah locked away in th' dungeon and I cannae get her out! He's comin' for her. Th' man intends to pour a vile potion down her throat, do ye ken? Now, get up!"

At the mere mention of Evan's name, warm blood pulsated throughout his body and the feeling of it amazed him. He parted his lips to speak, but failed in the attempt. The inside of his mouth lacked any sign of moisture. He worked up a bit of spit and then swallowed it down to lubricate his throat. He repeated the action several times before a semblance of normalcy returned.

"Listen to me, Cailen," Mairwen demanded. "Evan hid by th' river durin' th' time Murriah completed th' spell. While we were all in our weakened condition, he captured her and took her down to th' dungeon. I have tried many times to get her out, but I dinnae possess th' ability. Th' laddie put some kind of enchantment on th' door, and I cannae open it. He intends to force a potion down her throat that will make her forget ye! Do ye ken what I'm sayin' to ye? She will no longer know who ye are!"

"Mairwen!" The new voice sounded like it might belong to Aveline and she seemed quite alarmed.

"Evan has arrived. He's just now gettin' out of his car and headin' for th' gate," she said.

Cailen concentrated on flexing his muscles. They responded to his mental command far easier than he expected. First his legs and then his arm muscles contracted.

"Does he have his despicable potion along with him?" asked Mairwen.

"Aye, and he has it in some kind of cup that has a twist on lid. Th' lid has a spout protrudin' from th' top. I think he's goin' to force it down her throat with that pointy wee spout!" cried Aveline. "Are th' knights awake yet?"

Cailen stretched every muscle inside his body and in that same instant, his chest expanded in response to her question. With a mighty heave, he hurled his body upright. He forced his eyes open and then swung his legs off his bower. With sword in hand, he rose to his feet. He completed the maneuver without undue hardship despite the fact he hadn't occupied his mortal frame for centuries. Yet, 'twas as if he never left it.

For the first time in over seven hundred years, he took a deep breath of air and exhaled it. All the while, he gazed into the faces of his sister and her companions. A thousand questions popped into his mind, but none of them mattered, save one.

"Has th' bloody churl entered th' dungeon?"

A look of relief appeared on Mairwen's face as their eyes met and held. While he waited for her to speak, the deafening clamor of his knights rising to their feet behind him, entered into his ears. At any other time, he might've found a bit of amusement in the chaos.

"I dinnae know—"

Just then Alison popped into the room, she spared Steven a brief glance and said, "He's just aboot to th' dungeon door. Ye must hurry!"

Cailen rushed past the women who had remained in their spiritual form. He climbed over the top of the scattered, rocky debris that had entombed their earthly remains without giving a thought as to how or when the devastation occurred. His knights followed him as he made all haste to the dungeon. Once he arrived at his destination, he kicked the door off its hinges and rushed down the steps, taking them two at a time. The scene he encountered at the bottom made his blood run cold.

Elspetha stood beside Evan. A sadistic smile exposed her rotted teeth. Hatred filled her eyes as she whispered the incantations Evan repeated. The miscreant had already yanked Mariah out of her cell and had crushed her body against the iron bars. With one arm holding her captive, he forced the container into her lips and between her clenched teeth. All the while, she turned and twisted her head to ward off the assault. She choked and sputtered, but Evan gave her no quarter. So intent on his purpose, he didn't hear the rending of the door or the sound of their approach. Elspetha, though aware of their presence, urged Evan to hurry and complete his spell.

"Let her go, Evan!" he demanded as he closed the space between them.

Evan whirled around to face him while still clutching his victim. A mixture of astonishment, joy, and relief filled Mariah's eyes even as Evan filled his with malice. Elspetha shrieked her rage. For a brief moment, the laddie shifted his gaze to the witch. Yet, she offered him nothing in return but disdain.

"This is impossible," Evan spat. He tightened his grip around Mariah's waist and inched backward, dragging her along with him. "You're not supposed to be here. The spell cast you out of this realm, and you had no way to return."

Ignoring the idiotic comment, Cailen moved forward. "Dinnae try it, Evan, ye'll lose th' battle, just as ye did afore."

"You cannae have her, do you ken?" he screamed. "She doesn't belong to you."

Without warning, Mariah lowered her head and opened her mouth. She took a deep breath and then clamped down on Evan's arm. He screamed out in pain. In response, he grabbed her by the hair and brutally flung her to the side. Full of wrath, Cailen rushed toward him.

Just as his fist connected to Evan's jaw, sending him flying backward, Elspetha turned her vengeance upon Mariah. A flash of blinding, purple light accompanied Mariah's shriek of pain even as Mairwen and her companions converged upon the witch while chanting words he didn't understand. In the same instant, Evan prevented him from hastening to Mariah's side. He staggered to his feet. The lad screamed in fury and, head-first, hurled his body at his chest. Evan bounced off his armor, yet before he hit the ground, Cailen grabbed hold of his shirt and yanked him to his feet. He slammed him down on the table several times over, the force of which sent the lantern flying against the iron bars across the way. He then dug his elbow into his chest and pinned him there.

Though dazed, Evan struggled to free himself from his grasp, all the while spitting out a string of filthy curses and intense hatred for him and the knights. Ignoring his vile mouth, he held him fast. He turned his head away from Evan and glanced at his men. Duncan itched to get into the fight. "Duncan, fetch me th' cup that Evan had."

Evan's eyes widened in horror as Duncan swooped the cup from off the ground and strode toward them.

"Let me give it to him, Cailen," he said, locking his gaze on their opponent. Duncan's eyes gleamed in anticipation of the coveted assignment.

"I'll give ye a hand," Steven bellowed.

"Cailen," Mairwen called out. "Ye better come quick. Murriah needs attention right now."

"Dinnae worry," Duncan said. "We'll finish this here. See to your woman."

Evan choked and gurgled as his knights forced the

potion he created for Mariah, down his own throat. Cailen didn't know the effect it would have on him nor did he care. Not right now.

The ghostly women parted to let him through. Mairwen cradled Mariah's head in her lap. He knelt beside them and took hold of his lady's hand. "Murriah?" he whispered.

She didn't respond to his voice. He scooped her up into his arms and turned to face his sister. "Where's Elspetha?" he asked.

"We banished her from this realm using magic of our own," said Mairwen. "She cannae return. 'Twas our right to send her off to the same place she intended to send ye, Cailen."

He gave her a nod, dismissing the witch altogether from his mind. "Ye need to come with me, and tell me what I need to do." Never in his entire existence had he experienced such fear or ever felt so helpless.

Mairwen looked around for the knight closest to her position. "Malcolm," she said, in a voice that commanded. "Ye need to fetch a bowl of warm water and some towels from Murriah's bathroom. Edmund come along with me to Sybil's cottage. We need to borrow some of her herbs. Cailen, we'll meet ye back inside Murriah's room just as quickly as we can. Prop her up on her pillows because th' first thing were goin' to do is empty her belly, do ye ken?"

Cailen cuddled Mariah close to his heart as he carried her up the stairs, out of the dungeon, and into her room.

A flurry of activity followed. Mairwen prepared a brew that caused her stomach to purge itself with a violence that alarmed him. She followed that with another foul smelling potion intended to counter Evan's spell and heal any internal damage caused by Elspetha's vicious magic. Each time, getting her to drink the contents in her unconscious state proved most difficult. Nonetheless, at the end of her ordeal he and Mairwen removed her soiled clothing, cleaned her up a bit, and got her into a fresh nightshirt.

Darkness overtook the castle, and for the first time since their deaths, the knights needed conventional methods to light the torches so they could see. He could hear them all talking down in the hall, but not with the clarity to which he'd grown accustomed. He wouldn't leave Mariah's side in order to listen to their conversation, though. Time for talking would come soon enough.

Once he removed his heavy armor, retaining only his léine and surcoat, he sat down on the edge of the bed. He took hold of Mariah's hand and held it firmly within his own. By so doing, he hoped to transfer some of his strength and vitality into her weakened body. For right now, he had an abundance of both. He harbored the hope that when she opened her exquisite, azure-colored eyes, he'd see recognition and joy in her gaze.

Mairwen swept into the room then, and sidled up next to him. "She doesna feel overly warm, does she?" she asked.

He placed a hand atop her brow and shook his head. "Nay, th' temperature of her body feels normal enough to me."

Mairwen nodded. "Well, ye need to check on that oft. I dinnae have th' same ability to assess a fever as ye have now."

He took a moment to consider the miracle of his

renewed mortality. "Did ye know this would happen to us when ye had Murriah reverse th' spell?"

"Not with absolute certainty but I suspected." She paused for several moments and then said, "After several centuries of goin' over Elspetha's words, I came to believe that since she never completed th' spell, her wicked enchantment could be nullified. So, we started to pay attention to those who professed to practice magic, both for good and evil purposes. As ye might suspect, we gained quite an education over time. From these sorcerers and witches, we learned th' proper words and herbs needed to reverse Elspetha's spell. I just didna know if ye could reclaim your bodies or not. At th' verra least, I knew ye could leave th' circle to which ye were bound and go where ever ye might chose to go. I knew I would be able to speak to ye at long last, and tell ye all that transpired."

Cailen held up a hand to belay her words. "Ye dinnae need to speak of it, Mairwen. I know all this. Murriah shared all her dreams and sketches with me as I'm sure ye already know. Ye only wanted to keep us safe and that was a charitable thing for ye to do."

Mairwen tilted her head to the side as a small smile emerged. "I have heard ye say such to Murriah many times. Ye dinnae know how much your forgiveness meant to me—to all of us, and I thank ye for it."

"No. 'Tis I that need to thank ye for all ye've done. Ye've given me a second chance at life and provided a way for me and Murriah to remain together."

"'Tis th' least I could do, Cailen, after all my mischief." She leaned down and kissed the top of his head. "I'll leave ye to your lady. Duncan will want to speak with me, I'm sure. He has a few questions of his own."

"What did the lads do with Evan?" he asked.

She lifted a single shoulder. "After th' man drank his own potion, he lost consciousness. Duncan and Steven hauled his yeasty body out to his car, turned th' vehicle around, and pushed it a goodly distance down th' road. I dinnae think Evan will come back to the castle once he wakes up. Most likely, he will not remember why he came out here in th' first place."

"What effect do ye think his potion will have on him?" he asked.

"'Twill have th' same effect he wished upon Murriah, times three. When he wakes up, he will not remember that ye, or any of th' knights, ever existed. Mayhap he will find that he doesna believe in ghosts at all."

"What aboot Murriah? Will he still have feelin's for her?" he asked.

"I dinnae know for certain. But if any luv for her remains, it will not be near so strong. Once he sees her heart is taken by a big unsightly lout like ye. He will not pursue her, especially if he values his life."

****

Cailen refused to leave Mariah's side. He gazed down at her lovely face and willed her to wake more times than he cared to count. Yet, fear gnawed at him that when she did, she would think him naught but a stranger. That fear inspired him to pour out his heart. He reminded her of each and every conversation they shared. Throughout the days that followed, he called attention to their walks, their laughter, and the passion of their kisses. Despite all effort, she didn't even stir.

Then as the sun rose for the third time, he withdrew

her hand from underneath the blanket, placed it between his own, and gently caressed it. "I need ye to wake up now, my lady," he whispered. "I hunger to see your smile and hear your laughter. I hunger to see th' luv ye feel for me shinin' in your eyes. And ye dinnae ken how badly I want to respond by showin' ye mine. For I luv ye more than life itself. Please, Murriah, please—for me, open your eyes so I can tell ye, just how much I luv ye."

She remained motionless. After a ragged breath, he tried again.

"Ye cannae leave me now." He paused as he fought for control over his emotions. "I'm beggin' ye, Murriah, wake up. Please, wake up."

At once, she took in a deep breath, held it for a moment, and then slowly released it. Her free hand escaped the confines of the blankets and traveled up the length of her face. She combed her fingers through her hair and for just a tiny moment, she drew her brows together.

"My lady?"

She turned her head slightly in the direction of his voice as her eyes slowly fluttered opened. His freshly beating heart dropped deep into the pit of his gut as confusion leaped into her eyes the moment their gazes locked and held. Time stood still as they looked at each other. Tremendous fear seized his soul.

Did she not know him then?

No matter.

He determined in that infinite space of time that if such had occurred he wouldn't allow her to leave this castle until he captured her heart. He had done so once, he could—and would—do so again.

A lump formed in his throat. "Murriah?" he called in a voice barely above a whisper.

In response, she again drew her brows together. She lifted a hand to his face, just as she did the first time they met. Yet, she stopped just short of connecting. She cleared her throat, shook her head, and said, "Cailen, your surcoat is different, and why aren't you wearing your armor?"

He wanted to shout his elation. Instead he simply shrugged and said, "Because it was heavy, my lady."

"Heavy?"

He suppressed a grin and nodded. "Aye, verra heavy."

Her look of confusion delighted him. He couldn't resist the desire to gather her into his arms, draw her close to his body, and give her the kiss he had wanted to give her the moment she exited her car outside his castle gates months ago.

He could feel the shock engulf her as their lips met. For a miniscule second, she shoved her hands against his chest, wanting answers. He could see that. But not now. No, not now—

Instead, he merely deepened the kiss, knowing the answers would have to wait. In response to that burning desire, a gentle hand traveled upward from his chest to the side of his face, and into his hair. Simultaneously, her other arm curled around his neck and cuddled him closer still. She responded to his first mortal kiss with a fiery passion that matched his own.

Chapter 29

"Cailen, ye have a visitor," Duncan said as his eyes danced with mischief.

A slight smile appeared on the face of her beloved knight who nodded in return. "I'll be right back, my lady." He hastily rose from the edge of her mattress. She followed his exit as he rounded the bed and made his way out of the door.

Though curious as to who would visit this late in the evening, Mariah said nothing as he vacated her bedroom. Why bother? Nothing she said mattered much anyway. Despite all desire to the contrary, the man hadn't allowed her to rise from this bed for three full days, save to take her showers.

During her period of confinement, the castle residents served her meals and entertained her in shifts during all her waking hours. The incarceration and curiosity drove her mad. Her body might've borne some kind of malevolent assault but her ears worked well enough, and she could quite easily discern the sounds of furniture moving about the castle.

When she asked Cailen about it, he said they all needed a place to sleep now they were mortal again, did they not? He also told her they needed more than wooden benches to sit upon, and begged her pardon for not realizing that before. She so much wanted to be in the middle of all the excitement, to see what the furniture looked like and discover where it originated from, but "Oh, my no," she remained much too frail to get out of bed. And, somewhere in the back of her mind, she wondered what Laird McNaughton would think when next he visited.

She released an exasperated sigh just as Mairwen entered the room and took a seat at the edge of her mattress. Mariah welcomed her company. She'd grown quite attached to Cailen's sweet sister during her period of confinement.

"How are ye feelin' this eve?" she asked.

"Much like I did in the dungeon, only the surroundings and company are far more pleasant," she quipped.

Mairwen let out a bit of a laugh. "I know ye feel such, but 'twas imperative to give your body a chance to heal from th' inner wounds inflicted by Elspetha. She sought your death ye know."

"I know that, really I do. But still—" Mariah shrugged and left it at that.

"Well, you're healed well enough now, and ye will not be needin' my services any longer. So, I wanted to take this opportunity to tell ye goodbye, even though we will not be leavin' until sometime on th' morrow."

The smile in her eyes contained a hint of mystery, but Mariah didn't want to ponder over it now.

"What do you mean?" she asked. "Where are you going?"

"Well, th' time for us to move on has come, Murriah. After all these centuries of waitin', we have finally accomplished what we wanted to accomplish," she said. "We couldn't have done it without your help though, and for that I give ye my deepest, heartfelt gratitude."

Her throat tightened. She didn't know quite how to respond to that. "Does Cailen know you're going away?"

"Aye, he knows," she replied. "I spoke with him at length earlier this morn. He's verra happy for us, and I want ye to be happy for us too."

"I am, Mairwen, truly I am." She attempted a smile. "I guess I just found it pleasant to have a little bit of female companionship around here."

Mairwen waved a hand in dismissal. "Och, ye dinnae have to worry aboot that. At least not for th' time bein'."

"I don't?"

Mairwen leaned forward, placed a hand on top of hers, and said, "In case ye haven't noticed, Alison and Steven cannae keep their hands to themselves and th' same goes for Margery and Roger. So, they wish to remain behind for now. After all, what self-respectin' castle doesna house a ghost or two, aye?"

Mariah breathed out a laugh. "I don't know a single one. But, Mairwen? I'm really going to miss *you*."

Mairwen shook her head ever so slightly. "Dinnae worry, I'll check on ye from time to time, especially if I find ye need me." She wrapped her arms around her then and gave her a ghostly hug just as Cailen returned, holding a rather large envelope in his hand.

Mairwen rose to her feet, exchanged a conspiratorial smile with her brother, and said, "I'll see ye both a wee bit later."

"Ye look exhausted, my lady," Cailen said after his sister vacated the room. "I think ye should close your eyes and try to get some sleep. I want ye well rested."

She said nothing in return as he took possession of the remote and turned off the power to the generator. However, before he could snuff the light from her lanterns, she extended her hand in invitation. He sat down on the edge of her bed, twined his fingers around hers, and waited for her to speak.

"Enough is enough, Cailen," she said using the firmest tone she could muster. "I feel fine, really I do. In fact, I feel great! You can't keep me confined any longer. I've not had a headache or a stomachache for two full days. I'm going stir crazy in this bedroom. I need to paint. Go outside. Take a walk. Scrub a toilet—*anything* but stay in bed another day. Do you understand?"

During her little tirade, she could see the tremendous effort he made to hold a grin at bay and she really wanted to slug him for it.

"I'm verra happy to hear it, my lady, for I have somethin' I need to ask ye, now that you're feelin' up to hearin' it. And I'm hopin' ye'll oblige th' request."

"You want me to do something for you?" she asked, suddenly excited over the very prospect of doing something useful.

He shrugged and said, "Aye, I suppose ye could put it that way."

"What would you like me to do?"

"Take a wee journey to Thurso, and spend a few days with me there," he replied. "Th' work ye have left can wait that long, aye?"

The idea of taking a trip with Cailen, even a short one, filled her with pleasure. "Yes, the paintings can wait that long, and I'd love to go to Thurso with you," she said. And then as an afterthought added, "But why Thurso?"

"That's where th' weddin' will take place, of course," he said.

"Wedding?" she asked.

He simply nodded as if his words should make perfect sense.

"Who's getting married?"

"We are, my lady, if ye'll have me for your husband." He paused for a brief moment and then added, "I dinnae need to ask your father for your hand, aye?"

Her eyes widened and as she gasped her delight, she threw herself into his waiting arms. He chuckled in response, tightened his massive arms around her waist while she clung to him and cried. Then for several sweet, memorable moments, they shared the most wondrous kiss he had given her to date. Somewhere in the back of her mind, she wondered just how many different kinds of kisses he had in his vast repertoire— not that she had any complaints over a single one of them—

Once he ended the kiss, he drew back slightly, gently wiped the tears from her cheeks and smiled. "I take it ye have accepted my request then?"

She swallowed past the knot in her throat as she nodded. "Oh yes, I've definitely accepted your request."

"Good," he said. "Because all of th' necessary arrangements have already been made. We just have to arrive at th' church on time, so ye'll need to arise early."

"Really?" At once, her mind traveled to all the

tedious legal requirements. "Don't we need to get a marriage license or something first?"

He lifted his thick envelope and gave it a wave. "We have already acquired one."

"How on earth did you do that?" she asked.

He paused, turned his head to the side, and lifted a single shoulder. "Well, I have a friend who had th' means to—*provide* me and th' lads with all th' paperwork we need to establish our identity in your twenty-first century," he said. "In the same way, he also had th' means to expedite our license after I filched your driver's license and gave it to him."

She knew better than to ask questions, for obviously his friend wished to remain anonymous for understandable reasons. She wouldn't ask him to betray that trust and really, she didn't care.

"Do I get to see the marriage license?" she asked.

In response, he opened the envelope, removed the contents, and placed them all atop her lap, save one. Amidst a birth certificate, driver's license, passport, and various other credentials, lay the document that allowed her to become his legally and lawfully wedded wife. She picked it up, fastened her gaze on the certificate and savored each word.

After a few silent moments, she dabbed at a tear and sniffed. "This all seems so surreal to me. I never once thought I would have the honor of becoming your wife, Cailen"

"Nay, Murriah," he whispered. "'Tis ye who bestows th' honor, by consentin' to marry th' likes of me."

After another delicious kiss or two, maybe three, he looked down at the document he clutched in his hand. He offered it to her then, and said, "Och, I almost forgot. Your weddin' gift, my lady."

Confusion beset her as she took the document out of his hand and fixed her gaze on the page. A sharp intake of breath soon followed. "The deed to the castle?" she cried out. "But how? I don't—"

Cailen rested a finger against her lips to still her questions and winked. "I did just a wee bit a tradin' with MacNaughton. He selected a few trinkets from down inside our tomb in exchange for th' castle and th' means to furnish it. He seemed more than satisfied with th' bargain. Th' man said he was gettin' too old to worry aboot th' place anyway. Nonetheless, he told me to tell ye that he still expects his paintin'," he said.

"Oh, Cailen," she said as she wrapped her arms around his neck. "I'll paint him as many as he wants!"

****

Shortly after dawn, a subtle knock sounded on her door, followed by Cailen, calling her name. She zipped up her freshly packed suitcase and then opened the door. When he saw her standing there, wearing her almond, ruched-sleeved sweater dress, he grinned and shook his head.

"I dinnae think ye'd be awake, much less ready to go," he said.

"Seriously?" she asked, raising a brow. "After all the sleep you forced on me this past week? Come on, Cailen, it's our wedding day. I'm wide awake and excited to get on the road."

"Well," he said, "our means of travel will not be here for another thirty minutes or so."

While he spoke, it dawned on Mariah that Cailen no longer wore his medieval attire. He had dressed for their journey in a form-fitting black T-shirt and jeans. She supposed his mysterious friend must also have supplied him with a start to his wardrobe. Of their own accord, her hands traveled to his chest and then upward across his broad shoulders. She tilted her head, drew in a short breath and said, "Very impressive, Sir Cailen Braithnoch."

"Aye?" he asked with raised brow as he pinched just a piece of the fabric.

"Oh, definitely, aye," she said, knowing her comment as well as the expression on her face, pleased him.

"I return th' compliment to ye, my lady. Ye look beautiful this morn." He took her suitcase off the bed and with her hand tucked in the crook of his arm, he led her down the stairs.

As they stepped onto the main floor, Mariah scanned the room, now filled to capacity with knights dressed similar to Cailen. They sprawled themselves out over the sofas and chairs, which lay scattered about, talking amongst themselves. Several lamp tables sat hither and yon, with a wide variety of kerosene lamps sitting atop them. Although very lovely, she would need to do something about the disarray once she got home. *Home*—the word took on a whole new meaning then, and she smiled her contentment.

Cailen took hold of her hand, squeezed it, and said, "Th' room needs a woman's touch to be sure and a bit of modernization along with it." He shrugged. "We'll figure all of that out together a wee bit later, though."

Just as the words left his mouth, a succession of raps sounded against the door and Alan bounded from his seat to answer. A man stood there with cap in hand

and, while gesturing at the fleet of vehicles waiting just outside the gate, said, "We're at your service, sir, whenever you are ready to go."

Mariah's mouth dropped over the unexpected sight. Even so, she had no idea the waiting entourage simply began a series of delightful surprises.

The procession of cars escorted them to the charming town of Thurso by the seashore, and thence to a quaint little chapel. The most exquisite Celtic style wedding dress awaited her there, with all the accessories one could think of to go along with it. While surrounded by her exuberant female ghostly companions, Madam MacNaughton helped her dress in her finery, and then Duncan escorted her to the chapel. She couldn't erase the smile from her face as he walked her down the aisle—an aisle filled to the limit with the rest of her knights dressed in full armor. They stood at attention with their swords unsheathed, pointing downward on the floor. As she took in the faces of her guests, it seemed that more ghosts attended her wedding than did her mortal friends, who remained ignorant of their presence. But truly, she expected no less.

Any other detail of her environment missed her completely as she sought for and then found Cailen, looking ever the fierce, handsome warrior of his century. Her heart fluttered wildly and a host of butterflies soared uncontrollably as he took possession of her hand. He gazed at her then as if he believed her the most precious, most exquisite, most beloved thing on this or any other planet. She hoped her eyes revealed those same sentiments in return.

Cailen felt near to bursting with pride as he drew

his lady to his side and took hold of her hand. He had never seen her look so beautiful. When prompted, he repeated and truly meant every word the minister had him say.

"I, Cailen Braithnoch, take ye, Murriah Jennin's, to be my legally and lawfully wedded wife, to have, to hold, to luv and cherish, from this day forward—"

Without taking his eyes away from hers, he listened to the sweet vows she spoke in return—words that bound them forever together. At the end of those vows, he placed a diamond and emerald ring on her finger, and then gave the kiss that sealed the promises they made to each other.

After a prolonged reception that took far longer than he had patience, they arrived at the secluded little cottage Laird MacNaughton provided them. He would have to remember to thank his new friend for all his assistance and for Mariah's look of wondrous delight as she took in every detail of their honeymoon cottage. Her gaze meandered over the table filled with baskets of food, the roaring fire, rustic furniture, and finally, the canopied bed.

He turned her around to face him then and gathered her close in his embrace. Her heart beat in wild abandon as he took his sweet time gazing into her eyes, for he wanted to relish each moment spent inside this cottage. He brushed his fingers through her hair and grinned.

"Ye seem a bit apprehensive, my lady, now that I have ye here, all to myself," he said. He leaned down then, and nuzzled one side of her neck and then the other. "You're tremblin'," he whispered.

"Well—I must admit, you are a bit...big and

quite…overpowering in your mortal form," she breathlessly replied as her arms encircled his neck.

"Are ye frightened?" he asked as he cuddled her body closer still.

"Oh—absolutely terrified," she murmured as she grazed her lips lightly against his. And then, just as he would kiss her, she said, "I love you, Cailen, with my whole heart and soul."

"As I luv ye, my lady." He had so much more he wanted to say. He wanted to express his gratitude for all she did and all she endured to give him this second chance at mortality—along with everything that gift entailed. To tell her what it meant to have her as his wife for all time. He wanted to tell her how very much he loved her, and that surely no one on this earth loved as deeply, as completely, or possessed a love as unique as theirs. He wanted to share all of his thoughts, all of his dreams and make plans for their future.

But not right now. No, not right now—

A word about the author...

Debbie has always had a soft spot for fairy tales, the joy of falling in love, and happily ever after endings. Stories of love and make-believe filled her head for as long as she can remember.

When she is not busy conjuring her latest novel, Debbie spends time with the members of her very large family. She also pursues her interests in family history, mythology, and all things ancient and historic.

Visit Debbie at:

www.dk-peterson.com

www.ingramcontent.com/pod-product-compliance
Lightning Source LLC
Chambersburg PA
CBHW07080503026
47504CB00003B/699